Accession of the
Stone Born
By:
Ken Lange

Table of Contents

Acknowledgements

Special thanks

To Rick G., Steven M., and Eric A. You have been an incredible resource and more helpful in this endeavor than I could ever have hoped!

A very big thank you to Maxine Bringenberg for agreeing to be my editor in this particular labor. You are certainly blessed with a great deal of patience in order to deal with the likes of me!

Dedication

To my partner in all things and my better half, Kim. You always show me the way and help me be better than I was the day before. Thank you.

Author Ken Lange

Prologue

Wednesday, May 27th

And the angel of death flew across the ocean on wings of iron and steel. The thirsty gray metal beast drank its fill twice between the old world and the new. The New World objected to his impending arrival, sending a great wall of storms to stand in his way. The gray beast groaned and creaked as it sliced through the thunder and lightning. The New World's guardians wept as the prodigal son returned home. The devil was coming to collect his due, and there was nothing that could be done to stop it.

Blinding white light cut through the shaded visor of my helmet, startling me awake. Jerking to one side, I slammed my head into the metal wall of the cockpit. The resounding thud caused me to wince as it reverberated through my head. After several seconds of blinking, the world began to come into sharp focus. The scene before me showed lightning dancing all around us in a brilliant show throughout deep black gray clouds that blanketed the sky. I wasn't sure how the pilot was able to navigate through the garish display of Mother Nature's power. The aircraft shuddered as thunder rolled over us in waves, forcing the thin, white-gray metal wings to quiver.

The clouds roiled around us like putrid smoke, buffeting our small craft with violent turbulence. The overwhelming feeling of being an unwelcome guest washed over me like icy water. It was as if nature itself wanted me to stay away from the land I'd once called home. Considering how things had gone over the last few weeks, staying where I'd been for the last twenty-eight years was simply impossible.

I should consider myself lucky that I hadn't been locked up or conveniently killed. That was normally what happened to people like me. Frankly, a very large part of me wondered why it hadn't happened. Not that I wasn't grateful for being able to walk away, but I was curious to the why. So whatever temper tantrum Mother Nature was throwing, she'd just have to get over it, because no matter her opinion I was coming home, and there was nothing that could be done to prevent it.

We were flying in an F-15 that wasn't accustomed to such long flights or the inclement weather we'd run into over the Gulf of Mexico. The storm was so vicious that the helmet did little to keep the sound of rain crashing into the canopy or the rolling thunder from hurting my ears. Over the next hour things progressively got worse as we flew deeper into the heart of the storm covering Louisiana, Mississippi, and a good bit of Texas.

Luckily we were on final approach and the plane touched down with a rough bounce. Strong winds threatened to thrust us back into the sky, but the craft groaned as the pilot fought back, forcing us down one last time, and taxied the length of the runway. We were about a hundred yards out when he let out an audible breath as he allowed his shoulders to go slack. Looking out the window, I barely recognized the Naval Air Station of New Orleans, or more accurately, Belle Chasse.

We'd been stuck in flight for nearly twelve hours, and while I wasn't sure about the pilot, I was stiff, sore, and generally grumpy. My shoulders were unaccustomed to being shoved into such a small space for so long, not to mention my knees and legs were cramping up from being in such close quarters.

It didn't help that I'd been unceremoniously let go—fired—after twenty-eight years of loyal service. I "WAS" an employee of the Department of Defense, assigned to special operations for the navy and marines. All things considered, I hadn't been surprised by the decision, but it still hurt. I'd been through nine types of hell and back a few times because of them, but now that life was over.

The base commander in Naples was new and hadn't approved of the way I'd handled my last engagement. To be completely honest, that wasn't the only reason; the man hated me on general principle. In his words, I "represented everything wrong with the world today." Frankly, I thought he exaggerated just a little. Even so, I gave him the perfect excuse to "ask" me to "retire." It wasn't as if I really had a choice in the matter.

He gave me a one-way ticket to anywhere in the world, and I chose New Orleans, of all places. Something was nagging at the back of my mind that told me I needed to be there. I hadn't the foggiest idea why. For a moment I'd thought about going back home to Montana, but everyone I knew there was probably dead. Something was telling me to follow through with my hunch and stay in New Orleans until I figured it out. After that I'd move on to whatever was next.

On a rather depressing note, I was forty-five years old, and everything I owned fit into one knapsack. Hell, I even had a little room left over in there since I was wearing a pair of size twelve black Wolverine Raiders, blue jeans, and a white button up long sleeve dress shirt that hadn't seen an iron in weeks.

It wasn't that I couldn't afford more, but I'd never bothered with acquiring things…which was about to change very rapidly. Normal people needed phones, computers, cars, and a place to live. One thing I'd learned a long time ago was to blend in as best I could and not draw too much attention to myself. A hard thing to accomplish given my size, but one that I'd mastered over the years. I'd need to repeat that success in the civilian world if I was going to "fit in"; fitting in was survival.

The pilot turned his head to one side as he settled back in his seat and said, "We've arrived, sir."

I felt my lips curl into a crooked half smile as a one-breath laugh escaped my lips. "You don't have to call me sir, I work for a living." I clapped the back of his headrest harder than I meant to, making him jump in his seat. "Thanks for the ride."

The pilot's helmet moved forward a fraction. "You're welcome. If it had been up to me we would've landed somewhere else, but I'm under orders to get you 'here' ASAP." Unfastening his oxygen mask, he couldn't stop himself from chuckling. "Either you're really important or you really pissed someone off." He held up a hand for me to see. "I don't want to know which." He stretched his neck and yawned. "All I want is a shitter and then a shower before I sack out."

Grinning, I unclasped my mask and let it dangle from one side. "You're a wise man."

The kid in front of me was maybe twenty-five, with a lot of life ahead of him. I, on the other hand, had more in common with the aircraft we'd been flying…a large, out of date relic that was best forgotten.

The hangar doors were open, allowing us to disembark out of the downpour happening just a few yards away. The canopy opened and the pilot scrambled down the ladder, where an officer promptly escorted him away for "debriefing"; which meant that this flight never happened. I could only hope that it wouldn't ruin his career.

Climbing down the ladder and turning around, I stood there looking at a dozen of the biggest marines I'd seen in a long time, but even the tallest was a few inches shorter than me. Each of them wore full combat gear, right down to combat issue flak jackets. More than a few of them looked confused, while the rest appeared to be amused, as if someone were pranking them.

Only their sergeant wasn't amused or confused. He appeared to know who I was…or more likely, who I might be. The sergeant was nearly a head shorter than I was, putting him around 5'10", and maybe thirty pounds lighter at around 205. He eyed me with calculated intelligence, waiting to see what I'd do.

I took a few seconds to size up the situation as I stretched. Not including the sergeant, I counted a dozen marines who were most likely reservists, who'd probably never seen action. That meant they were well trained but had little to no experience…bonus for me. I noticed several exits I could get through without permanent injury….

Taking in a deep breath and told myself to focus. I wasn't in danger, nor was I going to be arrested…otherwise the flight would've been useless. They could have arrested me with less trouble and with veteran troops back in Naples. Releasing the breath slowly, I forced myself to relax.

I needed to cooperate with these men and go with the flow, or things were sure to get very bad very quickly. I reminded myself that I wasn't a wanted man and I shouldn't treat these men as if they were the enemy. I needed to allow whatever was going to happen to unfold naturally.

The barrel chested sergeant stepped forward. His voice was uncommonly high for a man of his breadth, and the deep southern accent made it sound even more annoying. "Mr. Randall, we are here to escort you to the commander's office."

Snapping myself upright, I yanked my bag over my shoulder and gave the man a curt nod. "Carry on."

Four men fell in front of and behind me, allowing the others to flank me as they escorted me through the base into the main building. It felt like a mini parade for the damned as the procession silently made its way. People stared and gawked as we passed through their cubical domains until we reached the commander's office. The sergeant, along with three of his men, escorted me through the door that stood ajar.

I forced myself not to duck as we traversed the opening, and the top of my hair brushed the doorframe. For most men this would be an oversized office, with a massive oak desk at the rear of the room. For me it was a comfortable size, with a desk befitting a man of my stature. Instead, the brass placard read Captain Scott R. Gootee. I could only guess that this was the commander of Belle Chasse Naval Station.

Captain Gootee didn't bother to look up until he finished reading a report. He was in his mid-forties, thin, and his dress uniform was immaculate. We stood there in silence, then he tore his eyes away from the paperwork. He stared at me for several seconds before looking over at the sergeant and with a curt nod dismissed him. "You can leave us."

The marine wanted to object, but he and his men snapped to attention and closed the door behind them. Captain Gootee continued to eye me closely as if he were trying to fit some sort of puzzle together in his head. "I thought you'd be bigger. I'm not sure how that would be humanly possible, but there you have it."

Standing at parade rest, I stifled a snicker. "I get that a lot more than you'd think."

Captain Gootee motioned for me to take a seat. "You've caused quite a commotion over the last eighteen hours."

With a step forward and to the side, I reluctantly took my seat. The burgundy leather chair creaked when my oversized form sank into the buttoned cushion. It was comfortable enough, but I'd just spent the last dozen hours on my ass and it was starting to hurt. "I suppose I have, but I'm only following orders."

The captain looked sympathetic as he nodded. "I know." He appeared genuinely conflicted, sitting there searching for the right words. "You don't know me, but I know of you. You saved some friends of mine in Iraq, and others in Afghanistan over the years." He grumbled as he picked up a sheet of paper and read it again. "I've got orders as well." He shoved the papers onto his desk with a disapproving thud. "I don't particularly care for them either."

I felt for him, but there wasn't anything I could do to make things easier. "It's okay, Captain; just do what needs to be done. There isn't anything either of us can do about it."

Captain Gootee nodded. He reached under his desk and produced a bottle of whiskey. "You drink?"

Tilting my head to the side, I checked the clock on the wall. It read 10:15 a.m. CST. With a crooked grin, I lithely waved a hand. "I'm game if you are."

The captain put two tumblers on the desk and poured three fingers of whiskey in each before raising his glass in the air. "To those we've lost and to those who have lost themselves."

We both pounded back our drinks and placed the tumblers on the desk. The captain smiled and fingered the papers in front of him. "I can't do anything else for you. I can't tell you that there's a man sitting in a blue sedan outside the gates that'll drop you off wherever you'd like, and I can't say thank you for your years of service." The captain poured himself another drink and tossed it back before looking at me. "You do have somewhere to go, right?"

I nodded. "I do."

The captain visibly relaxed at the news. "Good. The door's going to open in a minute and you'll be escorted to the front gates." He downed his drink and poured another. "Goodbye, Mr. Randall."

I knew my time was at an end and stood. "You can call me Gavin."

The captain downed the third drink and poured another before toasting me. "Have a great life, Gavin."

With a grin, I bowed my head at the captain. Turning, I stepped toward the door and put my hand on the knob.

As I opened the door the captain called out to me. "You know this is wrong."

I paused for a moment, locking eyes with the sergeant and forcing myself not to turn around, and nodded. Putting one foot in front of the other, I didn't look back and I allowed the marines to escort me to the front gate. Once I was outside the gates they turned and marched back to their barracks. A blue sedan pulled up and the driver beckoned for me to get out of the rain. He kindly dropped me off at the St. Charles branch of Chase Bank.

Chapter 1

While I was "away" I didn't have a need for money. Every paycheck was sent into my checking account, and at the end of each calendar year everything save five thousand dollars was transferred to a brokerage firm in New York. Over the years I'd seen a few statements and knew that I'd never have a want for money after my retirement if I didn't spend it lavishly. It took a couple of hours' worth of paperwork to make the sweep obsolete, and another hour and a half to get a debit card, temporary checks, and three thousand dollars cash.

The big problem was that I wasn't near retirement age, and the money I had set aside for my later years needed to be kept for just that. That meant I'd need to find a job sooner rather than later. For now, though, I had business to attend to here in the city. Hopefully life in the States hadn't changed so much that I'd burn through my available cash before I found something suitable.

That thought made me snigger, pushing the brushed aluminum handle of the plate glass door, I stepped out onto St. Charles Ave. What was "suitable" for a man like me? I was pretty sure the few skills I did have weren't in high demand in the "land of the free and the home of the brave." This very question was why so many of the people I'd worked with over the years hadn't fared well when they returned home.

Grimacing, I rolled through a few names of men who had retired from service over the years that now ran "security" firms, which were more like private armies for those willing to pay. My stomach turned at the thought of working for any of them. Their loyalties were to whoever had the fattest wallet. I'd rather burn in hell than live like that. Of course, living on the streets or being institutionalized wasn't high on my list of shit to do either.

The rain had stopped about an hour earlier, but angry gray and black clouds littered the blue sky above, and threatened another deluge. Thunder rolled in the distance, telling me that Mother Nature hadn't finished having her say. Walking out of the bank, I found the late afternoon air thick, hot, almost solid in form.

Moisture clung to my skin instantly, causing my long sleeved shirt to stick to my skin. I felt a trickle of sweat between my shoulder blades run down my back. Putting my bag on the ground, I rolled up my sleeves, revealing the deeply tanned skin underneath. The humidity clung to the hairs on my arms as I leaned down and grabbed my bag again. The shirt pulled oddly as the fabric clung to my chest, back, and shoulders in unflattering twists and folds.

Fortune was shining upon me; my destination was maybe six or seven blocks away through one of the prettier parts of town. The Garden District was one of the older sections, filled with the city's wealthy and influential. Great oaks lined every street, creating shadowy canopies, allowing the area to maintain its own ecosystem. If I had to guess, I'd say any of the outlying areas, such as Metairie or Kenner, were probably ten degrees warmer than where I stood.

St. Charles Avenue bustled with heavy traffic. The once lazy Sunday drivers that I remembered from my childhood were long gone, possibly due to the massive road repairs I'd noticed on my way to the bank, or perhaps the streetcar line being repaired. More likely, though, it was due to the fact Katrina had delivered a rude awakening to the men and women who had once been untouchable by nature or man. Now that they'd been touched by such a disaster they felt fear, mortality, and vulnerability.

Throwing the bag over my shoulder, I set off down Jackson Avenue. About a half block down historic homes jutted out of the land, surrounded by concrete and wrought iron fencing. Passing Prytania, I was greeted by larger two story homes reflecting the city's mixed heritage. After crossing the street, I paused long enough to pull a handkerchief from my pocket and wipe the sweat from my brow.

I didn't know how anyone lived in this sticky mess without needing a shower every five minutes. Considering I'd just spent the better part of three decades in the desert, it wasn't the heat that bothered me, it was the humidity. When I was a boy I'd visited New Orleans only a few times during the latter part of the year, which had been a welcome respite from the frigid Montana winters. Continuing my trek, I paused long enough to check the addresses before making a right onto Coliseum.

The houses here were owned by the city elite, the oldest of old money. Every house looked like it was straight out of a painting, or off a movie set. The attention to detail, from the fleur de lis on the black wrought iron fencing to historic color schemes, was evident in every house for the next several blocks. Bronze plaques adorned the more famous homes, denoting one thing or another. Across the street from my destination was one such plaque from 1881, describing Ferret's Folly.

I didn't read any further…I knew I was postponing a long overdue visit. Crossing the street, I checked my watch…4:45. I needed to hurry before they closed for the day.

The giant house before me was an old plantation style white two story home. A two-foot cement wall with three-foot black wrought iron fencing lined the front of the property. The giant eight-foot green hedges behind the fence had obviously been allowed too much freedom, as they'd shattered bits of cement and warped the fencing.

Still, it was breathtakingly beautiful. Tentatively I reached out and put my hand on the gate, and I felt a jolt of energy run through me. Obviously my nerves were getting the better of me and I hesitated another minute before I strode through, closing the gate behind me. Ten feet in I padded up the massive triple wide gray cement stairs leading to the wrap around porch. Corinthian style columns supported the massive second story balcony.

My footsteps made a low soft thud on the polished hardwood as I came up to the extra tall seven-foot french double doors, filled with the most spectacular stained glass I'd seen in years. The sweat pouring off me had nothing to do with the high temperature or the humidity this time. The smooth glass overlay protecting the intricate leaded glasswork had faded gold letters head high, which read, Old & Rare Books since 1965.

Remembering stories from my childhood, I knew that fifty years earlier a first floor conversion had created the bookstore that now stood before me. The second story was a beautiful sprawling home that used to be filled with the most amazing antiques, trinkets, and books that I'd ever laid eyes on.

Glancing at my watch again, I saw that it was 4:55. I cleared my throat, straightened my shirt as best I could, and pushed. The dark oak framed door swung in, and the top corner rang a bell, announcing my arrival. The bell's high-pitched dings pierced the silence of the massive front room. The chilled air from the oversized AC washed over me, causing my shirt to stick to me even more. When it swung shut, the bell chimed once more. Reaching up with one hand I silenced the annoyance.

The store was much like I remembered it. Shelves filled with the most amazing books lined the walls. Tables and shoulder high shelves filled the floor, showcasing things particularly special or unique, be it books or odd yet spectacular trinkets of all sorts. Bits of metal and glass glinted in the afternoon light. I nearly lost myself to the smell of old leather and shiny objects until I heard someone clear their throat loudly.

Scanning the room, I found what I guessed was an employee. The man was maybe in his late twenties or early thirties, a light skinned Creole with wild, unkempt charcoal curly hair swept up in a mess that actually looked good on him. It wasn't a look that many men could pull off, and was something I would never try. Such was the reason I kept my straight black (now littered with copious amounts of white) hair cut short on the sides and swept back on top. He was someone who would never "fit in," whereas I had to blend as best I could.

With a nod I raised my hand to wave, but no sooner had my arm left my side when he consciously made a decision to ignore me by checking his watch. His disdain for me and my presence was written all over his very handsome features. He made a show of lazily putting down a very old leather tome, giving me a distasteful once over. He purposefully exaggerated his facial expressions, leaving me with little doubt of just what he thought of me. When I didn't turn and leave instantly he let out a heavy sigh and a small groan escaped his lips.

Reluctantly he moved from the spot he'd rooted himself in when I arrived. His movements struck me instantly; every step flowed with such grace, power, and confidence. He and I were the same height. What surprised me, now that he was moving, was the fact that I'd seriously miscalculated his build. What I thought was a thin, lanky frame was actually heavily muscled; even so, he was about forty pounds lighter than me. He moved with such intensity that I was reminded of a beast stalking prey. Before I knew it he stood about four feet away from me, body angled and poised to strike out if necessary.

His voice was even, yet filled with contempt that his heavy southern accent only accentuated. "I'm sorry, sir, but we're about to close, and you obviously don't have an appointment."

Translation...I don't care who you think you are, you are unworthy, unwelcome, and should really get the fuck out of this store before I throw you out.

He was clearly the watchdog, and I was sure his little act had run off more than a few people who didn't "belong." Plastering my best smile on my face, I gave him a quick wink. "You're right, I don't have an appointment, but I need to speak with the owner, Andrew, before you close."

The young man was thoroughly unimpressed with my charms and literally scoffed at me. "I don't know who gave you that name, but the owner doesn't meet with 'street people.'"

Dropping my bag, which garnered me even more disdain, I shoved a hand into my front pocket and pulled out my wallet. Grabbing my government ID, I handed it to the man. "If you'll give him this I'm confident he'll see me."

The young man glared at my bag again before reluctantly snatching the ID. He read it and reread it before holding it back in my direction. All the haughtiness in his voice faded, along with the accent. "This is you?"

With a look I was sure would make Bart Simpson proud, I shook my head in disbelief, barely resisting the urge to say, "duh." "Last I checked."

He eyed my belongings again and simply nodded. His voice was tight as he was clearly straining to remain calm. "Wait here." He scurried off to the back of the building and vanished.

Picking up my bag, I felt even more nervous. It had been a long time since I'd been here. My parents had brought me for the last time when I was maybe eight or nine. I wasn't sure that my uncle would remember me. I knew he would recall having a nephew, but we hadn't seen each other since my parents' funeral, a few weeks before I graduated high school. It would be hard for him to forget his only living relative, but stranger things had happened. Over the years I'd sent him the occasional card and Internet emails here and there, but we weren't exactly close.

A few minutes later the young man made his way back up front, minus the ID. His voice was an octave higher and he was sweating slightly. "I'm Isidore Chauvin. Andrew will be down in a moment."

Isidore fidgeted with the nearest bobble that suddenly needed polishing. He worked his way around the room while never taking his eyes off me for more than a second or two, when he stole glances at the rear of the store.

Then a deep, rich baritone voice rolled over me like a warm memory, with only the slightest hint of a southern accent. "Gavin! I can't believe you're here."

I turned around to see my uncle looking surprisingly well for a man in his mid-seventies. The dingy white shirt and charcoal tweed slacks appeared to be a few sizes too big, giving him a gaunt, frail appearance, but otherwise he looked healthy. Even with a slight stoop, Andrew was an inch or two taller than me. His sapphire blue eyes sparkled behind the round, gold wire rimmed glasses, and the chiseled good looks I remembered only seemed more refined with age. His once salt and pepper hair was now white, while remaining thick. That, along with a respectable thick yet well-trimmed beard, gave him the appearance of a scholar or a professor. Which, given his profession, kind of made all sorts of sense.

I felt like a kid again as a big smile plastered itself across my face, and I opened my arms to take Andrew into a bear hug. "It's good to see you." I lifted the big man up in the air and squeezed. "You look great."

I couldn't help but notice that my aging uncle was solid muscle under the oversized clothes, and for a moment I had to wonder why he was hiding. Andrew flashed me a big smile and I returned it without a second thought.

His expression faltered for only a moment before giving me a knowing wink. "You've filled out!" Andrew gave me one last squeeze before releasing me and turning. "Isidore, this is my nephew Gavin. Gavin, this is my assistant Isidore."

Isidore eyed us suspiciously; by his expression I could've mistaken him for a jealous lover. He held out a hand formally in my direction. "Pleasure to meet you. Andrew didn't tell me you'd be dropping by."

I looked between them and beamed, holding my hands out in an effort to keep the peace. "Hey, if this is a problem I'll get a room for the night and come back tomorrow. I don't want to interrupt anything."

Isidore's eyes widened in horror, and he nearly choked on his own spit when he saw the look on my face. "Oh, dear God in heaven no! First things first! I'm young and handsome, and he's an old bag of bones. So not my type." He bit his lip as he eyed me again. "You, on the other hand, are perfectly aged, tall, with beautiful tanned skin, a strapping build, and those bottle green eyes are simply to die for!" Isidore looked me over with a real hunger in his eyes. "There's nothing wrong with you that a hot shower, new clothes, and a good polish wouldn't fix."

I blushed. "Well, thank you very much...."

Andrew chuckled. "Isidore...."

Isidore shook his head and pursed his lips. "What? I can't admire?"

The man's good nature was contagious. "Thank you for the compliment, but you have at least one too many appendages." I cleared my throat and stood upright. "I'm sorry, but I'll have to pass."

Isidore sighed longingly and dusted off his shoulder in a dismissive gesture. "Your loss."

And just like that he was over me completely. "I'm sure." Patting Andrew on the shoulder, I smirked. "He didn't tell you because I didn't tell him. I only knew I was on my way to New Orleans about twenty-four hours ago." I shrugged. "I've been away for a long time, and I thought a visit was in order."

Isidore gave me another appraising look and circled me. "Too clean to be prison, so I'm guessing military."

Andrew sensed my discomfort and turned to Isidore. "Would you be a doll and lock up on your way out? From the looks of things, Gavin and I have a lot to catch up on." Andrew glanced back with an appraising look and nodded. "You look like you've had a hard day. Care for some dinner?"

The mention of food made my stomach rumble, and from what I remembered Andrew was a fantastic cook. "Dinner sounds great! All I've had today is three fingers of rye whiskey for brunch."

Andrew snorted and waved at the back of the store. "You go ahead. I'll be up shortly."

Holding my bag close, I swept by, making my way to the stairs, and all the while Isidore admired the view.

Andrew cleared his throat to get his attention. "Make sure the front gate is locked. We don't need any of those tourists getting on the grounds again."

Isidore rolled his eyes. "Yes, Mom."

My amusement faded quickly when I glanced back at them.

Andrew advanced on the younger man, towering over him when he spoke. His tone was low and calm, yet every word carried weight. "I mean it." Isidore shrank back at Andrew's words. "I have a guest, and I don't want to be disturbed."

Isidore's fright was easy to read, and he quickly stammered. "I was kidding. I'll make sure everything is locked up tight. I promise."

Satisfied, Andrew stepped back, turned, and waved me onward. "You do remember the way, don't you?"

Surprisingly, I did. The third step from the top creaked every time someone stood on it. When I was a child I'd made a game of trying to make music with it, much to my parents' annoyance. Andrew was suddenly right behind me, closing the oversized seven-foot door as we stepped into the massive living room at the front of the house. Four large floor-to-ceiling windows flanked the french doors leading out to the spacious balcony overlooking the tiny front yard.

Deep reddish brown hardwood floors covered the upstairs. The vaulted twelve-foot ceilings gave me a sense of comfort, knowing that I wouldn't be knocking my head against anything important. The living room was maybe twenty feet wide and thirty long, and a massive burgundy Persian rug covered most of the room. A fashionable yet comfortable looking deep brown leather couch sat against the far wall, allowing a good view through the windows. Four wing chairs sat at one end of the room, three of which sat around a sturdy looking table covered in beautiful leather tomes, notebooks, and pens of all sorts.

At the other end of the room sat a large oak desk with a red leather office chair and two chairs in front. The desk was clean, with a box holding a few papers at one side, three framed pictures on the other, and a centerpiece of a glass case containing what looked to be a sapphire about the size of my fist.

I took in the photos on the desk with a curious glance. The one at the far left was a photo of my father, mother, and me. The second was a black and white photo of a dark skinned woman with the most amazing eyes, clean jawline, and delicate features…one of the most beautiful women I'd ever seen. She was stunning, and it was hard to take my eyes off her to look at the next photo. Finally, I moved on to see my uncle, the woman, and a man I'd never seen before.

Andrew glanced back at the door and snickered. "You're not going to try to play the *National Anthem* tonight, are you?"

I chuckled. "Not tonight anyway. Honestly, I'm tired as hell, but you said there was the possibility of food."

Andrew swept by me as he nodded. "Leftovers all right?"

Real food sounded wonderful. It had been a very long time since I'd had real food on a regular basis. "Leftovers sound divine!"

Andrew stopped suddenly and turned. "I've got to ask." He was quiet for a moment, searching for the right words. "I'm really glad you're here, but it's been awhile since your last visit. Is everything all right?"

I felt an urge to unburden myself and tell him everything, but that wasn't going to happen. Still I struggled with the urge for another half second before I could focus and form a complete thought. "I'm sorry about not visiting prior, but my work has kept me very busy."

Andrew appeared displeased before turning towards the kitchen with me in tow. "And what kind of work is that exactly?"

Again I felt compelled to tell him everything, but how could I? I hadn't exactly been employed by the warm and fuzzy bunny brigade. "Just work. Overseas mostly...." Exclusively. I hadn't been back on US soil in nearly twenty years. "But that's over now. That's kind of the reason I'm here."

The kitchen was spacious, with a massive restaurant sized stainless steel Viking gas stove and a double wide commercial stainless steel refrigerator on the opposite wall. Terracotta tiles covered the room. In the far corner, next to the window overlooking the neighbors, was a small breakfast table and four chairs. Again, one was against the far wall and three sat around the table. It was odd to see such an arrangement repeated without any type of explanation.

Andrew set to work pulling leftovers out of the refrigerator. "Red beans and rice all right?"

God, that sounded good. "Sounds great."

He ladled rice and beans into two bowls and placed them in the microwave. "All right, son, tell me what's going on."

Again the need to unburden myself swept over me. It was a hard thing to fight, but I wasn't about to confess my sins to anyone, especially not family. If he ever found out about me I'd lose the only person I had left in my life. Yet I couldn't stop the next words from falling out of my mouth. "I got fired."

Andrew looked back at me in disbelief. A part of me was unsure what he was surprised by…the revelation I'd been fired, or that I hadn't told him more.

"Care to elaborate?" he asked.

My mind wanted to betray me, but I quickly locked that desire in a small room without a key before I proceeded. The last twenty-four hours had been the culmination of a lot of very bad things, and I wasn't about to unburden myself to anyone, especially not someone as kind and gentle as my uncle. "The world changed around me and I didn't change with it."

Andrew raised an eyebrow. I read the confusion on his face and wrote it off to me being an asshole. He was trying to be there for me, and I wouldn't let him. Andrew didn't deserve that kind of weight on his soul.

Andrew gave me a curious look and painted a smile on his face. "That's remarkably vague."

The disappointment in his voice was clear and it made me fight back a frown when I spoke. "I suppose it is. Can we just say that my services were no longer needed?"

Andrew turned and pulled the bowls out after the microwave beeped. Setting one in front of me and the other next to him, he nodded as he put his hand on mine. "I just need to know that you're okay."

I was confused. No one had asked about my welfare in twenty-eight years. "What do you mean?"

Andrew looked sad if not a little pained when he looked into my eyes. "I mean, are you okay? Are you hurt? Can I do anything for you?"

I sat back, looking at the food and then at my uncle, and smiled before lying. "I'm fine." I pulled the bowl closer to me, unconsciously wrapping an arm around it. "I could use a place to sleep. I don't have a house here and I don't want to stay at a hotel." Truth be told, I didn't feel safe anywhere else. "It's not a matter of money. I've got three decades' worth of pay I haven't touched, so I can afford a hotel, but I'd rather be here if that's okay. And before you ask again, yes, I'm fine. I'm healthy, I'm not dying or anything. I just miss...." I didn't know how to finish that sentence. It was silly to say I missed family. My parents had died long ago, and I barely knew my uncle.

Andrew took a bite of his beans, considering my words. "I have a spare room, and I could use a helping hand here if you have the time."

Relief swept over me. "I've got nothing but time. Thanks."

Andrew beamed. "I have one more question."

"Shoot," I replied, and shoved another spoonful of food into my mouth.

Andrew never took his eyes off me when he spoke. "You could obviously have gone anywhere in the world; why here?"

I took a deep breath, leaned back in my chair, and considered his question for several seconds. He wasn't going to give up anytime soon. "I needed to see family, and you're all I've got. I've missed the feeling of being at home, of being safe."

That last bit slipped out.

"No wife or kids?" Andrew asked.

That was fucking ridiculous, and I shook my head. "There's been women, of course, just no one special, and as far as I know no children."

Andrew was ecstatic. "I'm glad you're here. Finish your food, and the guest room is down the hall on the left."

Shoving another bite of food into my mouth, I nodded. "I remember."

Andrew eyed my bowl. "Want some more? I have plenty."

My stomach was already feeling stretched to its limits, and I shook my head. "I think I'll save my appetite for breakfast."

Andrew bobbed and gestured towards the living room. "Go put your bag away, get a shower, and meet me in the living room for a civilized dessert."

Groaning, I leaned back in my chair and shook my head. "I'm not really into sweets."

Andrew pointed and said. "That wasn't a request. Now go get cleaned up, and come see me in the living room when you're done."

I made a right out of the kitchen to the end of the hall. Opening the door, I stood there for a moment trying to take it all in. Over the last few decades I'd become accustomed to a ten by ten room with a communal bath. The door opened to reveal a decent size living room, a kitchenette, and three doors at the back of the room. One led into a sprawling bedroom, another into a massive bath, and the final one held a small washer and dryer for laundry.

Throwing my bag on the bed, I pulled out a fresh pair of jeans and a clean blue polo before heading to the bath. After a piping hot shower, I slipped into some clean clothes, tied my boots, and headed for the living room. Andrew had cleaned off the table at the far end of the room and sat in one of the wing chairs, waving me over. On the table was a bottle of Dalmore twelve-year-old Scotch. Tumblers sat on either side of the bottle, with three fingers of amber fluid in each.

Andrew waved at the chair next to his. "I hope you'll be comfortable. I've been considering trying to find someone to live in there for the company."

That hurt. He was lonely and I'd been busy working, never even giving him a second thought. Grabbing the nearest glass, I held it up for a toast. "To my good fortune and to a good man."

Andrew blushed and took a drink. "Thank you, but I'm not so sure good would describe me. I've made plenty of mistakes...that's why I live alone."

The last bit was tinged with enough grief and remorse that it made my heart ache. "To the two of us together, then."

Andrew nodded. "To the two of us."

Taking another drink, I looked around the room and wondered how he maintained it. "How are you able to keep this place so clean? If I lived here it'd be dusty as hell and cluttered with shit from floor to ceiling."

Andrew actually hooted. "Says the man that can hold everything he owns in a single bag." I winced but he kept on. "But I don't keep up with it all. I have a nice lady, Heather, who works three days a week downstairs and cleans up here the other two." Andrew took a sip of scotch and his good nature vanished. "Do you recall the house rules?"

Indeed. It had been the one and only rule my father and Andrew had ever imposed on me. Everything past my uncle's bedroom was off limits. I could've run through the precious books downstairs with a fucking flamethrower and they wouldn't have cared, but if I took one step into the hall leading east they'd flip their shit. "I do. I've always wondered why."

Andrew only sipped his scotch. "Tell you what…if you stick around long enough I'll give you a personal tour of the entire floor."

Now that was tempting. I was always curious about my uncle and his very strange home. Andrew's bedroom was next to the living room, ensuring that no one could ever use trying to find him as an excuse to wander around unattended. What had struck me the most was the fact that given I had a propensity for ignoring rules all my life, I'd never once even dreamt of breaking this one.

"You may regret making that deal," I said.

Andrew chuckled. "Why do you say that?"

"I might be tempted to stay here indefinitely just to find out what's down there."

Andrew smiled. "Finish your scotch, get some sleep, and we can discuss it more tomorrow."

I held my glass out to Andrew before downing the rest of it. Standing, I gave him a quick bow and smiled. "Thank you again for taking me in tonight."

Andrew nodded and finished his drink. "Sleep well. See you in the morning."

I padded off to my suite and collapsed on the bed without getting out of my clothes, and for the first time in twenty years I didn't have the nightmare that had haunted me. Instead, I dreamt of my father talking to Uncle Andrew. It was the first time since his death that I'd ever dreamt of him.

Chapter 2

Thursday May 28th

My rest was fraught with twist and turns, which made the bed creak and groan under my weight. I awoke, clammy, hair soaked, and barely rested. Laying in a soft cushy bed felt...uncomfortable, weird, and unsettling. The soft mattress made me ache in strange places, as the old springs supported me in unfamiliar pressure points.

It was around midnight when I considered pulling the bedding off and sleeping on the laundry room floor. It was small, defensible, and smooth, but that was an impossibility since I was trying to "fit in." When I got a place of my own that was secure, maybe then, but now...now I had to pretend, I had to fit in. So I forced myself to turn over and try to get a few more hours of fitful sleep.

Rolling out of bed, I flipped on the lamp and headed for the shower. Again I couldn't help but feel out of place in the civilian world. The power never flickered, hot water poured out of the showerhead and never got cool. The room was oddly quiet...no background sounds of fighter jets overhead, gunshots in the streets, or far off explosions that I'd become so accustomed to over the years. After spending so many years in one warzone or another, I had become accustomed to the sounds, smells, and sights. Here in the States it was so quiet, almost tranquil.

I'd often been sequestered on base with at least two guards escorting me wherever I needed to go. The lack of guards made me feel somewhat lonely and gave me an uneasy feeling in the pit of my stomach. The barracks were full of conversations, laughter, and comradery. It wasn't as if I'd been included in any of it, but I did miss the sounds. Then there were the smells of the base and people who lived there. That may sound like odd things to miss, but there you have it. Not that I could smell anything, since a few hours after landing, the humidity and mold had me completely stopped up.

The furniture was so clean. I'd become accustomed to a thin layer of sand coating everything…no matter how hard you tried, it was always there. Shaking my head at the thoughts, I pulled out a clean set of clothes and mechanically pulled them on. I needed to get past this sooner rather than later if I was going to survive in the private sector. I finished dressing quickly and headed out of the room, leaving my dirty clothes in a pile in front of the washer. It was a few minutes to five when I pushed open the door and found Andrew in the middle of preparing breakfast.

Andrew glanced over at me and cocked his head. "Sleep well?"

Heading towards the stove, I lied. "Absolutely!"

Andrew paused, and eyed me again. "If that's what you look like after a good night's sleep, then you're going to either need several more such nights or to learn what a good night's sleep really is."

Ignoring his comment, I shrugged. "Anything I can help you with?"

Andrew gave me a haughty look. "You can sit your ass down, before I knock you down. You're in the south now and we take care of our guests."

I found myself following his instructions without a second thought. These new sensations I'd been experiencing since my arrival were very unsettling. The voice in the back of my head told me not to worry, which only made me worry more.

Reluctantly taking my seat, I said, "You don't have to wait on me. I'm old enough to make breakfast for the two of us."

Andrew pursed his lips and sucked in air through his teeth loudly. "The question is, can you cook?"

I felt my chest swell with pride. Cooking was one of the few talents I possessed that would actually be acceptable in the States. It was unlikely there would be bloodshed or deaths involved, which for me was a bonus. During one of my many recovery periods from a serious injury, they'd taught me to cook as part of my rehabilitation.

"I'm actually a really good cook." I said.

Andrew didn't appear convinced as he spooned potatoes onto the plates. "We'll find out tomorrow morning. You'll be restricted to the basics of what's in the fridge. If you can make something that I don't want to scrape off my tongue after, then you have my permission to cook. Otherwise, don't touch shit!"

That made me chuckle. It was a good sign that he wanted me to stick around. One of the things that kept me up last night was the fact that my current state of unemployment dictated that I needed a few things. "Uncle Andrew, do you know where I can pick up a cell phone and a computer?"

Andrew pushed a plate filled with crispy hash browns and two fried eggs in front of me before sitting down with his own. "I've got a perfectly good computer in the other room, if you'd like to use it."

Grabbing a fork, I was grateful for the offer, but I still shook my head no. "Thanks, but I really need to pick up one for myself. Something portable that I can use wherever I happen to wind up."

Andrew chewed his food silently, and absently stabbed a few more bits of potato with his fork before nodding. "There's an Office Depot on St. Charles not too far away if you need something quick. They should be able to help you with the phone and the computer." He paused, looked in my eyes, and smiled. "You know you're welcome to stay here as long as you like."

"Thanks," I replied.

Andrew continued, speaking between bites. "Is there anything else you need?"

The thought of spending so much of what was left of the cash in my bank account made my stomach tighten. "I'm going to need something to get around in. I can't bum rides from people every time I need to go somewhere, and New Orleans isn't exactly known for its public transit system."

A tiny derisive breath escaped him while nodding in agreement. "You make a fair point, but I might have a solution."

That perked my interest as I tore my eyes off the plate to look up at my uncle. "Oh?"

Andrew's smile faded, and he dabbed a paper napkin at the sides of his mouth. "I don't get out like I used to. Which means I have two cars rotting in the garage." He made a dismissive gesture. "It's an older model vehicle, but I assure you it's in great shape. If you want, I could sell it to you."

I kind of felt like I was taking advantage of the old man, making me feel even more guilty than before. "I couldn't take your car."

Andrew's eyes narrowed and his face lit up. "You wouldn't be 'taking it'! That's stealing. No, you'd be buying it. Don't worry so much. I have a second vehicle, and if I don't feel up to driving I'll ask you for a ride."

How could I argue with that logic? He had a second car, so when I needed to move on he'd still have transportation. Then there was Isidore, who'd take him wherever he needed to go if I wasn't there to do it. If he was willing to part with whatever was in the garage and it helped him in any way, how could I refuse? "Sounds good. How much do you want for it?"

Andrew was quiet for several seconds, pondering the question before settling on a decision. "I hate paying the insurance on it anyway. How about you give me twenty-five-hundred dollars and we call it even?"

Sticking a hand in my pocket I pulled out the wad of cash, counted out twenty-five one hundred dollar bills, and pushed them towards my uncle before pocketing the last of the cash. "Consider it done."

Part of me really hated buying something sight unseen, but I didn't like owing people. Having outstanding debts to family, friends, or people in general made me feel indentured to them, and I couldn't stand that. No, far better that I handle it right away and be done with it.

Andrew was quick to pocket the money with a smile. "When we go downstairs I'll show you the car before we head in and set up for the day."

Picking at the last of my food, I nodded. "I take it you've got appointments?"

Andrew spread his hands in a casual manner. "Someone is selling a copy of the *Dunlap Broadsides*, and I'm supposed to authenticate it."

I damn near fell out of my chair. "Someone is trying to sell a copy of the *Declaration of Independence*?"

Andrew shoved another forkful of potatoes in his mouth and shrugged. "There are twenty-six accounted for; after today there might be twenty-seven."

I obviously didn't understand what my uncle did for a living. How could he be so nonchalant about an original copy of the *Declaration of Independence*? My mouth had fallen open and I promptly closed it. "You're acting like this isn't that big of a deal."

Andrew swallowed another bite of his food. "It isn't." He chuckled and waved his hands around in a grand gesture. "In my line of work, you can't get all misty eyed every time some musty old document comes your way."

That was something I could understand. After a while, work could desensitize you to things that would baffle anyone else stepping into your shoes. "Well, it may not be a big deal to you, but to me it's pretty fucking impressive."

Andrew eyed my plate and his face brightened. "Finish up while I grab the title to the car. I'll have it notarized this afternoon so it will be all nice and legal."

His rush to put the car in my name made me a little nervous, but his excitement about it still made me smile. "No rush on my account."

Andrew looked all too happy with himself. "Hey, I consider this a great return on my investment. I got back exactly what I paid for it when I bought it used. It's not every day you can say that!"

Fuck! I'd bought a third hand car, and only God knew what kind of shape it was in if it's been sitting for a long time. All I could hope was that it ran until I could trade in the heap for a new car at the dealership.

Putting on my happy face, I smiled at my uncle. "Well, I'm glad I could be of service."

Andrew disappeared, allowing me to finish what was on my plate before going for second helpings of the hash browns. He returned a few minutes later with an envelope in one hand and a set of keys he promptly shoved into his pocket.

Chewing the last bits of my breakfast, I followed him down the stairs and out the back into the private park my uncle called a backyard. The lush green yard was perfectly manicured, broken by ancient oaks ringed with golden yellow, brilliant white, and shimmering pink flowers in full bloom. Whoever maintained the grounds could give the White House staff some pointers.

It was a good hundred yards to the white brick four bay garage. Andrew pointed at the far door. Leaning over, I grabbed the metal handle, giving it a hefty tug and allowing it to roll up and over, revealing the deep cavernous room beyond. My mouth fell open when my eyes adjusted to the gloomy interior. There in the early morning light sat a mint condition maroon aerodynamic work of art, better known as the Tucker 48.

The car was eighteen feet long, six and a half feet wide, and five feet high, and of highly polished smooth, curved steel. It had the standard headlights on either side of the front fenders, with the most recognizable feature of a third directional light in the center of the vehicle. A part of me felt the way I had when I saw the photo of the lady on my uncle's desk last night, as I couldn't tear my eyes off this amazing piece of machinery. Stepping to the side to get a better angle, I could see the white walls gleaming in the morning sun. The metal body was so polished I could see the dawn reflected in the maroon paint.

Andrew slid between the wall and the car before opening the door and slipping into the driver's seat. He turned the key and the engine purred to life...purred might be wrong, but it wasn't a growl. It was quiet, but the entire vehicle radiated power as it idled, taking stock of its new owner. A moment later Andrew turned it off, and I felt cheated not hearing its gentle purr in my ears.

He stepped out of the car and casually closed the door with a giant grin. "What do you think?"

Shaking my head, I felt numb, almost speechless. "I think I opened the wrong door." Stepping back, I started towards the next bay when Andrew grabbed my arm. "You're kidding, right?"

Andrew puffed out his chest with pride when he put the keys in my hand. "Absolutely not. This is yours."

My hands were sweating. I felt like the keys would slip and fall at any moment. "I can't afford this thing. There's no way twenty-five-hundred will cover it!"

Andrew brushed off my concerns. "Think of it as twenty-eight years of missed Christmas and birthday presents."

I nearly choked on the thought. "Uncle Andrew—"

Andrew waved me off with slight irritation in his voice. "Uncle nothing! You'll take it, and if you're a good boy I'll show you what's in there." He pointed at the closed door next to this one. "The third door…well, that's probably never going to happen, but boys can dream."

What the fuck! If this was the shitty toy in my uncle's collection, then I was in for a huge surprise one day. "Fine. I'll hold it for you until you see fit that you need it back."

Andrew rolled his eyes, amusement clear to see in his features. "If it makes you feel better, but I don't make deals I don't stand by." He chuckled more to himself than me. "Besides, it was worth every cent to see the look on your face earlier when you thought you'd bought some piece of shit Oldsmobile. You take good care of her and she'll take good care of you. Take her out for some fun and enjoy yourself." He stood between me and the garage and motioned towards the back of the house. "Later of course. We've got work to do this morning."

There were only fifty-one of these beauties made, and every one of them was unique in their own way. We stayed out in the garage till nearly seven as he pointed out all the features of the car, and there were many. Heading inside, Andrew clapped me on the back and smiled, and before I knew it we were setting up one of the clean rooms for use at 8:30 for the client with the documents that needed authenticating.

Isidore arrived around 7:30 and was surprised when he walked in to see Andrew and me setting up the room. He folded his arms and yawned. "I should've slept in." He cooed with a sly grin and a wink. "I see he's rooked you into doing the grunt work."

His attitude was infectious; I felt more at ease and relaxed in his presence. "It feels good to help where I can."

Isidore sauntered over and ran a hand across my shoulders, looking rather devilish while eying my uncle. "Don't let the old goat fool you; he's more capable than he appears."

It was then I remembered just how good of shape he was in no matter how much Andrew tried to hide it. I noticed the design of his tailored clothes hid the strength of the body beneath them. They were a couple of sizes too big, yet still very stylish. It occurred to me that he'd gone through a lot of trouble to create the illusion, and I had to wonder why.

Andrew padded over with a delighted look on his face. "Is everything all right?"

I felt as if there was something I wanted to ask, but I couldn't put my finger on it. "Yeah, everything's fine. Is there anything else I can do to help?"

Andrew shook his head. "Nah. You should talk to Isidore and get directions to the Office Depot."

Nodding, I went to speak with Isidore and before long I was out the door, walking to the store on St. Charles Avenue. After only a couple of hours I returned to the shop with the latest Samsung Galaxy S model and a Surface Pro combination tablet and computer.

Andrew pointed at the clock and beamed. "It's nearly eleven. Care to go find something to eat nearby?"

The thought of a proper meal made my stomach growl. "Sounds great!"

The bell on the front door rang as a UPS driver stepped through. He looked at the package and announced. "Is there an Andrew Randall available?"

Isidore instantly appeared concerned, moving to between the deliveryman and Andrew. "I'm sorry, but we normally don't take deliveries this time of day. Can I help you with something?"

The driver eyed Isidore carefully, cradling the package in a strange protective manner. "Are you Mr. Randall?"

Isidore took a tentative step forward, swelling to his full height. "I'm not, but I can sign for it."

To his credit the driver stood his ground, yet shifted his stance to keep the package out of Isidore's reach. "I'm going to have to insist on speaking with Mr. Randall. He will need to sign for the package personally."

Pulling out my ID, I strode past Isidore, who was quickly becoming annoyed. Handing it to the man, I nodded. "I'm Andrew Gavin Randall. Can I help you with something?"

The UPS driver visibly relaxed, handing me the package, allowing me to sign for it. "Thank you, Mr. Randall, and have a wonderful day."

I waited for the driver to leave the store before putting the package on the nearest table and waving my uncle over. "It's for you."

He was behind me in a moment, peering over my shoulder. "Apparently."

Andrew pulled a small penknife out of his pocket, deftly slicing the package open. He pulled back the cardboard, revealing a large leather bound book atop a stack of papers, and quickly closed the lid. He looked over at me apprehensively. "Is it all right if we order in? I need to tend to something personal."

He looked almost panicked by what was in the box. It was obviously very personal, and I thought it best to give him some space to handle it. "No problem at all. Want me to go pick something up?"

Andrew's hand shot out, grabbing my arm hard as he shook his head. His voice was taut and a little higher than normal. "Absolutely not!" Looking down, he realized he was holding my arm, and quickly released it. He regained his composure, forcibly staying calm. "Isidore, would you mind ordering something for us? I need to speak with Gavin alone."

Isidore's face was pensive, clearly worried about his boss, but he nodded in much the same way the sergeant had in Captain Gootee's office. There was a reluctance to leave their liege alone in my company. "Sure thing. Anything in particular?"

Andrew wasn't really paying attention anymore, and shook his head absently as he stared at the box. "Whatever you pick up is fine." He pulled out a couple of hundred dollar bills and handed them to Isidore. "Get yourself something as well, and bring it up when it arrives." Isidore started to walk off when Andrew spoke again. This time anger crept into his voice, creating a hard edge to his tone when he picked up the box. "Keep a watchful eye, and don't leave without letting me know first."

Isidore's face hardened, and he nodded. He somehow seemed to swell…there was something menacing just under the surface. It was then I understood that Isidore was a very dangerous man. I couldn't put my finger on it, but I'd bet everything I had that he was more than capable of putting a man in the ground without thinking twice about it. My uncle's agitation, fear, and anger spilled over into the younger man. Isidore was clearly loyal to my uncle, and whoever had upset him today better pray they he didn't find them first. Isidore stalked over to a table and opened the drawer filled to capacity with takeout menus. He started leafing through them and my uncle nudged me.

Andrew motioned for me to follow and we went upstairs. Hurrying after my uncle, I was well past the stage of concern. After years of situations where my handlers had similar looks on their faces, I automatically fell into that cold detached place in my mind. The one that allowed me to observe, listen, and carry out whatever tasks needed to be done without hesitation. Isidore might be dangerous, but I was in an entirely different category.

I'd earned a nickname while I was away, but it of course was shortened like everything dealing with the government, and they called me "The Grim." My mind relaxed, allowing every detail to soak in. My eyes darted around the room looking for possible threats. My voice was flat, even, and cold. "What's wrong?"

Andrew stopped and turned. His face registered that something had changed in me, but he couldn't put his finger on it. Shaking his head, he picked up the pace heading up the stairs. He sat the box on the round table and pulled out the book, reverently placing it next to the box, pushing back a few of the papers with one hand while never taking his other off the book. His face sank as he found what he was looking for and pulled a small jeweler's bag out of the box. He held it in the air before shoving two fingers into the opening. Turning the bag over, he dumped the contents. There was a soft hollow thud as metal struck the cover of the book.

His knees buckled and he rocked back, falling into the wing chair behind him. Andrew was unable to take his eyes off the tiny platinum and sapphire ring that now lay atop the book. Tears welled up, yet did not fall, and he struggled to catch his breath.

I recognized the combination of fear and grief instantly. I'd seen it often throughout the last three decades. Someone close to him was either in trouble, dying, or dead. His was the look of a man who knew the truth of something, yet refused to believe it.

Andrew fumbled for the phone, refusing to look at me. Looking into someone else's eyes would only solidify what he already understood. He couldn't lie to himself any longer if that happened. No, he must not look up. It was the reason why parents, spouses, and other loved ones wouldn't look anyone in the eye when something terrible happened. They wanted to hold on to that last few moments of hope, praying that whatever god was out there would make that terrible thing go away. It never worked.

"I need to make a call," he whispered as he dialed a number. He sat there silently for nearly a minute. I could see the silent prayers emanating from him. I'd seen it before…people not wanting to believe something they knew to be true, praying that they were wrong and whoever they were trying to call wasn't gone. The silent pleading with the gods above that they'd allow them to speak to a loved one once more. Then it sank in as no one answered. He hung up the phone, dialed another number, and waited.

"Hello, this is Andrew. Is Martha available?"

I saw the reaction from the unheard words. His body tensed, his face reddened, and his eyes fought back the tears, his spirit crushed as the news washed over him.

"I see. Thank you," he replied blankly.

Pain etched itself throughout his being and into his soul and his heart broke. I'd grown accustomed to the look over the years in my line of work. It was the look of someone losing the only thing they'd ever cared about; the look of lost and broken love, and of being left behind.

Andrew nodded, his voice barely audible. "I'll be there. Thank you again."

He hung up the phone and slumped in the chair, his eyes fixated on the book in front of him. There was nothing I could say or do. I left him alone long enough to go to the kitchen and grab a glass of water, and placed it next to him.

Sitting down, I bowed my head and solemnly spoke. "I'm so sorry for your loss."

His head snapped up, confusion on his face. "How do you know someone died?"

Swallowing, I bit my lip and tried not to let his grief overtake me. "I've seen that look a lot over the years. I assume it was someone close."

He reached out and picked up the ring. "She was my wife, but that was a lifetime ago. We've remained friends, but after.... Well, we split a long time ago is all."

It was clear that he wasn't accustomed to talking about her, and I felt like a piece of shit. Not only had my uncle been married and divorced, but something traumatic had caused it and I wasn't there. Goddamn, I had to win the shittiest family member of the year award several times over.

"I'm sorry," I whispered.

The words felt hollow, but they were all I had. I was never good with comforting and support. I'd never had to be. I was an orphan and my grandparents were gone long before I was in the picture, so no one ever passed the ability along to me.

"Is there anything I can do for you?" I asked.

Andrew shook his head, his eyes fixated on the book. "No, not right now. Because of her Jewish tradition the funeral is tomorrow morning and we'll need to attend." He looked up at me for a long moment, his face solemn. "I'm really glad you're here, Gavin. You have no idea how much it means to me. Thank you."

"I'm glad I could be here." That was the truth. For the first time in a very long while I felt like I was in the right place at the right time.

We sat in silence for the next thirty minutes until Isidore knocked at the door. I got up and found Isidore holding two pizzas and a bag of po-boys. He looked past me with anger in his eyes, clearly tense. "I didn't know what he wanted so I ordered a little of everything. What's going on?"

Standing there, numb and at a loss for words, I didn't know where to start. "I'm not sure if you're familiar with Martha?"

Isidore's scowl deepened and he simply nodded. "I'm familiar."

My heart dropped and my head dipped. "I'm sorry to say that she passed this morning." I took a deep breath. "The funeral is tomorrow...I'm sure that we'll be closing up shop if you want to attend."

Isidore growled...I mean that literally. It was odd.

He nodded. "I'll be there. Let me know if he needs anything else."

Fixing my eyes on Isidore I looked for the cheerful man I'd met yesterday, only to find that man missing and replaced by someone far more primal. "Thanks for the food. Don't forget to let us know when you're leaving."

He flexed his jaw and anger threatened to spill out. "Especially now."

"What's that mean?" I asked.

He shook his head. "He'll explain everything in time. I've got to go."

He turned and left and I closed the door. Heading to the kitchen, I set the pizzas on the table, brought the bag of po-boys into the living room, and placed it on the table next to the book. I pulled two fried shrimp and oyster po-boys out of the bag and nodded at my uncle to move the book, which he reluctantly did.

Looking at him, I handed him a wrapped sandwich. "You need to eat."

Andrew looked up with a blank look on his face and I knew the words barely registered. Slipping the ring onto his pinky, he took a deep breath and slowly let it out. "I suppose I do." Grabbing the sandwich, he unrolled it and took a bite. "Thanks. You should grab a drink; the french bread is dry from this place."

I did as I was told. He was right...the bread was dry and flaky, but the sandwich itself was amazing. We ate in silence for several minutes, just eating, drinking, and breathing. It was a ritual I'd seen over and over again. When people grieved they needed to remember the basics...food, drink, breathing, and sleep. Everything else would come as long as they were strong enough to handle whatever was next.

Chapter 3

Friday May 29th

Sleep evaded me, so I spent most of the night hours scouring the Internet for information. Ever since I arrived in New Orleans I'd had a sneaking suspicion that something wasn't quite right with the city. Even now I wasn't sure what it was, but after a night of cyber reconnaissance I was starting to think that New Orleans was something of an anomaly. Glancing over at the clock—2:45 a.m.—I decided it was time for me to wind down my evening's activities and start my day. Creating a hidden partition on the internal drive, I hid my notes, searches that I didn't want anyone to find, before heading to the bath.

After a hot shower I pulled on a pair of old jeans and a T-shirt and headed to the kitchen. It was thankfully vacant and I set to work making breakfast. I'd barely gotten the ingredients out of the fridge when Andrew stalked in. He didn't say anything as he pulled the tea pitcher out of the fridge and poured himself a glass before sitting at the table quietly. Changing tactics in an effort to expedite breakfast, I whipped the eggs into a fluffy mixture for ham and cheese omelets. Andrew smiled and thanked me as he mechanically took a fork and ate his meal.

When he finished his food he looked up at me, and I watched as he struggled with his grief. His voice was hollow and flat. "That was surprisingly good. Thank you." Standing, he clapped me on the shoulder when he passed on his way to the sink and dishwasher. "I need to get dressed, and so do you."

Getting to my feet, I followed his lead. "I'll be ready shortly."

I headed back to my room. There I pulled my black suit out of the closet. With Isidore's help we'd been able to get the wrinkles out yesterday afternoon, allowing me to look presentable. Due to my height and size, running out to buy a new suit was impossible.

Tying my shoes, I stood up and pulled on the jacket before reaching for the red tie. Flipping up my collar, I pulled the tie around my neck, but as I started to cross the silk noose I froze and pulled it off. If something went wrong, it would only get in the way. Folding the tie, I hung it over the chair next to the bed and headed for the living room.

Andrew was already at his desk looking lost in thought when I entered. I stood there watching him as he fiddled with a small, intricately carved wooden box. Clearing my throat, I fully entered the room and Andrew snapped his head around in my direction, giving me a woeful look.

He had changed his glasses from the old-fashioned gold-rimmed spectacles to more modern rectangular cut bronze half rimmed glasses. His sapphire blue eyes sparkled and shined through the tinted lenses. He sat there silently, unmoving, as if he were seeing me clearly for the first time, taking in every last detail of my person. At that moment he made a decision, scooped the box into one hand, and stood.

Power washed off him as he stood there palming the box with a determined look painted across his features. The tailored black two-buttoned suit fit his athletic form well without being tight. A thousand tiny details had transformed him from my elderly uncle into someone who could be mistaken for my older brother. What struck me the most was the sense of regal authority that cascaded through the room. I was reminded of some of the men I'd had the opportunity to meet during my career abroad…men who actually ran the governments of the world. Not the politicians or generals, but the scary shadow people who pulled the strings of those around them.

Over the years I had prided myself on being highly observant and normally the smartest person in the room, but I'd missed this by design. That simple fact scared the fuck out of me. I'd survived more lethal encounters than I'd care to count due to my ability to see who people really were. The patterns I saw all around me allowed me to control and manipulate almost every situation…until now. I had no idea who this man standing before me was, and I was frightened for the first time in over twenty years.

Andrew never took his eyes off me while he gave me time to fully process the situation. Then he spoke in a reverent tone. "We have much to discuss, but most of it will have to wait until after the funeral." Looking down at his hand, an old hurt crossed his face before he held the box out for me to take. "This belonged to your father; he would've wanted you to have it."

Forcing my mind back into gear, I stepped forward, taking the box out of his hand before sitting in the chair in front of the desk. "What's this?"

He collapsed into his chair and he let out a long breath. "This would've been so much easier after your parents' deaths, but you disappeared." Something about the man suddenly looked frail as his eyes met mine. "Where did you go?"

Shame and guilt forced me to stare at the floor; nervously I fondled the box in one hand. My voice shook and was barely above a whisper. "After my parents died, I needed to get away."

Andrew straightened up and the frailty I'd seen vanished. His hard blue eyes seemed to soften when he spoke. "Twenty-eight years is a long time to be away."

Shame rushed over me once more, coupled with a tinge of fear that caused me to shiver. "I'm sorry...."

Andrew's voice was soft and tears threatened to fall. "Where did you go that kept you away for so long?"

I couldn't look him in the eye so I focused on the painting just over his shoulder. "I started off on Parris Island."

He looked genuinely surprised. "You were in the marines?"

I didn't know why, but tears came to my eyes even as I fought to maintain control. "Not exactly. The Department of Defense looked at my tests and offered me a job."

Andrew folded his hands, placing them on his chest, and leaned back. "And what did you do for them?"

Memories of explosions, fires, the dying, and the dead flooded my mind and I forced them back into the locked room where they lived. There wasn't a chance in hell I was going to tell him what I'd done or where I'd been. All I could do was lie. "I solved problems, paperwork mostly."

Andrew's eyes narrowed, focusing on me as if trying to divine the information. "Open the box."

I'd forgotten about the small wooden box in my sweaty hands. "What's in it?"

Andrew shook his head and his features remained steadfast. "Open it and find out."

Pushing the box top aside, memories of my father swam through my mind and the tears came. There at the bottom of the box was one of his rings. It was an intricately carved platinum band with a ruby on one side and an emerald on the other. Running my finger along the edge of it, I felt a strange tingling sensation throughout my body. I didn't need encouragement to slip it onto the ring finger of my right hand. Sitting there looking at it, goose flesh erupted and I felt somehow more whole. The feeling subsided and a peace came over me as the world came back into focus. Everything seemed brighter, colors were richer, and I had to blink a few times because the light from the windows illuminated my uncle in a brilliant golden glow that hurt my eyes.

Andrew didn't say a word; he watched, and waited for me to process my emotions.

"I hadn't realized that I missed him so much. Thank you," I said quietly.

Andrew's eyes narrowed and the solemn look never left his face. "I have a few other odds and ends for you as well, but it'll take some digging to find them."

Something about his words didn't sound right. A voice in the back of my head whispered that he was hiding something. I put those thoughts out of my mind immediately, blaming them on the emotional upheaval of receiving something I never thought I'd see again. "I've got plenty of time. Maybe we'll find them on that tour you promised."

Andrew pushed himself forward and leaned his elbows against the desk. "About that...."

I waved him off and took a deep breath. I hadn't meant to make him feel guilty. "I'm joking. The tour will come in time

I'm sure, and I'll finally discover what you've got hidden over there."

Andrew visibly relaxed and looked down at his watch. Shaking his head, he stood. "It's after eight…we should get going, services will be starting soon." He paused for a moment and looked conflicted. "I know you probably want to get behind the wheel of your new vehicle, but seeing how you don't know the way, would you mind if I drove?"

Pulling the keys out of my pocket, I tossed them over and he deftly caught them. "I've got no objections."

It took us about twenty minutes to cut through the broken, battered streets of New Orleans. All things considered, the ride to Jacob Schoen & Son Funeral home was smoother than it should've been given the dated suspension of the Tucker. Another oddity was the fact that it was already thick, clammy, and wet outside, but I never once felt uncomfortable in the car with the windows rolled up. It was not like the thing had air conditioning.

Needless to say, Andrew wasn't exactly in a talkative mood so we made the trip in silence. When we pulled into the gated parking lot I found it curious that it was full of everything from pickup trucks to high end BMWs, Mercedes, and more than two dozen NOPD police cruisers, not to mention the other dozen or so unmarked vehicles. The list of odd/ interesting things that had taken place since I arrived at my uncle's house was growing exponentially.

Andrew pulled into a space at the furthest end of the lot. He sat there for a moment, as if he were trying to work up the nerve to walk inside. I kept my head on a constant swivel, counting more than two dozen police officers in dress blues with a black band across their badges. Andrew finally worked up the nerve and pulled the key out of the ignition, and in one fluid motion stepped out of the vehicle and shut the door quickly. It was as if he were afraid if the door stayed open too long he might chicken out and drive us home.

Following his lead, I closed the door and looked over at my uncle. "What's with the massive police presence?"

The question pulled Andrew out of whatever memory he'd been walking through. He glanced around the parking lot before nodding at me. "Oh, that. Martha was a *vigiles* for the Archive." He saw the confusion on my face and shook his head. "She was a sort of civilian overseer for the Uncommon Crimes Division."

I wasn't sure what a *vigiles* or an Archive were in this context, so I filed it away as something I'd have to discover later. Furrowing my forehead, I looked back at the police officers, trying to discern if the officers wore something that would tell me more about what they did, but found nothing. "Uncommon Crimes? Aren't all crimes uncommon?"

Andrew cut his eyes at me and shook his head. "Not in this city. But this isn't the time or the place to discuss her work."

Guilt ran through me, with that I closed my mouth and let my want for information fall to the side. "You're right, sorry."

Andrew stepped up beside me and clapped me on the shoulder, then guided me towards the front door. "Nothing to be sorry about. You've always been smart and very curious. Nothing wrong with either of those, but right now I need to focus on laying my wife and friend to rest."

I felt bad that I'd completely forgotten about Martha when the first new shiny piece of information that cropped up piqued my curiosity.

"Of course," I said.

I caught sight of Isidore's back before the funeral home door swung closed. Andrew steered us in the direction of the main entrance that was guarded by a middle aged, medium height, very fit black female NOPD officer. She barely glanced up at Andrew before waving him through. She scanned the clipboard in front of her and crossed something off a list. I was following close behind, but obviously not close enough as she reached up and placed a hand on my chest. Her deep nut-brown eyes were bloodshot, and a thin dangerous smile crossed her lips.

Her voice was soft if a bit husky, but it carried a clear authority that she was accustomed to wielding. "Name?"

Even though she'd only spoken the one word, it was clear to me that if I wasn't on the list and I tried to bypass her I'd be fortunate to wind up in a cell instead of a body bag. I'd seen this a lot over the years. She was the kind of officer that relished in the violence that her job afforded her. She'd bait someone and use her position as an excuse to justify whatever came next.

Choosing my tone carefully so I wouldn't challenge her any more than I already had by towering over her a good twelve inches, I replied simply, "Gavin Randall."

The officer huffed, her eyes darted over the paperwork, apparently praying that my name wasn't there, and those prayers were answered. She took a half step back, all pretense of pleasantness gone now. Puffing out her chest, she put a hand on the hilt of her weapon, with a curt nod that told me to return from whence I'd come. A tinge of excitement colored her voice as adrenaline pumped through her veins; she hoped I'd cause a ruckus. "This is a closed event and you're not on the list." With a nudge from her thumb she unsnapped the nylon strap on her holster. "I'm going to have to ask you to leave."

She'd positioned herself well enough for the average size man. But I was not exactly average size. I thought about snapping her neck, but I did the smart thing and held my hands up as I took a step back. "I'm sorry for interrupting. I'll wait for Andrew by the car if that's all right."

Her face contorted, her hopes for a fight being dashed. "You'll need to stand outside the gate."

By this point Andrew had swung around, and stood there watching the encounter with great interest. Now that things were quickly fading into a non-event, he stepped in. "Officer Trahan, I'm sorry I didn't mention it earlier, but Gavin is with me."

Officer Trahan whipped her head around and snarled at my uncle, jabbing a finger into the papers and holding up the clipboard for him to see. "He isn't on the list."

Andrew swelled to his full height and Officer Sonia Trahan visibly shrank as her face went ashen. His voice was hard and even as he stared down into her eyes. "I believe I'm awarded a plus one?"

Fear and anger swam across her features in equal measure. "Yes...."

Andrew gave her a big smile. He stepped around and put his hand on my shoulder, pulling me a foot past her. "Then Gavin will be my guest."

Sonia knew she'd lost, and wasn't above trying to get one last dig in before she was finished. Turning her attention to me, she held out her hand. "I'll need your ID."

Pulling my ID out of my wallet, I handed it to her and she scribbled down my information before waving me through. Once we were a safe distance away, I whispered to my uncle. "Security is kind of tight, don't you think?"

Andrew kept a steady hand on my shoulder. "The Uncommon Crimes Division is a very tight knit group and doesn't care for strangers."

If Sonia was any indication, that was an understatement. I kept my head and eyes moving, looking for something or someone that I couldn't put my finger on. Something felt wrong other than the obvious fact that someone was dead. "I can see that."

I'd been to presidential inaugurations with less security than I saw here. All the officers were in their best dress blues, but their weapons were a different story. Usually for social or important events dress blues would be accompanied with shiny new weapons they'd never carry in the field. These men and women were using their daily service weapons, all of which had seen more than a little action.

Andrew guided me through the front door, where we both had to duck. As I crossed the threshold I felt a weight come over me, dampening my senses and making me feel sluggish and unsteady. If Andrew hadn't had a death grip on my shoulder keeping me upright, I might have stumbled or even fallen. A half second later the sickening sensation was gone. Almost as if he knew what had happened, Andrew released me, allowing me to follow in his wake.

The packed lobby fell silent as people made a wide berth for Andrew, and myself by proxy. The scene reminded me of a nature documentary I'd seen when I was young about a pack of wolves. The other weaker wolves parted, allowing the alpha to move to the front to claim what was his.

Isidore was in the back of the room talking to a very large, powerfully built man with long black hair pulled back in a ponytail. The man stroked his scraggly beard and he nodded at Andrew before returning his gaze to the crowd. He looked out of place in the custom tailored suit he was wearing. Something about him spoke of a predator as he continued to scan the crowd. Isidore was doing the same, and I wondered if they too felt something was amiss.

A stout yet pudgy looking medium sized woman with mousy brown hair, porcelain white skin, and gray eyes was the only one who dared slow Andrew's progress. When she stood in his path it felt like the room took in a collective breath.

She stuck out a beefy hand to my uncle, craning her neck to look him in the eyes. "I'm sorry for your loss, Andrew."

Andrew mechanically took her hand. I thought I saw revulsion in his eyes for a microsecond when he looked at her. "Thank you, Ms. Dodd."

If Ms. Dodd noticed, she didn't show it when she stepped back and faded into the crowd. Isidore and his companion wore sour looks and their eyes tracked the small woman through the crowd. It was clear that they didn't care for her, and by the way Andrew unconsciously wiped his hand with a handkerchief from his pocket, neither did he.

The low murmur of people talking guided us down a double wide tiled hall to the chapel that held Martha's casket. This room was no different than the lobby had been. As soon as everyone caught sight of Andrew, they fell silent. Every head turned, watching Andrew pass through the double doors.

He never looked to one side or the other, just headed for the closed black casket in the front of the room. I watched as every man, woman, and child practically held their breath as he stalked through the room. I wasn't sure if it was respect or fear that kept them so fixated upon my uncle. Either way they were thankfully ignoring my presence completely.

It was then that I noticed Andrew still wore the sapphire ring on his pinky. He stood in front of the casket for a moment, and then lay his hand atop it and bowed his head. Sunlight glinted through the room, catching the sapphire and illuminating it just before he removed his hand. Turning, I found myself standing between my uncle and a shivering old man.

The stooped, heavily wrinkled old man in front of me had bloodshot, faded chartreuse eyes and surprisingly thick oily black hair. His gnarled left hand wrapped around the gold handle of an onyx cane with a rubber tip. As he glared through me to my uncle, I knew I'd found what had been troubling me since I'd arrived.

The old man coughed and wheezed when he spoke. "You should've stayed in your musty old bookstore, Andrew." Every word was laced with anger, hate, and loathing.

Something about the old man was dangerous, giving me the dual sensation of having my skin wanting to crawl off my body and an unhealthy desire to rip his head off. I felt Andrew's hand on my shoulder as he eased me back while sliding in front of me a half step. "You should go, Walter."

At the mention of Walter's name, a number of police officers got to their feet. One officer in particular, a tall, lanky man wearing a lieutenant's bar on his collar, barely twitched and four men surrounded the geezer. They were careful not to touch him, but made it clear that he was unwelcome. When he didn't move, a universal snap of weapons being freed of their bonds swam through the room. Every officer in the room had their hand on their weapon, and the four nearest him had theirs half drawn. It was clear that if he didn't move soon they'd execute him right there.

Walter didn't seem all that bothered that four men less than half his age were reaching for their weapons. He gave Andrew one last glare. "We'll be seeing one another again very soon."

He turned and hobbled out with his escort.

Andrew looked at the big man against the wall and nodded. The tall man returned the nod just before turning and leaving the room to follow Walter. Andrew looked down as he inspected me carefully. "You okay?"

His concern puzzled me. "Yeah. Are you all right?"

He turned and looked back at the casket before nodding. "I'll be fine."

We spent the next hour standing at the rear of the room shaking peoples' hands as they expressed their sorrow for our loss. Two hours later we'd interred her remains in a mausoleum not three miles away before heading home. An odd word to use... I hadn't called anywhere I'd been in the last twenty-eight years such a thing. There were places I'd stayed, places I'd been, but none of them were home...it was an odd yet powerful word.

Chapter 4

It was a little after 1:00 p.m. when we returned. Andrew vanished into his room without a word and I headed for mine to change. After slipping on a pair of jeans and a T-shirt, I headed for the kitchen and pulled the leftover pizza out of the fridge. I took a couple of slices and put them in the microwave, hit the one-minute express button, and waited for it to beep. Once it did I opened the door and closed it again, leaving the warm pizza inside for my uncle.

I pulled three cold slices out of the box, stacked them on the plate, and headed for the table. Over the last few days I'd encountered a very interesting problem with what I'd been eating. After nearly three decades of eating cold to room temperature food, anything even resembling hot food burned the shit out of my mouth and throat.

Sitting my plate on the table, I was barely in my chair when I tore into the first piece, devouring everything except for the crust. I was halfway into my second slice when Andrew pushed open the door. Simply pointing at the microwave, I inclined my head. "I warmed up a couple of slices for you."

Andrew eyed my plate curiously on his way to recover his food. Pulling his plate out, he sat down across from me. He took a bite of pizza and swallowed before speaking. "Are you holding up all right?"

All things considered it was a very odd question. Swallowing the last bit of edible pizza, I placed the burnt crust on the plate. "It wasn't my former wife that we laid to rest today. I'm far more concerned about how you are doing."

Andrew didn't say anything before taking a big bite of pizza, gesturing at the crust on my plate. "Are you going to eat that?"

Snatching my last slice of pizza off the plate, I pushed it towards him. "Absolutely not! I have to draw the line when it comes to filler."

He scooped the two pieces of crust up in one hand and pushed the plate back. "Thanks."

He was a little surprised at the cold crust when he tore off a bite. I finished off my slice of pizza before tossing the last of the crust onto the plate. I sat there for a moment, wondering where to start. This was hardly a typical day in the Randall household and I didn't want to push my luck, but I did have questions.

I'd felt this way when I was in school on the reservation back home in Montana; awkward, shy, not knowing where to put my oversized form that wouldn't upset those around me. "Uncle Andrew, I've got a couple of questions if you feel up to humoring me."

Andrew picked up the last piece of crust and leaned back in his chair. "What's on your mind, son?"

Where to start? I figured it was either go big or go home. "Who is Walter and what's his problem?"

Andrew held one of the pieces of crust in his hand and tore at it with his teeth, using the time to figure out the best way to answer the question. "Walter was a friend a long time ago. We had a falling out of sorts a few years before you were born." Andrew's features darkened. His anger was almost palpable and seemed to radiate from him in waves of heat. "Back then I wanted to kill the man." His face softened but his voice remained hard. "But Martha, being the kind and generous woman she was, made me promise not to harm him."

I didn't need all my years of training to sense the deep remorseful bitterness in his voice.

"And now?" I asked before I could stop myself.

He looked up at me with the closest thing to pure hate I'd seen in a long time. "And now, he simply isn't worth the effort."

There was something familiar in the tone, so matter of fact that it wasn't the act of taking someone's life that bothered him. It was clear he didn't have an issue with it, but it was more a matter that someone was such a waste of space that to acknowledge them would allow them credibility they didn't deserve.

I got up, grabbed the pizza box, and brought it over to the table, pulling out a slice as I set it down. "When we walked into the funeral home I felt weak, almost sick. You expected my reaction. How?" Taking a big bite of pizza, I sat there watching my uncle.

The anger faded from Andrew's face. He leaned over, grabbed another slice of pizza, and put it on his plate. "Let's finish our lunch before we get into something as complicated as that."

I raised an eyebrow in his direction. "It's not like I'm going to forget the question."

Andrew snorted at the comment. "I'd be worried about you if you did. Finish your lunch. After that we'll go into the living room, pour ourselves a drink, and have a nice long chat."

Finishing the edible part of the pizza, I placed the crust on his plate. Closing the box, I got up and put it in the fridge before my uncle could turn this into an all you can eat buffet. I washed my plate and hands in the sink.

Andrew finished his food before doing the same, then we headed for the living room. He went to the liquor cabinet and pulled out a bottle of Dalmore 15, and set it on the table with two tumblers. He gestured for me to take a seat in one of the wing chairs.

I didn't bother to hide the disbelief on my face and took my seat. Andrew uncorked the bottle and poured us a healthy measure. "You really enjoy your scotch."

His shoulders made a small dismissive twitch. "The little pleasures are all a man has to call his own."

He held up his glass in a silent toast to me, and I returned it before we knocked it back in one. He poured a second round and leaned back in his chair. He looked pensive for a moment and then relaxed as he apparently made a decision. "What do you know of our family history?"

What I knew of our history was laughable. "Not much. We're from St. Mary, Montana, which was what...population fifty?"

Andrew stiffened, realizing just how little I knew. "So that's it? You don't know where we're from or anything about your mother?"

Sipping on my scotch, I shook my head, confused by his remark. "Mom was a member of the Blackfoot tribe. From what I gathered back then, Grandpa Aatsista-Mahkan wasn't pleased that she'd married outside the tribe...or maybe it was my father in particular that he didn't care for."

Andrew snorted, lost in memories. "You don't have any idea how bad it was at first. There was a time I thought the tribal elders would murder your father and me in our sleep." He took a drink of scotch as he pulled himself free of the memory. "Anything else?"

It was clear he was looking for something, but I didn't have an answer so I shook my head. "I don't know what you want to hear. It wasn't as if either side of the family held a special class on our history or anything. As you know, I attended school on the reservation and after that...." Embarrassment and a tinge of guilt hit me. "After that I left home."

Andrew looked at me wistfully. "I was there that night. You were so pale, I thought you'd pass out. You were shaking when they called your name before parading you across the stage like a show pony. Once you didn't faint I was convinced you'd puke all over your grandfather and the other tribal elders."

The truth was I'd lost my dinner a few minutes prior to the ceremony. I'd always felt like an outsider. I was a half-breed—half "English" and half Blackfoot—but neither side accepted me. The townies didn't like my father because he'd married an Indian. They didn't like me because as far as they were concerned I was one of "them." The tribe, on the other hand, hated me because I was white in their eyes. One foot in either world, yet accepted by none.

Aatsista-Mahkan, my grandfather, particularly despised me and took every opportunity to remind me that I was proof that the touch of the English had ruined his daughter. Every time anyone from the reservation said English they made it sound like a curse word. To them English were filthy, uncivilized, and murdering bastards. And I embodied everything they hated.

I grimaced and nodded. I tried to keep the bitterness out of my voice, but from the look on his face I'd failed. "Such fond memories."

Leaning back in his chair, he fondled his glass thoughtfully. He was clearly working up to something, but he was trying to find a place to start. He nodded to himself as he decided on a course of action. "My father—your grandfather, Harold—and my mother, Ethel, came over from England, passing through Ellis Island before finding their way to Montana. They'd come to the United States for the promise of a new life. One with freedom to be who they were, which I'm sure you're thinking is odd but it's true. They left the old world out of fear, and braved an entirely new continent in the hopes of building a better life."

Leaning back in my chair, I took a healthy drink of my scotch. "I never had the pleasure of meeting them."

Andrew let out a long breath, before a wistful thought turned his lips up at some long lost memory. "Mom died when I was ten, from what I can only guess was malnutrition and exposure. Dad didn't handle it well and just wandered off one summer day a few years later, leaving your father and I to fend for ourselves." He took another stiff drink for courage before continuing. "That's when Zachary, your father, got a job working on the reservation and met Jennifer, your mother."

I leaned forward, placing my forearms on the table. "What did he do for them, and why did they even consider hiring him? They hate the English."

Andrew sat there calmly for a moment looking me in the eye. "Give me time to tell the story and all will be revealed. Afterward I'll take you for a tour. I think it's time."

Tilting my glass in his direction, I fixed my attention on him. "Then by all means tell your story."

Andrew returned my toast and he downed more of the scotch. "As I said, that's when Zack met your mother. They were able to keep their relationship a secret for two years before they decided to come out to her father and the tribe." He paused to pour himself another drink before continuing. "They wanted to get married, and it was with great reluctance that Aatsista-Mahkan agreed to their union. Your father was too important to the tribe to have him leave, taking Aatsista-Mahkan's daughter with him when he went. They were very happy together but wanted a family of their own, and fifteen years after their marriage you were born. I've never been able to figure out if Aatsista-Mahkan was happy about your birth or not."

Andrew shifted in his seat, clearly uncomfortable at having to tell this story, but he settled back with another swig of scotch and started again. "I need to roll back the clock a little…I got ahead of myself. Your father was a good man and your mother was a wonderful woman, but they were newly married and I felt like a third wheel. Right after my eighteenth birthday, I bought the family car from Zack and moved to New Orleans." He snickered as he sipped on his scotch. "In case you were wondering, the family car was the one I sold you."

That was a surprise but now it made sense why Andrew insisted that I keep it. "The Tucker belonged to my father?"

Andrew poured us another round. "Yep." He leaned back in his chair, joy and anger danced across his face before he took another swig of liquid courage and continued. "I wasn't here a month when I met Walter and we became fast friends. Two years later I met Martha and we married the same year. She was in school at Loyola for occult studies, and Walter and I were her pet projects."

And now he'd lost me. "I don't think I understand. What does one thing have to do with the other?"

Andrew held a hand out for patience and sat up straight in his chair. "I'm getting to that. Just relax." He set his glass on the table and his face became serious. "Now that you know a little about our family's origins, it's time you learned about your heritage and what makes us truly special." He never blinked as he spoke. "What do you know about the world of the occult? Magic, sorcerers, wizards, or more importantly, the stone born?"

Part of me wanted to laugh in his face, but I could tell that he was serious. Over the years I'd encountered some pretty weird shit, but nothing that would indicate magic was real. And in this moment, by his tone and his question, that's exactly what he was implying.

Leaning back in my chair, I kept my eyes locked on his. My voice was low but steady, and the Grim was on high alert, first with Walter and now this. "That's a broad question, but I'll answer as best I can. I've encountered a lot of strange beliefs throughout my travels, read a lot of mythology, and even encountered some spooky stuff. I can say, however, that I've never encountered anything that would make me believe that any of it was true, or that magic actually exists." Taking a sip of my scotch, I shook my head slightly. "As far as wizards and sorcerers are concerned, there is a lot of literature dedicated to their myth. I've never even heard of the stone born."

Andrew picked up his glass and drained it. Pouring yet another stiff drink he leaned back in his chair, staring at me for a full minute. "And if I were to tell you that they are real? That magic is real? And you are one of the rarest of the supernatural community, a stone born?"

A crooked grin crossed my face and I fought back actual laughter. "If you told me that you believed it, I'd have to pass it off as an old man who has had too much to drink for the evening."

Andrew frowned, his face turning sour. His eyes lit up as he sat his glass down. "Do you know how old I am?"

That was a bizarre question. "Seventy-four, I believe.

Andrew nodded. "And in this moment, how old do I look?"

Now that was a better question. It was one I'd been asking myself over and over again since I'd arrived. Funny thing was the thought always slipped from my mind. "That's something that's been on my mind since I saw you Wednesday afternoon." Taking another sip of scotch, I felt something tingling at the back of my mind. "I've been meaning to say something, but—"

Andrew quickly finished the sentence for me. "But you've gotten distracted and forgotten?"

Something in the way he said it made the back of my mind itch. It really hadn't been a question but a statement. He knew I'd been curious, but he also knew that I'd forgotten.

That was a combination of curious and annoying. "Care to fill me in on how you know that to be a fact? Or would you rather tell me why you look like my elder brother instead of my elderly uncle? Better yet, why don't you tell me why your clothes are tailor made to make you look frail and sickly?"

Andrew flinched. "I wasn't expecting...." He held up his hand and shook his head. "Never mind. You have valid questions. The best way to answer it is to tell you that as a stone born you age normally till you're about the age you are now. After that the process stops."

I looked at him in disbelief. "What do you mean, it stops?" I snorted. "You want me to believe that you simply didn't age after you hit forty-five?" I finished off my scotch and poured some more. "That's a fountain of youth that people would kill for, if it were true."

Andrew was more than a little peeved at my continued disbelief. "Look, I can't make you believe me if you refuse to do so. Allow me to point out that you've lied to me several times since you've been here." He grumbled more to himself than to me. "That's never happened before."

I couldn't help myself and I let out a chortle. "People lie all the time. You can't really believe that you're so special that no one has ever lied to you!"

He scoffed. "It would be a relief if they could, but that's one of my many gifts. Everyone...." He paused and looked me in the eyes. "Everyone—except you, it seems—is compelled to tell me the truth. They can't help themselves."

Now that I thought about his words, I did feel compelled to tell him certain things, but I'd chosen to ignore those impulses before consciously lying to him. Maybe he wasn't completely insane, but he was closely bordering doddering old fool territory. Then again, he didn't look old, and earlier he'd even felt powerful. Powerful enough to make me feel fear again. Odd....

Chewing on the words, I struggled to let it all sink in. "Let's say that we are special. That I have a fantastic heritage and I'm one of these stone born. What does that even mean? And just how do you know that I've lied to you?"

He poked a finger at the back of his head. "There's an itch way back here when you do it. It's absolutely infuriating!" He took another swig of scotch. "It's really impressive." He seemed relieved that I was actually considering his words instead of writing him off.

I knew the itch he was describing…it happened every time.... Damn! It happened every time I'd wanted to tell him the truth and I consciously lied about it. Now that was spooky as hell. "What does this mean? How do I fit in with what you're talking about?"

He sized me up like a prizefighter considering how best to devastate his opponent. "Where you fit in is here with me. The fact that you are impervious to my abilities makes you a very special person."

I held my hands close together. "Short school bus special."

Andrew sighed and waved me off. "I'm trying to tell you something important."

I was quickly losing my patience. I didn't like the feeling of not understanding, and this was something I truly didn't grasp. "Then just say it!"

Andrew was frustrated. It was obvious that he wasn't used to people not simply accepting what he had to say at face value. His eyes darted to his desk and he pointed at the far end of the room. "Do you see the sapphire?"

Now that was a segue! "What the hell does that have to do with anything?"

He didn't answer; instead he waved his hand. The sapphire on his desk glowed, emitting deep blue shafts of blue light throughout the room. The small ring he wore on his pinky finger glowed and pulsed in unison with the larger stone.

Before I could interject, a thin wispy light blue tendril slithered from the ring and shot across the room, to be absorbed by the massive sapphire.

The stone in the ring was gone, simply vanished before my eyes. I spent the next several seconds looking between the empty socket on the ring and back at the sapphire on the desk. I stood to go investigate, but things got even stranger.

The shafts of light flickered and converged in front of the desk, creating an image. It took a few seconds before I could make it out, but when I did I fell back into the chair behind me. There, standing in front of my uncle's desk, was a sapphire blue translucent figure of the woman from the photo I'd seen earlier.

She looked confused until she saw Andrew, and relief seemed to sweep through her. The sapphire form pixelated as she tried to move, only to suddenly stop when her eyes fell on me. Her expression changed from relief to instant trepidation. A weak yet pleasant voice emanated from her with a deep English accent. "Who are you?"

Andrew was on his feet in an instant, smiling at her before waving a hand in my direction. "Martha, I'd like to properly introduce you to Gavin." He sounded like a proud parent showing off his prize child to the love of his life. "He's all grown up."

Her form wavered and she groaned in pain. "It's too soon. I've got to rest...." She tried to say something more, but it was garbled and she vanished from sight, retreating back to the sapphire on Andrew's desk.

Setting my glass on the table in front of me, I shook my head. "What the fuck was that?"

Andrew beamed. It was the first time since I'd been there that he looked whole, happy, and content. His mind was far away as he kept his eyes fixated on the sapphire. "That was Martha...well, a part of her anyway."

My head was hurting. No matter how I tried to process what had just happened, I wasn't able to fully comprehend it. "I don't understand."

Tearing his eyes away from the desk, he turned his attention back to me. "When someone like us is born a gemstone is created. The parents look after the child and their stone until they are of suitable age to be responsible for themselves. Your father kept mine until I was eighteen, and after your father died I was to care for yours until your eighteenth birthday, but you vanished and I've been holding it for you ever since. Every gemstone is different; for instance, Martha's was a sapphire. Mine is a jade and emerald combination. Your father's was a half ruby, half emerald concoction, and yours is a golf ball sized diamond."

I felt weak. I couldn't stop blinking as my mind tried to process everything I was being told. Something deep inside of me told me his words were true, but how could that be? How could I be stone born? How was any of this possible? "I'm not sure how all of this works...I simply don't understand what's happening."

Andrew pushed his chair back and stood, waving for me to do the same. "Follow me."

He opened a locked door leading to a hallway on the forbidden side of the house. We were about halfway down the hall when he stopped and stuck another key into a door and opened it. Stepping inside the massive room, I saw hundreds of stones lining the walls, shelves, and tables. He guided me through the maze to the exact center of the room and pointed at a display case with a single flawless diamond the size of a golf ball hovering about three inches off the red velvet lining.

He flipped back the top and waved me over. "This is yours. Normally you would handle this for the first time when you are eighteen, but I've heard of people getting theirs later. Not twenty-seven years later, but still. Be warned...this will be painful, but I promise it'll be worth it."

I barely heard the words as I felt a thrumming inside my brain coming from the perfectly cut rounded stone in front of me. It called to me. This was what had been calling me to New Orleans. This was why I had come here. Everything Andrew said was true. For the first time in my life I wasn't in control of myself as my body acted on its own, betraying me.

I stepped forward, and holding out my left hand I slowly wrapped my fingers around its smooth polished surface. I felt power surge through my body as heat pulsated through the diamond into my hand. Its smooth surface erupted into thousands of tiny shards, slicing through the palm of my hand and fingers. Larger structures jutted out of its surface, through my palm, and out the back side of my hand. I screamed and the world around me shivered. I hit my knees, gripping my wrist in my right hand.

I didn't know how or why, but I felt it was important that my left hand stay over the case as blood ran freely from my hand down onto the red velvet. The stone stopped growing after the shard that penetrated my hand was about four inches long and had turned onyx. When I released the stone, it floated above the blood soaked velvet, now oddly shaped, jagged, and weeping. My head swam, darkness came for me, and I fell back into its warm embrace.

Twenty years earlier

The rough stone floor was cool against my face. An ever-widening pool of red-black fluid spilled out all around me as someone grabbed the back of my neck, yanking me upwards before slamming my face back into the floor. The thud was followed by an immediate sickening crack of one of my bones breaking.

The man behind me whispered in my ear with a thick Arabic accent. "You will tell me what I want to know!"

Thing was, I wouldn't…I couldn't, because I simply didn't know and he wouldn't believe me. "If I knew I'd tell you." I wheezed, coughing up blood.

He kicked me hard in the ribs and I felt one snap. "Liar!"

I didn't know how long we'd been at this today. It could've been minutes, hours, or days for all I knew. I'd long since lost track of time. They'd been interrogating me for what felt like years. A part of me knew that I wouldn't be able to take much more of this kind of abuse…that I was dying. It wouldn't be long now. I was drowning on my own blood from internal injuries. If that didn't get me, dehydration or malnutrition was close behind. More likely my death would come from one too many blows to the head or a rib puncturing my heart.

When the man grew tired of beating on me he would call for the guards. They would drag me down a long corridor and out into the center of their old mud and stone fortress. There they'd toss me into one of the many stone lined pits covered with ancient thick iron grates. During the day I'd bake in the sun, then shiver in the cold of the night. The sound of the medieval padlock snapping shut sounded akin to a nail being driven through steel. The sound of being one click closer to death.

At first this was how I'd kept track of the time, counting the days and nights, but soon the sweats, fever, and sun drove all reason from my mind. That, coupled with the daily beatings, had long since caused me to lose track of even what year it was, let alone how long I'd been there. The guards would relieve themselves over the grate in an attempt to humiliate me. But truth be told I secretly prayed for them to do so. I knew I was poisoning myself, but drinking the urine was keeping me alive. They threw rotten food or mildewed bread down for me to eat, and laughed as I scraped it into my mouth.

Reality crashed back to the forefront of my mind when my captor grew angry with my lack of cooperation and slammed his boot into my crotch. I coughed as a case of the dry heaves overtook me. Curling into the fetal position, I tucked my head between my knees as he continued to slam his leather boots into me over and over again. After several minutes he grew tired and knelt beside me, pulling me up by the hair so he could speak directly into my ear. "You'll die here very slowly if you don't tell me what I want to know."

I was still gasping for air. One of the broken ribs was grating against my lung. Now it was truly only a matter of time before it filled with blood and I drowned on my own fluids. I couldn't speak, and in his frustration he slammed his fist into the side of my head, sending me hard to the stone floor.

He said something in Arabic I couldn't understand and I felt myself hoisted into the air and drug back to the hole I called home. They tossed me in and I heard the familiar click of the ancient lock above, and my mind drifted.

The moon was high in the night sky when I heard something in the inky darkness. Instinct told me to move, forced me to investigate. I was rewarded for my vigilance with mind numbing pain as every inch of my body ached in a way that only the near dead could.

A childhood memory overtook me and I heard the beating of drums and a low steady chant building off in the distant reaches of my mind. At that moment I felt calm.

Then I heard a man's voice, which was smooth, comforting, and very English. "You're not going to die like this, are you?"

I realized that my mind had become unhinged because I knew no one was there. The drumming was a little louder and the chanting stronger, building and building, making my heart race along with it.

I coughed up blood and spit it on the ground in front of me. "I've got to hold out long enough for my people to come get me."

The man laughed. It was rueful and angry. "You don't believe that lie anymore, do you? They are never coming for you."

The drums and chanting grew even louder and I felt my chest vibrating with every beat.
I couldn't move for fear of pain. "I have to. It's all I've got left."

I felt someone touch my shoulder and grip it tight. "That's not all you have, boy! You know they're not coming. If you want to live you're going to have to do something about it!"

The drumming was so loud now, and I chanted along with the chorus of angry demons. The pain faded and I felt stronger. "I don't know what to do."

I could barely hear him over the drums as he whispered in my ear. "Kill them all!"

For the following twenty-nine hours I acted as the angel of death made manifest, hours that became etched across my soul and burned into my memory. The two men who pulled me out of the pit died first. From there I sought out every living soul, saving my tormenter until the end. He suffered for only a matter of hours before he passed with the dawn of the following morning. They still haunted my dreams...their screaming, pleading, and crying for mercy, begging to be spared, but the rage that took hold of me wouldn't allow it.

Before I left this special hell on earth, I doused it in diesel fuel before setting off all the ordnance I could find. Little did I know that the shithole was built atop a natural phosphorus deposit. It could be seen for weeks afterward, burning like a miniature sun on the horizon.

It took me another three days to find the nearest base, which happened to belong to the Israelis. They tended to my wounds and contacted my handlers, who took their time in collecting me. A few months later I learned I'd been a captive for 113 days, and that the Iraqi government blamed the Kurds for killing every last man, woman, and child housed at the forward base. No survivors were left to tell the tale; a practice I would maintain throughout the remainder of my career.

After that no one ever looked at me the same. I ignored the whispers and snide glances. They hadn't been there and never would be. They didn't have the right to judge me. The one other thing I learned that I wasn't meant to was the fact that my people knew the moment I'd been taken, and had written me off. I wasn't worth the effort to retrieve. That's when they'd given me the pet name of the Grim Reaper.

Friday May 29th

Fear overtook me and I didn't want to open my eyes. I didn't want to find out it was all a dream and I was still back in the pit. Still, I forced my eyes open slowly and saw Andrew leaning over me, holding my head in his hands and looking scared to death. He kept repeating the same thing over and over again. "What have I done? Please be okay...please wake up."

When I stirred he visibly relaxed, but I was still concerned about the pain. It had been so real, as if it were still happening, but when I moved my arms…nothing. I was fine, thank God. I was not in a hole dying, choking to death on my own fluids.

Something in the back of my mind remembered the black diamond shards slicing through my hand and out the back of it. I steadied myself, preparing for the worst…a ruined hand that would have to be lopped off to save the arm. But when I looked down it was healed—heavily scarred, caked in blood, but functional and healed.

With a little help from Andrew I got to my knees. "What was that?"

Andrew pulled me close, hugging me before allowing a tentative smile to cross his face. "I'm not sure. I've never seen anything like that. Are you all right?"

Shifting my weight, I allowed Andrew to help me to my feet. "I don't know."

Andrew's eyes flashed over at the display case, filled with pear shaped blood red garnets…the tears I'd seen just before I passed out. The once perfect spherical diamond was now a jagged mess of a dozen different colored shafts, the most prominent of them being a four-inch black diamond covered in my blood.

Andrew's voice was hoarse, his hands shook, and he looked genuinely frightened. He kept a steady arm under my shoulders, keeping me upright. "I'm not sure what happened. It wasn't supposed to be like that. I've never even heard of something like this occurring." He looked down at me and shook his head. "Is there anything I can do for you?"

My stomach was tying itself in knots and my intestines churned as the old memory danced through my mind's eye. I'd spent years trying to forget that night, and now it was as if it happened yesterday. "Got anymore scotch, and maybe a washcloth?"

Andrew half carried me back to the living room before pouring me a double. He disappeared into the nearest bathroom and returned with a wet cloth and a towel. He waited for me to clean my hand before vanishing again to dispose of them.

He sat at the table next to me and poured himself a double, then refilled mine. "That, my boy, was the strangest thing I've ever seen."

Downing my drink, I held it out for another as I swallowed. "I take it that wasn't normal."

Andrew filled my glass again. "The inductions are never violent. Normally they're peaceful, uplifting experiences." He poured himself another scotch and downed it as he waved a hand back towards the hall. "Nothing like that is ever supposed to happen."

Downing my drink and holding out my glass for another, I grimaced. "I'm a violent man, and I deserve a lot worse than I got."

Andrew shook his head. "It's not like that, Gavin. Your mind is supposed to awaken, not do whatever the fuck that was."

He was right…I'd awoken. I'd spent years trying to forget what I could now recall with perfect clarity. How I wish that wasn't the case. Everything that took place over those six months, the before, during, and after, had all rushed back to me in a matter of seconds.

Other things floated through my mind as well. What my uncle had said earlier I now knew as truth. We wouldn't age like those around us. The world vibrated with an unseen energy, but even now the glowing sensation of certain items of power were fading from my vision. Sensations and the knowledge that there were things out there so much greater than I'd ever seen were now just around the corner. A weight fell upon my shoulders, and I knew that I was being called to something much greater than I'd known or done before. At that moment, though, I needed a drink…several drinks. I needed time to process what just happened.

Chapter 5

Saturday May 30th

Jerking awake, I turned my head to the side and saw the clock read 6:15 a.m. As I rolled out of bed my head felt heavy, sluggish, and to top it off I had cotton mouth. If I were a hopeful kind of man I'd think the large quantities of scotch, I'd consumed last night were responsible for my fatigue. I was not a hopeful man, however, and I knew it was the nightmares and the ghosts of the dead that haunted me.

Even now I heard their screams in the deep recesses of my mind. Clenching my jaw, I stretched and stood, swelling to my full height. I forced the voices and screams to be silent. They may rule my dreams, but here and now, in this world, I was in control. They would remain silent until such time they could escape their cages to haunt me again.

When I brought my arms down I caught sight of my mangled hand. My palm and fleshy parts of my fingers were heavily marred with scars. It gave my hand the appearance of a melted wax figure. It looked as if the artist was able to make a roughhewn shape of a hand, but the detail work was beyond them. Over the years I'd seen soldiers who were much worse off than this. I at least got to keep the use of my hand, no matter how messed up it might appear to the outside world.

This was physical proof that I was in New Orleans, twenty years removed from my time as a guest of the Iraqi government. Once in a while I had doubts. A little voice that hid in my deepest fears would taunt me saying that I'd never left the pit and I was still a prisoner, that all of this was a figment of my sun stroked mind.

No, the voice was a lie and this, this was reality…my scarred hand, my uncle, and this miserable humidity. This was real. Running my fingers across my hand and feeling the scars again.

More than the scars, the weight settling itself on my broad shoulders told me that this was reality and it weighed heavy on my soul. I didn't know what was coming, but it felt important. Something that would forever change me in ways that I couldn't even begin to fathom. At this point, the things I couldn't fathom were easy enough to come by. Most importantly, though, I was cared for, and for the first time in more years than I'd care to admit I was not alone.

Grabbing the last pair of clean jeans and shirt out of my bag, I headed for the shower. The unfortunate reality of having to do my own laundry was upon me. But that could wait till I got something in my stomach. After dressing I trudged down the hall and through the kitchen door. Andrew was at the stove making breakfast. He glanced back, giving me an appraising look, and returned his attention to the stove.

"Breakfast will be ready shortly," he said over his shoulder.

Placing my elbows on the table, I dropped my face into my hands and rubbed. "Thanks."

Keeping my face firmly in my hands, I massaged my forehead and eyes, trying to give myself a little relief. Whatever Andrew was making filled the air with the aromas of sizzling salted butter, pepper, and a hint of seafood. The smell alone was enough to make me feel better.

It wasn't long before I heard the plate gently clinking against the hardwood of the table top and sliding in front of me. Slowly lifting my head out of my hands, my eyes were bleary from the pressure I'd been applying to ease my headache. A few seconds later the world fell into focus, revealing crab cakes topped with perfectly poached eggs smothered in a thick golden hollandaise sauce.

My mouth watered at the sight. Sitting up straight, I looked over at my uncle, genuinely impressed. "Wow!"

Andrew looked pleased with himself as he gestured at the plate. "I assure you, it tastes far better than it looks."

Picking up the fork, I tore into it with fervor. Turning the utensil on its edge, I sliced through the egg, allowing the liquid gold yolk to gently cascade over the crab cake below. A second motion freed a good portion of the crab cake, egg, and a generous helping of hollandaise. Letting the flavors mix in my mouth, my eyes rolled back in ecstasy. The rich thick hollandaise sauce danced across my tongue with all of its buttery rich flavor, yet highlighting the more delicate hint of lemon and cayenne pepper. The crab cakes themselves were high quality lump crab meat and little else.

I chewed slowly, savoring every morsel of food before finally swallowing and going in for my second bite. I'd finished my first cake when I realized my toes were curled unnaturally inside my boots. Forcing myself to relax, I glanced over at my uncle. "Damn! I don't think I've ever had anything quite so delicious." A fleeting memory of a dinner I'd had in Tokyo flitted through my mind. "There was one meal with real Kobe steaks, but this may match that!"

Andrew watched and waited. Then, before I could tear into the second cake, he spoke. "Would you like to talk about it?"

I knew what he meant and I really didn't want to, so I thought I'd play stupid. "I thought we just did." I pointed my fork at the plate. "This is amazing."

Andrew savored his food with ecstasy. His tone turned harder when he spoke. "That's not what I meant." He used his fork to point at my hand. "How does it feel?"

I held it up for him to see, turning it around so he got a good look at both sides as I flexed it open and closed. "Everything seems to work fine. No lasting damage." Grimacing, I looked at the mutilated hand. "It's a little ugly is all. Nothing to concern myself with."

Andrew raised an eyebrow. "No chance you want to talk about what happened when you passed out, is there?"

My stomach churned and I forced what little breakfast I'd been able to swallow to stay put. "Not a single chance in hell."

Andrew wasn't happy with the answer and continued to press me for more information. "You said something very interesting...about you being a violent man and deserving worse." He kept his eyes on me. "Care to shed light on that subject?"

He reminded me of the shrinks I'd seen over the years. They had a way of asking the same question in many different forms. I didn't like them nor the way they did things. This was my uncle, however, a man who cared for me.

I owed him something. Not the truth, but something. I shoved another forkful of food in my mouth and swallowed. "Tell ya what. I'll give you the answer I'm comfortable with and you'll have to be satisfied."

I sat there and waited for him to nod in agreement before I continued. "Over the last twenty-eight years I've traveled the world. I've seen and done things, not all of them good. I'm not a good man, but I'm not a bad one either. Everything I've done was in service to what I thought and believed was a higher cause. I won't second guess what I did. I can't." I took a big draught of tea and washed down the acid in my throat. "All I want from life now is to be the best person I can be. I'd like to be kind, gentle, and overall a nice person. Please don't make me relive the nightmare that is my past."

I could see understanding cross Andrew's face; he didn't like being shut out but he understood it. When he spoke next his voice was calm, flat, and hard. "I wish you the best of luck." He raised his tea glass in my direction and drank. "Know that your desires, while admirable, may not be possible." He sat the glass down and took a deep breath. "A man's past has a way of catching up to him eventually. Be ready for it when that happens."

I doubted my past would catch up with me anytime soon. Most of it was dead and buried. The men I'd worked for had chosen to wash their hands of me instead of putting a hole in my head or dropping me off in a padded cell somewhere. If by chance it did rear its ugly head in my direction, I'd deal with it as I always had. I'd kill it, burn it, and set fire to the world if need be. I was never going to be held prisoner by my past, nor was I ashamed of it.

Of course I didn't say any of that. Instead I gave my uncle a level look before turning my attention to my food. "If it shows up I'll be ready." Cutting out the biggest bite the fork could handle, I gave my uncle a wink. "I'm a survivor. It's what I do." And shoved the food into my watering mouth.

Concern crossed my uncle's face, but he said nothing while he ate. Finally, after he finished, he leaned back in his seat and chewed on his thoughts for a minute longer before speaking. "It's obvious you are accustomed to a much different life than one that should've been afforded you had your parents lived." I started to speak but he held up a hand to stop me. "From what I can gather you're more acclimated to this city than most."

Swallowing the last of my food, I felt uncertain at his words. "I don't believe this city is a full-fledged war zone."

Andrew didn't appear to be convinced by my observation. "Perhaps not in the way you mean, but there is no mistaking that there has been an ongoing war since the city was founded." He took a drink of tea before continuing. "New Orleans is often ranked in the world's most dangerous cities. Then there is the unseen world 'they' know nothing about. Our world. Make no mistake, we are as brutal and dangerous as the humans that live all around us."

Pushing my plate forward, I allowed the Grim to pose the questions that had plagued us. "About that.... How many others are like us in the city?"

Andrew pushed his plate away and leaned back in his chair as he thought. "As far as I know there are three...myself, you, and Walter—if by us you mean stone born."

The mention of Walter gave me pause, but I had more pressing questions to deal with before returning to that particular asshole. "I take it that there are other...." I pondered which word to use before I settled on the obvious. "Species?"

Andrew pursed his lips, raising his shoulders in a dismissive nature. "Many. These are the highlights though." He put up a finger and began counting them off. "There are witches, sorcerers, shamans, monks, elementals, shapeshifters, werebeasts, vampires, nephilim, and guardians, better known as angels."

I waited for the joke that didn't come. He had to be joking, but the look on his face told me he believed it. After what I'd been through in the last twenty-four hours, I supposed anything was possible.

Allowing the Grim to analyze the situation, I posed another question. "You're serious about the others?" Pausing to let it sink in, I continued. "There are vampires, werewolves, and witches? Not to mention the angels."

Andrew stood, grabbing our plates and dropping them off in the sink. He gestured towards the door. "This is best discussed in comfort and within reach of reference material."

Getting to my feet, I bowed slightly as I waved my uncle ahead of me. We traipsed into the living room and sat at the table. Thankfully the bottle of scotch was nowhere in sight. Not that it was bad, but the constant flow of alcohol since I'd arrived was sure to kill my liver sooner rather than later.

Andrew had obviously prepared for the morning's conversation. The table was covered with a dozen ancient looking leather tomes. He took a seat and waited for me to follow suit before continuing. As soon as I was seated he pulled a medium sized black leather book with a silver buckle out of the pile and flipped it open, turning to a premarked page. When he held it out for me, I took it and turned it around so I could read the handwritten journal.

Race	Age Rate Against the Human Standard	Abilities
Human	Standard 1x1	None/ cattle
Angel/ Guardians	Immortal	Exceptionally powerful within their own territories. Their abilities are far too numerous to go into depth. They are able to wield power over all elemental spheres. Omnipotent within their own territories. No known weakness.
Elemental	Age normally but can reverse the	Able to manipulate and wield an element, earth, fire, or water.

	aging process every 40 years, extending their lives indefinitely.	They are able to absolutely control that element for as long as they wish. Rare cases have been documented where they can wield two elements. Other attributes depend upon their assigned element. Earth wielding elementals are immensely strong. Air elementals are fast. Water elementals have a high stamina. Fire elementals combine strength and endurance. Known weakness opposite elements.
Monk	The physical form ages per human standards, yet live indefinitely through sheer willpower and meditation.	Highly disciplined well trained martial artists. They have the ability to manipulate Chi, the energy all around us. _Very dangerous._
Nephilim	1x5 One year for every 5 human standard	Massive, strong, hard to kill, high stamina. Able to regenerate limbs. Some have limited elemental abilities. Others have limited telepathy. Best pressed into service or killed quickly. Removing of the head or fire are best practices.
Shaman	Age normally till the end of puberty. After that 1x30.	Wide range of abilities. Summon, commune, and control any animal. Some sway over weather. Minor use of elemental powers. Best kept in service or avoided.
Shapeshifter	2x1	Shapeshifters live fast and die early. They can shift into any form, be it human or animal and occasionally the mythical. If they can dream it they can become it. They are a sickly race and not

		known for their endurance.
Sorcerer	*Age normally till the end of puberty. After that 1x50.*	*Ability to learn and wield 'magic' without the use of a focus item, item of power.* <u>*Dangerous.*</u>
Stone Born	*Age normally till the mid 40's. After that essentially immortal.*	*Random. Variations are too vast to even list. Stone Born are rare and must be pressed into service as soon as possible to ensure the safety of everyone.*
Werebeast	*Age normally till puberty. After that 1x20.*	*There are as many variations of this creature as there are animals in the world. Werebeasts are born not created as many myths state. They are strong, fast, high stamina, and generally powerful.* <u>*They rarely exhibit intelligence and should be either kept as pets or put down.*</u>
Witch	*Age normally until puberty. After that 1x5.*	*Witches need focusing tools or items of power to store and use 'magic'. Without such an item they are essentially long lived humans. Multiple items of power can be created throughout their lifetime. Most do not take advantage of this and focus on a single object in an effort to amass as much power as possible as quickly as possible.*
Vampire	*Immortal after being turned.*	*Vampires are most recognizable by their gray eyes. They all have them. They feed on the energy of other living creatures, be it blood, actual life force, or other less*

| | | *pleasant ways. Depending on the type of vampire you are dealing with they can be highly intelligent and mentally manipulative. Their saliva is a neurotoxin that paralyzes their victim. Sunlight has no effect on them. Only silver or beheading truly works for the long term. A stake through the heart more or less paralyzes them, keeping them in a suspended animation until it's removed or they are dispatched.* |

I will add further species as I get time. Lazarus.

My head was starting to ache in the left temple as I read. Keeping my finger in the book to mark the page, I closed it and looked up at my uncle. "As in THE Lazarus?"

Andrew nodded. "Yes. He is a very unique man."

Shaking my head, I could barely believe what I was hearing. "You speak as if he's still alive."

Andrew took a deep breath and squirmed in his seat. "About that...he is still alive. In fact, he is the defacto leader of our kind around the world."

"The world?" I asked.

Andrew pointed at the book in my hand. "If you'll turn to the next marked passage it'll be easier to understand."

I flinched when I looked down at the charts, and my head started to hurt. They actually had entire organizational charts with lines and everything for me to see.

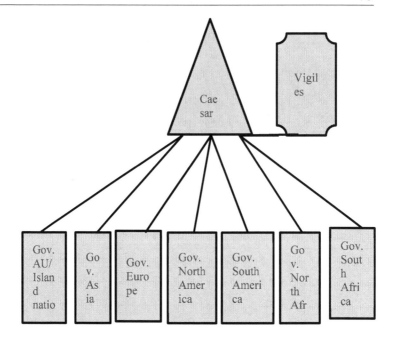

Caesar, vigiles urbani, governor, and triumvirate offices are for life. Every governor is given a vigiles urbani to keep the peace in their respective territories. Prefects are also given vigiles urbani for their sectors. Vigiles urbani answer only to higher ranking vigiles urbani. Caesar's vigiles is responsible for keeping the others in line. Governors are given three prefects, nine triumvirate members, and eighteen council members to fairly rule their territories.

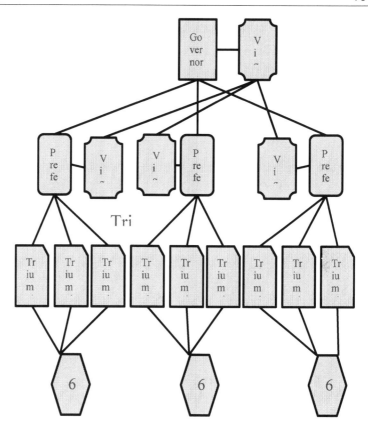

After staring at the drawings for a moment I shook my head. "Could you give me the abridged version?" I held up the book in my hand. "I'm still trying to wrap my head around this."

Andrew looked more than a little amused at my bewilderment. "Lazarus created what we call the Archives throughout the world." He looked frustrated as he searched for the right words and facts to convey this as simply as possible. "He's ancient, and as such he set up our government in accordance with the Roman Empire. He is the caesar. There are seven governors throughout the world: one in North America, South America, Europe, Asia, North Africa, Southern Africa, and Austria, in conjunction with other island nations. Each governor oversees three prefects, three triumvirate members, and six elected council members." He looked nervous as he shifted in his seat again. "The caesar, governors, prefects, and triumvirate are lifetime appointments."

Something clicked in my mind and I interrupted. "You said that Martha was a... *vigiles*?"

Andrew's confidence grew as he could answer a question better than teach an elementary class. "Yes, a *vigiles urbani*, to be exact. They were the original police and fire department for ancient Rome. That's a lifetime appointment as well."

"How are any of these people chosen?"

Andrew looked disappointed and I could see that he struggled with the answer. "That's a closely guarded secret and one that I don't know. Lazarus has designed a system in which the applicant is tested, and if they are deemed worthy they are appointed and marked for life."

Relief spread through me suddenly. The fact that I didn't have to worry about any of this for the foreseeable future was liberating. "Damn good thing I won't be meeting anyone in an official position for a while. Let alone a vampire or a werebeast."

Andrew's face went blank and he looked me dead in the eyes. "You've already met one werewolf, seen a vampire, and a few other races as well. Not to mention the prefect of the Southern United States and Mexico...same woman, by the way."

Now I did laugh at the sheer absurdity of his words. "Please! I'd know if I'd met a vampire or a werewolf. As far as politicians go, I'm sure they are easy enough to miss."

Andrew chuckled as he nodded. "I'm sure Ms. Dodd will be glad to hear that."

My forehead furrowed as I tried to recall the name. The tiny woman who'd stood in Andrew's way at the funeral. "That mousy haired little woman is a—"

Andrew finished the sentence for me. "A vampire who happens to be the prefect for this section of the country." He paused for a moment, and almost as an afterthought said, "And Isidore is a werewolf!"

That last bit explained a lot. I'd often gotten the feeling that Isidore was a predator, and one couldn't get much more predatory than a wolf. As far as Ms. Dodd was concerned, she'd shown up for Martha's funeral, which confused me. She was important as any elected official in this supernatural government. Why had she bothered, and why did she feel the need to speak to my uncle?

"Why was someone of her status at the funeral of a *vigiles*?" I asked.

Andrew blushed as he chewed on his lip, searching for an answer. "There is only one *vigiles* for every governor and prefect. They are on equal footing and are the tiebreakers in all votes."

There was more to it than he was telling me, but I let it go. "The *vigiles* are important, I take it?"

Andrew nodded. "They are extremely important. They keep order, enforce our laws, and make sure that the humans are treated fairly by our kind and vice versa."

Trying to piece all the parts together, I made an assumption. "I take it that Lazarus will be arriving soon?"

Andrew shook his head. "No, he rarely leaves his home inside the Vatican."

"I thought you said that he devised, and from what I gathered implemented, a test for all the lifetime appointments."

Andrew sniggered. "He did. It's not what you think. There is an entire process that I'm not privy to, but once the candidates are chosen they are given a test of sorts." He shook his head as he couldn't find the words to describe it. "You'll see soon enough, since a new *vigiles* must be chosen."

Setting the book down, I wanted to turn the conversation to something more personal. "I would like to change the subject for a few, if that's all right?"

Andrew looked relieved, quickly nodding his assent. "By all means. What do you want to know?"

There were so many questions, but I knew where to start. "You said that people couldn't lie to you."

"True," he said. "Except you."

Closing my eyes, I reluctantly agreed. "Except me. You also mentioned that it was one of your many talents." I chewed on the last few words before letting them rush out of me. "What can I do?"

Andrew brightened at the question while looking completely bewildered. "I haven't the foggiest. Other than being immune to mental manipulation and the ability to lie to me, both of which are huge, I have no idea what you're capable of. Normally you would've been inducted on your eighteenth birthday, and if your abilities hadn't appeared by then you'd be tutored by either your father or other mentor he felt appropriate." Frustration overtook his features as he threw his hands up in defeat. "As far as I know, no one has ever gone this long before taking their stone."

My chest deflated and my head slumped. "I see. Then I might not have any abilities."

Andrew gave me an incredulous look. "If the reaction I saw last night with your stone is any indication, you will be exceptionally powerful. We just have to figure out what it is you are capable of doing."

Death, destruction, and general mayhem. That was what I was good at. I'd always healed quickly and somehow made it out of situations I shouldn't have, but I doubted seriously that my superpower was luck.

Andrew caught the look of concern on my face and waved it off. "Don't worry, we've got next to forever to figure it out." Pausing, he thought for a moment before his mind landed on an idea. "Tell you what. Close your eyes, let your mind stretch out, and tell me what you feel."

Following his instructions, which was harder than he made it sound, after about a minute I began to see the room in my mind's eye. The table and books radiated traces of something, but I couldn't make out what it was. Then as my senses expanded, my brain cried out as if it were being scorched by the sun and I jumped back, nearly toppling my chair over. I winced as I tried to open my eyes again. My head hurt and the fear I'd felt earlier returned. "What the hell?"

Andrew sat there quietly, patiently. "What did you feel?"

"It made my skin tingle, my brain actually hurt, and something in the back of my mind kicked in, yelling 'danger Will Robinson, danger.'"

Andrew nearly choked on the breath he was taking in and tried not to laugh in my face. "That's a first!" His face was full of humor while he mulled over my words. "The older a person gets the more powerful they become. There are a lot of factors that increase a person's power, such as items...," he held up his hand and flashed his ring, "enchantments, and so much more."

I snickered. "Well, this should be interesting. Can you try and see what you sense with me?"

Andrew looked amused. "Sure." Closing his eyes, he sat there for a moment and then the smile faded. I could tell that he was straining, and then his eyes popped open. "That's odd."

"What's that?" I asked.

"It was as if you weren't there. No, that's not the right way to put it. It's like there was a hole where you're sitting. I couldn't sense anything. Nothing at all."

My heart sank. I wasn't like my uncle. I wasn't special after all. I was human. "You mean like I'm human. Right?"

Andrew was quick to shake his head. "Not at all. Humans register. You can sense them like one can sense a dog or a cat or even a table. No, that's very inhuman. I've never even heard of such a thing being possible." He paused for a moment then shook his head. "It could explain a few things."

"Such as?" I asked.

He gestured at the walls and the ceiling above. "This place, the entire grounds, are actually covered in enchantments to keep other people's thoughts out of my head." He grimaced as he thought about it. "Even with all that, I can still hear the muffled sounds of their thoughts from all the houses around me." He suddenly looked ashamed. "That is until you arrived. Since you've been here I've been able to sleep uninterrupted by other people's thoughts, dreams, or anguish. Even at the funeral it was as if the world around me was dialed down to a whisper. That's why I didn't realize Walter was there until he was right in front of you."

Okay, wow! That had to suck, and not just a little. To never have peace must be hard. "I'm glad I could help." Trying to change the subject, I thought of a new topic. "The fact that stone born don't age after forty-five has me a little confused."

"Really? It's a simple concept," Andrew snarked.

"Can you explain why Walter looks like he's ready for the retirement home?"

Andrew's face darkened. "You get right to the heart of the matter, don't you, boy? Still, it's a fair question." He shifted in his seat, stalling while he searched for the right words. "The way our bodies reveal themselves to the world is a direct reflection of who we are." He gestured at my hand. "Your hand is a perfect example. It doesn't mean you're a bad person, it just means you've been through a lot in your life. Now, if you were to go around and torture people, rip out their souls or murder them for fun, your body could and probably would reflect that. There is a cost to everything we do. If we do the right thing—and that isn't always what you think it might be— then the universe credits you. If you are an evil bastard, the universe debits your account. Not that anyone has any real proof one way or another in Walter's case however."

That last bit was highly disappointing. Leaning back, I took in a deep breath before slowly letting it out. "Why would anyone willingly do that to themselves?"

He didn't even hesitate to answer. "Power!" His voice was full of anger and disgust. "And everything that comes with it. Some people can't be happy unless they are hurting others. That's Walter's problem, he likes to hurt people." His face contorted as he waved a hand. "Again, not that we have any proof."

"Why hasn't anyone found proof? Either the *vigiles* or the Uncommon Crimes Division?" I asked.

Andrew held his hands up in a show of confusion as he shook his head. "The UCD is more of an after the fact type of unit. As for the *vigiles*, Martha.... Well, either she couldn't prove it or she was held back for one reason or another." He grumbled as anger rolled over his features. "I can't say why for sure, but perhaps Ms. Dodd and her next *vigiles* will be able to tend to that 'situation'."

"Perhaps," I intoned.

Andrew stood, waving for me to follow him. "Let's take a proper tour."

We headed back to the room that held hundreds of gemstones. "Where did you get all of these? Who did they belong to?"

Andrew's features swelled with pride as he straightened his shoulders. "They belonged to our family through the generations. When one of us dies the nearest family member holds onto their 'essence.'"

"Why?" I asked.

"As you saw last night, a shadow of their former selves is accessible for consultation. In today's terms they would be artificial intelligence. Kind of a crude term, but it works."

"So it doesn't involve their souls?"

Andrew stiffened. "Not exactly, no. Once a person has passed, nothing short of a really disgusting ritual of pure evil can be performed to trap the soul before it travels to whatever is next. Necromancers are a pretty bad bunch."

Looking around the room, I felt awestruck. "So my father's stone is here."

Andrew pointed near the center of the room. "Right next to yours."

"And your father?"

Andrew shook his head. "When he left he took his stone with him. He left the others in your father's care, but those fell to me after he passed away."

He turned and left the room with me in tow, and we visited several other rooms. One was filled with parchments, deeds, and an old family crest. Another contained rows of bottles, tubes, and other containers filled with potions. At the back of the house was a large ornate room with a long table and maybe a dozen chairs around it. They were all equally fascinating in their own right.

Seeing how the tour was done, I clapped him on the back, guiding him back to the living room. "What are we going to do today?"

"Heather should be by later with the groceries and other essentials. If there is anything you want, you'll need to add it to next week's list."

"You don't get out much then?"

Andrew's cheeks flushed red. "I can't...not really."

It dawned on me after he said it. "I'm sorry."

He pointed at one of the wing chairs and grabbed a bottle of scotch. "Care for a drink?"

Looking at the bottle, I looked at my watch and said, "It's not even eight in the morning."

He didn't reply before pouring us a drink. "Welcome to New Orleans." He sat back in his seat and relaxed. "It's been nice having you here. I didn't realize how much it weighed on me to have all those noises in my head until they weren't there."

Picking up my glass, I toasted him and took a sip. "Again, glad I could help." With another drink I couldn't help but feel optimistic about the future. "So, I guess I'm some sort of wet blanket to your abilities...that's my superpower!"

The comment almost made him spit out his drink. "I doubt that seriously. It's more likely a side effect of something else. Don't worry, we'll figure it out soon enough."

Sitting there staring at my glass, I watched as the scotch stuck to the sides, pulling itself down the glass and creating the most beautiful lines as I slowly swirled it around. I had to wonder what was in store for a man like me. Walter looked like hell, but I didn't see any twisted, melted skin on his body. It wasn't as if I'd taken pleasure in my job, but I never shied away from it either. Only time would tell.

Chapter 6

Andrew was on his fourth round of scotch while I was nursing a second at 10:00 when Ms. Heather Broussard arrived, arms full of groceries. It took the three of us twenty minutes to unload the car and carry everything upstairs. It wasn't a bad job, as I got to watch Heather glide up and down the stairs.

Heather was a tall—about six foot one—classic kind of pretty that would've given Audrey Hepburn a run for her money. Her blue green eyes sparkled behind her tortoise shell horn rimmed glasses. Her refined features stood out against the black long sleeved Under Armour workout shirt that fit tight across her ample chest and hugged her taut stomach. The medium length pink running shorts hugged her hips, accentuating her rock hard bottom and showing off her long, shapely, yet muscular legs. Her auburn hair was cut in what I was once told was a shag cut, and parted to one side. I'd always assumed it was called that because the women who wore it looked as if they'd just been well shagged.

She moved with old world grace and elegance, making her appear strong, sensual, and sexy. The most wonderful thing about her was the fact she didn't seem to either know or care that she was stunning. She was such a genuinely pleasant woman, and I couldn't help but be happy in her presence. A part of me was surprised that she hadn't taken up modeling, and another part of me was grateful that she hadn't. I wasn't sure how my uncle had ever convinced such a woman to clean his house and work part time in his bookstore, but I had to give the old man considerable credit for doing so.

After we dropped everything in the kitchen and living room she shooed us away, insisting that we let her get to work. Andrew and I returned to our scotch, allowing Heather to disappear into the kitchen and guest quarters.

About a half hour later Heather appeared behind Andrew with a wry grin, wagging a finger in my direction. "You obviously didn't notice the perfectly good hamper in the bath. It's just under the tall cabinet next to the sink."

Blushing, I hadn't actually given it any real thought that the guest quarters was actually my room. "I'm sorry," I stammered. "I'd planned on doing the wash this afternoon."

A brilliant smile spread across her face as the sunlight danced across her eyes. Her voice was a rich alto that lilted with only the slightest of southern accents. "It's already in the wash." Her laughter danced across my insides, making me both excited and nervous. "Is that everything you own? I looked around but didn't find anything else."

Blood continued to rush to my cheeks as I turned an even deeper crimson. "Yeah, that's everything." Gaining a little bit of dignity, I cleared my throat and nodded. "I'll need to go shopping soon and pick up some new stuff."

Heather let out a chuckle as she ran her tongue along the inside of her cheek, shaking her head. "I don't think you'll be able to find stuff in your size off the shelf."

Andrew perked up as a thought popped into his mind. "She's right."

He appraised me as if for the first time, taking full stock of my size. While it was true he had a couple of inches of height on me, I was thicker. My dense broad shoulders led off to beefy arms. My chest swelled out from the heavy muscle mass before creating a deep v towards my trim muscular waist. My legs were akin to tree trunks, ensuring that everything I wore needed to be custom tailored to my unique form.

He groaned, half in appreciation and half in shock. "Damn boy! What did they feed you?" He chuckled as he waved off my attempt to answer. "Never mind. I'll give George Nguyen a call and he'll take care of you."

Tearing my eyes off Heather, I turned my attention to Andrew. "Who's George Nguyen?"

Heather pivoted in her white tennis shoes with pink laces that squeaked against the floor, heading for the kitchen, calling out over her shoulder. "He's the best tailor in town. He's made a lot of my clothes."

I couldn't—well, wouldn't—stop watching her sashay out of sight. Once she was gone I turned my attention to Andrew, who was watching my expression with great amusement. "What?" I asked.

Andrew tried to remove the knowing look off his face but failed. "Nothing. Nothing at all."

He reached for the phone and held out a hand for me to hold that thought. Dialing a number, he waited for someone to pick up. "George...? This is Andrew.... Good morning to you as well. I hate to ask this of you on such short notice, but I have someone who is in need of your services.... Today would be best, if you can fit him in.... I'd consider it a personal favor.... Really? Outstanding, see you at three."

Andrew hung up the phone and looked over at me, raising his glass. "George will be happy to stop by at three to get your measurements. After that he can retire to his shop and have a full set of clothes for you sometime next week."

A lot of questions went along with my feeling of imposition I'd just placed upon my uncle. First, I was curious as to how the maid/ part time employee afforded tailor made clothing. Hell, I was curious about how I was going to afford it. The other was, other than the obvious, why did my uncle have a tailor on speed dial? And how was he able to convince the man to drop everything on such short notice to come see me this afternoon? I was sure the man had a business to run, not to mention other customers' orders to attend to, before making such an exception for me.

"I'm not sure I can afford a full line of custom made clothing." After the briefest of thoughts, I paused. "Maybe a couple of pieces, but I need to find a job before spending all my cash on clothes."

Andrew's bemused look told me I wasn't getting out of this so easily. "Don't worry, you'll receive a steep family discount."

That made me laugh. "Last I checked, neither of us were a Nguyen."

Andrew rolled his eyes at me. "Not his family. Our family discount." He could see that I clearly didn't understand.

"I do a lot of work for Mr. Nguyen, and in return he tailors my clothing, and now yours, at no cost."

I snorted in disbelief. "That must be a hell of a job that you do for him."

Andrew's face was quite serious now. "It is." He held up his scotch and took a drink. "Now don't worry about anything. Besides, from what I've seen of your clothing, you definitely need a more refined set. The suit was nice, but hardly befitting a man of your station."

"And what station is that?"

He cut his eyes towards the kitchen with a devilish glint in his eye. "Besides being struck dumb by a beautiful young woman? You're my nephew! And you'll need to dress appropriately when you register at the Archive next week."

That gave me pause. What made me being his nephew so special? "Are you sure I'll need to register so soon?"

Andrew sat his glass on the table as he hardly considered the answer. "Absolutely. You can't go traipsing around in someone's territory and not register with the local Archive. It's just rude, not to mention it could be considered a crime after thirty days. Not that we currently have a *vigiles*, but the next one might take offense, just to be an asshole."

Holding up my hands in defeat, I understood the point. "All right, I'll register as soon as possible."

Heather finished her duties and joined us in the living room at around noon. She took the seat nearest to mine before leaning forward and stretching out her delicate hand in my direction. "I know we exchanged names when I first arrived, but that's hardly a proper introduction." She locked those sensual blue green eyes on mine. "I'm Heather Broussard; and you are?"

Trying to keep my reactions under control, I kept the blushing to a minimum as I took her soft, strong hand in mine. "I'm Gavin Randall."

She held my hand for a moment longer as she gave me a wink, glancing back at Andrew. "Any relation?"

Andrew didn't appear to be bothered as he casually replied. "He's my nephew."

Still holding her hand, I grinned stupidly and repeated. "Nephew."

Great, now I'm repeating my uncle. Way to keep cool!

Heather released me and sat back in her chair, turning her full attention to my uncle. "You never said anything about a nephew." Swiveling back to me, she eyed me with great curiosity. "If he'd mentioned you were coming to visit I would've picked up a few things."

Dropping my head slightly, I blushed. "Don't be upset with Andrew, he didn't know." Looking up at her sheepishly, I felt the blood rush into my cheeks again. "This visit sort of just happened."

Her eyes flitted to my left hand for the third or fourth time since she'd arrived. "And where were you that kept you away for so long?"

The back of my mind started to itch, the amusement left me. "Naples, Italy."

Sweat beaded on her forehead, her breathing became labored, and her eyes bulged. Groaning, she fell back in her chair, wrapping her long fingers around her face as she tried to rub away the unseen pain. "Goddamn it!" Lifting her eyes, she looked at Andrew. "What did I do wrong?"

Andrew suddenly looked like a man who'd forgotten to hide his porn. "Shit!" He shook his head as he tried to find the words. "I'm sorry, dear, I should've told you when you first arrived that Gavin is somewhat of a special case."

Quickly putting away the love struck act, I found myself irritated at being the center of this conversation. "What seems to be the problem?"

Andrew waved a hand towards Heather as he regained his composure. "Heather is a very clever and powerful witch." He blushed crimson as the slightest of smiles crossed his lips. "Her mother, Kim, is a very dear friend and asked me to tutor her." Looking back at Heather sheepishly, he nodded. "He's a blank to me as well."

Heather forgot about the pain in her head as her mouth fell open, and she looked absolutely dumbstruck. "I didn't think that was possible."

Andrew wore a look of similar disbelief and took a drink of scotch. "Neither did I."

What little buzz I had instantly faded during Heather's attempt to pluck information out of my mind. Looking between the two I finally gave up, picked up what was left of my scotch, and downed it. "I'm going to assume that I've missed something important and move on."

Heather turned her head in my direction and gave me an exasperated look as she took a deep breath. "Your uncle has been mentoring me in the art of telepathy." She rubbed her forehead again as she leaned back in her chair, apparently with a raging headache. "It's been a rough go of it so far, but this is ridiculous."

Andrew piped in. "It's not for everyone, dear."

She frowned at him before turning her attention back to me. "If it wasn't for the fact that I couldn't read you I'd swear you were human." She took a deep breath and closed her eyes, and then looked at my uncle, perplexed. "It's as if you're not even in the room. I know you're here because I can see you, but on an energetic level you're non-existent. It's just so odd!"

Leaning forward, I grabbed the bottle of scotch and poured another dram. Raising my glass in her direction with a wink, I took a healthy drink, letting the amber fluid cascade over my tongue with its wonderful flavors before sliding down my throat. "Furniture can't drink and enjoy a good scotch." She smiled and I returned it. "I'm sure my lack of presence is due to the fact I've only just discovered my heritage."

She relaxed, but the look on her face betrayed her thoughts as I saw a desire just under the surface. "Perhaps."

With that simple look, thoughts of her in stages of undress suddenly danced through my mind. "Perhaps, indeed."

Heather winked at me before turning her attention back to Andrew. "I've got to pull the clothes out of the dryer, as well as a few other odds and ends to tend to before I leave. Is there anything else you'll need?"

Andrew looked far too happy with himself for my comfort. "Thank you again for the assistance, but I think that'll be all."

Heather stood and held out her hand, which I took. "It's been a pleasure to meet you." She turned and put her hand on Andrew's shoulder. "Call me if anything comes up, and remember I'll be busy Sunday night. I have that wedding to attend."

Andrew patted her hand and nodded. "Have a great rest of your weekend."

Heather sauntered out of the room, and even though the boyish crush I'd had was already gone I couldn't help but watch. She was a spectacular looking woman, and had an equally fascinating and personable demeanor.

She wasn't out of sight for more than a second before I turned to my uncle. "Should I concern myself with Isidore trying to read my mind as well?"

Andrew looked annoyed by the question but brushed it off. "I'm sorry about that. She is a wonderful girl, but eager to try and expand her horizons. As far as Isidore is concerned, he's a ninety-year-old werewolf, and telepathy isn't in their repertoire of skills."

That bit of news came as a comfort and I instantly relaxed. I downed my scotch and poured another. "I suppose that's good news." A peculiar thought crossed my mind. "Why did she start to sweat and her breathing become labored? Is that normal?"

Andrew looked pensive. "I'm not sure. She's always struggled with the ability, but I've never seen her react that way before. Perhaps it's something specific to you, or perhaps she was just straining. Either is possible, I suppose."

A really crappy thought occurred to me as I recalled the handwritten journal, and I paused. "Is Isidore a pet?"

Andrew nearly choked on his drink and anger flashed in his eyes. "No! Why would you ever ask such a horrible question?"

Grabbing the journal off the table, I started to open it. "Well—"

Andrew growled. "For fuck's sake, son. That particular book is over eight hundred years old. You can't take things like that seriously." Andrew took a breath as he composed himself. "Look, Lazarus is ancient, and as such he has some very peculiar, if not outdated, thoughts, but even he has moved beyond the whole 'werebeasts are pets' thing." The wind was taken completely out of him as he hung his head. "There are others, though, that still use these old laws as excuses to abuse others."

Looking at the book, I flipped through a few pages and wondered why my uncle would have such an ancient and rare tome. "I suspect copies of these are rare?"

Andrew appeared to be thoroughly amused by the question. "There are maybe seven in the world."

"Why do you have a copy?" I asked.

He didn't even blink as he gestured at the room around him. "It's my life. If you haven't noticed, I deal in rare and antique books. Hell, it's even on the door downstairs."

And there we were. I might as well run my stupid flag up a pole and shout about it. "Yeah, there is that."

Again his amusement was clear in his voice. "Besides being a unique sort of employer, having a powerful witch and an old werewolf on the payroll keeps the things that go bump in the night from coming to my door."

I seriously doubted he needed to hide behind either Heather or Isidore to deal with anything that would cross the threshold of this house, but it couldn't hurt. "I can see the logic in that line of thought."

A half hour later Heather strolled through the living room on the way to the door, pausing to catch my eye. "If you need a tour guide let me know." She looked at Andrew with a wry smile. "Andrew has my number if you ever want it." Looking down at my hand, she smiled again. "Perhaps I'll ply you with drinks, and then you'll tell me about your hand." She waved at me and then Andrew. "You always know the most interesting people."

Heather didn't wait for a response as she strode through the door, closing it behind her. She was confident in who she was and happy with or without my company. If I called, I called, and if not she'd find someone else to entertain her.

Andrew wisely kept his attention on the bottle of Dalmore and poured us another round before checking his watch. "We should grab a bite to eat before George arrives."

It dawned on me to ask the question rumbling around the back of my head. "What's so important about George? I'm sure there are other tailors that you wouldn't have to call in favors to come see me on such short notice."

Andrew held the door to the kitchen open for me as I passed. He waved me into a seat at the table as he rummaged through the fridge for leftovers. "As I said earlier, I have many unique abilities. One of them is that of an enchanter." He grabbed the last of the red beans and rice out of the fridge. "I tend to all the enchanted material he uses every year, and he takes care of my clothing needs." He gave himself a hapless shrug of his shoulders before giving me the Vanna White wave at himself. "I haven't had a lot of need of his services in years, so he kind of owes me."

"What do these enchantments do that make them so vital?" I asked.

Andrew rolled his eyes and snorted. "Boy, you haven't been listening, have you? There are dangerous things outside the gates."

Leaning back, I looked at my uncle with a sudden realization; there were things that frightened him outside his home. I kept my opinions to myself. "Is it really that bad out there?"

Andrew's features turned serious as he gazed out the nearest window. "At times." He sighed. "There's absolutely no reason to take unnecessary chances."

There was more to his fear than the thousands of voices he would encounter. I could tell that he felt genuinely afraid of something out there, as if there were a target painted on his back and he wasn't willing to admit it. "Anything you'd like to tell me that you haven't already?"

Andrew went still for a moment as he gave the idea of it considerable thought. "For now I think you've got quite enough on your plate. Not to worry though, I'm quite safe within these walls. No one intending me harm can enter."

I wanted to argue the point. This was what I was good at. This was something I could help with. The argument died much where it had started, and I felt it was important to let him have this, at least for the time being. "If you change your mind I'm here, and if I can help I will. If there is anything or anyone I should be aware of, let me know."

Andrew's hand shook as he put his glass on the table. "Let's keep things simple for now. I'll teach you what you need to learn, and you can decide what scares you later. Deal?"

"Deal," I agreed.

George stopped by about an hour later and measured me for what he called adult clothing, and not the droll civilian clothes I was currently wearing. On his way out he assured me I'd have a full set of clothing by Monday afternoon, and to try and not get myself killed between now and then.

It was 5:15 by the time George left, and I was starved. Heading to the kitchen, I found Andrew pulling something out of the oven. He glanced back, giving me an appraising look. "Excellent! How did it go?"

I waved a dismissive hand at myself and grunted before trying to get a better look at what was in the dish, but with no luck. "No idea. George was exceptionally displeased with my current attire."

Andrew turned his attention to the long glass baking pans on the stove. "George is a bit of an elitist when it comes to clothing."

"He said something odd on his way out."

"What was that?" He asked.

I repeated George's final instructions. "'Don't get killed between now and Monday.' Why is that even a thing?"

Andrew turned pale before regaining control of his features. "As I mentioned, the clothing is enchanted. They provide a great deal of physical protection, against things such as physical trauma or fire or...hell, any number of other things."

I had that annoying itch in the back of my skull that couldn't be scratched. He was lying to me, but it was clear he wasn't about to divulge anything further. "So stylish body armor."

Andrew made a face as he thought about it and tilted his head in acquiescence. "More or less."

"You're the only enchanter he uses?" I asked.

Andrew straightened up as pride filled him. "Enchanters are rare. Very rare, but I'm sure he could use another if he wanted. But that would require all new tools."

That was peculiar. "Why is that?"

Andrew spooned some food onto a plate and spoke thoughtfully. "Because only the enchanted tools that I've provided for him will cut or pierce the material. Every enchanter is unique, and as such require unique tools to work the fabric."

Andrew turned and brought two plates heaping with beef enchiladas with red sauce to the table.

I was skeptical, of course. "You wearing any of it now?"

Andrew unrolled the sleeve of his shirt and buttoned it before putting it on the table. Gesturing at the fork, he nodded. "Go ahead and stab the shirt, and let's get that over with before our dinner gets cold."

I didn't have to be invited twice, and I stabbed his arm as hard as I could. The fork warped and bent in my hand, leaving a little red sauce on his white sleeve, which he simply wiped away. "It's also stain proof," he added. "Grab another fork out of the drawer and toss that in the recyclables."

Now I was becoming more concerned about the city I'd chosen to visit. "Who would need this kind of protection? I mean, it can't be that bad out there, can it?"

Andrew took another forkful of food and grunted. "There are lots of others out there besides Heather, Isidore, you, and me. There are literally hundreds that live in the city, and maybe a couple thousand in the surrounding cities, and they are the nice ones." He took another bite of food and swallowed. "There are a lot of vanilla mortals who'd kill for that ring you're wearing, or mine for that matter. A hundred years ago they would've killed Heather simply because she was a witch. Not to mention Isidore's blood is worth a fortune to the right buyer. We are constantly in danger from the standard humans and other paranormal entities that would do us harm simply because of who we are or what we can do for them, alive or dead. This isn't a safe place to begin with, but when you add in greed, a thirst for power, and the general desire for brutality, you learn to protect yourself."

I'd nearly finished my food when I stopped and mused. "If it's so dangerous here, why stay?"

"God, you really do sound like your father." That thought brought a combination of joy and sadness to the man. "Because this is where Martha was, and now that she's gone.... I don't know. There's still a house and plenty of land back home, but I'm not sure I'd want to go back there alone. At least here there are others I can speak to. I'm not your father. He could go days, weeks at a time not speaking to another human being and not be bothered. I, on the other hand, would miss Isidore, Heather, and my other friends."

I guess I was more like my father than I ever realized. I'd spent the last twenty-eight years with absolutely zero friends, and nothing more to look back on than what was in my bag in the other room.

"The house is still standing?" I asked.

Andrew looked almost offended. "Of course it is. I enchanted the entire place before I left, and your grandfather wouldn't let his daughter's home fall into ruin even after her death." He took another bite of food and pointed his fork at me. "You're going to need to contact him and let him know you'll be up there sooner rather than later."

I blinked. "What? Why?"

Andrew tskd me. "Because he's family even if you two didn't get along. He'll be happy you're alive."

I suddenly felt full and pushed the last of my food away. "I'll finish that later." Grumbling more to myself than to

Andrew, I said, "I'd like to get settled in here before you ship me off to see 'him.'"

Andrew held up his hands letting me know he wouldn't push the matter further. "I don't know what transpired between you two, but he never seems angry about it when I go up there to check on the place."

That surprised me. "You've seen him?"

"It's hard not to. I stick out like a sore thumb, considering the city has a population, as you said, of fifty, and none of them consider me a resident. The locals have gotten used to seeing me on my once a year pilgrimage, but that doesn't mean they don't call the chief every time I get within a hundred miles of the place."

I tensed and let out a low growl of displeasure. "He always had the place under his thumb. To be honest, I thought he would've passed away by now."

Andrew instantly understood why I hadn't brought my grandfather up before now. "He is a shaman." Saying it like it were the most obvious thing in the world.

I vaguely recalled the journal again. "Oh...I see."

I didn't remember the math, but even though he was ancient he'd grow to be much older before he died of natural causes.

Andrew beamed. "Don't worry, you'll get accustomed to this world soon. I've got plenty of books for you to familiarize yourself with so you can fit in."

Fitting in was of primary importance. "I'll start reading the journal tonight."

We heard a knock at the door and Andrew looked a little puzzled. We marched into the living room and I went to open the door when it swung open, revealing Isidore carrying two overflowing banker's boxes precariously stacked one atop the other. Picking up the pace, I grabbed the top box and followed Isidore over to the table.

Isidore was clearly irritated. He turned to Andrew. "Captain Hotard from the UCD is here to see you." He gestured at the boxes. "He has several more downstairs, and insisted that I take them 'off his hands.'"

He might as well have finished that sentence by calling the man an asshole. From the expression on my uncle's face he appeared about as pleased as Isidore with the situation.

Andrew glowered. "He's already cleaned out her office?"

Isidore's cheeks were flush when he gestured at the boxes. "Apparently he couldn't wait. He said he needed the office space for 'actual officers, doing actual work.'"

Andrew swelled to his full height, irritation written all over his face. "Where is the bastard?"

Isidore pointed at the floor. "Downstairs. He is 'insisting' on speaking with you." Isidore hesitated. "I was about to head out for the evening…should I wait till you finish with the 'captain'?"

Andrew grumbled as he waved off the idea. "I think Gavin and I can handle it from here. Besides, it's only a few days to the full moon."

Isidore's eyes darted to me and back to Andrew in a panic. "He knows?"

Andrew looked at Isidore as if to say "of course." "It's all right, Isidore. I don't believe Gavin is going to hold it against you."

Holding up my hands in a sign of nonaggression, I said, "After the shit I've seen and done in my life, I can't see how being a werewolf is any worse than anyone else."

Isidore's focused on my heavily marred hand before looking up at me curiously. "What happened to you?"

Looking down at the melted skin, I raised an eyebrow at him. "Had a hard night."

Isidore's eyes lingered on my hand, shaking his head in disbelief. "That looks like more than a hard night, but I really do need to get home. I'll be by in the morning to make sure you two are okay."

Andrew and I followed Isidore downstairs to meet Captain Hotard, who was, much to my chagrin, accompanied by Officer Sonia Trahan. I'd seen but not met Captain Hotard at the funeral. He was a chubby man, nearly a foot shorter than myself, placing him on the short end of normal height.

From this angle I got a good look at the terrible comb over of his obviously dyed deep brown hair. His round face lacked a chin, and his forest green eyes darted all around the room as if something were about to jump out of the shadows. Sweat beaded on his forehead and he continuously blotted it with a heavily stained yellowing handkerchief.

Sonia looked much the same as she had at the funeral, only now she wore a defiant smugness on her fat face. By the way she stared at me it was clear she hated my guts, for what reason other than breathing I couldn't possibly tell. Her expression wavered when she looked at Andrew. Something about him scared her, even though I had a good eighty pounds of muscle on the old man.

Andrew glared at the dozen boxes littering the floor all around the captain and his henchman. "Bryan, you couldn't wait until I could send someone to collect her things?"

Captain Bryan Hotard turned crimson as anger crept into his voice. "Mr. Randall, I'd appreciate it if you'd address me by my proper rank!"

Andrew took a step closer and both of the officers shrank back. "Do you really want to get into a dick measuring contest with me, 'Bryan'?" Andrew held their gaze for a moment longer. "We both know who'd win."

Bryan huffed as he flattened his uniform shirt against his massive belly. "That may be, but as I told your boy—"

Andrew cut in. "His name is Isidore. Don't disrespect him again." He let the threat hang.

Bryan blanched, and his hands shook either from nerves or anger, or perhaps both. "Fine! As I informed Isidore, we need the space for actual police business!"

Andrew stared holes through the little man. "You realize that it's only a matter of time before a new *vigiles* is appointed."

Bryan puffed out his chest and his jowls shook with every word. "I... we at the NOPD don't believe we will be needing the assistance of a *vigiles* in the future."

The dark look that crossed Andrew's face should've terrified the little man. His voice could've cut diamonds when he spoke. "Oh, really?"

Bryan apparently hadn't notice the change in my uncle and continued on with his rehearsed speech. "I think we can get by very well on our own. We thank you for your assistance, but it's no longer required."

Andrew stepped forward, slamming a finger into the man's pudgy chest, causing his man boobs to jiggle and Bryan to cough as the air was forced out of his lungs. "You forget your place."

Sonia stepped back so quickly she tripped over one of the boxes, falling over with a thud against the hardwood floor.

Andrew's voice was quiet, hard, and easily heard throughout the room. "I've put up with your arrogance and ineptitude out of respect for your grandfather." Andrew loomed over the much smaller man, forcing Bryan to strain his neck to look up at my uncle. "He's long since passed, and you'd do well to remember that my authority far exceeds yours."

Bryan stepped back and his form shook, causing his big belly to bounce. His face was a putrid purplish red. "If you're going to insist on a new *vigiles*, then I demand we have a hand in choosing them!"

Andrew's ability to humor the little fat man was fading quickly. "Have you lost your mind?" Andrew looked into the man's eyes and shook his head. "Someone's been filling your head with ideas, Bryan. Who?"

Bryan glared at the floor as he back peddled to the door, with Sonia right behind him. "That's not important! Stay out of my head, Andrew! I'm warning you."

And that was it. Andrew had finally had enough. "Bryan, you should leave now. You should forget about whatever line of shit someone is feeding you, and realize that being the captain of the UCD, in your case, is purely ceremonial. If you challenge me on this, I swear I'll destroy you and everything you hold dear. Am I clear?"

Bryan reached behind him with a pudgy hand, gripping the doorknob as he sneered at Andrew. "You can only do that if you're still in charge of things." Sonia was out the door when he turned halfway around and looked back at my uncle. "That may change soon, now that Martha's no longer here to protect you."

Bryan was out the door and gone before Andrew was able to make a reasonable reply. It was clear that the captain thought he knew something that we didn't.

We followed them out a few minutes later to lock the gates. Returning, we lugged up the dozen plus boxes to the apartment. The living room was crowded with boxes filled with what appeared to be random files. When they were in file cabinets I was sure they'd been well organized. Opening one of the files, I saw that they were highly detailed, precisely marked, and easy to follow. Whoever had emptied her office didn't care that they'd probably destroyed years of painstaking care and organization.

Andrew quickly grew frustrated and waved a hand at the sapphire on his desk. The thin blue mist version of Martha appeared a few feet in front of the desk. She looked only slightly better than the first time I'd seen her.

Andrew spoke softly, and his face fell as he watched her standing there. "Evening, Martha."

Martha gave Andrew a kind look, and then her face dropped when she saw the boxes on the floor. "I see Bryan didn't waste any time ransacking my office."

Andrew's face darkened. "Clearly."

Martha's form pulsed and glitched in place. "I'm sorry I can't stay longer, but you need to go through the files. I've been working on a series of murders all across the country...." Her voice broke and reverberated for a moment. "I can't stay, but they are somehow related to you." She looked at Andrew with fear in her eyes. "Someone's coming for you!"

Her form shimmered and vanished from sight. Terrific; someone had to go and piss in the Cheerios right after we threw the police out on their ass.

Chapter 7

Sunday May 31st

Waking up, I felt like staying in bed for several more hours, but the aches and pains of sleeping on such a soft mattress told me it was well past time to get up. Rolling over, I saw it was five minutes to five. Three hours' sleep would have to do. I'd left Andrew in the living room after I helped him pull two rolling blackboards out of a storage closet in the back.

He'd promised to get some sleep, but even as he said it I doubted that he meant it. My stomach growled and groaned, telling me I needed food. Stopping in the kitchen, I found a plate of lukewarm eggs and dry toast waiting on me. Making short work of breakfast, I headed for the living room in search of Andrew, and as I turned the corner I froze, awestruck.

While I'd slept Andrew had lined up the blackboards next to one another. He'd affixed newspaper clippings, notes, and other articles to the boards with tape. On top of the articles he'd attached his own notes via bright yellow Post-it notes. Long white lines connected different articles, while blue scribbled text explained how they were connected. I found the boards both fascinating and more than a little disturbing. I could already see the connection between more than a dozen "deaths," and if Martha's doppelganger was correct they were somehow connected to my uncle.

Taking my eyes off the boards I found Andrew typing away at the Surface Pro on the table. He was viewing an article now, studying it, and pushed one paper after another to the side, glancing down to read text. He was calm, methodical, and precise. The way he moved spoke volumes about his character. There was no fear to be found, only a man driven to find the people behind the conspiracy. After that it was only the simple matter of ending the threat permanently. This was a man who would have none of it, and was ready to defend himself against any challenger.

I'd made it halfway to the table when I announced myself. "I'm guessing you didn't go to bed."

Andrew barely acknowledged my presence as he waved me over. "Not yet." He pulled a sheet of paper off the table and read it carefully as he glanced back at the screen to confirm the words. "I'm trying to fit all this together."

The room was covered in papers and open boxes. I was thoroughly impressed with how he'd been able to make sense of it all. "You really need to get some rest."

Ignoring my comment, he stood, walked over to the farthest chalkboard, and taped the paper he was holding to the black surface, then drew a white line between the nearest file and the paper before scribbling in blue chalk an explanation of how they fit together.

Andrew reluctantly tore his attention away from the boards to look at me. It was easy to see the exhaustion in his eyes, yet he willed himself to go on.

"I'll get some rest shortly. I'm close to something. I can feel it," he said.

Putting a hand on the old man's shoulder, I shook my head. "You said that at one-thirty this morning." Pulling him away from the blackboard, I forced Andrew to keep his attention on me as I tried to make myself clear when I spoke. "Thank you for breakfast. Now go crawl in bed and get a few hours sack time before you lose your mind!" Taking in the enormity of the task at hand, I was forced to stifle a shiver. "I'll carry on in your absence." Looking at the heaps of papers, I sighed. "Care to tell me how you have it arranged before you crash out?"

Andrew stared at the chalkboards in frustration. "Someone out there is apparently pretty serious about wanting me dead, and now you just want me to go get some sleep." He gave me a withering glance before turning back to the blackboards. "You might see how I find that counterproductive."

The man did have a valid point and the scene was more than a little overwhelming. During most of my career I'd skipped the investigative part of the job and mostly did the hands on work. Even so I'd like to think I could figure this out and piece the puzzle together in his absence for a few hours.

I fixed a hard look on Andrew and pleaded my case in a slightly different manner. "Give me a chance to run through a few of the leads without you. I might see something you didn't. Get some sleep, come back with a fresh set of eyes, and we'll see where things go from there."

Andrew hung his head, realizing I wouldn't be swayed. Grumbling, he desperately looked around the room for a suitable defense but found none, and he reluctantly caved to my request. "I suppose a few hours wouldn't do any harm." He looked around the room almost longingly before heading for his room. "Don't let me sleep too long. I need to be here."

"I won't; now get some sleep," I said, pointing to his room.

Andrew forced himself to put one foot in front of the other as he padded off to his bedroom and closed the door. It was only then that I realized he hadn't given me a clue as to how he'd sorted all this shit. Oh well, time to figure it out on my own and hope for the best.

Grabbing an empty notebook off the table, I walked around the room and scribbled down notes about each of the piles, then headed back to the computer.

Martha was very organized. Most of the articles were listed in chronological order, but the confusing part were the leaps she'd made to connect different events over the last fifty years. I spent the next two hours compiling information and sorting through the chalkboards before adding more clippings to the opposite sides. Three hours later I was beginning to see the pattern Martha found. I still wasn't sure I understood, but there was a bit of good news for Andrew…his death was only a means to a goal. There was a significant wrinkle to their plan, and that was me. I would have to wait for Andrew to wake up to confirm the theory.

I was in the kitchen making lunch when Andrew drug himself through the door and collapsed in the nearest chair. "What are you making?"

"Leftover pizza, want some?" I said.

Andrew glanced back towards the living room before turning his attention to me. "Sure." He swallowed hard and looked back at the door again. "I saw some progress when I came through. Anything of interest?"

Putting a plate in front of my uncle, I took in a nervous breath. "I think so, but I need more information before I can be sure."

"I'm sure we'll find it in the papers given enough time."

I furrowed my forehead. He'd misunderstood, so I pointed my finger at him and said, "I need information from you."

Andrew looked at me, perplexed, and swallowed a bite of pizza. "What do you think I know that isn't in the papers out there?"

Out of simplicity or stupidity, I pointed towards his room and the back of the house before taking a bite of my slice. I got the words out between bites. "The stones down the hall."

"What about them?" he asked.

I tossed a crust onto my plate and Andrew leaned over and swiped it. Taking a drink of tea, I swallowed and looked at him. "Can you please explain, for lack of a better term, the rules surrounding them? For instance, you said no one can touch either of ours while we are still alive, but what about the rest of them?"

Andrew finished his first slice of pizza, looking more than a little lost by the question. "I don't understand what this has to do with anything." He looked irritated by such a childish question. "Once a stone born dies, one of their living relatives picks it up and stores it for future use."

Now I felt frustrated. Not by the answer but by the lack of further information. "But what if there wasn't a living relative, like Martha?"

Andrew looked highly annoyed. "She could give it to someone, like me, for instance. I don't understand how this is important to solving our current problem. I told you before we have next to forever to figure all this out. That is unless someone kills me in the meantime."

Closing my eyes, I pushed my irritation down, trying to keep it out of my voice, and continued. "I'm getting to the important part if you'll just bear with me a bit longer." Yep, I still sounded like an asshole. "For instance, if you died, could someone walk in and take possession of the stones?"

From the absurd look on Andrew's face the answer was a clear no. "Not while you're alive...." Realization etched itself across his features. "You think they are after the stones?"

I sat down and looked at my uncle, who was fully awake now. "What would happen to someone touching a gemstone while I still drew breath?"

Horror etched itself across his features at the thought. "If someone were to touch any of the stones back there they'd suffer greatly before having their body torn apart at a cellular level and sprayed across the room."

Well, wasn't that a pleasant thought. "I'm guessing not a lot of people know about me?" I asked. "Heather seemed surprised to find out we were related."

Andrew gave me one of those you-can't-be-serious looks. "Not really. You were always either at school or simply gone."

That made sense, even if it was depressing. "And who knows about that room?"

Andrew scoffed at me and his face turned serious. "Besides you?"

I gave him a duh look and nodded. "Yeah, besides me."

"There was Martha of course...it wasn't as if I showed the place off to people."

"What about Isidore or Heather?" I asked.

Andrew jerked back like he took offense to the question. "No, neither of them could enter the hallway without my permission. I've had it heavily enchanted since before you were born. No, the only person who ever saw it other than you was Martha."

In a desperate attempt to pin this on a known enemy and to thwart my mounting disappointment, I asked, "Walter?"

Now he was offended. Andrew slapped an open hand against the tabletop in frustration. "Not sure how many different ways I can tell you that I've only shown the room to you and Martha. Besides, he and I stopped being friend's years before I built the room. There's no way he could know about it."

Pulling a small notebook out of my back pocket, I tossed it to him. "I don't think he saw it here. Whoever this is, Martha seems to think that they saw it back in St. Mary, Montana when my father was still alive."

Andrew's confusion was apparent. "I can't speak to who your father would've allowed to see the stones, but I'd wager it wasn't many. I can assure you that he wouldn't have shown it to Walter, considering how much he didn't like the man."

I really wanted a concrete link to Walter because he was a known entity, someone that could be dealt with. Unknown enemies were hard to combat since they were, by the very definition, unknown. The way Captain Hotard had acted indicated an outside influence, but by the same token it had been the NOPD that escorted Walter out of the funeral. On the other hand, it had been the NOPD that had let him into the funeral in the first place. This was feeling more like a group effort than a single individual.

Looking back at Andrew, I thought back to prior nights' events. "When Sonia and Captain Hotard were here, were you able to get a reading on who was feeding him information?"

Andrew's face fell. "He doesn't know. I heard raspy voices over telephones. Saw photos and documents that meant nothing to me but were important to him." He pushed his chair back as he stood. "What's on your mind?"

Picking up Andrew's plate, I put it in the sink and headed for the living room, waving for Andrew to follow me. I spoke as we walked. "I'm thinking that there are a lot of moving parts." Gesturing to the nearest chalkboard, I shook my head. "There may be a mastermind behind it all, but there are too many things happening at once to be only one man."

I pointed at two of the articles dated the same but in separate parts of the country. "These are two enchanters that went missing two years ago. They were abducted on the same day a thousand miles apart." Pulling both files off the board, I laid them on the table. "They were both missing for forty-two days before being found dead in their homes of 'natural causes.'"

The fact of the matter was some of these cases stretched back fifty years. Someone, or perhaps several people, had been working in concert for at least that long in an effort to acquire the stones just down the hall. The first few decades the cases were filled with outright murders. Later, as they got cleverer, the victims started dying of "natural causes," mostly heart failure.

Martha had tracked several of the murders back to stone born across the country; people who had no living relatives, and whose stones were always missing. Which lent credit to the theory that someone wanted the treasure trove being held by Andrew.

Andrew listened to my theory as he read the reports, scanned the computer, and finally, with much reluctance, arrived at the same conclusion I had. "They really want me dead."

I wagged my finger and snorted. "Correction…they want US dead, but why. What would they gain?"

The look Andrew shot me said he found my humor distasteful. "Not like many people know you exist, but yeah, they want us dead. As for what they'd gain? Knowledge and each stone under their control would bolster their power." He walked over to the board, pulled down the notes about a couple of enchanters killed over the years, and mused, "Why kill these people? They aren't stone born."

That had been the first thing I'd worked out after I discovered their goal. "For the same reason George only uses your services…for the enchantments."

Andrew looked at me as if I were the dumbest human being on the planet. "What?"

Straightening myself, I moved towards the boards like a professor about to start class. "From what you've told me about your work with George, enchanted cloth needs specific tools." I watched my uncle's face for affirmation before moving on. "Then there's the fun fact that this house and the grounds are enchanted as well. Whoever is behind this would need a way to counter them."

Andrew continued to stare at me as if I were ignorant. "What in the world would ever make you think that?"

Walking over to the table, I picked up a file labeled Neil Nunez. I pulled out a photo and showed it to my uncle. "Any chance you know this man?"

Andrew rubbed his chin and said. "It's possible I've seen him, but I don't have a clue as to who he is. Why?"

Opening the file again, I pulled out a receipt and a handwritten note of Martha's interview with George Nguyen. I handed the receipt to Andrew. "That's a receipt for the blue shirt he was wearing when he was murdered."

Andrew barely looked at it before handing it back. "I don't understand how this relates to the subject at hand."

Taking a deep breath, I remained calm as I spoke. "Neil was stabbed through the heart with a long silver dagger, according to eyewitness accounts."

Andrew stared at me, still not comprehending the situation. "A lot of people get stabbed in this city."

My irritation grew and I felt it creep into my voice. "Not everyone is wearing enchanted clothing that's supposed to prevent that very thing from happening."

Andrew flinched, snatched the receipt out of my hand again, and looked down at the photo. "Are you sure that's the same piece he bought from George?"

I held out the handwritten note to Andrew. "I don't have to be. George identified the article of clothing." I motioned for him to keep reading. "You'll see that Martha did some testing on it as well, and discovered that no matter how she tried to puncture the shirt, nothing penetrated it."

Andrew fell into the chair next to the table. "That's impossible."

Irritation still in my voice, I replied, "Yet it happened."

He was frustrated and poured over the notes again in hopes of finding a discrepancy. "But it shouldn't have."

"I know," I replied.

Andrew sat the note atop the file. His face twisted in anger, fear, and finally acceptance. "It would take years, as well as a deliberate attempt to undo someone else's enchantments. It's bad form, not to mention highly counterproductive. There are laws that prohibit such actions. Why would anyone do such a thing?"

Taking a seat across from him, I pulled the file close and skimmed it again. "That would explain the need for so many enchanters over the years. One building on the others work." I saw the defiance on his face, his objections and arguments mounting by the second. "You've got to remember a lot of people died. Many of them were missing for long periods of time. Trust me on this, given the proper motivation, torture for instance, people will do things they normally might not." I stood and walked back to the chalkboard and removed a file. "This one was missing for nearly a year before they turned up face down in the Arkansas River. Martha has a note here about an Aaron Lopez from Honduras that has been missing since April of last year."

Andrew was having a hard time accepting this. "I'm not sure—"

I cut him off quickly so he couldn't rationalize it away. "Look, we know that it did happen. We may not know how or by who, but we know it did happen. You really need to accept that so we can formulate a suitable defense."

Andrew's head hung limp at his shoulders for a moment longer before he raised it and looked at me. "What are you proposing?"

Leaning back in my chair, I stroked my chin. "Nothing yet. Let's go over what we know. Someone has been killing off stone born and stealing their stones over the last five decades." Putting up another finger, I pointed at the closed door. "You have a massive collection of them just down the hall, and until recently no one knew you had a living heir, so it stands to reason that you'd be on that list." Another finger popped into view. "We know they have a weapon or weapons that can penetrate some, if not all, of your enchantments. So your usual safeguards are out the window. You'll need to develop new defensive strategies."

Andrew shot me an absurd look. "That's easier said than done. Enchantments like that take months to complete."

I responded a bit more flippantly than I'd intended. "Then you'd better get started. The one big thing we have on our side is the fact we know about it and they don't know about me."

Andrew's posture told me he wasn't so sure about our advantages. "That's one way of looking at it." He looked me over, and noticing my calm, he furrowed his forehead. "This was probably the last thing you believed you'd get caught up in when you came home. I'm sorry I've put you in danger."

I laughed. I hadn't meant to but I couldn't help it. This was a life I was accustomed to. This was where my skills blazed into existence and made me a force to be reckoned with. "Don't worry about it. This is something I understand. This is something I can help with."

Andrew became concerned at my words. "Just what did you do all those years over there? I'm doubting it was pushing paperwork as you've suggested/ lied to me about."

There was that sensation again. The one that made me want to tell him all my deepest, darkest secrets, but that was never going to happen. "Let's just say that this is an area in life that I excel at and leave it alone." I left the last bit unsaid...*Pray that you never have to witness the kind of man I can be when everything goes to hell.*

I felt the dark part of my soul stir as I finished that thought. The old familiar Grim begged to be released. It wanted out, it wanted to find the people responsible for these crimes and make them pay. Soon, I promised, soon.

The sensation lessoned and I looked up to see my uncle staring at me in a peculiar way. The look on his face was a combination of concern, fear, and awe.

"Are you all right?" he asked.

Brushing off his concern, I sat up straight and tried to mask my old friend. "Of course, I'm fine. Why do you ask?"

He looked at my hands and then my face before slowly letting out a long breath. "I thought I saw something, but it must be the lack of sleep catching up to me."

We heard a knock at the door and we both jumped. I was on my feet heading across the room when it opened. Isidore stood there on the landing with two small parcels under his arm. He saw me coming and hefted the parcels in my direction. "I'm glad you're here. George called me earlier…he didn't have your number." He handed me the packages and turned his attention to Andrew. "Is it all right if I come in?" Then he caught sight of the living room and stopped in his tracks. "What the hell is all that?"

Andrew looked tired but he stood and waved at the boards as he explained what Martha was working on. He went into detail about the enchanters and the stone born that had been killed, and how since many believed he was without an heir he was on the list. Andrew was careful to leave out the room full of stones, and instead implied that they wanted only his and probably mine now if they knew about me.

In an instant all the joy and lightness that normally oozed from Isidore ceased, replaced by something quiet, calm, and deadly. It was as if his physical form became denser as his body became clearly defined under his silk shirt. His voice was lower, with a hard edge. Every syllable was calculated as he fought to control his emotions. "Do you know who it is?"

Andrew barely looked away from the board as he continued to piece it together. "We don't, but as Gavin said we know about it now, which is more than I could say two days ago." He looked over at the table and pointed at the file belonging to Neil Nunez. "It appears whoever this is has a weapon that can pierce the enchanted clothing we're wearing."

Isidore picked up the file and quickly skimmed the notes. "Just the one weapon?"

Andrew put up his hands, clearly at a loss of further insight. "I don't know."

Isidore thought for a moment, looking back at me and then Andrew again. "I can stay in the room downstairs if you want."

Andrew appeared to quickly consider his offer before accepting it. "That might not be a bad idea."

Isidore turned and looked at me. "I'm sorry you came home to this."

I found it odd how they both were so accepting of the danger placed at their doorstep, yet somehow felt a need to apologize because it involved me. They needn't worry though…this was my specialty. "This isn't the first time someone has wanted me dead. I didn't oblige them, and I don't think I'll oblige whoever this is either."

Isidore looked curious but turned his attention to Andrew. "I've got to grab some things from home. Should I call Heather?"

Andrew shook his head. "No, she's got a wedding tonight and will be back tomorrow. We can tell her then."

Isidore clearly didn't like the idea but accepted it. He turned on the spot and headed for the door. "You two be safe until I get back."

We walked Isidore out the front door and locked the gate behind him. Once we were up the stairs I looked over at Andrew and asked. "How's Isidore staying here going to help?"

Andrew found the question far too amusing for my taste. "We are two days away from the full moon, which means it'll take more than a sharp pointy stick to put the man down. That, and the more people we have here the better I like our odds."

Like I understood any of that, but I accepted his words. In the package I found a new pair of black slacks and a cobalt blue long sleeve button up shirt. I tossed them on the bed and went back to work trying to figure out who was wanted to kill us, and how the UCD captain was involved. Why had he asked to be involved in choosing the next *vigiles*, and why did he say that Andrew's opinion only counted so long as he was in charge? How did being in charge of a bookstore even rate a visit or a rant from the pudgy little man?

Isidore returned with his hackles up and ready to rip off someone's head with the slightest provocation. Andrew was obsessed with digging through the boxes attempting to uncover the next clue. I, on the other hand, was ready to go pay a visit to the one man I was sure had his hand in the mix, Walter. If that didn't pan out, I was sure I could find the appropriate pressure to apply to Captain Hotard to get answers. He knew more than Andrew had picked up, of that I was sure. There were phone records, notes, and photos that could point me in the right direction.

The phone rang about a quarter to six. Andrew answered it and then handed it to me. "Heather says she needs your help."

Squinting at my uncle, I took the phone. "Hello?"

Heather sounded a little panicked. "I hate to ask this, but my 'date' bailed on me five minutes ago, and you're the only other single man I know."

Weddings weren't my thing, but I figured I'd try to let her down easy. "You could always meet someone there."

She growled. "That's exactly what I'm trying to avoid. One of my old friends will be there, and if I don't show up with a date she's going to try and fix me up with an old 'family friend.' I'm sure the guy is nice, but your uncle and he were probably born in the same decade." She sniffed. "Please, will you just do this for me? I'll owe you one."

Hanging my head, I knew I'd been beaten. The first sniffle had done it. I hated to see or hear women and children crying. "Fine. Where and when?"

She relaxed and I could almost see her smile. "I'm not far away; how fast can you dress?"

Damn! "I'll be down in fifteen."

"Can you make it ten?" she asked hopefully.

"Sure."

Hanging up the phone, I looked up at my uncle. "It appears I'm going to a wedding tonight."

Andrew didn't look pleased. "Are you sure you want to go out with everything going on?"

I smiled and patted him on the shoulder as I headed for my room. "Relax, I was going to be going out one way or another tonight. At least this way I'll be with Heather and not looking into Walter."

Andrew huffed. "That's not comforting at all!"

I was changed and downstairs in eight minutes. Heather pulled up in a Kia Sedona two minutes later and waved me in. We were off to the Elms Mansion on St. Charles Avenue for an evening of rich people spending a ton of money on a party instead of a new house or car or god forbid, student loans!

Chapter 8

As if the bride and groom had planned it, the sunset occurred at the close of the ceremony, bathing them in the last vestiges of the day...talk about pretentious. That was about an hour ago, and since then the giant ball of flaming death had disappeared over the horizon allowing the temperature to drop several degrees. That and the small yet welcome breeze out of the north permitted me to remain somewhat comfortable under my dark suit jacket. The humidity was at a reasonable level for New Orleans, which of course meant I felt clammy, but not so much so that it was noticeable.

I'd worn the cobalt blue shirt and black slacks I'd received from George earlier. I'd finished the look by pulling on my black suit jacket I'd worn to the funeral, along with a red silk tie. Heather wore an emerald green form fitting silk dress that landed just above her knees. The matching five-inch heels put her at eye level with me. I'd always thought there was an unspoken rule that you weren't supposed to look better than the bride, but if that were the case I was certain she wouldn't be invited to many weddings.

As to be expected from the city's exceptionally wealthy, the evening's events were lavish beyond comprehension. The wedding itself was an overdone yet beautiful ceremony decked out in rare flowers, white silk, and all the other trimmings money could buy. The seven-inch Samsung tablets set atop the finest floral china place settings obscured the white linen tablecloths. From what I gathered, the tablets were the party favors for the guests. Obviously someone had more money than sense.

Shortly after dusk dinner was served atop the antique china, along with actual sterling silver utensils. The most unfortunate part of the evening thus far had been the fact that Heather's original date was a vegan, forcing me to choke down stinky tofu specially imported from Japan with many,

many vegetables. How I prayed for a burger or a steak during the entire ordeal.

After we'd finished, Heather stood and drug me to my feet. "Come with me."

Wiping the corners of my mouth, I dropped the napkin and stood. "Where are we going?"

She turned, holding my hand, and pulled me along behind her. "I need to introduce you to my mother."

That drove ice through my gut. "I'm not sure I'm the kind man you want to bring home to Mom."

She paused a moment, looking back at me with a mischievous glint in her eye. "We're not going home...yet." She let out a giggle as she guided me through the crowd. "Besides, she's just over there."

I caught sight of our intended destination several seconds before we arrived. The woman we were approaching was nearly identical to Heather save for the blonde hair. She wore a yellow version of Heather's green dress, and a massive rock on her ring finger.

Heather waved at her mother, and she turned to take us in, me in particular. Her eyes cascaded over me as she appraised my worth. She seemed happy enough to see me trailing behind her daughter.

Heather pulled me up next to her, practically glowing with excitement. "Mom, this is Gavin." She looked back at me and waved at her mother. "Gavin, this is my mother, Kimberly Broussard."

I gave her a slight bow and gently took her hand in mine. "A pleasure to meet you, Mrs. Broussard."

Kim's voice was raspier than her daughter's, yet no less pleasant. "The pleasure is all mine." She looked thoughtful for a moment and asked, "Didn't I see you with Andrew at the funeral Friday?"

I nodded. "Yes, ma'am."

She sucked on her cheek for a moment. "If you see Andrew, would you tell him how sorry we are for his loss?" She made a face suddenly. "We didn't want to interrupt him after that nasty business with Walter."

"When I see him again I'll let him know."

She appeared pleased, leaning forward to give Heather a kiss on the cheek. "I've got to make the rounds and pay our respects, since your father had to 'work' tonight."

Heather's beautiful face contorted for a fraction of a second at the mention of her father. When she spoke her voice was heavily laced with sarcasm. "You'd think being the head of surgery would have its perks."

Kim's face turned sour quickly before she regained her composure. "It does. He doesn't have to attend funerals or even weddings if they inconvenience him in the slightest."

Lesson one: when women are discussing their husbands or fathers in a negative way, never interject your opinion. It never goes well for anyone, especially me.

Kimberly gently squeezed my forearm as she swept by.

Heather's eyes widened and her face became brighter. "She likes you!"

"Is that a good thing?" I asked.

Heather rolled her eyes and she guided us back to our seats next to the wrought iron fence near St. Charles. "That's a great thing! I don't have to allow myself to be set up with some old geezer that my father would approve of and my mother would hate." She grabbed a crystal flute of champagne when the waiter passed. "The man I was supposed to come with tonight is one of those set ups by my father." She took a long draught of her champagne and anger flickered across her delicate features. "My father desperately wants me to get involved with the creepy little shit that works for him." She shook her head in disgust. "I only agreed to the date tonight with him to shut my father up! Then the fucker turns around and stands me up at the last minute."

I wisely kept my mouth shut and sipped on my Coke and ice in a rock glass. Just because I'd left the safety of the house didn't mean I was going to be reckless. Drinking when people wanted you dead was a sure fire way to allow it to happen.

We took our seats at the end of the table, allowing us to watch the traffic on St. Charles Avenue and still have a view of the overdone gazebo where the band was playing. Some of the guests were still picking at their food while drinking and generally being rowdy...well, as rowdy as rich folks got, I supposed. Our table was empty now, allowing us to have a proper conversation without having to either whisper to keep from being overheard or yell at one another.

She kept her face serene while she swirled the champagne around in her glass, watching the crowd swell and thin at an odd rhythm. Finally, she turned her eyes back to me. "So, what did you think?"

Her question forced me to stop scanning the crowd for possible security issues. "Of the wedding?"

Heather's pink lips twitched and she let a delightful giggle escape. "Of course, the wedding!"

I'd seen this type of thing a lot over the years and I hated every minute of it. The vast waste of money combined with arrogance and ignorance of it all pissed me off. "Honest answer?"

She fixed me with a stern look. "We literally just met yesterday. I'd greatly appreciate it if you didn't start our friendship by lying to me." Her face screwed itself up as she downed the drink and grabbed another from a passing tray. "Actually, if you could promise not to lie to me at all that would be spectacular."

I took a drink of my Coke, never actually agreeing consciously. "I hated every last second of it!" Grabbing my new tablet off the table, I held it up in disgust. "The money they poured into this 'party' could have paid for a very nice house and a car." Looking around at the decadence, I felt uncomfortable. "I've always felt that people throw these type of parties to brag and tell others how special they think they are."

She sucked her lips into her mouth and bit down and she tried not to laugh. Finally, the fit passed and she gasped. "Oh, thank the lords above!"

Setting my glass on the table, I was suddenly curious. "I thought these were your friends and you were sort of required to like it out of, I don't know, camaraderie or something."

She waved a hand around airily, in an effort to utterly distance herself from the event. "These are more my father's friends than mine." She made a face as she caught sight of the bride drifting around the front tables, fawning over the more special guests. "My mother and I show up for appearance's sake, but honestly, I hate these things and so does she."

I was treading into dangerous territory, but this was the second time her father had come up in such a negative manner. "And these being your father's friends, is there any reason he didn't wish to be here tonight?"

Anger and bitterness clouded her beautiful features before she downed another gulp of champagne. "My 'father' does his best to avoid anything he considers beneath him." She glowered and leaned forward. "These are simply the children of one of his more influential friends. A suitable gift was purchased in each of our names and sent to the bride. A task he surely delegated to the help, and then Mother and I are sent as his emissaries, bearing the news that he was just too swamped with work, otherwise he would've surely made it."

It was clear from her tone that she held a deep resentment for the man, and was even more bitter about being used in such a fashion. Holding up my glass, I toasted her and gave her a big smile. "The one great thing about this evening is you got me out of the house, and possibly saved my liver in the process."

That snapped her back to reality, placing her champagne flute on the table and she took my rock glass, sniffing it before taking a drink. "What the hell?"

Her mock outrage was amusing. "What?" I said innocently.

She pointed across the lawn to the open bar. "You may not know this, but it's a cardinal sin to refuse an open bar here in New Orleans."

Taking my drink from her, I pulled a face that made it clear I didn't mind sinning. "Andrew has been pouring scotch down me by the liter since I arrived." I waved a hand at the Coke on the table. "I needed a break."

She let loose with another fit of the giggles, which I assumed was brought on by the onslaught of champagne she'd drank since we arrived. "The old man can put them back." She beamed at me again as she looked back at the open bar. "It's a real shame you didn't take advantage, but I can sympathize." She fondled her tablet for a moment longer before tossing it back onto the table in disgust. "You're right about this being a way to show off." She looked over at the band and smirked. "The cost of the band could've paid off my car."

Leaning forward, I put my weight on the table. "I just assumed you were well off."

She shifted a little in her seat. "My mother's father was wealthy and set up several trust funds for me, which I don't touch unless I have to." She scrunched her face as if she'd smelled something foul. "My father is definitely well off, but that's his money and he takes every opportunity to remind everyone of that fact." She shivered at the thought. "I'm well enough off, I suppose. I inherited my grandfather's house, and I've got money from when I used to model, but I have bills like everyone else."

Wanting to change the subject, I shifted gears. "How did you go from modeling to working for my uncle?"

And just like that she perked up and her mood instantly lightened. "That's a long story, not to mention several years apart. However, Andrew used to date my mother, and my father has never forgiven him for it! So when I was looking for a mentor, my mother, of course, suggested Andrew. I was floored when my father not only approved but encouraged it."

Now, that was odd to have such a massive shift of opinions. Perhaps the old man wasn't a complete piece of shit and truly wanted the best for her. "I see."

Heather grumbled. "You don't, but after you meet my father you will." She paused and glanced around to make sure we were alone. "Are you really his nephew?"

The question caught me off guard and I stammered my reply. "As far as I know. Why do you ask?"

Her eyes went big lighting up in excitement. "Are you like him? I mean, are you one of the stone born?"

I felt myself stiffen at the question, and a part of me wanted to avoid it. "To be honest, I have no idea what I am. As for being like him, I doubt it. He appears to be on a scale of power that would far exceed my own." I frowned and suddenly wished I was drinking scotch. "I have no idea what I can do other than being impervious to his mental manipulation…and yours, for that matter." I inhaled, catching the scent of jasmine far off in the distance. "I've only been introduced to this world two days ago."

She leaned forward, glancing around again as she whispered. "Really?"

Trying not to make a big deal about my ignorance, I put my drink on the table. "Really. I've been away a very long time, and well, Andrew only told me about my family after the funeral Friday." I leaned forward in my chair as I looked around to make sure we were alone. "If you'd told me anything close to this before then I would've thought you were mental."

Her languid smile brightened the evening, and she gently tossed her hair back with a flick of her hand. "Some days I feel a bit mental anyway." She bit her lip as her eyes traveled down my arm to my left hand. "Care to tell me how that happened?"

I thought about the promise I'd never actually agreed to earlier but still felt obligated by, and chose to answer as best I could. "I'd really rather not."

She pushed out her bottom lip in a pout, yet her eyes were full of amusement. "Perhaps you'd feel up to answering what you do for a living."

I suppressed a silent titter. "At the moment I'm gainfully unemployed." I held up a hand to stop her follow up question. "I may not have family money, but I'have have three decades of paychecks I haven't touched. I'm looking for a new career, but not today, since I've also got thirty years of vacations I need to catch up on."

She pursed her lips, giving me the stink eye. "That was terribly unrevealing!" She clucked, finished off her champagne and waved for the nearest waiter to bring another. "In that case, would you care to tell me what you did that kept you away from this great city for so long?"

My smile faded. Shaking my head, I sat my glass on the table. "I think that falls into the same category as my hand."

With that answer she felt obliged to pick up two glasses. "That category being the one you don't want to talk about?"

I touched my finger to my nose, indicating she'd guessed right. "Correct."

She shook her head as her wry grin reappeared. "You're definitely different than most of the men I know."

"And how's that?" I asked.

Heather's face turned devilish, she shook her hair, allowing her sultry eyes to find mine. "You're not tripping over yourself to please me."

That wasn't hard to believe. She had the face, body, and attitude that could melt most men. In a different world I might have been one of them, but my sins were far too great to be casually shared. "And this pleases you, I take it."

She set her glass down with a snort. "God yes! There's something so appealing about a man with a spine."

The way she looked me over made me feel naked. Needless to say, I liked it. I liked it a lot, but she was drunk and whatever was on her mind wasn't going to happen. Looking down at my watch, I considered the time and her sobriety. "Where do you live?"

The smile that crossed her lips spoke of passion. Waving a languid arm towards St. Charles, her eyes sparkled with lust. "I'm only a few blocks away." She chewed her bottom lip in anticipation. "What's on that mind of yours?"

Shaking my head, I said, "Nope!" I held my hand out in her direction and said, "If you were sober we would be having a much different conversation, but you're not." Still the thought of being twisted naked in the sheets with her swam through my mind. "Save whatever it is you're thinking about until you're single and sober."

Her eyes lit up like it was Christmas, and the smile on her face couldn't have spoken more clearly if she'd used a thousand words. "I've never been turned down before." She pushed her chair back and waved me ahead of her. "I'm either far more drunk than I thought or I really like it! Either way, I'm good with it."

Again, it wasn't hard to believe her when she said such things. She was a beautiful woman, and I'd probably kick myself tomorrow. But the thought of taking advantage of a woman who was angry at one man and at the very least tipsy made me feel dirty. Not in that good fun way either. Not that I was against drinking and sex, but not for the first encounter.

She suddenly frowned, reached for her glass, and pounded it back. "As for 'Brad.' You need not concern yourself with him. The man is more in love with my father than me. He wouldn't come to the wedding at the last second because he thought it would make our 'relationship' too serious." She grimaced, grabbed the second flute, and took another drink. "He and my father may still have something going on, but as far as the two of us are concerned, we were over before anything ever got started." She waved her hand at the other guests. "This was a pity date."

I put my arm out to steady her before walking us towards the gate. "Let's get you home, and perhaps tomorrow will be a better day."

She looked back at the band again as she leaned her warm, soft body against mine and smiled. "I think today was pretty damn nice!"

A boyish smile came to me and I leaned my head against the top of hers for the briefest of moments. "It's been a very nice evening."

She nuzzled against me before pulling herself fully upright and waving a delicate hand towards the gate. "Our chariot awaits!"

Just a few feet from the gate I was nearly overcome by the exotic scent of jasmine all around us. It made me cough and my nose itch in irritation. "Do you smell that?"

Heather sniffed the air curiously and turned to me with a blank look. "McDonald's?"

Pulling a handkerchief from my pocket, I dabbed my nose, concerned she didn't pick up the overpowering stench. "Nothing else?"

She took in another deep breath. "Just New Orleans...." She giggled. "What's up?"

With the next breath my stomach rolled and threatened to revolt at the putrid odor. "It's like jasmine gone bad."

She looked around and made a face as she shook her head in mock disbelief. "You sure you haven't been drinking?"

I wiped my nose again and stuffed the handkerchief back in my pocket. "Come on, let's get you home."

She tugged at my arm and leaned against me. "You're in an awful hurry to get me home and not do anything about it."

I blushed. "That may be true, but I'd like to get you home nonetheless."

The off duty policemen working the wedding detail waved us through, telling us to have a good night. All the while the smell continued to get stronger. I didn't know why, but the scent had placed all my senses on high alert.

I heard the quiet thud of soft-soled shoes rapidly pounding the sidewalk behind us. My body tensing, I grabbed Heather in my far arm, swinging her around me and holding her at arm's length, which allowed me to spin around and face the runner. The small yet handsome Asian man barreling our away was barely five feet tall. The officer reached out for him, but the runner ducked and planted a palm into the man's chest, sending him sprawling through the open gate where he landed hard on his back, slapping his head against the black stone walkway with a sickening crack.

The Asian man seemed at odds with himself, moving like a young man but appearing to be in his mid to late thirties. His bald head gleamed in the moonlight and his focus was on Heather. Increasing his speed, he pulled out a long silver dagger. He was fast, muscular, and most importantly, a threat.

Our attacker hadn't anticipated Heather being spun around, several feet out of reach, and his blade pierced my coat and shirt, allowing its razor sharp edge to leave a long shallow gash across my ribs. It wasn't life threatening, yet the warm blood trickling down my side was annoying and a little itchy. He pulled the blade back and flicked his wrist, and slamming the ridge of my hand against the man's throat, I lifted him off the ground, propelling him several feet back.

He was unarmed now, the dagger seemingly vanishing from sight, and it registered in my mind that I hadn't heard it hit the ground. Discovering the weapon's whereabouts was secondary to handling the man who wielded it.

He fell back gracefully, pulling his knees up, rolling over his shoulders and neck back to his feet, prepared for a fight. He was dazed and slow, which was bad news for him. I sped towards him in a low footballer's stance and he kicked out a foot, landing hard against my shoulder.

He wasn't heavy enough to slow me down, and I grabbed the leg. Catching sight of the fence, I changed tactics. Forcing myself upright and pulling his leg along with me in a nasty twist, I heard it snap at the ankle and knee before I felt it give way as I pulled it from the socket. He lurched back as I swept a leg underneath him, forcing him around and allowing his face to plow into the wrought iron fence, which was forced downward with all his body weight and a good shove from me. A long black iron *fleur de lis* erupted from the back of the man's head, causing him to convulse in an oddly rhythmic fashion for several seconds. Finally, the twitching stopped and he slumped against the fence with his knees on the sidewalk, resembling some sort of gruesome prayer to an uncaring god.

Suddenly the world sprang back to life with people screaming, others being sick, and yet more scattering in whichever direction would allow them to vacate the scene fastest. Two more off duty police officers who'd been working the same detail joined their friend, helping him to his feet.

It occurred to me that Heather wasn't where I'd left her, and I looked back to find her laying on the ground with the silver dagger protruding from her stomach. Her mother was already atop her, carefully removing the foreign object before casually tossing it aside. It clanked against the pavement, skidding to a halt against the curb at a weird angle.

Stepping off the sidewalk, I stalked over to where Heather lay and twisted my ankle on a chunk of cement. Stumbling back, I stepped on the dagger, snapping it in two with a loud pop and a large bright green spark that made everyone jump.

Coming up behind her mother, I could see Kim applying pressure to her daughter's wound. Heather shivered as sweat poured off her forehead. Taking a knee, I held Heather in one hand and put the other over the wound. Kim looked up at me before giving me a curt nod.

She pulled a phone out of her clutch and dialed 911. "This is Kimberly Broussard. There's been a stabbing at the Elms Mansion on St. Charles. I need an ambulance dispatched straight away, and our destination is Touro." She paused long enough to get whatever answer the operator gave her before hanging up and dialing another number. "Robert...Heather's been injured. Gut wound. Prep the OR and be ready. We'll be there shortly." She paused again as sirens rang in the background. "I've got to go; the ambulance should be here any minute."

She ended the call and looked up at me, really seeing me for the first time. She stuck a hand out and pulled back the jacket, revealing the blood soaked shirt. "You've been hurt."

Glancing at my chest and then back to her, I tried to alleviate her concern. "It's minor." I looked down at Heather, who was in and out of consciousness. "Will she be all right?"

Kim's face twisted in fear at the unknown. "I'm not sure, but the knife wasn't too deep." She grimaced as she looked at her daughter's stomach. "It's a gut wound; it can go either way."

I'd seen enough gut wounds over the years to know that she was right. People could get treatment right away but still go septic and die anyway.

Just then the paramedics pulled up and came to a screeching halt next to us. The first EMT jumped out and tried to muscle his way between Kim and Heather. "Excuse us, ma'am, we need to get in here." He gave me a distasteful look and snarled. "You'll need to step back as well."

I gently lay Heather back, allowing the man to take my place just as Kimberly swelled to her full height. "You don't recognize me because I'm not in scrubs today, but I know you." The man shook his head. "I'm the head nurse for Touro, and in case the dispatcher didn't inform you, that's our destination." She listed off Heather's condition in great detail while the driver wrote down everything she said in a notebook.

I was getting to my feet when two of the officers came up with their hands on their pistols. The officer who'd been shoved to the ground was checking for the Asian man's pulse. The fact that a large iron spike was sticking through the back of his head should've been the first clue the fucker was dead.

The bigger of the two officers in front of me looked down at Heather and then back at me. "We need to speak with you in private."

They were poised and looking for a fight, so I just nodded and I held my hands out so they could see them. "All right, where are we headed?"

Kim whirled around on the officers as she reluctantly allowed the paramedics to move her daughter. She moved between me and the officers, wagging a finger at them. "You're really going to harass a man who was nearly killed by someone you should've seen coming?" She glared at the man and then turned her attention back to me. "Don't say a word. I've got to make a call." Turning back to the officer, she growled. "You'll want to answer your cell when it rings."

She strode off and got in the back of the ambulance with one hand on her daughter and another holding the phone to her ear, leaving me to be escorted into the main house, where I was handcuffed and sat in the Louis XVI room. One of the officers stood at the door, while the other two attended to the mess outside.

The manager was going to be pissed about the bloodstains on the upholstered white furniture. The cut wasn't too deep but I'd probably need a couple of stitches. I wasn't about to inspect the wound given the situation. Weird thing was I'd either gotten used to the blood trickling down my chest or it had stopped. I was hoping for stopped. That would mean fewer stitches. At this point, however, it was never going to close properly since it wasn't being tended to right away. I'd bled through my shirt and jacket and was sitting in blood soaked pants, very uncomfortable.

A few minutes later the officer standing guard jumped when his phone rang. He fumbled around in his pocket before retrieving the phone and answering it.

"Hello?" He paused. "Yes sir.... I know, but...." He looked back at me and shook his head before looking at the couch and groaning. "Yeah, he's hurt too, but I...." He held the phone away from his ear as I heard crackling and a squeaky voice saying things I couldn't make out. "I'll tend to it right away." He paused and put his ear back to the phone. "It's cut and dry…I saw the whole thing, but we couldn't.... Yes sir. I'll make sure I apologize." He glowered back at me, shaking his head, letting me know that wasn't going to happen. "Thank you, sir. I'll file the paperwork before I leave for the night."

He stalked over to me, pulling out a set of keys. "Hands." I held out them out and he removed the cuffs. "You'll need to have someone look at that." He pointed at my chest. "I'm not calling an ambulance for you. If it was that bad you would've said something earlier."

Rubbing my wrists, I stood and nodded. I wasn't sure what to say that wouldn't piss the guy off further. "Stay safe tonight."

With that I pulled my phone out of my pocket and dialed my uncle. I let him know what happened and that I was taking Heather's car to the hospital to check on her. I left out the fact that I'd been injured and told him to stay put. I didn't want him out in this mess until I could figure out what was going on.

Ten minutes later I was at the hospital. I took a minute to duck into the nearest bathroom and pulled up my shirt. To my surprise the six-inch gash had closed on its own. It was still sore and it was downright painful if I touched it, but it was closed. Pulling my shirt down, I kept my jacket on while I sat in the waiting room.

Two hours later Kim came out to speak with me. I noticed that she had changed out of her dress and was wearing surgical scrubs. She looked tired but steady, flashing me a quick smile in an effort to put me at ease. "It appears she's going to be all right, thanks to you." Craning her neck, she looked at my chest. "Did you get that looked at?"

Mustering up my most reassuring voice, I gingerly got to my feet. "Yeah, all put back together. Everything will be fine."

Kim was clearly distracted by her daughter and patted me on the shoulder. "Good to hear. I'll let her know that you were here."

I fished Heather's keys out of my pocket and handed them to Kim. "I parked it in the garage on level 3."

Kim dropped the keys into her shirt pocket and nodded. "Thanks."

She waved before turning and heading back through the ER doors, disappearing from sight. I headed out through the lobby for home.

Chapter 9

Monday June 1st

The cool night air traveled all around me on a gentle zephyr from the north. The walk back to Andrew's place wasn't a long one, but it gave me plenty of time to think. The last few days had been eventful to say the least, and I did my best thinking when I put one foot in front of the other. That's why I'd left Heather's car with Kimberly.

It was nearly 3:00 a.m. when I turned onto my uncle's block. My senses were dialed to eleven, and I felt rather than saw someone standing in the shadow of the hedge at the far corner.

Keeping my pace slow and steady, I approached the gate leading into the front yard. About ten yards out I came to a stop and gave a small wave. After that I waited for my newest "friend" to show themselves. "You might as well step out, so we can have a proper conversation."

I heard the rubber soles scrape against the cement just before the man shuffled out of the darkness into the light of a nearby streetlamp. He was short, thick, and shapeless. His blond curly hair was matted to his head, and the freckles on his face and neck obscured the details of his muted, soft rounded fatty features. His stumpy arms hung out to his sides oddly while he leaned heavily on a thick black wooden cane. From the looks of his swollen legs, diabetes had taken hold long ago and the cane was necessary to get around.

He wiped the sweat off his forehead with one pudgy hand. Every word he spoke was between deep, wheezing whistles. His voice was thick and gooey, as if the fat had somehow oozed into his vocal cords. The deep French/Canadian accent didn't help. "I've been sent to speak with you."

It was clear from his tone that he disapproved of being tasked with such a menial job. His bright green eyes looked at me with a haughtiness, if not downright disgust, at being forced to speak with someone he deemed unworthy.

Allowing my senses to expand, I took in everything, waiting for whatever was coming next. "And you are?" I asked.

The fat man huffed as if I'd just insulted him. "Who I am is of little importance. What I'm here to offer, however...."

A strange coalescing of shadows swirled at the tip of his black cane.

I took a deep breath, allowing my body to relax yet remain agile enough to move when the time called for it. "I'm listening."

Slowly I moved a few steps closer. It was clear he either didn't notice or didn't care.

His lips stretched, forcing a smile, showing his mismatched uneven teeth. "My employer would like to double whatever offer Mr. Randall has on the table, for you to simply walk away."

This was interesting. Whoever was behind all this had no idea of who I was, and I wasn't about to inform them. "Really?"

The man was all too eager to mistake my question for agreement. His agitated movement caused his big jowls to slap against his formless neck. "Name a price, any price, and you can simply be on your way before you get any further into something you can't get out of."

The shadows at the tip of his cane swirled now and were about the size of a softball. "Out of curiosity, what has Mr. Randall gotten me into?"

Sweat ran down his face in rivulets. He shivered and shook so much that he splashed the salty fluids all around his bulbous form. He sneered in my direction and spewed spittle when he spoke. "Your kind couldn't possibly understand!" He steadied himself as he ran a hand down his heaving chest and his rounded belly. "How much for you to walk away?" He paused for dramatic effect to frighten me. "While you still can."

Something in the back of my brain started to itch as he stared at me. I didn't like it. He was maybe twenty feet away as I calmly took another step towards him, pretending to contemplate the offer. "How much would it be worth to you to have me gone?"

That was obviously the final straw. I'd crossed some unseen line by asking the question. He heaved himself back on his heels, lifting the cane off the ground a fraction of an inch before slamming it down. "You're nothing but a goddamn monkey, and you dare negotiate with me?"

The spinning ball of shadows flew up from the ground, expanding and exploding against my chest. I rocked back on my heels and my vision was obscured for several seconds as the ball of darkness enveloped me completely. Thousands of tiny black things slithered across my body, searching for a way in. I felt their malevolence coating me in an ichor. Then I felt their fear and trepidation as they grew weak and began to fail. They died by the hundreds, vanishing in puffs of smoke until I stood alone on the street facing my attacker.

I could hear his labored breathing as he sweated and swayed so hard he could barely stand. His eyes bulged out when he saw me standing there unscathed. He was so winded that he was unable to cry out when I sprinted forward, slamming my open hand around his throat and lifting him off the ground. So weak he couldn't maintain the grip on the cane, it clattered uselessly to the ground. Pulling him in close, I whispered in his ear. "You have no idea who I am! If you can put one foot in front of the other to leave this place, you might just live."

With all my strength I shoved him away from me, allowing my grip on his throat to loosen. He flew several yards before skidding across the sidewalk and out into the street. Stooping over, I swept up his cane into the palm of my hand and stood there. He struggled to get on his feet before turning tail and heading away at his fastest waddle.

It was then that the realization of throwing a rotund man several yards registered. I was a big guy, but I was not Superman by any stretch of the imagination. I waited to ensure that the fat man was gone before unlocking the gate and letting myself in. I paused at the bottom of the stairs and dialed my uncle, letting him know that I was coming in. Last thing I wanted to do was hurt him or Isidore if they were surprised by my arrival.

Pushing the upstairs door open, I found Andrew and Isidore seated in the wing chairs at the far end of the room. Andrew focused on me, and concern crossed his face. "What's that?"

I'd forgotten about the cane and I held it up to get a good look at it. It was covered in strange markings, and it vibrated ever so slightly in my hand. "Huh." I felt my face contort…something deep inside me really hated this thing. "Some asshole stopped me outside and wanted to pay me off."

The thought of someone trying to buy my loyalty pissed me off more than I could say. Flipping one end into the palm of my other hand, I slammed the cane down and raised my knee, snapping it in twain. A brilliant red light filled the room, followed by a powerful shock wave that threw me through the door, splintering it before depositing me on the landing with enough force to crack the floorboards.

Forcing myself up with a groan, I got to my feet while trying to dust off the broken door. "That was dramatic."

Andrew got to his feet, helping Isidore up before they turned their attention to me.

Isidore's features were clouded with rage and anger, shifting his gaze around the room. "What the hell was that?" He kept a wary eye on me, yet gave me plenty of room. Even from my position I could sense his fear.

Andrew focused on the broken cane. Crossing the room, he snatched the two halves off the floor and carefully inspected the shattered pieces. "Someone just let you take this from them?"

From his tone he was obviously skeptical. I suddenly felt like a kid who'd broken their mother's favorite piece of china. "Not exactly."

Andrew held his ground, glaring at me. "Then what? Exactly!"

My face burned crimson and my chest clenched. "Some fat guy stopped me outside the gate and offered to buy me off. I somehow insulted him, and he hit me with a swirling black orb that creeped me out. It was like thousands of tiny snakes trying to burrow through my skin." Hanging my head, I mumbled. "After that I may have gotten pissed." Seeing the look on his face, I held out my hand reassuringly. "I didn't kill the bastard…I did toss him down the street with enough force to make him skip down the sidewalk, but I didn't kill him."

Andrew appeared to be relieved. "I don't need to call for a cleanup crew then?"

I slapped my hand against my pants, trying to remove the dust. "No." Then it struck me. "Why would you have access to a cleanup crew?"

Andrew waved a dismissive hand in my direction. "Don't worry yourself with that. Tell me more about this shadow 'thing.'"

I described it to him, from the swirling mass at the tip of the fat man's cane to the thousands of tiny tendrils that tried to burrow through my skin. Finally, I bowed my head, then looked up and found Isidore staring at me with his mouth slightly agape. Then I flicked over to Andrew, who wore the same shocked yet rapt expression, his attention locked onto my every word.

"I'm not sure what it was, but I didn't care for it in the slightest."

Andrew slowly shook his head and closed his mouth. "I guess not."

Isidore's nostrils flared as he caught a scent in the air. "You've been hurt."

That was just plain creepy! I waved a dismissive hand in his direction. "I was cut earlier, but it's pretty much healed at this point." The fact I hadn't needed stitches was a fantastic bit of luck. "The cut has nothing to do with the fat man's rant."

Andrew stalked around me, appraising me as if I were a prime cut of meat. "Please take off your shirt."

My embarrassment grew but I did as I was asked. "I don't see the problem." Again Andrew and Isidore circled me, making me feel like a prize calf up for auction. "Would you two care to tell me what you are looking for? Maybe I can help you find it."

Isidore pointed. "I thought you said you were cut."

Confused, I could only assume they'd missed basic anatomy in school. "As I said, it healed up." Then I looked down and saw a fine white scar just above the blood soaked skin. "It wasn't like that earlier."

Andrew stepped closer, poking at the white line on my ribs. "I see plenty of blood and a thin white line, but no cut."

Looking down again I felt heat rush to my cheeks. "As I said, it wasn't like this earlier. When I checked it at the hospital it was scabbed over but not healed."

Andrew ran a finger along the scar, furrowing his forehead. "Now that's interesting."

His finger sent a charge through me as he brushed against the new skin.

"What's that?" I asked.

Andrew stood upright as he looked back at Isidore, who came close yet did not touch me to appraise the wound. "You were cut? By what exactly?"

"A long silver dagger." With a quick thought, I handed the bloody shirt to Andrew. "This is one of George's creations." I allowed that to sink in before continuing. "Our assassin wanted Heather, but I'd moved her far enough away that I took the first hit." The memory of the man kneeling in prayer to the uncaring god sent a chill up my spine. "He was fast though. I was able to dispatch him with little trouble, but he'd already landed what could be a devastating wound to Heather."

Andrew looked concerned. "Did you get an update on her condition?"

The night's events, blood loss included, were starting to take their toll, and weariness sat in. "Her mother said things were looking promising. Fact of the matter is she received a gut wound, so it could really go one way or another. Kim seemed confident that they'd been able to stabilize the situation."

Andrew barely registered the words. He and Isidore continued to circle me like I was some sort of specter. Andrew put his fingers against my neck and felt my pulse. "And you're sure you feel all right?"

Anger welled up inside me. The adrenaline was quickly wearing off and I needed rest. "I'm fine! Why do you two keep looking at me as if I'm patient zero in the impending apocalypse?"

Andrew stood upright, ripping his eyes off my wound. "Because you should be dead."

That made me laugh as I gestured at my healed chest. "It was merely a flesh wound."

Andrew threw up his hands impatiently. "Not the cut," he seethed. "The 'labebantur mors serpentium,' or sphere of shadows."

The reverent way he said the words left me feeling even more lost. "I don't understand! That didn't do anything more than piss me off."

Frustrated and clearly at a loss for what to do next, Isidore flopped onto the couch, and a memory seemed to overtake him. "I saw someone use that incantation maybe thirty years ago. The man was ripped apart from the inside out. His family spent the next week cleaning up the blood and chunky bits out of their yard."

Andrew paled at the shared memory. "I remember."

Pulling the jacket over me, I rolled my shoulders in a sheepish fashion. "What are you talking about?" Suddenly my head hurt and I held out my hand in defiance. "You know what, never fucking mind. I need a shower and a change of clothes. After that we can talk."

Twenty minutes later I was dressed and back in the living room. I found Andrew and Isidore at the desk, going over the broken pieces of the cane with a magnifying glass.

"What are you doing?" I asked.

Andrew looked up and handed the magnifying glass to Isidore, who kept looking at the cane. "We're looking over the souvenir that nearly killed us."

Furrowing my brow, I thought they were being funny at my expense. "That's even more dramatic than the cane blowing up in the first place."

Andrew looked exasperated at my ignorance. "You haven't got a clue what's going on around you."

Sitting at the table, I poured myself a scotch and gave him a look like he should damn well explain. "I don't feel up to trying to decipher what you're pissed about, so just tell me what I've done wrong and we can all move on already!"

Andrew threw his hands up in the air and gave Isidore a pleading look. "Kind of my point!"

Downing the drink, I poured a second. "I can see that you're pissed off, but I don't know why. Care to fill me in?"

Andrew came over and collapsed into the chair across from mine, then poured himself a drink and waved Isidore over. "I'm sorry for being 'dramatic,' as you call it, but after what you said about the attack outside and then the cane...." He gave me a dismissive wave.

Sipping my drink, I just stared at him blankly. "That wasn't an attack so much as an attempt at terrorism. An attack would imply that he meant to hurt me."

Isidore tossed the cane on the table. His impatience getting the better of him, he raised his voice several decibels. "He did!"

Andrew shot Isadore a nasty look as he pulled the broken cane towards him. "Let's start with the cane."

I finished my second drink and poured a third. "What about it?"

Andrew took a deep breath and took the tone that a parent would take with a petulant child. "Isidore and I have inspected it and determined it's a focusing object, something those of us who wield 'supernatural' powers use."

"Focusing object?"

Andrew ignored me and continued. "Most objects of this nature are something that the person would have on them all the time, such as a ring, or in this case a cane. Something that wouldn't draw attention. It allows its owner to gather power and store it for later use."

"All right," I said. The lecture was nice, but the surge of energy from earlier was starting to fade and my patience was coming to an abrupt end.

Andrew sighed. "These objects are virtually impossible to destroy. When they are, very bad things tend to happen. It's like setting off a tiny atomic bomb."

I tilted my drink in his direction. "Then you're wrong about it being a focusing object. I mean, sure there was a light show, but—"

"But nothing!" Isidore growled.

Andrew glared at him, and he fell silent. "But the fact that you were able to snap it like a twig and so little energy was lost leads me to entirely other questions."

I stifled a yawn as sleep threatened to overtake me. "I'm exhausted. Can we get to something resembling a point?"

Andrew looked annoyed and more than a little put out by my ignorance. "The point is this house should've been leveled and we all should be very dead. Then there's the sphere of shadows cast by your newest fan out front."

Letting out a groan, I slammed my glass onto the table. "I keep telling you that wasn't an attack. An annoyance sure, definitely creepy, but not an attack."

Andrew got to his feet, utterly annoyed with me. I'd seen similar looks on my grandfather's face when he was about to prove a point at my expense. "Would you mind if I tried something?"

This wasn't the first time someone had thought me too dense to understand words and resorted to the dreaded show and tell. "If it will let me get some sleep sooner rather than later, go for it."

Andrew's left hand suddenly glowed violet. He stood there a moment, letting the glow get brighter, and then slammed his palm against my chest. The light engulfed and blinded me for a few seconds before fading away. Andrew stumbled back, with sweat pouring off him and panting, barely able to stand.

I could barely see, my eyes ached, and now my head hurt even more. Needless to say, I wasn't happy. "What the hell?"

Andrew coughed and struggled for breath. "I don't understand."

My anger evaporated when my eyes cleared and I got a good look at my uncle. "Are you all right?"

Isidore was quickly behind him with a steady hand, ensuring he didn't fall down, and helped Andrew into the seat. Andrew took a minute to catch his breath before looking at me. "I'll be fine in a bit." He coughed and took a big drink of tea before leaning back in his chair. "That's very strange."

I felt a new surge of energy running through me and I instantly perked up. "What was that?"

He still looked pale and tired, but his strength was returning. "That was a defense spell designed to repel one's attacker." He craned his neck as he pushed himself upright and color flooded back into his cheeks. "That obviously didn't happen."

"Obviously."

He shivered for a moment. Every passing second he looked more and more normal. Both he and Isidore leaned forward and looked me over. "Odd," Andrew said before looking back at Isidore. "Did you see that?"

Isidore's face clouded with concern and curiosity, which forced him to lean in closer. "I think so, but what was it?"

Andrew looked genuinely puzzled. "Not the faintest idea."

The surge of energy faded quickly and I was getting tired again. Not to mention my annoyance of being left out of the conversation. "Care to fill me in?"

Andrew snapped his head back as he fought to find the right words. "It was strange. It was as if a shadow passed over your features, slightly obscuring them, making them almost misty. I don't know, maybe I'm just tired, but still it's odd."

I felt my forehead furrow, considering the implications. The sudden burst of energy was now utterly gone and my uncle was looking normal again. "I'm tired, and you two have been up all night so I'm guessing you are as well. Maybe we should get some rest and talk about it after we get some sleep."

Isidore kept a healthy distance as he shook his head in my direction and made the sign of the cross. "You're a very strange man."

Standing, I finished my drink. "You're not the first to tell me that." I headed to my room.

Andrew stood and yawned before nodding at Isidore. "Gavin's right, we all need to get some rest. Would you be a doll and hang a sign letting everyone know we are closed for the day?"

Isidore nodded. "I'll take care of it."

Chapter 10

It was just after noon when I rolled out of bed. My head ached, my back was sore, and the thin white scar itched. This was why I didn't drink…I hated hangovers! The thing was, something in the back of my head told me this wasn't a hangover, but had more to do with my fat friend and my uncle's prodding last night. I couldn't put my finger on it, mind you, but none the less the information was there even if I couldn't figure out what to do with it.

I stepped out of the shower, and as I dressed my stomach growled. Rubbing my eyes as I headed down the hall, I heard Andrew and Isidore's muffled voices in the living room. Pushing the kitchen door open I made my way to the fridge, rummaging for leftover enchiladas. Scooping out a couple onto a plate, I didn't bother heating them. A few minutes later I patted my stomach and finished my tea before heading to the living room. I was not fit company when I was hungry.

Opening the door, I found we had company. Mrs. Broussard sat in one of the two chairs in front of my uncle's desk. An older yet refined looking gentleman sat next to her, eyeing Isidore with great distaste. If I were a betting man I'd bet that this was Heather's father, Robert.

Kimberly leaned forward in her chair, speaking to Andrew. "I'm grateful that your man Gavin was there, but Robert and I are at a loss as to why she was attacked. From what I saw she was clearly targeted."

Andrew started to open his mouth when I decided to intervene. "Good afternoon, Mrs. Broussard. Am I to assume this is your husband?"

Kimberly and Robert turned their heads. She stood and her husband reluctantly followed. Her face lit up in greeting. "How's that side of yours? I didn't see in the reports that you'd gotten treatment."

I patted my chest and gave her a casual roll of my shoulders. "After sitting for so long at the Elms and the cut being so shallow, I really didn't need it." For the record I'd only agreed not to lie to Heather; everyone else was fair game. "How's Heather doing?"

Robert stepped around his wife, hand out, and that's when it struck me that the man had to be a good foot shorter than myself. His voice had that grating tone of arrogance combined with entitlement, mixed together in equal measures. "I'm Robert." Taking my hand in his, he gave me a weak, limp wristed, and moist handshake.

"I'm Gavin."

Something about my tone—or perhaps it was the many calluses on my palm—caused him to jerk his hand back before wiping it on a convenient handkerchief. He sneered, tucking the white cloth into a pant pocket. "I know."

Kimberly glared at the top of her husband's head and she spoke over him. "Heather's prognosis looks good. We believe she'll make a full recovery."

Robert scowled, his face purpling. "We were here asking why our daughter was attacked." He gave me an appraising once over, and practically accused me of being at fault. "Would you happen to have any idea?" He waved his hand back at Andrew. "He clearly doesn't know."

It was a sad state of affairs when I'd known someone less than sixty seconds and I already want to throw them out a window. I took a deep breath and forced myself to remain calm. "I haven't the faintest idea."

Robert huffed, staring daggers through Isidore. "I've got at least one very good idea why she'd be attacked." His anger and hatred flowed out of him, turning on Andrew. "And it's all your fault for making her associate with his kind!"

Fury flared deep inside me. The man disrespected not only Andrew, but Isidore as well. Stepping between Isidore and Robert, I looked down at the man. "Care to be more specific about 'his kind'?"

Robert looked appalled at being spoken to in such a manner, and quickly lumped me in with Isidore. "Let me guess; you're one of the filthy beasts as well!"

It dawned on me he was angry about Isidore being a werewolf, and I couldn't stop myself from laughing in the man's face. "You have a problem with werewolves?"

Robert felt emboldened. He stepped forward, shoving a finger into my chest, sneering at me. "Werewolves! That implies your kind have a human form! You're nothing but filthy dogs that need to be disciplined, or better yet put down so the rest of us don't have to deal with your horrid stench!"

Kimberly grabbed her husband's shoulder and spun him around. "You forget where you are!"

Robert whipped his head around at Andrew. "Why should I bow to him when he associates with such filth?"

Kimberly stepped closer to her husband, her voice dropping. "I've put up with your bigotry for a long time, but you've stepped over the line." She pointed at the broken door. "I think we need to go home and have a serious discussion."

Robert glared at me and spat on the floor. "Filthy beast!"

It was everything I could do not to punch the man in the face, but that would be a waste of effort. His kind would never see the light no matter how hard I tried to beat it into him. So I changed gears and smirked at the man. "If that's how you feel about werewolves, then count me in!" A cold rage flared in me, causing me to take a step forward. "Just remember, a filthy beast saved your daughter's life last night! And considering it wasn't even a hundred years ago that your kind was burned at the stake, I'd get off your fucking high horse!"

Robert snapped his head towards my uncle. "You're going to let your dog talk to me like that? I should've never allowed you to train Heather."

Kimberly glowered down at Robert and her voice threatened violence. "You didn't allow her to do anything. It was on my blessing that she came here, and she will continue to do as she pleases." She stepped away from the little man. "Soon you'll be able to do the same." She turned to Andrew and forced a smile. "I'm sorry you had to witness this." She spun on her heel and headed for the door. "It's time we left, Robert."

Robert turned and pointed at the door. "This is what happens to your home when you let rabid dogs off their leash for too long!"

Kimberly's heels were stamping out an angry rhythm as she went down the stairs. Robert, suddenly realizing he was alone with the three of us, hurried after her.

Fucking coward.

Andrew's face contorted in amusement, irritation, and shock before he followed them out.

Isidore flopped into the chair Robert had vacated earlier and chuckled. "Why did you tell him you're a werewolf? He's going to hate you...even more than he would've. That piece of shit hates everyone!"

"Fuck him!" Plopping into the chair next to his, I felt disgusted by the racist. "And for the record, I never said I was a werewolf." I flipped the empty doorway the bird. "I may have implied it, but it's his own fault for making the assumption." Turning to Isidore, I gave him a flat look. "Does everyone hate werewolves?"

That made Isidore grumble and he shook his head helplessly. "More do than don't."

I started laughing. I couldn't help it. "So you're a gay black man who happens to be a werewolf...God was having fun with you!"

Isidore eyes fluttered. "That's why he made me so handsome."

Andrew reappeared, shaking his head in complete disbelief, stepping through the broken door and heading for the desk. "Gavin, if I haven't said this lately...I love you! God, I've wanted to tell that asshole off for years."

Looking over at Isidore, I smiled. "And God made me irresistible."

Andrew started to open his mouth but closed it, and held out his hands to stop any sort of explanation. "I don't even want to know…don't ruin the moment for me. All I want is to etch the look on Robert's face in my memory."

Looking at the busted door, I groaned. "I really need to fix that. Where's the nearest hardware store?"

Andrew looked at me incredulously before forcing himself back to reality. "The local hardware store doesn't exactly carry those in stock." He gave it a dismissive wave. "Don't worry…I've already called the maintenance man to come by. I'm sure he'll have a new one up and in place by the time you get back."

Pushing myself up straight, I gave my uncle a curious look. "Get back from where?"

Andrew pointed at Isidore and puffed out his chest. "Isidore will be taking you across the lake to the Archive to pick up a few things for me." Andrew gave me a nonchalant wave of his hand. "And while you're there you can register with Ms. Dodd. She'll be expecting you."

Isidore leaned forward and groaned, clasping his head in his hands in dread. He didn't bother to look over at me when he spoke. "Thank God I'm driving, since I like air conditioning. I'll need a cool place to sit while you register and collect whatever Andrew asked to be pulled."

Okay, this was sounding like a setup. If they planned on having me lug down God knew how much shit on my own as some sort of haze the new guy, I simply wouldn't play their game. "No need to have you sit out in the car. You're welcome to come in and help while I fill out paperwork."

That's when I noticed Andrew shifting in his seat as if he were sitting on hot coals. His voice was low as he tried to hide his embarrassment. "He can't help you…Isidore can't step inside the Archive."

Now this was really starting to sound like a load of crap to razz the new guy. I huffed, looking between the two as I asked the obvious question. "Really? Why not?"

Andrew shifted again, clearly uncomfortable with the subject. "He's a werewolf, and as such can't enter the Archive. It would kill him." Anger crossed his face in a storm. "That's why he's driving you." He hung his head, his voice still low. "If you were registered and knew the way I wouldn't bother sending him, but since you're not and you don't...you get Isidore as a guide."

What the fuck? Seriously, the magical world was this far behind the game in equal rights? I looked over at Isidore and felt a little ill. "He's joking, right? You two are just fucking with me, aren't you?"

It was clear by the sour look on Isidore's face that this was for real. Clearly he was more accustomed to being treated like a second rate citizen, but I could see it still pissed him off deep down. "Wish he was. To be honest, he may be sugarcoating the situation."

I got the distinct feeling I'd traveled back in time several decades. The world obviously hadn't moved forward on all fronts at an equal rate. Honestly, I shouldn't have been all that surprised, things weren't much different back home. I'd been at the receiving end of similar bigotry due to my mixed heritage. Once I was overseas people hated me just because I was American. It amazed me just how little one person needed to hate another.

I grumbled. "I'm not sure I want to be a part of the club if this is the way they're going to act."

Andrew held up a hand to try and reassure me. "I wish there was a choice in the matter, but there isn't. Things are changing for the better."

Isidore interjected. "Very slowly."

Andrew cut his eyes at Isidore, who simply raised his hands dismissively and stepped back. "Very slowly," he repeated. "But over the last twenty years' things have actually changed for the better." We both looked over at Isidore, who simply made a face that said yeah, things are better, not great but better. "The truth of the matter is you have to register...it's the law."

With a long breath, I put up my hands in surrender. "Fine, I'll register. I can only pray there isn't too much paperwork involved."

Andrew mumbled. "Not as much as there used to be."

Isidore snickered. "It got changed twenty years ago when they had a mass influx of my kind. We may not be welcome inside the building, but we are at least granted a portion of citizenship in the Archive now."

That was a start, I supposed, and much better than nothing at all. Considering how much I actually knew about the situation that didn't exactly carry a lot of weight. "Nothing like having to fill out a bunch of paperwork to find a better way to do it." Looking up at Andrew, I sighed. "Is it just werebeasts that can't enter the Archive?"

Andrew looked serious. "There are a number of others. Some truly less than desirable creatures, such as demons, shapeshifters, and others who are not particularly social creatures."

I was perplexed by Andrew's attitude. "Seriously, you're going to lump groups together as well?"

Isidore sat up straight and shook his head. "Before you get your panties in a bunch, you should remember that they are called demons for a reason. As for the shapeshifters, they are born into a fast life, and they burn through everything they can. They start life as grifters, thieves, and sell their services to the highest bidder. I've never even heard of one being remotely sane. Something about their makeup pretty much insures their insanity."

With those words, I gave up. I wasn't as sold on the idea of groups all being shitty, but it was obvious I didn't have a chance here. "Fine. I'll register. Just for the record though, I don't like being earmarked like cattle."

Andrew conceded the point with a small gesture. "Our kind have to give a little to get along with the humans and others that inhabit this world. Registering allows us to have access to our people when certain governmental agencies get involved, be it here in the States or elsewhere in the world."

"Great."

Isidore cut me off. "We better get on the road if we plan on getting back at a decent hour."

The conversation being over, I grabbed a bottled water and followed Isidore downstairs. He drove a large silver extended cab pickup truck. It took a minute to get out of the Garden District due to the size of the vehicle and all the road construction. After we got on the interstate, it was smooth sailing across the Causeway Bridge that spanned Lake Pontchartrain to Covington, Louisiana.

When we came off the bridge, it was painfully obvious by the smooth roads, copious amounts of shops, and higher end retailers that this was the wealthier side of the lake. Sure, New Orleans had the Garden District, but the Northshore had several small cities and villages that were almost equal in splendor. It was clear that New Orleans was the "old money" side of the equation, while the North Shore was all about the "new money."

Isidore's demeanor changed from happy and carefree to nervous and almost paranoid. Both hands gripped the wheel, and he never so much as broke a traffic law once we were off the Causeway. It was clear to see that being this close to the Archive made him very nervous. I had to wonder how many years he'd been forced to live that way before things changed to what they were now. And was the here and now all that better?

Several twists and turns later we pulled up outside St. Tammany Parish Justice Center/ 22nd Judicial District Court Office. It was a large, generic looking, multi-story brick and tan stucco building that looked like every other modern courthouse I'd seen over the last thirty or forty years. It was as if the United States had purposely chosen to build the new court system in the blandest, dullest way possible.

Isidore pulled around to 26th street, where he found a parking spot at the farthest end of the lot. Sweat beading up on his forehead, he gripped the wheel with one hand and pointed with the other. "The Archive is on the 3rd floor." He pulled an envelope out of his back pocket and handed it to me. "You'll need to give Ms. Dodd this for your uncle. After that she'll get you the files and books he's ordered." An afterthought occurred to him and he pointed at the glove box. "I was saving this for a rainy day, but its usefulness is about to run out."

Pushing the button on the compartment, it popped open. "What am I looking for?"

He pointed at a clear plastic case containing a blank looking CD. "That's a copy of Bon Jovi's upcoming album due out next month."

I pulled it out and flipped it over in my fingers with more than a little confusion. "What am I supposed to do with this? I'm not exactly a big Bon Jovi fan."

He rolled his eyes. "It's not for you, idiot! Give it to Ms. Dodd. It'll earn you tons of brownie points!"

Flipping the CD over in my hands, I felt a little weirded. "All right...want me to tell her it's from you?"

His eyes nearly bugged out in panic and he looked around the parking lot, making sure we were alone. "Not unless you want to get thrown in jail." He was fidgeting as he glanced around again. "And if you could hurry I'd be very grateful."

I unbuckled the seatbelt and pushed open the door. "Thanks."

It took less than a minute to cross the lot before I stood in front of the generic plate glass doors that led into the courthouse. I had to take off my boots, ring, and belt, and empty my pockets before I could pass through the metal detector. Once I was dressed again, I looked around the bland lobby and sighed. How goddamn boring!

I took the stairs up to the third floor two at a time and stepped out into the unimpressive landing covered in peel and stick squares of blue carpet. The place had that new building smell that was a combination of paint, glue, plaster, and cement. The floor gave me the willies; I didn't see or hear a soul stirring. It was as if I'd found myself on an abandoned floor, but a few seconds later I saw my destination. The large glass walls showed one after another in yet a further example of boredom in office design.

One of the offices midway down had all their shades dropped and closed. Stenciled on the plate glass door was the word Archive in big gold lettering. Trying not to yawn, I pulled the door open and stepped inside. The interior lighting nearly blinded me as it reflected off the surgical white walls, floors, and ceiling. The room consisted of a small waiting area, a heavy steel security door leading into what I could only assume was the Archive, and an ancient metal desk that sat at the far side of the room.

Ms. Elizabeth Dodd sat at the desk, and looked simultaneously irritated and nauseous, her gray eyes fixated on me. She wasn't what I'd consider attractive, with shoulder length wavy mouse brown and white hair. Adjusting her horn rimmed glasses, she wiped her fingers on a nearby napkin and waited. It was clear that she expected me to go away if she didn't address me.

She took a deep breath and slowly let it out. When she spoke, her voice was full of contempt and arrogance, mixed with just the right amount of disgust to let me know she wasn't pleased I'd forced her to speak. "I'm sorry, sir, but you've clearly got the wrong office."

Nothing about her tone or demeanor told me she was in the least bit sorry. I resisted the urge to walk across the room and give her a good solid slap across the face. Exactly how would I explain to my uncle that I'd slapped the prefect before uttering a single word to her? Instead, I plastered on a smile and reached for the letter I'd put in my back pocket. "Afternoon, ma'am."

She closed her eyes, shaking her head as if it were taking all of her willpower not to scream at me to get out. "You obviously didn't hear me when I said you were in the WRONG office."

This time the annoyance was gone, replaced by something more dangerous.

Making sure I didn't make any sudden movements, I stepped closer and handed her the envelope from Andrew. I made sure that I kept the animosity off my face, trying to be as pleasant as possible. "Andrew Randall sent me over to pick up a few things." His name made her sit up straight and pay attention. "He implied that he'd called ahead, and told me there would be some items I needed to pick up."

Ms. Dodd kept a wary eye on me as she took the envelope out of my hand. She opened it and scanned over its contents before placing it face down on her desk. Then she glanced at the letter and back at me. Her eyes focused in on my left hand as she pointed. "What happened there?"

By chance it was the same hand I was holding the CD with, and I placed it gently on her desk. "I come bearing gifts."

She raised an eyebrow at the CD. "And just what is that?"

"It's an advance copy of Bon Jovi's new album."

Ms. Dodd blew air through her nose in disbelief. Picking up the CD, she stepped closer to the combination CD alarm clock at the far end of her desk. She put it in and hit play, and smiled as soon as Jon's voice came over the speakers. "Where did you get it?"

Relieved that she'd forgotten my hand, I stood up straight. "A good man never reveals his secrets."

Her eyes twinkled with delight. "Is there anything else before I get Andrew's order?"

I felt stupid and even more than a little embarrassed when I spoke. "Andrew mentioned that I would need to register with you before returning to New Orleans."

She glowered, shoving a finger onto the stop button of the player. "That isn't funny."

Her response took me by surprise, and I stammered, "I wasn't trying to be funny. He insisted that I register today."

Her face turned sour, and she scrunched up her nose as if I'd shit on the floor. "I was willing to let this 'incident' go without complaint, but this is too far over the line! You inform Mr. Randall that I'll be lodging a formal complaint about this! I don't care who he is! He can't just send humans into my office asking to be registered!"

What the fuck was her goddamn problem?

"I'm sorry?" I asked.

Her pale skin flushed the slightest shade of pink as she shoved her pudgy finger in my direction. "You damn well should be!" Her face continued to darken as it twisted itself into utter disgust at the sight of me. "You tell Andrew that I don't appreciate him sending monkeys to my office."

I was so lost. What the hell was she talking about? "Monkey?"

She glared, rubbing two fingers across her forearm, and whispered. "It's sad how little your kind knows, filthy fucking humans!" She waddled off to the back without another word, and returned a few seconds later with two bankers boxes and slammed them against the desk. "I shouldn't let you have this, but since the mutt can't come up and collect them, you'll have to do. Make sure you don't damage anything!"

And there it was. Not only did these people hate werewolves, shapeshifters, and other less desirables of their own kind, but they seemed to really hate humans.

I picked up the boxes and gave her my best smile. "Thanks for trusting me with such an important task," I said with as much contempt and sarcasm as I could muster.

It was clear she hadn't heard it, and she almost smiled as if she were looking at a retarded child. "It's always so cute when monkeys learn their place." She shooed me away. "Now go before I change my mind."

I'd wanted to slap the tubby little bitch when I walked in, and now I wanted to punch her. I refrained, however, as I wasn't sure how I'd ever explain my actions to Andrew, or Isidore for that matter. He was nervous as it was, and that would just push him over the edge.

Exiting the building, I found an animal control truck parked next to Isidore's truck, with the driver sitting in his vehicle taking notes. Opening the door and putting the boxes behind my seat, I climbed in.

Thumbing back at the driver of the next car. "What the fuck does he want?"

Isidore rolled his eyes. "Ms. Dodd thought it would be amusing to have animal control check the lot for a dog locked in a silver truck."

What a fucking whore. This woman was unfucking believable. "From the sounds of things though, she likes you far more than me."

Isidore shot me a strange look. "How do you figure that?"

Once again I felt embarrassed and slightly ashamed. "When I asked to register she got all worked up and started calling me a monkey. That's the second person to do that today."

Isidore's eyes bulged as he nearly choked on his drink. "She thinks you're human?"

I looked out the window as we pulled off into traffic. "Apparently, and they don't register my 'kind' there." Chewing on my lip, I sighed. "I think I got Andrew into some hot water as well. She said she was going to file some sort of formal complaint."

He burst out laughing, gunning the car to pull into the far lane of traffic. "That's rich! Andrew's going to have her ass if she does."

That comment caught me off guard, and I turned to look at Isidore. "How is that going to happen? Isn't she the prefect?"

Isidore snorted. "First off, you're not human; that much is painfully clear to anyone caring enough to dig below the surface. The fact that she refused to register you will put her in far more trouble than anything she could possibly whine about." He thumbed back at the boxes. "That's some research material to help him figure out who and what you are." His fit of laughter completely subsided. "As for how Andrew will take her down a notch or two, that is an entirely different story. One person or another has been after him since he became governor back in '71, and after '95 people are beyond pissed."

The last comment didn't register. "Since when did Andrew have shit to do with Louisiana politics?"

Isidore tore his eyes off the road and stared at me for a full second like I was the dumbest person on the planet. "What?"

"The governor of what, exactly?" I asked.

Isidore glanced over at me, trying to see if I was joking or not. Then realization crossed his face. "Holy shit, you don't know, do you?"

I threw up my hands in such a manner that made it clear that I didn't. "Know what?"

Isidore snorted and he fought back more laughter. "Andrew is the governor of North America, and answers directly to Lazarus. Anyone filing a complaint against him will have to do so at their own peril! Lazarus doesn't take well to insubordination." His features turned serious. "And I would prefer to piss off just about anyone up to and including every prefect in the US before I'd piss off your uncle. He's a dangerous man."

I sat there dumbfounded, trying to assimilate the information. "Andrew is the governor of North America?"

Isidore was exceptionally amused at my ignorance. "Yeah."

I tried to sort through the chart I'd seen in the book, and it dawned on me then why he even had it. Lazarus had given it to him. "Is that why Robert and Kimberly were at the house today?"

Isidore frowned when he recalled the incident. "Yeah, they are both on the triumvirate. The two of them broke protocol by bypassing the prefect, Ms. Dodd, and speaking to a higher authority, the governor."

I remembered how Robert had spoken to Andrew and I got angry. "I thought Robert was there just to yell at you, and if Andrew is so important why would he speak to him in such a way?"

Isidore's frown deepened. It was clear that he didn't like the man or anything to do with him. "Robert is part of the old guard. He lost a lot of power when Andrew took over. He'd enslaved an entire clan of werebears and was forced to release them from service because of Andrew. He's hated him ever since."

"Wow! That guy's a bigger asshole than I'd thought."

Isidore snickered. "You don't know the half of it, but ever since then people have been gunning for your uncle."

"This isn't the first time someone's tried to kill him then?" I asked.

Isidore shook his head. "Andrew doesn't get angry often, but when he does bad things happen on a pretty big scale. The last time someone came for him Andrew buried the man's entire family just to make a point. No one has openly moved against him since then. That was thirty years ago."

Well damn, the old man had a mean streak in him. "I see."

It took us nearly an hour to get back to my uncle's place. I carried in the boxes and Isidore locked up behind us. At the top of the stairs I found a new door in place of the one I'd broken. I had questions for my uncle but they'd have to wait till we had some privacy. With Isidore coming and going I wasn't sure when that was going to happen.

Chapter 11

Tuesday June 2nd

Sweat covered me, I sat up and swung my feet off the side of the bed, letting my bare feet touch the cool hardwood floor. Easing myself out of bed I stretched and stood, hearing my joints pop and creak as I extended my arms and legs. Adjusting my shorts, I strode out onto the private balcony. Silver light cascaded over my skin, highlighting dozens of scars. I looked out over the side of the house past the fence and into the neighbor's immaculate yard. It was hard to believe that just over a day ago I was fighting off an attacker not more than half a mile from here.

The peaceful night air wrapped itself around me, and I heard the call of something dark and familiar in the back of my mind. I shivered hard enough to snap me back to reality. Fighting off a sense of foreboding that beckoned for me, I went inside for a cool shower. Twenty minutes later I was in the kitchen, grateful to be alone.

About ten minutes passed before I heard the door swing open behind me. I didn't need to turn to know Andrew was there. "You going to just stand there or make us something to eat?" he asked.

Grabbing eggs and bacon out of the fridge, I set to work making breakfast. "Did you find anything worthwhile in those boxes?

I heard Andrew take a seat, the aged wooden chair creaking from his weight. "Not yet."

The door opened a second time and I turned to see Isidore rubbing his eyes and sniffing. "Scrambled."

"Aye aye, Captain," I replied.

It didn't take long before I had breakfast on the table. Isidore was busy nursing a hangover from the looks of things, and Andrew was sifting through a book he'd brought with him. Breakfast was eaten in blissful silence.

Andrew closed the book he'd been reading and, frustrated, he tossed it on the table. "Still nothing!"

It was clear that I could offer absolutely no help, so I picked up the plates and rinsed them off before placing them in the dishwasher. I waved for my uncle and Isidore to follow me into the living room. "Let's take this in the other room and see if we can't sort through the pieces together."

Andrew reluctantly got to his feet and Isidore slowly followed, trailing several steps behind.

Once at the table Andrew put the book he'd been reading aside and picked up another before instantly putting that one down as well, only to select another at random.

Isidore watched him for several seconds and finally intervened. "What are you looking for?"

Andrew looked at the pile of books, completely lost. "I haven't the foggiest idea." He looked over at me, even more puzzled. "For starters, I'd like to know why you don't give off a standard signature."

Well, that was absolutely cryptic to the new guy in the room! "What the hell does that mean?" I asked.

Isidore picked up the nearest book and flipped it open with a grunt. "It means that no matter how hard any of us try, we can't sense you." He waved the book around with every word. "For all intents and purposes, you don't exist on an energetic level. That's why stupid people think you're a human. Most of us have to really search to feel them, but they are there. Most don't bother to search for anyone they can't sense right away, thus not discovering that you are an anomaly. It's as if you are a hole in the universe."

Andrew held out a hand in Isidore's direction as if to make a point. "Exactly!"

Like that made it fucking clear. Looking between the two of them, I sighed and waved for them to continue. "Okay...."

Andrew could see that I didn't understand. "All right, let's just put that aside for a moment. There are several other issues at hand, all of which are fairly substantial."

Oh, this was going to be supremely enlightening...or more likely not. Leaning back in my chair, I wondered, "Such as?"

Andrew leaned forward with hope in his eyes, like he actually expected me to catch on. "Such as, snapping an item of power and we're all still alive. Like I said the other night, they are damn near indestructible. The fact that you snapped it like a twig and we all lived is downright amazing."

Isidore looked lost in thought as he interjected. "I put in a call to Lieutenant Baptist, and he told me that the dagger that was used was also broken." He pointed at me. "According to the other officers, Gavin stepped on the dagger and it snapped under his weight."

Andrew looked at Isidore curiously at the revelation. "Really?"

Isidore gave Andrew a sober look. "That's what I'm being told."

Andrew fell back into his chair, allowing the book in his hand to rest on his lap. "That's fascinating."

Giving them both a hard look, I waited for the explanation to follow. When it wasn't forthcoming, I spoke. "Care to share with those of us that are on the short bus?"

That pulled Andrew out of his thoughts. "The dagger was clearly enchanted since it was able to pierce not only your shirt but Heather's dress." He paused to see if I understood. I didn't, and that point must have been made abundantly clear by the stupid look on my face. "Enchanted items fall under a similar category as the aforementioned items of power...they're nearly indestructible, and they release a lot of energy. Nothing like the cane, but still a significant amount. At the very least you should've lost a leg."

That made me tense. I'd seen a lot of men lose legs over the years due to mines or gunshot wounds or makeshift bombs. I didn't like the idea of losing an appendage, and I regarded my leg before looking at Isidore with concern. "Are you sure that the dagger fell into that category?"

Isidore gave me a weary look. "Very sure."

I wasn't sure how to feel about the oddities that continued to pile up at my feet, but it was better than losing a limb or blowing myself up. "Perhaps neither item was crafted using any significant power."

Isidore outright laughed in my face. "That's doubtful."

Andrew appeared to be in complete agreement with Isidore. "He's right, it would be highly unlikely. Even the weakest of items carry significant power. That's what has me so perplexed about you." He waved a hand in my direction. "I don't even know where to start! In all my years I've never heard of such a thing. I'm not sure how it's possible."

By this point it didn't look like Andrew and I would have a private moment anytime in the near future, so privacy and tact were out the window. Not that either of those things were one of my strong points. Leaning forward, I cleared my throat. "You heard how things went yesterday with Ms. Dodd."

Andrew grumbled. "Don't worry about her. I'll take care of that later."

"About that...when were you going to tell me that you are the governor for North America?" I pulled the journal he'd given me out. "And why didn't you tell me this was a gift from Lazarus?"

Andrew's face scrunched itself up as he looked back at Isidore. "For the record, the book was mailed to me...."

"From?" I asked.

Andrew ducked his head and mumbled. "Lazarus."

I raised an eyebrow. "Kind of skirting the question, aren't you?"

Averting his eyes, he let out a long breath as he mumbled. "Yes, I'm the governor for North America, but it's not that big of a deal."

Fixing the man with a look that had to tell him how stupid that statement was, I continued. "Because there are so many of you, right?"

The wind was taken out of his sails. "Fine, it's a big deal." He stood up and started to pace. "Martha had just become *vigiles* and the previous North American governor died in a plane crash." He grumbled more to himself than me. "Not sure why he did that when the gates were available."

That utterly confused me. I hadn't read anything in the books about gates. "What are gates?"

Andrew waved a hand in the air as he spoke. "Travel gates allow our kind to move from one part of the world to another without having to take conventional methods such as planes, ships, or trains." He looked around for something to help him explain, but didn't find anything handy. "There is at least one in every country in the world, sometimes more depending on the size of the country in question. You step through one gate and are sent to your desired location gate via enchantments."

"I see." I didn't, but I'd figure it out soon enough.

Andrew appeared slightly rebuffed. "As I was saying, I took over as governor in 1971, and have been striving to make a change in the way we treat our people."

Looking over at Isidore, I gave him a half understanding look. "Like the werebeasts."

Andrew nodded as he waved a hand at Isidore. "Like the werebeasts. I was able to pass a law in 1995 that allowed them to have rights and not be subjugated as pets or worse." He looked back at Isidore and then me. "Things have been changing, even if that change is slow."

Andrew's phone rang, which caused us all to jump in our seats; it wasn't even 7:00 a.m. yet. He leaned over and picked up the receiver. "Good morning." He paused and nodded. "I see." He paused again as he let out a long breath. "If you insist, go ahead and set it up for the twelfth. That should give everyone enough time to make adjustments to their schedules." He hung up the phone, looking ill.

I waited, trying to let Andrew get his feet under him before asking, "What was that about?"

Andrew turned a nasty shade of white. "As I told Captain Hotard the other night, we will appoint a new *vigiles,* but it appears that Robert and the triumvirate are pushing for it to be sooner rather than later." He looked at Isidore and shook his head. "Of course, Robert has a few people he wants moved to the front of the line."

The thought of Robert or any of his buddies assigning the new *vigiles* made my head hurt. "I have to say, anyone that prick would recommend seems like a shit idea." I barely thought about it before the next words rolled out of my mouth. "I could volunteer if you think I'd pass for a *vigiles*."

Isidore and Andrew both snapped around to look at me.

Isidore whispered, "Careful what you volunteer for."

Andrew shot a dirty look at Isidore and waved him off. "Are you serious? You do remember it's a lifetime appointment?"

Isidore got to his feet, glaring at Andrew. "He doesn't know what he's getting into, and you know it!"

Andrew stared daggers through Isidore. "Let him speak."

Leaning back in my chair, I chewed on my bottom lip. "If it means that Robert's choices aren't picked, yeah, I'm dead serious!"

Isidore closed his eyes and fell back in his seat. "You simply don't understand...."

Andrew looked at me, all amusement stripped from his face. "Are you sure? This is a lifetime commitment. Your subordinates can retire, quit, and generally say fuck off, but you would have to serve as *vigiles* until the day they bury you."

That gave me pause, but I nodded anyway. "I need a paying gig. It's not like there's a ton of work for a guy like me out there in the world." I paused again and looked at my uncle. "Would I be stuck here forever?"

Andrew tried to appear understanding as he came closer and put a hand on my shoulder. "Not necessarily. You can transfer to another district or take over a larger territory, but yes, in the beginning you'd be tied to the area."

Relief filled me and I looked up at my uncle with hope. "So I wouldn't be able to go home and visit my grandfather right away?"

Andrew gave me a shrewd look. "You would have responsibilities here, but you could travel for a week or so to handle family business. If you took the position, I would require that you handled that as soon as possible. Especially since Aatsista-Mahkan is a member of the triumvirate up north."

Isidore nearly choked as he looked between Andrew and myself. "Your grandfather is Aatsista-Mahkan?

Turning, I gave Isidore an annoyed look. "Yeah."

Isidore beamed at Andrew, shaking his head. "You're never going to find what you want in these books. I got a feeling that you're going to need to speak to his grandfather to shed some light on the situation."

Andrew opened his mouth and shut it again, looking confused, and then snickered. "Damn, I never even gave that so much as a thought." His eyes were glassy, lost to the idea. "You're probably right though. Whatever this is most likely relates back to that side of the family."

Looking between them, I tossed my hands in the air impatiently. "Are we going to do this *vigiles* thing or talk about my grandfather all day?"

Andrew gave me a mystified look. "You still want to do it?"

Cutting my eyes at him, I growled. "Yeah, I don't see that there are a ton of other options."

Andrew got to his feet and stopped in his tracks, looking down at me with tempered hope. "There's no guarantee that you will be accepted."

Isidore nearly choked, cackling at the man. "I very much doubt that. He has the power and the will to use it, from what I've seen in the last few days."

I looked over at Isidore questioningly. "What do you mean?"

Andrew looked slightly deflated. "What he's talking about is me. I have the ability to be a *vigiles*, yet it refused me. It readily accepted Martha because she had the will to use her power in a manner that I will not."

Isidore snickered. "In plain English, Martha was more of a hands on girl, whereas Andrew here would rather direct the orchestra. Both of them are stupidly powerful, but only one of them had the will to use it in the way the coin saw fit."

Coin...what the fuck were they talking about? Now that I was totally confused I looked up at Andrew. "Coin?"

Andrew didn't answer right away and padded down the hall next to his bedroom, calling over his shoulder. "You'll see shortly."

Isidore looked over at me and groaned. "I'm not sure you should do this."

"Why not?" I asked.

Andrew reappeared before Isidore could answer. He held a small velvet bag in his hand, and as he approached he nodded at me. "Hold out your hand."

Looking up at Andrew, I snickered and held out my right hand. "This is it? No ceremony, no badge?"

His smile was gone. Now his face was strained. He was nervous. "The ceremony will have to wait till everyone is here next week, but I do have a 'badge' for you." Andrew looked back at Isidore. "You'll be my witness."

Isidore grumbled. "Do I have a choice?"

Andrew shook his head. "Not really."

Isidore gave Andrew a level look and waved a hand in my direction. "Get on with it then."

Andrew pulled the string on the bag and it fell open, and its contents fell into my open hand. It was a single silver denarius, with a wreath and crossed swords on one side and the symbol for Pax Romana on the other.

Something stirred in me. I felt my head swim and a rhythm building all around me. Brilliant blue flames erupted in the palm of my hand, spreading around to encompass everything from my wrist to the tips of my fingers. The coin began to melt and the flesh of my hand seemed to groan in agony of being burned from the inside out. I wrapped my ruined left hand around my aching, flaming right and my breathing became labored.

I felt the coin awaken...it was alive, sentient, and highly intelligent. It peered into the dark recesses of my mind and took stock of my soul, and rejoiced. The tension inside of it eased, its consciousness expanding alongside my own. It was comfortable for the first time since it had been birthed into this world, and it knew as well as I did that it was home.

The flames danced across my hand, unfolding themselves and stretching out into a long, thin reptilian snake-like creature with wings. It coiled itself around my forearm, sliding up my arm, around my elbow, and up to my bicep. There it pulled its head back and drove itself into my deltoid hard enough to knock me out of my chair, sending me crashing hard into the floor. It burned a hole the size of a quarter through the sleeve of my shirt, burrowing through my flesh.

Then, just as suddenly as it had started, it ended; blissfully, thankfully, and mercifully, it was all over. I found myself curled into the fetal position on the floor. Unwrapping myself, I slowly pulled my left hand away from my right and stared at the palm. There in my big meaty paw I found the Pax Romana seal branded deep into the flesh. Instinctively I flipped my hand over to find yet another brand. This one was of two crossed swords cupped inside of a wreath. Unlike most brands I'd seen in my life, these were highly detailed with fine thin lines, almost as if they'd been cut into my flesh instead of burned into it. Then I remembered I wasn't alone in the room, and looked up to see Andrew and Isidore leaning over me looking worried.

I groaned, rolled over onto my back, and held out both hands. "It appears that fate has seen fit to give me a matching set."

Isidore put out a hand and helped me back into my chair. "Are you all right?"

Looking over at him and then back at Andrew, I nodded. "I think so. Why do you ask? Did that not go as planned?"

Andrew's concern was clear to see as he eyed my right shoulder. "Can you pull up the sleeve so we can get a better look?"

Grabbing the bottom of my ruined sleeve I pulled it back, and there emblazoned on my shoulder was the ancient

Roman standard, Aquila or Eagle, grasping crossed lightning bolts. Both men crowded around me to get a better view.

Andrew looked at Isidore as he pointed. "Ever seen anything like it?"

Isidore shook his head. "Never."

Looking down, I looked back at them as if they were taking the short yellow bus to school. "It's an eagle."

Andrew looked down at me with utter amazement, as if I'd uttered the dumbest words in the world. His voice was full of the Bart Simpson "Duh" when he spoke. "I can see that, you dolt!" He shook his head and fell back into his seat with a thud. "I've just never seen it appear on a *vigiles*, or anyone else for that matter."

Isidore stood behind my uncle as he kept his eyes fixated on the ancient symbol. "I've dealt with a few *vigiles* in my life, but I've never even heard of such a thing." Finally raising his eyes to search my own, he said, "You seem to be a very unique, if not an extraordinary man, Gavin Randall."

As I looked down at my hand, the being inside my head shared its knowledge with me. Anyone could carry a badge, but only a true *vigiles urbani* could wear the true mark. Looking over at my shoulder, it saw the Aquila through my eyes and squirmed in delight. "Hail Caesar!" flooded my mind as I unrolled the sleeve and pulled the ruined cloth over it as best I could.

My mind expanded and I felt the other *vigiles urbani* who'd carried the coin before me, their knowledge just out of reach for now as the connections were so new and tenuous. Other minds popped into view for less than a second before fading into the background, to be sorted and filed later by my new friend. Then a new consciousness rocked me back in my chair as it took hold and released me nearly instantly. It was pleased, and then it was gone.

Shaking my head, I shook the feeling of the overwhelming consciousness off and looked up at Andrew. "Sorry about the coin." As soon as I said it I knew that this was the way it was supposed to happen. "You knew it would vanish."

Andrew looked at me curiously. "I did, but how did you know?"

I shifted in my seat uncomfortably. "I... just knew. It's as if there are things that I understand now that I didn't before."

Concern crossed Andrew's face as he looked back at Isidore. "Could it be happening already?"

Isidore appeared slightly panicked by the idea. "Not this fast. It never happens this fast."

As I heard their words I understood their conversation. The connection between the person and the *vigiles urbani* contained within the coin normally took months to develop, sometimes years to fully emerge as a fully functioning tool of the Archive. For some reason this wasn't taking days, weeks, months, or years, but seconds, minutes, hours, and at most days.

Shaking my head, I grumbled. "But it is happening right before your eyes."

Isidore's concern was written across his face, much like my uncle's, as they both eyed me. Isidore nodded. "I suppose it is." He snapped to attention as he slammed a hand over his chest. "All, hail the *vigiles*."

Andrew stood and they both intoned the next phrase together. "All hail Caesar!"

Isidore continued to stare at me for several more seconds before looking over at Andrew. "You know that Ms. Dodd and the triumvirate are going to be pissed about this."

Andrew snarled. "They can be pissed all they like. It's within my rights as governor to place people in positions that need to be filled." For a moment Andrew looked to be smelling garbage. "Besides, it's only Robert who is chomping at the bit for this. He has designs on becoming governor one day."

Obviously Robert had missed the memo. "I take it he doesn't know about your whole age impairment."

Andrew glanced over at Isidore with a conspiratorial face. "Not many people do. As stone born we don't go around advertising it." He waved at Isidore. "It's hard to hide from someone who has known you for fifty years, but yeah, it's not common knowledge."

That made me think. "Unless he does and he's got a hand in the plot to kill you."

That wiped the satisfied look off his face as he considered my words. "That would be very bad for business, but all things considered equal, not out of the question for the little shit."

Making a mental note to return to this conversation later, I shifted gears. "Now, as far as Ms. Dodd is concerned, how much fuel will this add to her fire when she files that report against you?"

Andrew's face told the story of just how little he cared about that report. "I have a duty to assign people to an area. If anyone is stupid enough to volunteer for such a position and they are capable, then I'm duty bound to see that it happens. I'm perfectly within my right to do what's best for everyone."

Isidore snickered. "It isn't exactly politically savvy, but since you are not an elected official it doesn't matter."

Andrew blew out a breath and eyed Isidore. "As Gavin pointed out, they could be plotting to kill me."

Isidore's form shifted slightly, he slammed his hand into the table, cracking the wood. "Don't even joke about that!"

Andrew winced. "I was only kidding!"

Isidore growled. "And I find that shit extremely funny."

Putting my right hand on the table, I looked between them. "You two need to sit back and relax. Consider that my first order as *vigiles.*"

Isidore's form returned to normal and he leaned back in his chair. "Sorry about the table."

Andrew didn't seem to be bothered by the outburst. "It's only wood. Besides, I've needed a new table for years."

Isadore looked around sheepishly. "You seriously need to update this place!"

Andrew closed his eyes and steeled himself against what was obviously an old argument. "Don't even start with that shit. I'll call the carpenters and have them repair the table."

Isidore's eyes grew wide ashe started to envision remaking the apartment. "You could update this place with a more modern style."

I looked around the room and made a face before looking back at Isidore. "I like the decor."

Isidore sighed. "Fuck me, and you're the new *vigiles*. I was hoping you'd have good taste."

I waved my hand around the room. "What do you call this?"

Isidore didn't even hesitate. "OLD!" he grumbled. "I'm older than either of you and I wouldn't be caught dead in this place. There's so much wood, and even more wood as far as the eye can see. Then there's that leather atrocity that you call a couch."

Andrew huffed. "You're a fucking werewolf…don't go all vegan on me!"

"I don't care about the leather, it's the design. It looks like something I'd find Edison owning."

Andrew looked truly offended. "That was low! You know I despise that man!"

Isidore dismissively waved off my uncle. "It isn't as if you knew him!"

Andrew pulled his shirt straight. "That's not the point. He was a thief! I hate thieves." Andrew turned his attention to me. "Thieves deserve a special place in hell! As the *vigiles* for the Southern United States, I expect you to be extra tough on them!"

I didn't care for thieves, but I didn't like being told how to do my job. "This seems like an old argument and one that I'll stay out of." Looking at my uncle, I smiled. "But when it comes to the job I'll do what needs to be done."

Andrew barely acknowledged my words. "Good man."

The three of us sat there for several hours, talking about the rules and regulations for the Archive, both locally and globally. I was beginning to see why Isidore had tried to talk me out of it. It was a little late now…I'd already agreed and been marked for life.

My first task would be to find out what really happened to Martha and the others. Once I'd done that I'd be within my rights to put that person in the ground. The UCD would be useful up to a point, but if I were right about who was behind these crimes the perpetrator wouldn't survive the encounter. There was, of course, the second option…that the council would need to find a new *vigiles* at the meeting next week because I'd been killed. Either way things would come to a head very soon.

Chapter 12

At around 2:00 p.m. Isidore needed to go out for supplies and to pick up a few things from home. Just before he was ready to leave I asked if he could drop me off at Touro so I could check on Heather. I'd meant to drop by yesterday, but with the trip across the lake and all the reading I'd lost track of time. I wasn't going to do that again.

Andrew was clearly hesitant about me going out and he made several excuses for me to stay, the best of which was about my new position. "Do you think it wise to taunt Robert the first day on the job?" he said.

While his concern was touching, I really needed to visit Heather. Andrew wasn't thrilled when I waved and followed Isidore out the door. "Don't worry so much, I'll be fine."

Andrew made a point to follow us down, a ruse to lock the gate behind us. Stopping, I turned to face my uncle. "The fact I'm the newest *vigiles* means I have new responsibilities, the first of which is to save your life, and by extension, my own."

Andrew reluctantly agreed. "If you could avoid a confrontation with Robert that would be fantastic."

He was right, of course, but there was an even chance that wasn't going to happen. "I'll do my best."

It was a clear, bright, hot, and very humid afternoon in the city. The black pavement radiated heat like giant hotplates. We pulled up outside the hospital and I thanked Isidore for the ride as I hopped out. Ducking as I passed through the sliding glass doors, I wound my way through the lobby until I found the information desk.

The elderly woman at the information desk was probably in her late 60's or early 70's, with white hair, thick glasses, and hands that shook. Her voice quavered as she spoke on the phone, and I waited until she hung up. She looked tired and feigned cheerfulness when her old bloodshot blue eyes fell on me. She flashed me a mechanical smile as she ran her arthritic fingers across the keyboard, speaking in a bored tone. "How may I help you?"

Giving the older woman the most cheerful look I could muster, I stepped closer. "I'm looking for Heather Broussard; could you tell me what room she's in?"

Again she flashed me a mechanical, insincere smile and slowly typed in Heather's name. The smile faltered before turning into a frown, and she looked back at me with suspicion. "She's in a private room with strict instructions not to be disturbed." She saw the look on my face and she held up a finger in my direction. "In simple English, I can't tell you where she is."

That was odd, but then again her father was the head of a department and her mother was the head of another, so it wasn't too far out of the question. Fortunately for me, I was large enough to easily glance over at the monitor and see the room number for myself. "That's all right, ma'am. Thank you for your time." I turned to leave and stopped, looking back at the woman. "Where's the cafeteria?"

She instantly relaxed, thankful I wasn't going to press her further on the issue. Her nose scrunched up as she pulled a face. Leaning forward, she whispered just loud enough for me to hear. "You don't want to eat there. The food is terrible." Leaning back in her seat, she raised her voice, pointing down the hall. "Just follow the hallway till the end and make a right. You can't miss it."

I gave her a wink as I touched my nose and nodded. "Thanks for the heads up."

When I turned to leave, she gave me a sly grin and raised a shaky hand to wave. "Have a wonderful day."

I took the hall she'd pointed out, but instead of making the right I made a left and hit the nearest set of stairs. Slowly pushing the door open, I stepped out onto an old fashioned if not generic and tired looking fourth floor landing. The carpets were threadbare and the floor smelled like an old folks' home. I found the placards on the wall denoting room numbers; rooms 400-425 were to the right.

Of course, the lower numbers were nearest the outer wall, which meant I walked most of the hall before finding room 404 second to last on the right. When I put my hand on the door I heard raised voices on the other side. It was clear by Heather's tone that she wasn't pleased with her guest, and seeing as how I was the new *vigiles* in town, it was my job to ensure she got her rest.

The door stuck a little when I pushed it open. As the gap widened I caught sight of Heather sitting up in bed and red faced as she wagged a finger at the man standing over her. Heather's "friend" looked to be in his mid-40's, with long black hair pulled back into a ponytail in an attempt to be hip, but mostly looking old. He appeared frail, waiflike, and his pallor was sickly white.

He pointed a long boney finger at Heather and huffed. "You should consider yourself lucky that I'm even willing to take you back after you embarrassed me by taking a mutt to the wedding!"

Heather's eyes bulged as she growled at the little man, making him wince. "We were never dating, you dolt!" She waved her hands out in exasperation. "We went out a couple of times because Dad forced me to!" And then she finally processed the rest of the sentence and looked at him blankly. "What are you talking about, a mutt?"

Ah, Brad! So this was the vegan who didn't want to attend the wedding with her.

Brad rolled his eyes. "Don't be daft! I know you took that mutt from Andrew's to the wedding!" He huffed and a vein popped into view on his temple "How could you stoop so low as to be seen in public with a werewolf? Are you trying to prove your father right?" His voice was suddenly full of venom. "That you're some kind of fucking whore?"

And we're done! I tapped my big knuckles against the door hard enough to make them both jump, and stepping into the room fully, I let the door close behind me. Looking at Heather, I gave her a once over. "Afternoon, Heather." Turning my head slightly, I glared at Brad. "You must be the vegan."

His head snapped back as if I'd slapped him and he puffed out his chest as he tried to intimidate me. "I thought Robert placed sigils around the hospital to keep your kind out!"

Wow, Robert's a bigger asshole than I thought. If a werebeast was injured they couldn't be treated at a regular hospital…well, at least not this one. That was low.

I took a step closer and he stumbled back. "I'm betting the man hasn't got a clue about 'my kind.'" Just to be an asshole I stuck out my hand in his direction. "I'm Gavin."

He recoiled, nearly tripping over his own feet. He looked back at Heather, who was busy trying not to laugh, before whipping his head back at me. "You're obviously too dull to understand how much you're upsetting Heather! You should go now before I'm forced to remove you."

Brad ran his thumb against the ring on his index finger, clearly his focus item. I stepped closer, looked down at the weasel, and snarled. "I'm not the one leaving." Pointing at his ring, I looked him in the eyes. "Try it and I'll rip it off and shove it down your throat." Looking over at Heather, I smiled, allowing my tone to soften. "You're okay with me staying, aren't you?"

She pulled her eyes off my right hand and a conspiratorial look came over her before she flashed me a warm smile. "I would like that very much." She turned to Brad. "You really should go and find someone who wants your company."

Brad squeezed between the bed and me, scrambling towards the door. "You wait till your father hears about this!" He paused. "If I walk out of this room, we're over!"

Heather lifted a hand and waved. "Bye."

Brad stormed out in a huff, and a moment later the door closed with a soft click, very anticlimactic.

I looked down at Heather and chuckled. "Sorry about that, but he was kind of being a dick."

She snickered. "No kind of about it; he was being an asshole." She beamed up at me. "Looks like you've saved me twice in less than a week."

I blushed hard and took a seat on the edge of the bed. "I do what I can." Making a more thorough inspection of her, I shrugged. "You look a lot better than the last time I saw you."

She snickered and grasped her stomach. "Don't make me laugh, it hurts." She flattened the sheets. "Besides, something about not gushing blood from an open wound can do that for a girl." Her lips twitched, yet she fought back the case of the giggles. "So why does Brad think you're a werewolf?"

"Who says I'm not?" I asked.

Her head tilted in such a way as to tell me that she wasn't about to buy into my bullshit. "The fact you're a *vigiles* makes that clear." She folded her arms and waited. "Care to fill me in on what's going on outside these walls?"

I ducked my head, blood rushing to my cheeks. "Your father may think I'm a werewolf since he met with Andrew yesterday." She sat there waiting for me to explain myself. "He may have been a dick to Isidore, and I may have implied that if that's the way he felt about werewolves, he could count me in."

Heather's lips curled up in the cutest crooked smile that allowed the slightest chuckle to escape. "You told my father that you were a werewolf?"

Shaking my head, I held out my hands defensively. "I never said it, but I never denied it either."

She winced as she laughed a little too hard, and she punched me in the arm. "That's for making me laugh!" She wiggled under the sheet, trying to get comfortable. "No one's called since I've been in here."

"That's because your father has you on restricted access. It took some doing for me to figure out which room you were in." Looking around the room, I searched for her mobile. "Where's your phone?"

She grimaced. "I think my father took it."

Pulling a phone out of my pocket, I handed it to her. "Use mine."

She took it and tucked it under her thigh before she looked up at me. "What are you going to do for one in the meantime?"

With all the skill of a day one magician, I made a show of pulling a second phone out of my pocket. "I signed up for Google Fi last week, and got my new Nexus phone last night."

She raised an eyebrow in my direction…I'd like to think she was impressed. "You know this whole werewolf scam is going to go south very quickly when he finds out you're a *vigiles*." She looked around the room and whispered, "You do know he's one of the triumvirate members."

And there goes all the feel good in the room. Sighing, I closed my eyes. "About that; do you think you could avoid telling him about my new position for a few days?"

She held out her hands, indicating how helpless she appeared. "I'm in no condition to fight with him, so your secret's safe with me." She glanced over at the door and shivered. "You know that Brad went to find my father and have you thrown out." She rubbed a hand gently over her stomach and suddenly changed the subject. "From what Mom said, I'm going to have a pretty nasty scar."

All I could think of was that it was a scar I'd like to see. "Scar's give a person character."

She pursed her lips and waved a hand in my direction. "Maybe for a man, but I'm fairly certain men like their women unmarred by such things."

I nearly choked at the comment. "Then they aren't men worth having! Besides, I have never known a man that got a woman naked and saw such a minor flaw that said nope, not gonna happen. I can promise you at that point it's not your stomach they're focused on!"

It was her turn to go crimson. "Thank you again for being there the other night." She paused for a moment, taking in a breath. "If Brad had been there I'd probably be dead."

Glancing back at the door, I sighed. "I really want to disagree with you, but after meeting the man I'm fairly certain you're right."

Her mouth fell open, feigning offense at the words. She looked back at the door and up at me sheepishly. "I don't want you to go, but it might be in your best interest to do so. I'm sure my father will have security with him when he arrives."

That was probably a safe bet. Stepping away from the bed, I allowed myself to get to the reason I'd come. "I'll go, but before I do, any idea why someone attacked you?"

That sucked the joy right out of her. She had clearly given it a lot of thought but still hadn't found a reason. "Honestly, no. I really wish I could help but I'm at a loss."

I'd guessed as much. If she'd known anything Kimberly and Robert wouldn't have shown up on Andrew's doorstep. "You've got my phone; use it as you see fit. And if anything comes up my number is already in there under speed dial 1."

She gave me one of those "Oh really" looks. "Speed dial 1...I guess you think pretty highly of yourself."

And with that she was happy again. Gripping the handle of the door, I turned back. "Someone has to. If not me, then who?" Stepping out the door, I held it open. "Get back on your feet quickly, and remember, call me or Andrew if you need anything."

She waved. "I will."

Taking the nearest staircase down, I avoided the roving security guards that seemed to be on high alert. I guessed Brad had found Robert and cried on the old man's shoulder. Ducking out of a side door, I hustled off the hospital grounds and blended into the Garden District's afternoon health enthusiasts. The elderly strolled through the shaded streets next to new mothers jogging with strollers, trying to get back into trophy wife shape as quickly as possible.

For a fleeting moment I thought of going to the UCD, but all things being equal I had no idea where they were stationed, let alone who to speak to. No, it was best for me to return to Andrew's place, do some digging through Martha's papers, and see where that took me. While I was at it, I needed to do a bit more research on my new position. Fact of the matter was I'd gone into this job only slightly less knowledgeable than my last. Considering how that turned out, I should probably focus on not fucking this one up. Sweat coated my forehead and ran freely down my back by the time I returned home to find Andrew sitting with Isidore at the living room table drinking scotch.

Walking over, I plopped down in the seat next to Andrew. "I've got a stupid question."

Andrew snickered, poured himself a scotch and took a hit. "All right, shoot."

That's just great, I've already got the boss drinking every time I ask a question. I'd never liked discussing money, but this was important. "The *vigiles* position...is it a paying job or will I need to find additional employment?"

Andrew and Isidore looked at one another with great amusement.

Andrew straightened his shirt and put on a professional demeanor. "As the *vigiles* for this area you'll be given a base salary, and from what I understand it's fairly substantial." He grabbed a fairly modern looking handbook and tossed it to me. "You'll be expected to travel to maintain control of the region, and as such that will be fully comped by the Archive." He pointed at the book. "The specifics are in there." He mumbled the last bit. "They also cover housing should you see fit to move out of here."

Setting the book to the side, I ran my hand over my face and head. "I'm sure there will come a time that I'll need to find my own place." Grabbing Andrew's scotch, I toasted him. "For now, however, I'm happy staying here until I can get my feet on the ground."

Andrew relaxed, grabbed another glass, and topped off all three. "Here's to you taking your time about that." We all took a drink and he looked over at me. "The peace and quiet you bring to the house is a most welcome change."

Isidore set his glass down and turned his curious attention to me. "Did you see Heather?"

Swallowing my scotch, I sucked in my cheeks, enjoying every last sensation of the amber fluid before answering. "She's doing all right." Remembering Brad, I felt irritation creep into my voice. "I also ran into her 'friend' Brad while I was there. Robert didn't waste any time telling people I was a werewolf."

Isidore snorted, and unconsciously his eyes flickered over my right hand. "They are going to be in for a rude awakening."

Of that I was sure. Taking another drink, I savored the rich flavors before turning to Andrew. "Why aren't the werebeasts allowed to be a *vigiles*?"

Andrew's face darkened. Setting his glass on the table, he fumed. "For the same reason they can't enter the Archive; people like Robert fight against progress. That being said, they can become a decanus." Andrew must have seen the blank look on my face and quickly followed up. "Think of it like a deputy in service to a specific *vigiles*, but that's about the extent of it."

Well, that's convenient. Turning my gaze to Isidore, I straightened up, trying to appear competent. "Want a job?"

With an uncomfortable look between him and Andrew, Isidore reluctantly answered. "Sorry, but I've already got a job taking care of your uncle." The pride in his face was hard to miss. "I work for Amelia, your boss."

It shouldn't have surprised me to learn that I had a boss, but hearing it spoken out loud caught me off guard. "Amelia?"

Andrew winced. Quickly leaning forward, he downed his scotch in one and poured another. "Amelia is the *vigiles* for North America."

"And who is her boss?" I asked.

Andrew and Isidore turned to one another, shrugging in unison. It was clear by their reaction they rarely gave the situation much thought. Andrew tilted his glass, slightly uncomfortable. "Lazarus hasn't had a personal *vigiles* in nearly a thousand years. So to answer your question, technically Lazarus."

What the hell? The local Archive was pushing for someone to replace Martha in less than two weeks. How could Lazarus wait a thousand years to find someone? "Why hasn't he chosen a new *vigiles* by now?"

Andrew considered the words carefully. His face suddenly serious, I saw him searching for an explanation. "The higher the rank the more significant the power needed to fill the spot." He waved a hand at the door as he spoke. "In Amelia's case, she's a 357-year-old sorcerer of immense power." He stared off into space, lost in thought. "The *vigiles* serving the other governors are equally as powerful, and some even more so. After Naevius Sutorius Macro was killed, no one has been strong enough to take up the mantel and the position has remained open."

At the mention of Naevius' name, Isidore's face darkened. "From everything I've heard about the man he was a complete asshole! It was at his urging that all the werebeasts were marked as slaves, pets, or in his words 'to be put down.'" He slammed back his drink. "He used to like betting on the fights he set up."

Anger flared up inside me as the thought of people being forced into cage matches due to their birth sickened me. "Sounds like the guy was a complete douche."

Andrew shook off the anger, and turning the glass in his hand, he watched the amber fluid stick to the sides. It was clear he was still lost in thought when he spoke. "I'll need to contact Amelia; she'll want to meet with you soon." Taking his eyes off the glass, he turned to me. "I'm sure there's some sort of orientation for you to attend."

That was somewhat comforting. I tossed back my scotch and stood, grabbing the book he'd given me. "I'm heading to my room. Is there anything else I need to read while I'm at it?"

Andrew swelled with excitement. "Tons! I took the liberty of putting many of them on the desk in your bedroom."

I felt like I'd returned to school, so I shouldn't be surprised that I had a massive reading list. Trying to keep a positive outlook, I eyed the bottle of scotch longingly. "Great. Got a set of cliff notes laying around?"

Andrew shot me a stern look. "Those are the cliff notes editions."

My stomach fell and the nerves kicked in. "Fantastic." Steadying myself, I tucked the small book under my arm before grabbing the journal and heading to my room. "If you two will excuse me, I've got some serious reading to do."

Andrew raised a glass in salute. "When you get through all of those, I've got some others for you in the library."

I loved to read, but somehow I doubted this would be enjoyable. Still, I forced a cheerful expression and waved.

Sitting at the desk in my room, I sifted through the books until I found one that made my right hand tingle. Pulling it out of the stack of books, I read the title—*Vigiles Urbani Guide to the Archive*—and of course it was in Latin. Fantastic! Andrew should've told me I'd need to order one of those learn a language kits.

Closing my eyes in frustration, I felt a sense of calm wash over me. When I opened my eyes again and looked at the text, it was in English. No, not English. It was still in Latin, but now I understood the words on the page. Well, hot damn! While I doubted this worked like *The Matrix*, something told me that I'd be able to read most languages.

The denarius was quickly adapting to my brain, creating a new interface that would allow me to access vast amounts of information. If a previous *vigiles* held the knowledge of werewolves or other creatures, I'd have access to it. The same went for deductive reasoning, cyphers, codes, and other similar things. Even if it was a new cypher, the knowledge of old ones could be used to break and read any new codes encountered. It was a sort of amplified intelligence.

Over the next several hours I discovered that the triumvirate and prefects were chosen in a similar fashion to a *vigiles*, but with ascending currency. Coins were used to carry necessary information from one generation to the next. This ensured that if a chosen officer died, or was otherwise deemed unworthy of continuing their work, vital knowledge and wisdom were not lost. Unlike the *vigiles*, none of the others were visibly marked, allowing them some anonymity.

The *vigiles urbani* were the first combination fire brigade and police force of the Roman Empire, and were known as the watchmen of the city. They were originally meant to guard Rome's citizens from all sorts of dangers while they slept. The Archive adopted a lot of the ancient Roman culture and adapted them into what it used today. *Vigiles* were given equal weight with the prefects due to political backbiting and general assholery. It was the *vigiles'* job to ensure things ran smoothly and keep the Archive a secret from the general populace by any means necessary.

That I could do.

As the need arose new coins would manifest themselves, as in the case of the Americas. When one of the hosts passed away, their coin would manifest in the possession of the most powerful official in any given sector, which was why Andrew had Martha's coin instead of Beth.

She would totally lose her shit when she found out that, not only was I NOT a dirty little monkey, but I was her *vigiles*. It wasn't uncommon for a governor to live within a prefect's base of operations. It was actually encouraged to cut down on travel and to ensure decisions were made quickly.

I spent the next several hours reading the different laws regarding the killing of our kind. Needless to say it was frowned upon and carried a death sentence. Killing someone in self-defense was reasonable, but murdering a fellow Archive member, or even conspiring to do so, normally demanded that the *vigiles* end the offending perpetrator. The denarius would assist the *vigiles* in acting as judge, jury, and executioner. The seriousness of the offense dictated other punishments, including stripping someone of their abilities for a period of time, to be imprisoned with the human population.

Chapter 13

Wednesday June 3rd

Pain shot through my neck and down my back, jolting me awake. The sudden movement only made things worse. Rubbing the sleep out of my eyes, I raised my stiff and aching head off the desk. Quickly putting a hand on the page stuck to my cheek to keep from ripping it out, I slowly brought myself into a sitting position. Pins and needles erupted down the arm I'd had against the lip of the desk for God knew how long. Giving it a good shake, I forced myself up onto my feet and ambled to the shower.

While I dressed, a plan formed. During my breaks last night, I'd delved into one of the portable drives. Martha had created a hidden partition, effectively rendering two files invisible. There wasn't a lot there, just an address for a warehouse out in Metairie and a couple of notes on Neil Nunez. She had obviously suspected someone, but never committed it to paper.

By the time I got myself together and meandered to the kitchen, it was 4:30 a.m. Pushing the door open, the smell of bacon wrapped itself around me, making me a very happy man. I found Isidore standing at the stove cooking breakfast for what looked to be a small army. Three long aluminum cookie sheets were on the counter, lined with bacon that he was pulling off with tongs to rest on crisping racks.

He glanced over long enough to acknowledge me before turning his attention back to the cookie sheets. "Eggs and toast will be up shortly." With a slight tilt of his head at the meat, he said, "If you're hungry grab a few strips of bacon…there's plenty."

The moment I'd smelled the smoky, salted meat my stomach twisted itself up in knots, letting me know the depth of my hunger. My mouth watered, so I snagged a couple of pieces and chomped down on them like a meaty candy bar. "Don't mind if I do!" My stomach mollified, I took in a large bowl with a dozen eggs cracked, ready to be whipped into omelets or scrambled eggs. "We have guests, or are you just that hungry?"

Isidore's eyes flashed and I thought I saw the beast just under the surface. "It's that time of the month, so to speak." He blushed, realizing what he'd said, and tried to backtrack. "The full moon...it's time for the full moon."

Barely able to keep my glee contained, I grabbed two more slices. "Anything I can help with?"

He eyed the bacon in my hand with envy. "You can save me some of that!"

Blowing him off, I mocked. "There's got to be four pounds of the stuff, and you're going to cry over four slices?" Swallowing, I waved at the counter. "Seriously, anything I can help with?"

He considered my offer for a few seconds before rolling his shoulders. "Nope. I've got it under control." He gestured towards the table. "Sit back and enjoy the show."

It was clear he didn't want to part with any more bacon, so I obediently took a seat.

His head popped up, suddenly remembering something. He waved a spatula in my general direction. "George dropped off several packages for you last night." He ladled some eggs into the pan with a low sizzle. "He kept apologizing about being late."

With everything that was going on I'd completely forgotten about George. "The man worries too much."

Isidore poured the remaining mixture into the pan. When he finished he piled three plates to overflowing with eggs, bacon, and several pieces of toast. He made several trips between the counter and the table to get everything before he sat down and started shoveling food into his mouth like he hadn't eaten in weeks.

The denarius whispered in my mind that during the full moon and other significant changes for a werebeast, their metabolisms accelerated. They needed the extra calories and food to sustain them before, during, and after a shift.

Finishing my breakfast, I cleaned my plate to leave before I actually lost a hand. Heading out of the kitchen, I stopped at the door and turned to Isidore. "I'll collect my things before running errands. I'll be back sometime later today, probably in the afternoon. If I'm going to be late, I'll call."

Isidore didn't look up as he gave me the thumbs up. As I headed into the living room I could see that George wasn't kidding about a full wardrobe. There were a half dozen garment bags filled to capacity, along with another seven boxes packed with clothes. In an effort to save time, I dumped one of the boxes onto the bed and found several pairs of jeans and some pull over polo's. The last box I'd brought in was heavier than the others, clunking loudly as I'd dropped it on the floor. Opening it, I was surprised to see an exact copy of my Wolverine Raiders at the top. Considering there were smaller boxes containing shoes for every occasion, I was betting this was what had taken the extra time George was so concerned about.

While George's shirt hadn't saved me from acquiring a new scar the other day, I figured it best not to tempt fate. Stripping down, I quickly redressed in the new attire, which was incredibly comfortable. Grabbing the car keys off the dresser, I headed downstairs and out the back just before 9:00.

The aged metal garage door slid up quietly, revealing the Tucker sitting there in all of its glory. Every time I looked at it I was in awe, but gawking at it wasn't going to accomplish anything. Pushing on the gas, I turned the key and it purred to life, and I idled it out into the driveway before getting out and closing the door. Pulling out of the gate, I stopped long enough to lock up before heading for the suburbs.

I'd plugged the address into my Nexus before I left the house, and was on my way to 521 Elmwood Park Boulevard. It took about thirty minutes to cut through traffic, navigate road construction, and learn how to do what I'd dubbed the Louisiana left, which was a U turn.

Pulling into the parking lot of what appeared to be an abandoned warehouse in Elmwood, I cut the engine and got out. From the faded and reversed sign, this was a hub for the now defunct DHL company. The building itself looked as if someone had kept up with it since DHL pulled out a few years back, but otherwise it looked abandoned. The long, narrow, gray cinderblock building was closed up tight. The wind had blown paper, plastic, and other trash that collected in all the corners, from the loading docks on up to the front door. What struck me most was the odd quiet that settled around the property. My flesh erupted in goose flesh from some unseen force of nature, one that I wasn't entirely sure was peaceful.

Coming around to the front of the building and the blacked out plate glass doors, I stood in front of a keypad. Looking down at my phone, I pulled up the notes I'd made from the files I'd found. There at the bottom was a series of numbers, which I punched in. A second later I heard the magnetic lock give way as the door popped slightly ajar.

When I stepped inside, the florescent bulbs came to life as motion sensors alerted them to my presence. I was at once thankful and concerned that the air conditioning was working. If the building was empty why would anyone bother with A/C? That's when I heard the sound of someone very large running at top speed, their boots slapping against the hard tiled floor in rapid succession. I heard the screeching of rubber soles sliding across the slick surface, followed by the thud of someone slamming into a wall before the padding of feet hitting the ground a half second later.

For my part I remained very still, raised my hands, interlocking my fingers, and setting them atop my head. I didn't have long to wait, maybe five seconds, before a gigantic man shoved open the two metal doors that led into the rear of the facility hard enough to shatter bricks from the impact.

I was 6'6", and this guy towered over me, his massive frame packed with lean hard muscle. His skin was so dark that it made it difficult to make out details of his face. In stark contrast, his eyes were a brilliant green and were trained down the sight of a specially modified AR-15 semi-automatic service rifle to fit his enormous size. The light glinted off his bald head as he moved the rifle towards the wall, indicating for me to move. When he spoke it was in a low, rumbling baritone.

"Against the wall."

He was calm, focused, and highly trained for such a young age. I turned and faced the wall.

"I'm here on business," I said calmly, not wanting to provoke the man.

He came up behind me and with a foot kicked my legs apart. "Hands on the wall."

I followed his instructions. "If you'd give me a chance to explain, I'd be happy to identify myself."

There was silence behind me, and then he spoke again. "You can turn around, but do it slowly and keep your hands where I can see them." I turned and he kept his eyes fixated on my right hand. "*Vigiles*?"

I nodded and stuck a hand in his direction. "I'm Gavin Randall."

He sniffed, lowered his weapon, and took my hand. "Gabriel." He looked back at the door and then down at me. "You alone?"

Again I nodded, trying to keep things peaceful. "Yeah."

He suddenly looked heartbroken, keeping his eyes locked on the door. "Martha's dead then?"

The tone of his voice made me hurt as I lowered my gaze from his. "She passed away late Thursday night." Looking towards the now open metal doors, I quickly wondered just how alone we really were. "Anyone else with you?"

He pulled the magazine out of the rifle and ejected the live round out of the chamber. "I'm alone."

"Sorry about Martha," I said.

He shoved the magazine into a back pocket and waved for me to follow. "It was bound to happen sooner or later," he rumbled, pulling the doors closed behind us. "That's the lot of a *vigiles*, they always die. One way or another."

"Where are we headed?" I asked, following in the big man's wake.

He gestured to what had once been a conference room. "The armory." Stopping outside the heavy metal security door, he punched in a code and the door popped open. He waved at the long conference table. "Take a seat and I'll be with you shortly."

Gabriel went to the nearest locker and pulled the clip out of his pocket, reinserting the round he'd ejected earlier before locking it up. Then he placed the rifle in the rack with a dozen other normal sized AR-15's. He turned around and came to sit at the head of the table in an oversized chair to fit his form.

He leaned forward, elbows on the table and hands together. "Related to Andrew Randall?"

"He's my uncle," I replied.

He looked thoughtful for a moment, and when he spoke his voice cracked. "How did my mother die?"

I went numb. No one had ever said anything about her having a child, and it was obvious that no one had bothered to inform him. "No one knows for sure. I'm so sorry for your loss." I stammered. "No one told you?"

Bitterness painted his features. "Mom didn't exactly go around telling people in the Archive about me." He gestured at himself. "My kind are not exactly welcomed with open arms."

It struck me as the little voice inside my head spoke to me: *nephilim!* "I'm new to the Archive myself, so you'll have to forgive my ignorance. Why not?"

Gabriel appeared to be shocked by the question. He sat there dumbfounded for several seconds. "You must be new. The law is clear that all nephilim are to be either pressed into service—a nice way to say enslaved—or killed."

Then it dawned on me what he was doing here. "Martha slid around the rules by having you work for her."

He grunted in assertion and spread his hands out. "That's right." Thinking about his situation, he frowned. "Now that she's gone I don't have many choices. I can run, be enslaved, or be killed." He looked up at me and shook his head. "What would you do?"

My answer was instantaneous. "Or you could opt to make a similar deal with the new *vigiles*." I pointed at my chest. "Me."

Gabriel's face broke into a big toothy smile as he eyed me carefully. "You don't even know me. Why would you do such a thing?"

"Because it's the right thing to do." And it was. Looking up at the big man, I nodded. "It may not be popular, but it's the right thing to do."

He laughed, a big, hearty, joyous thing. "You really are new." He looked me over a bit more carefully as he waved a big beefy hand at me. "How can that be? No offense, but you look older."

His joy was infectious; it lightened my heart and gave me a sense of contentment. "I've been away on business, and have only recently been introduced to the Archive."

Gabriel relaxed. "It's good to meet you." He stuck a meaty paw out and I took it. "When did you become *vigiles*?"

Right to the point then. This made things simple, though I hung my head at the awkwardness. "Yesterday morning."

He considered my words and glanced around the room. "You found me pretty quick."

His tone changed suddenly from acceptance to one of suspicion. I held up my hands again as a sign of nonaggression. "She had the address for this place in a hidden file on one of her portable drives. I only showed up here out of curiosity." He still wasn't convinced. "She was working several cold cases before she died. I'm here to find more information, because I think it's what got her killed."

Suspicion danced through his eyes as he got to his feet. "Come with me." He leaned over, grabbing a pistol on the way out. "If you're lying to me I'll put a bullet in your skull."

It didn't take a brain surgeon to see he wasn't kidding. In the words of Ron Burgundy, "that escalated quickly." Getting to my feet, I followed the man. "Show me the way."

He guided us through a couple of hallways until we reached a black metal security door. He waved me ahead and pointed at it. "Place your right hand on the door. If it unlocks you live; if it doesn't...."

My chest tightened and I fought back panic. There wasn't a palm scanner in sight, and even if there had been I was confident I wouldn't be granted access. But the gun leveled at the back of my head was a great motivator to do what was asked of me. There was a series of clicks, pops, and gears whirring as the door lock popped and it swung open. Then it struck me...magic. The scars on my hand must contain a unique signature to grant me such access.

I heard Gabriel click the safety on the weapon before holstering it. "Welcome to Casa De Morte."

Stepping through the door, I found myself faced with dozens of individual rooms built out of boxes, crates, and artwork. At the far end of the warehouse were a few cars. All but one military style oversized Hummer with tinted windows were antiques. Another section was littered with weapons of various types displayed in cases, on tables, and hung on the wall. Just past that were racks of what looked to be different types of body armor, coats, and other miscellaneous articles of clothing.

I couldn't keep the shock out of my voice. "What's all this?"

He swept his hand out in a grand fashion. "These are the belongings of the previous *vigiles*." He pulled a face as he thought about it. "They keep things that belonged to their predecessors for either sentimental reasons or practical ones. Sometimes one *vigiles* will adopt things from prior ones. It belongs to you now...look around and see if anything strikes your fancy." He pointed at the far end. "I'll place my mother's things at the end down there."

I followed his hand and saw that there were already several things there. "You started already?"

Gabriel's face clouded with emotion as happiness and sadness danced with everything in between. "She lived here part of the week to spend time with me." He walked me down to the spot Martha called home. He shined, waving me over some invisible line. "It's been like this since I was a child. She would come and stay. I've been to her house." He looked down into my eyes, making sure I understood. "That was never her home." He waved back to the open room and beamed. "This was home. I think she had more of HER things here than the place she had in the city."

Regarding the makeshift room, I couldn't help but admire the ability to turn such a place into a real home. "Either way, I'll be paying her place a visit at some point in the near future. Is there anything you want me to bring back?"

He never hesitated. "There's nothing there I'd ever want." He nodded at the big recliner for him and a smaller wing chair seated next to it and smiled. "All of her photos, notes, and other essentials were kept here."

Trepidation crept onto his face when he realized that this place was now in my care. Putting a hand on the big man's arm, I looked up at him. "Whatever you do, don't change it too much. This is just as much your home as it was hers, and that's not changing."

The dread subsided if only a little. "Are you going to turn me in?"

Pondering how best to handle the situation, I did my best to offer him a job, while still letting him know that he couldn't stay hidden. "I will eventually have to tell people about you, but as *vigiles* I can employ you. Just say the word."

Gabriel mulled it over for all of five seconds before agreeing. "Sure. Not like I have a lot of choices."

He was right, he didn't, but the denarius was very insistent that I needed him to be clear. "You're going to need to be explicit in your answer. Which means yes or no."

He stood up straight and said, "Yes, I'll do the job."

The denarius instructed me how to proceed, I moved to stand in front of the big man. Grabbing his left arm, I turned it so the bottom of his wrist was up. Placing my right hand over it, I felt power surge through me and into him, leaving me dizzy and weak for a moment. When I lifted my hand the Aquila appeared.

Gabriel gawked at his wrist. "What's this?"

The denarius whispered inside my mind and I repeated. "That mark means that you are a centurion and a ranked servant of the *vigiles*, and me in particular. It grants you certain rights within the Archive." I held up my hand to stop his questions. "Not that I know what they are at the moment, but it has to be better than those of a rogue nephilim."

The puzzlement on his face was clear. "You can do that?"

Allowing my eyes to linger on the Aquila, I shrugged. "Apparently."

He staggered off to the big recliner and fell back into it, ogling his wrist. "Thank you."

I hated to burst his bubble, but I needed him to understand some hard facts. "Don't thank me yet."

"Why not?" he asked.

My heart fell when I saw the anxiety on the man's face. "Because I don't have a clue what I'm doing. If I die, so does the sigil on your arm." Pulling my phone out, I saw it was nearly eleven and my stomach was growling. "Any chance of finding lunch around here before I start looking around?"

Gabriel perked up at the mention of food and got to his feet. "No, but if you don't mind waiting, I can order pizza. You could look around till it arrives."

Reaching in my pocket, I pulled out a hundred. "Order whatever you want for yourself, but I'm a big fan of meat lovers."

Gabriel took the money, heading for the door. "I'll take care of it." He stopped just before reaching the door and turned back. "It's good to see that there's another *vigiles* so quickly."

The way he said it made me wonder. "Why is that?"

His eyes darted around the room, afraid of being overheard. "No one wants to let Andrew handle the investigation into my mother's death." He visibly quaked in fear at the thought. "No one."

The distinct awe and fear people felt when speaking of my uncle disturbed me. "He can't be that scary."

The look of disdain he shot me was clear. "It's obvious just how little you know your uncle."

With that he stuffed the cash in his pocket and strode out of the warehouse. While I may not have been as familiar with my uncle as some people, I couldn't have possibly misjudged him that badly. Could I? It didn't matter at this point, because it was now my job to handle things and that would remain so. From what I could tell from the books I'd read last night, the only person who could countermand any order, judgement, or opinion that I may have would be Amelia. Normally one *vigiles* didn't get involved in another's territory unless the *vigiles* in question was somehow outside the law.

Skipping the individual rooms that were created by the makeshift walls of boxes, crates, and artwork hung on latticed rebar, I headed for the weapons. When I was talking to Gabriel, I'd kept seeing light glint off one of the swords, as if it were calling to me via Morse code. At the back of the room atop a dusty table lay a gladius, a type of sword used by the ancient Roman infantry.

I took the handkerchief out of my pocket, running it down the length of the black blade and wiping away the dust. The hilt was made of ebony wood with an onyx pummel. From tip to pummel it was two and a half feet long. The stone was surprisingly dust free, which meant that it was what had refracted the light. Grasping the hilt, I pulled it off the table and it vibrated in my hand as if it were alive. The denarius rejoiced as I flipped the sword over in my hand, getting a feel for the weight of it. Grabbing the scabbard, I sheathed the weapon before tucking it under my arm.

It wasn't the only item calling to me. I followed the pull of something else as I scoured the tables before ducking under one to pull out a wooden crate. There lay a wakizashi, two feet of gently curving Japanese steel coated in silver, with a plain wooden handle. When I picked it up with my free hand, it reacted to me much the same way as the gladius but with a higher frequency. Sheathing the weapon, I tucked it under the same arm before heading out. Just before I left I picked up a metal folding knife that I clipped onto the pocket of my jeans.

Stopping at the next little shop, I found a set of chestnut brown leg and chest armor. It wasn't something you'd find at your standard Renaissance Fair, but was something I could pass off as motorcycle gear if it came down to it. I looked around for a bag, and of course found no such thing. So I went back and grabbed the now empty wooden crate I'd gotten the wakizashi from, placing both swords and armor into it for ease of transport.

Lugging the crate back to the front, I found the armory door open with Gabriel sitting at the far end devouring a sausage pizza. He waved a hand at the closed box and grinned. "All yours...I can't stand pepperoni."

With a quick nod, I opened the box and pulled out a slice before plopping into the nearest chair. "Did Martha have an actual office here or just the place out back?"

Gabriel waved a greasy hand to something out the door. "Take the first left, and two doors down you'll find where she did almost all of her work."

"Thanks," I replied.

Two slices later I was in Martha's office sifting through notes, not just about this case but others she was working as the *vigiles* of such a large area. Finally, I stumbled upon a couple of files she'd stuffed into the center drawer of her desk. The first was labeled Timothy Miller. When I opened it I found a photo of the fat man who'd confronted me Monday morning on orders from his employer. The file told me he was hired muscle out of Vancouver. His long and varied rap sheet spanned breaking and entering to attempted murder, which he had served time for. After he was released he left Canada, and had become an employee of Walter Percy nearly ten years ago.

Fuck me! Walter was involved in this shit, and now I had proof!

The next file was labeled Chan Wong. The photo revealed him to be the man that attacked Heather and I Sunday night. Mr. Wong was a shapeshifter out of China, who'd escaped the authorities there two years ago and now worked for Walter Percy. I was surprised to see that Mr. Wong was only sixteen years old, and then I remembered that shapeshifters aged at twice the rate of normal humans.

Things were starting to fall into place; I didn't have enough to confront Walter, but that wasn't very far in the future. First I needed to get my hands on Timothy, and hopefully have him give me information about Walter. Not that it would gain him a reprieve.

First things first, I needed to speak with Andrew and Isidore and visit Martha's home to see if there was anything else I needed to be aware of. Finding a clean file, I slipped a few of her notes and the photos inside for safekeeping. Grabbing the file and the crate, I waved my goodbye's to Gabriel and headed back into the city, hitting rush hour traffic.

Chapter 14

The glare of the early evening sun beat down on the city as I turned off St. Charles onto 3rd. Two blocks later I made a right onto Coliseum just to double back on 4th. New Orleans was full of one-way streets, making it virtually impossible to make it anywhere without making U-turns and or going around entire blocks to make it home.

Midway down 4th Street, standing in front of the gate leading into Andrew's driveway, stood the very man I wanted to see, Timothy Miller. Slowing, I idled into a parking spot across the street and threw the car into park. Taking my time as I turned off the engine, I watched Timmy, who looked anxious as he sweated bullets fidgeting there in the heat. Finally, I stepped out of the car, pocketing the keys, letting gravity close the heavy metal door behind me.

Spreading my arms wide in welcome, I couldn't help but smirk at the fat man's discomfort. "Good to see you again, Timmy."

Timothy snapped his head back in shock at the mention of his name. He moved his greasy hand around his backside to produce a Glock 9mm, which he leveled in my direction. "How do you know my name, monkey?"

Leisurely crossing the road, I held my arms bent at the elbow, raising my hands about shoulder high. "You're from Vancouver, right?" Bending a finger in his direction, I watched him shake. "I'm pretty new here so at first I thought you were Cajun, but now I know better."

His hands quaked, and every time he spoke he waved the gun around like an idiot unaccustomed to handling such a weapon. The fool was more likely to shoot himself than me.

His voice quivered as he spewed spittle in my direction. "Where's my cane?"

And now we'd found the heart of the matter, the cane. He didn't care that I knew his name and where he was from; his overriding motivation was the cane.

Cocking my head to the side, I scowled down at him, just out of arm's length. My lips pursed, I scrunched up my face in one of those "Well" type of looks. "Funny story. After I went upstairs the other morning, I snapped it in two." With an unconcerned wave of my hand, I moved slightly closer. "The good news is you're here, and I needed to speak with you."

Screaming at me in utter despair, he gripped the weapon tightly and pulled the trigger, missing me by a couple of feet, the bullet marring the neighbors' red brick privacy fence. "Liar!" He put both hands on the gun, trying to steady the weapon. "Tell me where it is!"

Sweat ran into his eyes, forcing them closed. That's when I struck. Wrapping my hand around the gun, I jerked it hard to the left and pulled. At the same moment I pulled the knife off my pocket, thumbing it open. I slid the steel blade between two ribs, scraping against the sternum before striking the heart.

With a vicious twist I heaved the little fat man off the ground as I ripped the pistol out of his hands. I brought him close and whispered in his ear. "A little advice for your next life. Don't threaten to kill someone, just do it!"

With a hearty shove I pulled the knife free, letting him sink lifelessly to the ground. The gates flew open as Andrew stormed out of the drive. Power washed off him in waves, pulsating across the ground with enough force to move Timothy's body several feet. Isidore strode out from behind Andrew, his face twisted, preparing to transform into the beast he kept just below the skin.

Leaning over, I wiped my blade clean on Timothy's shirt before checking for a pulse. Not that I expected to find one, it was a gesture to calm the others.

Pushing myself up to my feet with a grunt, I clipped the knife in place. "He's dead, guys."

With a great deal of effort, Andrew forced calm onto his features. "Is this your friend from the other morning?"

"Yeah, he came looking for the cane."

Isidore shoved a shoe under Timothy's head and lifted. He shook his head. "I don't recognize him."

Andrew focused on the face before Isidore removed his foot. "Me either." He brimmed with questions. "Any idea how he is connected to all this?"

With a brusque nod, I gestured at the corpse. "His name is Timothy Miller, a hired thug out of Canada."

Andrew's face turned sour. His eyes fixed on mine, trying to force the information out of me. "Do you know who hired him?"

There was that itch in the back of my head again, telling me just how badly he wanted to know. Fighting off the compulsion, I glared at him. "I do, but we got a few things to tend to prior to delving into specifics."

Andrew stalked over to me and shoved a finger hard into my chest. "You'll tell me who it is and you'll tell me now."

Knocking away his hand, I took a step back and gave him an uncompromising look. "How about we deal with the dead body first, and then we can talk?"

Andrew scowled. He wasn't used to being denied information, but reluctantly agreed. "I'll call Lieutenant Baptist." He stepped back, glowering at the lifeless form. "He'll be able to clean this up without too much trouble."

Ten minutes later the first cruiser pulled up and blocked off 4th Street. It took another ten minutes for the UCD to arrive. Andrew was speaking to the lieutenant when I felt someone's hand grab an arm to spin me around. Whoever this was didn't have the strength to do so, but I followed its pull. That's when I saw Captain Hotard glaring up at me.

He was crimson and the top of his head glistened through the thinning hair and bald spots. His voice was low and threatening as he sneered at me. His fat finger pointed at Timothy being zipped into a body bag. "You're responsible for this?"

To say I wasn't happy with the man's attitude would be an understatement, but the denarius was far more offended by the man's tone and arrogance. It took a bit of effort after my encounter with Andrew to keep myself in check, but I kept my voice even as I stared down at the porky captain. "If you'll notice, he did try to shoot me."

The captain folded his chubby arms, his face turning sour. "That's your story, but I'm not sure that's the truth." While I was sure I hadn't personally done anything to the man, hatred radiated from him. "I've taken the liberty of having Sonia dig into your past, Mr. Randall. It won't be long before I'll know what type of degenerate you really are!"

The fact that he was digging into my past gave me pause, not for myself but him. The people I worked for wouldn't take that type of intrusion lightly. The audacity of it made me gleeful to see how it would end. "I'd be very careful if I were you. You never know what you might find."

The look of triumph on his face was palatable. "I knew it! You do have something to hide."

Glowering at the shit stain, I sniggered. "Not in the least." Dropping my voice so only he could hear my words, I continued, "However, the people I used to work for probably do, and I doubt seriously they'll take kindly to you sticking your nose in their business."

His bloated face filled with rage. "You must think highly of yourself! Who in the fuck do you think you are?!"

With a smirk, I lifted my right hand. "I think I'm the newest *vigiles*." That caused him to stagger back, and he visibly paled. "I'd appreciate it if you took it down a notch."

His shock was complete and he looked ill as he undulated, clapping a hand over his mouth. He stammered and pointed at my hand, mumbling more to himself than me. "How? I thought it wasn't happening until next week."

Without so much as a goodbye he waddled away into the crowd of officers, making a beeline for Andrew. More and more things about the captain weren't adding up…the conversation the other night, and now he had knowledge of next week's events. All of this was very curious.

The tall lanky lieutenant I'd seen at the funeral appeared in front of me, sticking his overly long thin hand out. He spoke with a heavy Russian accent. "Good evening." He paused, glanced down at the body bag, and sniffed. "Well, as good as an evening as one can have after having to end someone so abruptly." He looked me over again to make sure he had the right man, blinking several times in the process. "Mr. Randall, isn't it?"

The man's disheveled dark hair matched the unkempt beard. His suit, however, was perfectly pressed. His blue-green eyes were clear and his demeanor was competent and pleasant.

Taking his outstretched hand, I nodded. "Please call me Gavin."

He smiled, showing me his bright white teeth. "Da! I'm Lieutenant William Baptist."

With an accent that thick? I twisted my head in surprise. "Baptist?"

He shrugged. "My mother married a Cajun man when I was young, and changed our name when I was still in diapers."

"I see," I replied. "How can I help you today, Lieutenant Baptist?"

He waved an unconcerned hand at the captain's back. "Don't worry about the captain. He'll get used to the idea soon enough." Something strayed through his mind that made him chuckle before looking back at me. "And if he doesn't, fuck him!"

Apparently Lieutenant Baptist didn't care for the little shit any more than I did. His comment made me hoot. "Thanks."

He turned and pointed, and I followed his finger. "We've reviewed your neighbor's surveillance system…clear case of self-defense."

I couldn't help but make one of those I KNOW faces. "That's what I tried to tell the captain."

Lieutenant Baptist didn't look particularly bothered, but tried to explain away the captain's problem with me. "Yes, but look at it from an outside perspective…this would be the second death attributable to you in less than a week."

Cocking my head, I acknowledged the accusation. I surmised that the captain's hatred of me had nothing to do with the two dead bodies and had more to do with his dislike of Andrew. Even so, I couldn't help but state the obvious. "In my defense, both men were trying very hard to kill me." Keeping my features stoic, I gestured at the body bag. "Personally, I think I should get credit for saving the taxpayers some money."

He tittered at my comment. "While I may think so, the captain does not. He is trying to get promoted out of the UCD, and these incidents are shining a spotlight on our division."

"Not a good thing?" I asked.

The lanky officer did a belly laugh, reached up, and patted me on the shoulder. "Not when you're trying to get out of the UCD." He proudly looked at the other officers. "He doesn't take pride in what we do. He thinks that the Archive is a travesty, if not a crime against humanity itself."

From the sounds of things bigotry was rampant on both sides of the fence. "Most of the Archive doesn't think much of the humans either. I guess fair is fair. People seem to be shitty no matter their affiliation."

He struggled to find an argument but found none. "I suppose that's true." His face went blank and he looked up into my eyes. "Mind if I ask you a personal question?"

The way he said it made me cautious. "You can ask, but I reserve the right not to answer."

He pulled out his smartphone and showed it to me, pressing the play icon in the center of the screen. It was queued up to the point when Timothy fired the gun, and Baptist let it play for several seconds before he poked the screen, making it stop.

Pocketing the phone, he cocked his head to the side. "You didn't even twitch when he fired." He looked at the marred brick wall across the street. "It was obviously loaded with live rounds."

Raising an eyebrow, I waited. "Is there a question."

The man's blue-green eyes sparkled. "Care to tell me why you are so accustomed to gunshots?"

Over the last three decades I'd forgotten just how curious people were and I found their constant intrusions annoying. "I really don't, but if you want a hint I'd hang around the station. Once Sonia pulls my records I'm sure some unpleasant people will stop by to give her a piece of their mind."

Baptist's face darkened under his scraggly beard. "Who gave her...?" He looked over at the captain and shook his head. "I'll handle it."

Nodding my appreciation, I said, "I'd be very grateful."

He produced a card and handed it to me. "If you need anything let me know."

Taking the card, I shoved it into my back pocket. "I heard the captain cleaned out Martha's office. If there is anything he missed, I'd like to get my hands on it."

Baptist nodded as he thumbed back at Andrew. "Andrew informed me of your new position." He thought about my request. "I'll look to see if he overlooked anything in his haste. Will you be needing a desk in the near future?"

I shook my head. "I don't think so."

Baptist cut his eyes at the captain. "Don't let him run you out of the precinct if you want to work there."

The very idea that the captain could run me out of a wet paper bag amused me. "Nah, I'm good."

It was true. I wasn't sure why Martha had invested herself so heavily into the UCD, but I had a feeling that there were larger problems at hand. Problems she may have missed by being so ingrained into the local police force. And it was clear that the UCD had leaks, two of which were Sonia and the captain. God knew how many others there were.

He seemed disappointed at the answer but accepted it. "In that case I've got a full evening of paperwork. Keep in touch, and don't forget to call if I can assist you."

"Sure thing."

William strolled off without looking back to tend to the crime scene such as it was. It took nearly another hour before I could pull the car into the garage for the evening. Now that the NOPD were gone, we could get down to the real problem at hand…Walter Percy.

Isidore was still downstairs when I walked into the apartment and found Andrew at his desk wearing the old gold rimmed glasses. He waved me over. "Have a seat."

I suddenly felt like I'd been called to the principal's office when I took a seat in front of the desk. "Evening."

He grabbed a bottle of scotch and poured us both a stiff drink, pushing my glass across the desk to me. "About earlier—"

"Don't worry about it."

He raised a glass in my direction in a toast. His voice was calm and even. "I'm still curious as to who…Timothy, wasn't it?" He looked over at me for confirmation and I nodded. "Who did Timothy work for?"

Now we were back to where we'd started a few hours ago. I sat up straight in my seat, taking a long drink of the amber fluid. "I've got a few questions first."

Andrew looked only too pleased to accommodate me. "By all means, ask away."

I heard Isidore coming up the stairs and opening the door. Keeping my eyes focused on Andrew, I leaned forward. "As far as I can tell I'm the *vigiles* for the southern district of North America. Is that right?"

Andrew waved Isidore over and poured him a drink. "That's correct."

Taking another drink, I toasted Isidore. "As such, I answer directly to Amelia in this case, right?"

Andrew made an unpleasant face but grudgingly agreed. "Only if there was something you need clarification on, but I'm sure I could be of more assistance considering I'm right here."

Making a deliberate show of sitting the drink on the desk and the file in my lap, I eyed my uncle. "In that case, I'm going to insist that you let me do my job." Andrew started to object but I held a hand up to stop him. "Look, I don't mind keeping you informed, and I'll even give you the information you want. Make no mistake, however…this is my job and I won't tolerate you getting in the middle of it." I kept my eyes fixated on him to ensure he understood how serious I was. "If you can agree to those terms I'll give you the file. If you can't, I'll be out of here tonight, and when it's over we can talk. The choice is yours to make."

Isidore was ashen and tried his best to be invisible, drinking his scotch very quietly, looking between the two of us.

Andrew chewed this over. He clearly wasn't happy with the arrangement. "Very well."

Both Isidore and I let out an audible breath. I put the file on the desk and scooted it towards him. "There are two files in there...one of them on Timothy, whom you just met, and the other one is on Chan Wong, the man who attacked me on Sunday evening."

Andrew took the file and leafed through the pages, skimming them for the information he wanted. After several seconds his mouth parted and his face darkened. He glanced up at me and then back down at the page. "Walter?"

"That's what it looks like." Andrew started to get up. "Sit down!"

Andrew stayed seated. "We've got work to do."

Shaking my head, I gestured for him to hand the file back. "I've got work to do." Looking over at Isidore, I glared at him. "If I'm right, your job is to keep Andrew safe?"

Isidore scrambled back in his seat. "Don't bring me into this."

"Answer the question," I demanded.

Isidore moaned, hanging his head in defeat. "Yeah, that's my job."

Releasing Isidore from my gaze, I turned to Andrew. "I can't let you go out there. Let me do my job or you're going to make me forcibly restrain you."

Andrew considered me for a long moment, thinking I might be joking. Soon he realized I wasn't. His shoulders slumped when the fight left him. "What can I do to help?"

Tension seeped out of me. I'd been prepared to follow through with the threat if necessary and that wouldn't have been pleasant. "I'm going to need more information." Pulling the clip and single round out of my pocket, I pushed them across the desk. "Can you tell me if these were enchanted?"

Andrew picked up the bullet, focusing his attention on it for several seconds, then shook his head. "They're standard ammunition as far as I can tell."

Retrieving the items, I took another drink. "I'm guessing he didn't have a secondary focusing item since he didn't use magic."

Andrew sneered. "Some witches are arrogant like that." He looked over at me with a smirk. "Not that I think it would've made much of a difference if he had."

From the sounds of things Andrew was developing a notion regarding my abilities. "What do you mean?"

Andrew poured himself a second glass, letting his thoughts flow with the whiskey. "It's just a theory, but I think it's a pretty good one." He took a long drink. "The gash you received from Chan on Sunday night was healed up by the time you got to the hospital, right?"

Shifting in my seat uncomfortably, I replied, "Mostly...there was still a scab and it was tender, but yeah, the bleeding had stopped."

Andrew wore a eureka expression. "And then you met Timothy later that morning and he hit you with a significant amount of power."

"I suppose."

Andrew gave me a quick eye roll for my disbelief, then continued. "After that you snapped a focusing object with little more than a broken door to show for it."

"True," I replied, wondering where the hell he was going with this.

Andrew's face turned serious. "When you showed us the cut it was little more than a scar." He set down his glass, trying to puzzle it out. "You seem to absorb other people's abilities, using them to heal, become stronger, and God knows what else." His laugh was dry, yet lacked all humor. "You are essentially immune to every type of magical energy that can be sent at you...at least thus far."

After I thought about it, I couldn't help but agree with him. Every time I was exposed to magic, I felt better, stronger, more alive. "I can't argue the point."

Isidore looked ill and a shiver ran up his form. "You'd better keep that superpower quiet."

Glancing over, I gave him a questioning look. "Why?"

Andrew's voice cut through the silence with a hard edge. "Because you are the Archive's worst nightmare." He struggled with the thoughts that swam through his mind. "They've spent years, decades, and in some cases centuries learning their craft. They've developed entire defenses based in their own power and how to defeat magic." He looked up at me and I thought I saw terror. "And here you are immune to it all. They have nothing that can stop you and you're one of us." He visibly paled. "They'll panic."

I was sure that a bullet between the eyes would stop me pretty quickly. Yet I could see his point. "How about we all agree to keep this between us?"

Andrew looked at Isidore, who quickly nodded, and then back to me. "I've got a feeling that there's more to you than that, but you have our word that it won't leave this room."

I still felt highly uncomfortable, but felt a need to change the subject to satisfy my own curiosity. "Thanks." Turning my attention to Isidore, I asked, "Can I see your wrists?"

He appeared uncomfortable looking over at Andrew, who nodded his approval. He pulled back the sleeves of his shirt, exposing his writs. They were heavily mutilated, but I could still make out the Pax Romana sigil in the same place I'd seen the Aquila on Gabriel.

Pointing at the sigil, I asked. "Amelia's mark?"

His face flushed. "If by Amelia you mean the *vigiles'* mark, then yes."

Looking at him inquiringly, I thought he must have misunderstood my question. "Vigiles' mark?" Then again, maybe he hadn't. "You mean they're all like that?"

Isidore frowned and looked at the mark again. "Every one I've ever seen."

The Aquila couldn't be that rare, could it? "And how many would that be?"

He thought about it for a minute and grunted. "Maybe a dozen or so. Why do you ask?"

Clamping my mouth shut, I shook my head and lied. "I was curious about something I read in one of the books. They didn't have a picture, so I thought I'd ask to see yours."

Andrew cleared his throat, drawing our attention back to him. He gave me an odd look. "And where have you been all day? Where did you find this file?"

"There was an old storage unit Martha used out in Metairie that had a small treasure trove of information and a few items." I thumbed back at the wooden crate containing the swords and armor.

Andrew focused on the crate, noticing it for the first time. "I didn't know she had an office out there."

Scrambling to cover, I said, "It is more of a storage unit than an office."

Isidore's stomach growled loud enough for us to hear. He raised his hands as if to say "What do you expect?" "Anyone else hungry?"

I was starved! Andrew got up and headed for the kitchen with Isidore and me in tow.

Chapter 15

Thursday June 4th

Sleep escaped me most of the night. When I did find it, on those rare occasions it was full of dark and disturbing images. Waking with a start one last time, I gave up the pursuit of something that was obviously not going to happen. I stopped at the dresser long enough to pull out a fresh set of clothes before heading into the bath for a long hot shower. Twenty minutes later I was dressed and sitting at the desk, looking through some of the older books trying to find the Aquila. If what Isidore said was true, and there was no reason to doubt him, the Aquila marking was unique.

Glancing over at the clock—4:00 a.m.—I got up and headed for the living room, but as I passed the kitchen I heard someone. Pushing the door open, I found Isidore pulling food out of the fridge.

"Need some help?" I asked.

Isidore jumped, nearly dropping a pack of sausages. "Jesus!" He tossed the sausage onto the counter before grabbing another. "Don't sneak up on people!"

I should feel bad about spooking him but I didn't. "Old habits die hard."

Craning his neck around the door, he gave me an alluring gaze. "Still not going to tell me where you got those habits?"

Blowing out a puff of air between my lips, I squinted. "Not today."

He feigned disgust and shooed me away from the counter. "Go sit and I'll whip something up for us to eat." He turned back questioningly "You are hungry, aren't you?"

I patted my stomach. "I could eat."

He harrumphed. "Damn straight you can eat!" He held up one of the white packets of sausage in my direction. "Made this myself! Nothing beats homemade breakfast sausage."

I was more than a little impressed he'd gone to the trouble of making his own. "Seriously? I haven't had homemade sausage since I was a kid."

Ripping off the white butcher paper, he beamed with pride. "Then you are in for a rare treat." He waved a hand in the air casually. "I'm not sure what they fed you on the reservation." He beamed back at me brightly. "You did live on the reservation, right?"

Shifting in my seat, I forced a neutral expression onto my face. "No, my parents had a place about ten miles away. But for all the time we spent there, I might as well have."

If he noticed my discomfort, he didn't show it. "Well, I don't know what they made there, but this is my own secret recipe."

Pushing the chair back onto two legs, I gave him a thumbs up. "Can't wait to try it."

He placed an old cast iron skillet on the gas burner and set to work making breakfast. Holding an egg in one hand, he gave me an exasperated face. "Fried?"

With a sheepish expression, I nodded. "If it isn't too much trouble."

He groaned at my request with a twinkle in his eye. "You and Andrew like the strangest shit! It's like you've never experience the glory of scrambled eggs."

Being the kind and generous man that I was, I felt a need to point out recent history. "You made scrambled eggs the other morning."

He swiveled around with a look on his face that bespoke the mock horror at the memory. "I know, and you still didn't appreciate their awesomeness!"

Okay, he had a point. Something about a runny yolk made me feel all warm and fuzzy. "I suppose that's true."

He tossed six patties into the pan with a sizzle and the aroma of herbs and spices filled the air. He nudged each of them with a spatula before looking back at me with a serious expression. "I take it you didn't sleep well because of what happened last night?"

Raising an eyebrow at the man, I said, "Huh?"

He turned to nudge the sausages again before shifting his gaze back to me, looking apprehensive. "You do recall shoving a knife through someone's heart last night, right?"

Oh, that. I suppose that might make some people lose sleep. I wasn't one of them, mind you, but I could see his mistake. "You mean Timothy?"

Making sure not to burn the sausages, he grumbled. "Yes."

Letting my chair click against the floor, I kept my voice steady. "Sorry to say that he never crossed my mind in such a way to keep me up at night. He was a clue and now he's dead. Nothing more, nothing less."

Isidore winced at the callous tone. "I'm guessing that wasn't the first time you've been in a position to take someone's life."

That was the world record of understatements. The last twenty-eight years had been spent honing very specific talents. I was the boogieman to more than just the Archive because of my unique skills.

Fixing my gaze at the back of Isidore's head, I responded. "That would be a fair assumption."

Isidore flipped the patties and focused on the pan, not daring to look back. "From what I can tell you're handy with a knife." He made a show of waving the spatula around in the air. "I saw a couple of swords in that crate you hauled up. Got something against guns?"

Pushing the chair back onto two legs, I puffed out a breath. "Guns are fine, but swords, knives, and other such items never run out of ammunition." I made a face as I thought about it. "Guns are loud and impersonal. Edged weapons make the whole affair more intimate, if not meaningful."

He considered the words while pushing the patties around in the skillet. "I suppose that's true." He risked a glance over his shoulder. "What kind of swords were they?"

I couldn't stop the crooked grin that painted itself on my face. "One is a wakizashi, a Japanese short sword. The other is a Roman gladius. Both of which are genuine antiques from what I can tell." Shifting uncomfortably in my seat, I spoke to the floor. "I believe that unless you're willing to be up close and personal and have your victim's warm blood rush over your hands, you shouldn't own a gun. Guns make killing people easy and highly impersonal."

Isidore didn't speak right away. Pulling a plate out of the cabinet, he folded paper towels to cover it, then put the patties on it one at a time. He finally found his voice. "Killing people is always personal, whether or not people realize it. Death visits their families, breaks hearts, and sheds tears. Death is always personal!"

Raising my tea glass in his direction, I nodded. "Agreed."

Adding more sausage to the pan, keeping his tone low and even, he spoke. "Considering the swords are antiques, what are you going to do with them?"

Throwing my hands out, I sniggered. "Use them, of course!" Rocking my chair back and forth, I considered my next words carefully. "They are the very symbol of my office." There was more to it than that. I felt a need I couldn't explain to use these swords in particular. "Perhaps not as easy to carry around as a pistol, but still."

Isidore snorted. "Three feet of gleaming steel is harder to hide than a pistol."

My mind drifted back to the sniper rifles I'd used over the years. Even broken down, most of them were over three feet long, which meant that carrying the gladius or the wakizashi shouldn't be that difficult. I'd spent years creating covers for my old weapon of choice. It shouldn't be that difficult to modify those to carry the swords.

I took another sip of tea. "It shouldn't be that difficult to handle when they are needed."

Isidore flipped the patties again before pointing the spatula at my hand. "Remember the markings on the other side of your hand...you are to create and keep the peace."

Nodding, my face became serious. "It might surprise you to know that 'the peace' is normally created through the willingness of a few to do great violence in its name."

Isidore plated the next round of sausages, struggling to disagree but failing. "It has been known to happen that way." He paused as he patted the sausages with a paper towel. "It's good to see that you can keep Andrew in check. I was concerned that with Martha gone that might be an issue."

There it was again, the irrational fear of my uncle. "Is he really that bad?"

Isidore nearly dropped the spatula, whipping around to face me. "I told you that he wiped out an entire family just to make a point, or isn't that scary enough?" Turning back to the stove, he shivered at the thought. "Forget about it. It isn't as if you can truly comprehend what he's capable of."

"That's not very informative," I replied.

He turned the eggs, glancing over his shoulder to make sure I was paying attention. "Imagine a man who can tear your mind apart." He shuddered. "Or make you believe that you're on fire, make your blood boil. Then there's my personal favorite, ripping someone apart at the cellular level." He plated the eggs as he turned to face me. "And that's all before he gets angry."

Leaning forward, I let my chair hit the floor with a loud clack. Okay then. I was starting to see the picture. No wonder everyone shits their pants when it came to Andrew. It also painted Robert in a whole new light. Goddamn, that man was stupid. "How did Martha keep him in check?"

Isidore placed two sausage patties on my plate before handing it to me. "He loved her! He couldn't bring himself to defy her wishes." He pointed at the food. "Eat up before it gets cold."

Giving him the thumbs up, I tore into my breakfast. He was right, the sausage was incredible.

I'd just washed off my plate when Andrew stalked into the room. He didn't look well. "Could you come with me?"

With a faint smile I waved Andrew out the door. "Sure."

He led me down the hall and into the room with all the stones. He waved his arm out at mine as he pointed at the bottom of the case. "You see that?"

The first thing I noticed was that the misshapen diamond was a bit larger, but marginally so. Then I found what he was talking about. There atop the sea of blood red tear shaped garnets lay two pristine pear shaped aquamarine stones. My stomach churned as the implications hit me.

Standing upright, I looked at my uncle. "I see them."

Andrew's face was taut, his voice shook, and a slight tremor overtook him for a moment. "The only thing that's changed since the last time I was in here are those two stones, and the fact that two men have died at your hand." He looked down at the red stones and back at me. "Do you think that's a coincidence?"

There wasn't any point in lying about it. I shook my head and my shoulders slumped. "You believe there's a correlation, and I'm betting you're right."

Andrew leaned over, peering through the glass walls of the box as his eyes widened. When he spoke again his voice was somber. "I can only imagine how hard your life has been over the last twenty-eight years." He stood up straight, looking down at me as his eyes threatened to let loose tears he was barely holding back. "I'm here for you if you ever need to talk. I won't judge. I can't judge."

Keeping my expression neutral, I nodded.

The heartbroken smile he gave me made me feel a measure of comfort. He clapped me on the shoulder hard and pulled me in for a hug. "Remember, men of real character have always been made out of hard choices and harder lives. It appears that you've had both." He waved for me to follow. "Some of us haven't had breakfast yet."

"You go on. I'll catch up in a minute."

He looked back at me one last time before turning to leave. I waited for the door to close behind him before scouring the room. A few minutes later I found a large swath of black velvet, which I draped over the display case. If I was right, there would be several more stones to join the pile before this was over.

When I made my way back to the kitchen, Andrew and Isidore were in the middle of eating breakfast. Looking down at

Andrew, I gave him my best smile. "Think you could tell me where Martha lived?" I grimaced. "No chance you'd have a key to the place as well?"

Andrew suddenly didn't want his breakfast anymore and dropped the fork onto the plate, shoving a hand into his pocket. He pulled a key off the keyring and tossed it to me. "She lived at number 11 Audubon Place." He picked up a napkin and dabbed it at the corner of his mouth. "I'll make a call after breakfast so they can put you on the list."

"A list?" I asked.

Isidore sniffed. "You're about to visit one of the most exclusive neighborhoods in all of New Orleans. You better believe there's a list!"

Damn! Just what I needed, a bunch of nosey rich people with their overpriced security dogs up my ass while I worked. Smiling, I gave my uncle a thumbs up. "Great!" Thumbing back at the hall, I said, "I've got to grab a few things from my room. Let me know when I can head over."

Returning to my room, I picked up the wooden crate and placed it on the bed. Pulling the leather armor over my legs and chest and looking in the mirror, I saw that I looked like an overly enthusiastic biker. Removing the leggings didn't help, so I stuffed the entire outfit into a duffle bag along with both swords. Lugging it downstairs, I tossed the bag into the back seat of the car before heading up to wait on Andrew.

It was just after 7:00 when I got clearance to visit Martha's, and I headed down St. Charles Avenue following the Google navigator. When I was about a block away I noticed a massive twelve-foot-high brick wall running next to the road. Turning onto Audubon Place, I was stopped in front of a very practical, heavily armored but fashionable iron gate manned by armed NOPD officers, who stepped out of their little air conditioned brick gatehouse to inspect my ID.

Several minutes later they waved me through, telling me to keep my speed under fifteen miles per hour and not to deviate from my destination. To ensure that I not only understood their directions but followed them, one of the officers escorted me to my destination. Lucky me! I pulled down the long cobblestone drive that stretched the length of the property and parked in front of the garage.

A shiver ran up my spine as I shut off the engine. A giant oak blocked the view of the second story from where I sat. Opening the door, goose flesh ran up my arms and back. The hair on the back of my neck stood up and my gut twisted.

I wanted to grab the duffel bag out of the back seat and strap on the armor, but the NOPD officer that parked at the end of the drive was keeping watch. Pulling the key out of my pocket, I headed for the back door a good hundred feet away. As I slipped the key into the lock I thought I heard something above me. Twisting the key, I pushed the door open and stepped back to get a look. For a split second I thought I saw Brad, but then my world went white.

Fire enveloped my body, the world sounded like it was being torn apart, and the shockwave lifted me off my feet and sent me sprawling. Instinctively I threw my arms in front of my face as glass, wood, and brick pelted my body. The sickening feeling of freefalling through the air out of control caused my stomach to lurch into my chest. Then the massive nine-foot hedge lining the neighbor's yard slowed my descent as I crashed through it and landed with a heavy thud, tearing a large swath of grass out of their perfectly manicured lawn.

I hurt and it took me several seconds to take full inventory of my body parts. My hands, face, and arms were cut, scratched, and bruised, but I'd live. Thankfully the long sleeved shirt that George made me had taken most of the abuse. Things would've been better if I hadn't rolled up my sleeves earlier, but that was being absolutely ungrateful. Standing, I stumbled back through the hedge, nearly colliding with the NOPD officer who'd run down the drive to check on me.

He looked me over and pointed at the ground. "Take a seat, son." He clicked the radio on his shoulder. "Dispatch, we have a survivor." He looked at me oddly and then clicked it again. "He appears to be disoriented...tell them to step on it!"

The funny thing was the closer I got to the house the better I felt. Looking down at my arms, I saw that the majority of the cuts were closing. I wanted to get inside but that was impossible. The fire may have started out magically, but now the house itself was on fire. While I might be immune to the source of ignition, actual flames would still hurt like hell, and given the opportunity would kill me. Whatever magic was in the air quickly faded, leaving me scraped and bruised but otherwise okay.

The officer put a hand on my shoulder. "Sir, I'd appreciate it if you'd take a seat." He pointed at the ground again. "I've got a job to do."

The fire truck arrived in record time, but there wasn't any hope of putting it out before the house collapsed on itself. Now it was a matter of making sure the neighbors' houses didn't burn down with it. As for me, the EMT's were insisting that I go to the hospital. I, on the other hand, wasn't listening. Instead, I sat there for two hours until they cleared my car and let me pull out and head back to Andrew's.

According to the firemen they were guessing it was a gas leak, and when I'd opened the door it had ignited. I'd dealt with explosions, a lot of them, and this wasn't gas. Someone had set the fire using magic, intending to kill someone, and I was betting it wasn't me they were after. Andrew needed to beef up security, and do it quickly.

Chapter 16

It was around noon when I pulled through the gate, locking it behind me before backing into the garage. The large oak tree that prevented me from seeing Martha's house had protected the Tucker from the flying debris when the place exploded. I wasn't sure what type of insurance Andrew had, but I was fairly certain they wouldn't be pleased with me destroying it on my second trip out.

Once inside the house I took the stairs two at a time, landing on the third from the top and causing a loud creak. Pushing the door open, I found Andrew and Isidore at the desk going over paperwork.

Isidore pulled a face as he sniffed the air, and he looked at me with enormous disgust. "What in the hell have you been burning?"

Andrew looked up from his paperwork, his eyes flicking across me and settling on my arms, face, and neck. He laid down his pen and leaned back in his seat. His voice was steady, calm, and full of concern. "What happened?"

Glancing at my arms, I shrugged at him haplessly. "Martha's house blew up before burning to the ground. Sorry about that. The 'official report' thus far is a gas leak."

Andrew raised an eyebrow as he studied me. "But you think otherwise."

I wanted nothing more than to grab a shower and change, but this had to be handled first. "I've dealt with a lot of explosions over the years, and I can assure you this wasn't gas." Stepping closer, I held up my forearm to show them a long jagged gash that was rapidly healing. "I was pretty cut up from the explosion, but as you can see I'm left with mostly brush burns and a few bruises."

Andrew leaned forward, taking in the information. "It was magical in nature then."

Keeping my gaze fixed on Andrew, I continued. "That's the theory I'm working under at the moment. I'm fairly certain, however, that I wasn't the target."

Isidore snapped his head up immediately, understanding the implication. "Who do you think they were after?"

Cutting my eyes at Isidore, I quickly returned my full attention to Andrew. "Well, I was driving the Tucker, and let's face it, there aren't many people who'd be visiting Martha's now that she's passed away."

"You mean murdered!" Andrew growled.

My gaze never wavered. "Murdered." Letting the word sink in, I said, "If you think it through you'll come to the same conclusion I did."

Andrew took in a deep breath, slowly letting it out. "Me."

Standing at parade rest, I waited for the reality of it to truly hit home. "While I respect the fact that you're a powerful person in your own right, and that you've enlisted Isidore's round the clock assistance, I'd strongly advise finding a few trustworthy individuals to beef up security."

Andrew wanted to argue with me, but he could tell that I wasn't going to take no for an answer. He looked over at Isidore and nodded. "Could you give Alexander a call for me? Tell him I'm in need of his services."

Isidore got to his feet and pulled a mobile out of his pocket. "I'll take care of it."

Isidore was out the door and down the stairs before I could say anything. Looking back at my uncle, I eyed him curiously. "You can trust this Alexander?"

Andrew leaned forward and dropped his head into his hands, mumbling, "Without question."

"You're sure about that?" I asked again.

Andrew raised his head, closing his eyes slowly. "He feels indebted to me." He shifted in his seat. "Alexander and his clan have sworn a blood oath to protect me," he mumbled more to himself than me.

For a split second I thought about inquiring but decided against it. Waving a hand at myself, I thumbed back at my room. "I'm going to get cleaned up and put on some fresh clothes before I head back out."

Clean up took a bit longer than normal due to the fact I was sore and bruised from head to toe. My back had taken the brunt of the impact when I tore a large section out of the grass. It was still scraped and I had a really nice black and purple bruise from my shoulder blades to the top of my ass.

After dressing I gingerly made my way back to the living room, where I found Isidore and Andrew at the table. "Afternoon, gentlemen."

Isidore winced at the sight of me trying to walk. "You going to be okay?"

Raising my hands in a what-choice-do-I-have manner, I meandered over. "I'll be fine in a day or so. I'm just a little sore."

Isidore snorted. "Most people would be a little more upset."

Trying to sit made me flinch in pain. "This isn't the first time and I'm sure it won't be the last, especially considering the job." Trying to make myself comfortable and failing, I finally turned my attention to Andrew. "You've got everything handled here?"

Andrew's demeanor was easy to read. He wasn't happy with the arrangements and that was putting it mildly. "Alexander and his people will be here within the hour."

With more than a little effort I turned to Isidore. "You know this Alexander?"

Isidore looked confused when he answered. "Very well."

"He can be trusted?" I asked.

Isidore scoffed. "Absolutely!"

Keeping my eyes fixated on his, I said, "I'll hold you to that."

Isidore blanched. "I promise you have nothing to worry about."

"Good…." Grunting, I turned back to Andrew. "Considering my best two leads have either died or burned to the ground, I need to work on finding new leads." Putting a hand on the arm of the chair, I started to push myself up. "Let Alexander know I'll be back before sundown."

Andrew held up a hand for me to stay put. "Where do you think you're going?"

Giving him one of those you-have-to-be-kidding looks, I got to my feet. "I've still got work to do."

Andrew let out a breath. "I think you should stay put until things calm down."

Leaning over, I stared down at Andrew. "And just how's that going to happen? It isn't like someone else is going to handle it." Groaning, I pushed myself upright. "You've got our roles mixed up, Governor. You're the one that needs to stay put, and I need to go out there and find the bad guys." Softening my features, I tried to appear sympathetic. "Please let me do my job." Before he could mount a suitable offense, I waved and headed for the door. "Have a good afternoon."

After plugging Walter's address into the phone's navigator, I pulled out onto 4th Street. Twenty minutes later I was on Lake Avenue enjoying the cool breeze coming off the lake. Massive houses of every conceivable shape and size littered the street, with no sort of rhyme or reason to their designs. Everything was mismatched as each owner tried to be more outlandish than the next. My destination was no different.

It was a pretentious and gaudy expansive white cement stucco building made up mostly of one floor. I say mostly because the main entrance, such as it was, made up a second story. The monstrosity stretched out for nearly an entire city block. The equally massive muted U shaped drive centered on the entrance was made out of a stark white cement that created a nasty glare in the afternoon sun. White marble statues stood in the tiny lawn near the street, while their massive counterparts stood like Atlas against the walls of the home, holding up the flat roof.

The intent was obviously to impress, intimidate, and belittle visitors. I, however, felt sad that someone needed to spend so much cash in an effort to compensate for what I had to assume were their own shortcomings. Walter shouldn't have bothered…much like his frail and twisted form, Mother Nature would have her way with this eyesore as well. Mold would creep into the stucco, causing it to chip and crumble. The flat roof would collect water, eventually caving in under its own weight, and finally the wind would tear it apart bit by bit.

I brought the Tucker to a stop at the apex of the drive, about thirty feet from the double oak doors that led into the home proper. Leaning over the seat, I grabbed the duffle bag and dropped it next to me. I strapped on the leather armor before securing the gladius and wakizashi at the waist. This was my first official house call as *vigiles*…I might as well look the part.

Striding up to the front door, I found it slightly ajar, and with a gentle push it silently swung open. Cautiously, I stuck my head through only to find the foyer empty, and when I say empty, I mean four walls and a floor kind of empty. Taking a deep breath, I focused, dialing up my senses and preparing for any unseen danger before taking the first full step inside. The following three rooms were equally barren. The next room held the first and only piece of furniture…a small, round dinner table at its center. From where I stood I saw a cavernous room that was meant to be a den and should contain sofas, chairs, and people. The massive double french doors framed a picturesque lawn and a view of the lake.

Approaching the table, I caught sight of an old flip phone laying there. It began to ring about the time I noticed the camera at the far end of the room. With a smile and a wave, I picked up the phone. Flipping it open, I placed the receiver to my ear, strolling towards the electronic eye.

"Hello."

I recognized Walter's voice instantly. It was raspy, winded, and genuinely intrigued. "Good afternoon." He paused as he took in a long ragged breath. "Gavin, isn't it?"

Stopping a few feet from the wall, I looked up at the camera as I nodded. "Good job, Walter."

He tittered, which caused him to wheeze and cough. "You're smarter than I've been told."

Raising an eyebrow at the lens, I smirked. "That's normally the case."

I could hear him shifting in the background. I imagined he was leaning closer to the monitor. "I'm curious…do you mind if I ask you a few questions while I have your undivided attention?"

Wagging my finger at the camera, I shook my head. "Not unless you want to answer a few of mine. A sort of tit for tat type of thing."

The shifting in the background continued, and I heard the whir of oxygen being pumped into a tube followed by a chunky, chest rattling cough. "I'll go first."

Of course he would. Asshole. I raised an impatient hand at the camera. "All right, shoot."

His ragged voice grated through the receiver. "I've got to know. Are you a disgusting human, or one of those filthy werebeasts?"

Cocking my head to the side, I snorted. "That's just rude."

His voice became hard and angry. "That wasn't an answer!"

With my free hand I pulled the wakizashi, swinging it high and cutting the camera in two, causing it to spark as the lens crashed to the floor. "It's a question I don't feel is worthy of an answer!"

He croaked and groaned, and I heard something slamming against the floor in the background. "You're one to talk about rudeness after invading my home and then destroying my equipment!"

"I don't like being watched. Especially by an old man that is constantly doing the heavy breathing thing in my ear."

He coughed and wheezed again. "Too bad we can't continue our conversation, but you've been a very bad man."

He paused for just a moment and snorted. "I'm surprised that Andrew would employ someone of your nature."

Jerking the phone away from my head, I glared down at the thing before putting it back to my ear. "And what the hell is that supposed to mean?"

His laughter was dry and rattled around in his chest like it was going to break something. "I hope you've made peace with God, son. You're going to meet him very soon."

The line went dead, the room went unnaturally dark, and I felt a tingling throughout my body. Looking down at my hands, I watched as cuts and bruises healed and vanished. It didn't take long for me to feel normal again as the inky blackness poured into the room, trying to blot out every last bit of light. The power wrapped itself around me, coursing through my veins, and I felt an odd sensation creeping through me. The darkness engulfed me, wrapping itself around me ever tighter, and I felt my body begin to change and morph into something new.

My skin tingled, and I lifted my left hand. I watched as it began to glow, elongate, and turn into something less flesh and blood and more akin to living blue flames. Looking over at the right hand that held the wakizashi, I saw that the flesh had turned into an armored onyx glove. In the light of my left hand I saw the gray black long flowing robes enveloping my body. The sight of it chilled my heart as the spectrum of my vision changed.

There in the darkness stood a dozen souls. I don't mean that figuratively. I could see the glowing orange outline of Chan and Timothy standing out amongst the other mortal souls in shades of blue and gray. The one thing they all had in common was the fact they'd all died at my hand in the last month. Frankly, I was surprised that there weren't more of them.

The little girl at the front of the spectral horde was no more than ten years old. She had a hole about the size of my pinky on her left temple, and another about the size of a grapefruit at the back of her head where the bullet had torn through. She'd been the first to die twenty-one days ago. I'd pulled the trigger and splattered her brains all over her friends that stood nearby, just before the IED (improvised explosive device) that she was wearing blew up, causing a chain reaction that leveled an entire city block. Now she and the others were here for their pound of flesh.

Taking a deep breath, I looked at them and shook my head. "Please don't."

I wasn't pleading for my safety, but theirs.

The little girl's specter wailed, shattering windows, and then she charged me with vengeance in her eyes. Waiting until she was within arm's length, I snatched her up with my left hand. She howled in pain as the flames charred the spectral flesh. Her claws tore at me, passing through the enchanted cloth and digging into my flesh, allowing blood to flow freely. The blue flames intensified and her neck glowed orange, then red, before fire engulfed her form. She screeched, twitching in agony. Instinct kicked in and I thrusted the wakizashi up through her gut and out her skull, and with little more than a puff of smoke she simply ceased her existence.

Tendrils struck out from the billowing gray-black robe around me, pulling the tiny puff of smoke that had once been a soul into its swelling form. I felt her power added to my own and the others howled their displeasure. Several darted out of the crowd to score vicious blows against my midsection. I brought the wakizashi down again and again, cleaving souls in two only to have their remains pulled into the living remnants of the death shroud I wore. Even so my blood ran freely to the floor, but I wasn't about to leave this world without a fight.

Chan took off in a run, ducking into a footballers' stance, lodging a shoulder in my gut and driving me back several feet. Grunting, I brought my hand down, slamming it between his shoulder blades, knocking him to the floor hard enough to shatter the marble. I followed up with a kick that lifted him off the floor, and he flew at an odd angle into the others.

Charging ahead, I brought down the wakizashi in a big slash, slicing several specters in half, allowing their essences to heal my wounds and embolden my attacks. My left hand shot out and caught Chan by the back of the neck. I slammed him into the nearest wall and shoved the wakizashi up through his right side and out through his left collarbone, causing him to turn into a blazing orange and red mist that wrapped itself around me.

A jolt of energy passed through me, my eyes felt hot, and the world turned to shades of orange and red. Red lightning poured out of me in every direction like power from a Tesla coil, enveloping the nearest souls that were still standing and instantly extinguishing them. The red lightning wrapped itself around Timothy, pulling him closer. It turned him around to face me and I opened my maw, tearing into his spectral flesh with my teeth. He howled for perhaps a split second before his form erupted into the same orange and red mist as Chan.

Power continued to course through my veins, but there was no one left to kill. No souls left to devour, yet my hunger was everlasting. Now it was me who howled in rage. The hunger and power left me in a rush. I felt the house rumble and the walls around me shatter. Making a mad dash for the double french doors leading out into the backyard, I crashed through the glass at top speed. Rolling to my feet, I looked back as the center of the house caved in on itself.

I guessed I didn't need to wait for nature to run its course!

A few minutes later the world returned to normal. The robes faded and I watched in fascination as the flames receded and my hand returned to its naturally marred state. This hadn't been a complete waste of time...I now knew for certain that Walter was behind all of this.

Pondering the implications of someone being able to summon souls from whatever lay beyond to do their bidding unnerved me. That and other thoughts made the drive back to Andrew's place a long one. Walter hadn't been what I'd expected.

Chapter 17

The late evening sun hung low in the purpling sky above, keeping the air thick and steamy. I pulled off St. Charles Avenue heading for Coliseum. Making the block, I turned into the drive only to have my progress stopped by a man who made me look small by comparison. My first thought was that Timothy had a friend, but then I remembered with a personality like his I doubted he had those. On the other hand, Andrew had called for additional security and this man would certainly fit the bill.

Throwing the car into park, I stepped out of the Tucker to greet the bear of a man. It was then that I had a vague recollection of seeing the man with Isidore at the funeral. This had to be Alexander.

Even though he only had an inch or two on me in height, the massive barrel chest and body to match made me look puny standing this close. The additional fifty pounds of muscle rippled through the loose fitting jeans and long sleeved flannel shirt with every movement he made. An equally long beard matched his long black hair. His eyes were a deep chestnut brown that seemed to peer through me.

The man had a Hell's Angel vibe mixed with something more gentle, yet far more dangerous. Sticking one of his massive hands in my direction, he gave me the slightest of smiles and a gentle nod. His voice was a deep, rumbling thing. "You must be Gavin." He gave me an appraising eye. "You were at the funeral with Andrew."

When I took his hand, I was surprised to find that the big man's grip was firm without being a vice. He clearly had nothing to prove to the likes of me. "I am, and I was."

He waved a hand and two men I hadn't seen earlier pulled the gates open. "I'm Alexander." Keeping his grip firm, he waved back at the drive. "When you get settled into the job I'd like to have a word."

Keeping my eyes on his, I was instantly concerned and a little curious. "Is there a problem?"

Alexander's chest heaved as a big belly laugh came rolling out of him. "Not at all." He clapped me on the shoulder hard enough to knock me a few steps to the side. "It can wait till this is handled." His amusement faded as he locked his eyes onto mine. "If you need assistance with anything, anything at all, you let me know." He pulled out a card and stuffed it into my hand. "I've got plenty of people, all of which want to help should it be needed."

It didn't take a genius to figure out that wasn't an offer he made lightly or often. "I'll keep that in mind if things get hairy."

His face went blank and the big man stood up straight. "Did you just make a werepeople joke?" The edges of his mouth started to twitch, and then he laughed as he smacked me on the shoulder again. "Just joshing ya, son!" He waved me back to the car. "Go on and get upstairs. Andrew's been looking for ya."

Pointing to the dashboard of the car where my phone sat, I said, "He could've called."

Alexander chortled. "He still isn't used to those things."

Grumbling, I moved the car into the garage. When I pulled the door closed I turned to thank Alexander, but he and the men were gone. Scanning the yard, I expected to see them walking around the side of the house, but I was wrong. I saw no trace of them. Heading through the back door I thought I saw someone, but when I turned there was nothing there. Spooky as hell.

Opening the door to the apartment, I found Andrew at his desk talking to Isidore and looking particularly amused. He gave Isidore a knowing glance and Isidore turned and let out a chuckle.

Andrew couldn't keep the mirth out of his voice. "Welcome back."

They were absolutely full of themselves. Glancing behind me before closing the door, I turned to face them, annoyance building.

"Did I miss something?" I said flatly.

Isidore pushed himself around in his chair and snickered. "Have fun out on the Lakefront?"

Closing my eyes in frustration, I groused, "I suppose my trip to Walter's house has somehow preceded me?"

Andrew sniggered. "You could say that. There was a report of my...your car being spotted at 1601 Lakeview Drive just before the place collapsed." Andrew couldn't hide his delight.

Taking a seat, I threw my hands up in disgust. "Before you get upset, the place was empty when I walked in." My frustration with the visit got the better of me. "It didn't stay that way however. Shit got weird fast."

Andrew's amusement slipped. "What do you mean?"

The denarius told me to tread carefully. "What I mean is Walter is a fucking necromancer."

Andrew's face tightened and his back went rigid. "Are you sure?"

My confusion and anger flowed together as the words rushed out. "Yeah, I'm sure." A part of my mind fought to keep me from saying that ghosts were real. "Walter was able to summon Chan, Timothy, and several others from beyond the veil."

Isidore shuddered, his voice hollow. "A necromancer? You're sure?"

Andrew remained rigid, his voice tight. "You're positive?"

Sitting upright, I glared at them. "Unless there is some other creature out there that can summon the souls of the dead to do their bidding, then yes, I'm fucking sure."

Andrew winced, his voice grave. "I've heard rumors, but no one has ever been able to prove it until now."

Leaning back again, I felt the denarius pulsate in anger. With effort I turned my attention to Andrew. "This is just one more crime in a long list against the bastard."

Andrew turned a nasty shade of green when he spoke. "How did you escape, let alone survive the encounter?"

The denarius urged me to answer with caution. "I used the wakizashi; something about the weapon allowed me to destroy them."

Isidore was incensed, getting to his feet. "You did what?" He stammered as he looked at Andrew. "How is that even possible?"

Looking up at Isidore in confusion, I heard the denarius whisper in my mind. *Do not tell them the truth! They can't know!*

It needn't have bothered. There wasn't a chance in hell that I was going to tell them I'd shifted into some sort of soul eating monster. I did feel obligated to remind the self-righteous asshole about the situation. "Don't forget these specters were doing their best to kill me at the time, and I used the wakizashi in self-defense."

My words did little to sway the look on Isidore's face. He looked at Andrew for support. "Aren't you going to say anything?"

Andrew shook his head in disbelief. "What am I supposed to say?" He closed his eyes as he shook off a thought. "He's fortunate to have found such a weapon."

Absolute horror never left Isidore's face. "That may be true, but those poor people—"

Andrew motioned for Isidore to sit down and let him handle the situation. Once Isidore took his seat, still fuming at me but silent, he continued. "Is there anything further you'd like to add?"

The denarius was alert, whispering facts and figures into my mind. Necromancers summoned souls from whatever lay beyond, and forced them to serve their new master. Under normal circumstances, these specters couldn't be dispatched or dispersed without powerful counter spells or the death of the necromancer that summoned them.

It was clear to everyone in the room I didn't know the first thing about counter spells. And with Walter still being amongst the living, option two hadn't occurred. Since I'd given the wakizashi full credit for handling the situation, I could see why Andrew was skeptical. The denarius pointed out that it had never encountered anything like this previously.

The denarius was frightened yet highly intrigued by my abilities. It also cemented the fact I needed to stick to my story. The best lie always lay hidden in the truth. "As I said, I used the wakizashi I acquired from storage, which seemed to cause them to melt into a strange mist that faded away."

That was the truth…mostly. Of course, I'd left out the fact that the mist in question wrapped itself around me in the form of whatever it was that I'd taken on. That was something they didn't need to know. Not only did I not understand what had happened, I also didn't know the implications or repercussions of divulging too much.

Andrew sat there looking at me questioningly for a moment before falling back in his seat. "I see." His face was hard as he stared at me, trying to search out the truth on his own before letting out a long breath. "Have you found the law regarding necromancy?"

It was fucking hard to miss; it was the second law, after all, and stated that necromancy was strictly forbidden.

The denarius spoke quickly to explain why necromancy was such an affront to nature itself. Lazarus was a perfect example as to why it was forbidden. He'd died long ago and a powerful sorcerer/ necromancer and a dozen of his followers performed a perverse ceremony over a course of three days that pulled his soul through the veil and forced it back into his body. The result brought Lazarus back from the dead, but changed. He came back with the powers of the stone born, vampire, sorcerer, and others; each of his new powers corresponded to the men who'd resurrected him. He was something that should never have been, and it enslaved Lazarus to this world for all time with the inability to die.

A much noted side effect unknown to any other living creature was the fact it had magnified Lazarus's power several hundred fold. Even so, Lazarus was heartbroken and wished nothing more than to return from whence he'd been ripped away. He'd not wanted to return to this world. It was then that he created the Archive to regulate our kind and keep us under some sort of control. Necromancy had never been used in a way to benefit anyone other than the necromancer.

Part of me wanted to know how the denarius knew all this since I was certain that no other living creature, save for Lazarus, had ever heard this story. But that was when Andrew cleared his throat to get my attention.

Tearing myself away from the denarius, I turned to my uncle. "Yes, I know the law, and yes, I'm aware of the penalty."

Andrew was exhausted. "Good...."

Isidore looked between us with his mouth agape. "That's all you're going to say?"

Turning to Isidore, I scowled at him. "Look, I understand that those poor things didn't have a choice in the matter, and believe me, I don't like it any better than you, but what the fuck do you want? It was either me or them, and so long as I draw breath I will always choose me."

Isidore opened his mouth to respond and then shut it again. After several moments he found his voice. "I'm glad you survived, but it's just hard for me. They were forced into—"

"They were, but people like Chan and Timmy aren't worth mourning. The others weren't either," I growled.

Andrew glared at Isidore, who quieted down. "You understand what you need to do?"

Shooting Isidore a dismissive glance, I turned my full attention to Andrew. "There was never any question about what I needed to do. This just makes the paperwork easier."

Andrew blinked. "How do you plan on proceeding?"

The way Isidore kept looking at me made me feel somber. Taking a deep breath, I shrugged. "With an abundance of caution. First things first, I need a shower and a change of clothes before heading back out." Getting to my feet, I stretched. "Met Alexander earlier. Seems like a good guy from what little I've seen."

Andrew visibly relaxed at the change of subjects. "He's one of the good ones unless you've crossed him, and then he is a very difficult person to deal with."

Stepping around the chair, I placed a hand on Isidore's shoulder. "I'll get cleaned up and be back out there shortly." I looked down at Isidore. "For what it's worth, I'm just as horrified by what happened as you. I just don't have the luxury of second guessing myself."

The righteous indignation rushed out of him. "Of course you were right to defend yourself, and I'm glad you survived." He took a long breath as he looked over at Andrew and then back up at me. "You sure you want to go back out tonight?"

A small chuckle escaped my lips. "Don't tell me Andrew's swayed you to thinking I'm some sort of helpless child."

He gave me a dry laugh and shook his head. "Not at all, but you should know that necromancers are far more powerful after sundown, and if Walter could conjure up that many souls in the middle of the day, just imagine what he can do after the sun sets."

Flashing him a frown, I turned to look at Andrew, who only nodded in agreement. "Isidore is correct in this matter."

While it was nice to have people suddenly concerned for my welfare, it was starting to give me a headache. "Even so, I've got to go back out. I don't really see a way around it."

Without another word I headed for my room. Standing in front of the washer, I dropped my blood soaked clothes in to be washed when I got back. I was fairly certain Heather wasn't going to be up to doing my laundry for a long while. Speaking of Heather, I really needed to call her and check in, but that could wait till after a shower. Something about calling a girl while naked and covered in my own blood seemed a little creepy.

It took a good half hour of scrubbing to feel even remotely clean. While it wasn't surprising, I was still caught off guard by the distinct lack of visible wounds. After toweling off I found a clean pair of jeans and a pullover T-shirt and got dressed. I left the leather armor on the floor. It had done little to protect me, so why bother lugging it around?

Before pocketing my Nexus 6 I dialed my other number. It rang twice before Heather answered. Her voice was coy and full of mirth. "About time you called."

Laying back on the bed, I smiled. "Last I checked your fingers weren't broken."

She snickered. "True." She hesitated and I heard sheets rustling in the background. "Everything all right over there?"

Swinging my legs over the side of the bed, I sat up. "Yeah, why do you ask?"

She hesitated again as worry crept into her voice. "I heard that Andrew was involved in an accident at Martha's."

News traveled fast, even if it was wrong. I got to my feet. "And who told you that?"

She lowered her voice. "I overheard Brad talking to my dad outside the door." She suddenly sounded somewhere between pleased with herself and angry. "That little shit won't come in since you ran him out of here the other day."

"Brad?" I confirmed.

"Yes!" she huffed.

It was then that I remembered seeing someone upstairs. At the time I'd passed it off as wishful thinking or even manufactured memories from taking a sharp blow to the head when I landed. Of course, hadn't I seen him before things blew up? It was hard to remember now. "Don't worry about Andrew. He's safe and sound here at home. I've made him beef up security. Which means he brought in someone named Alexander."

Her intake of breath was audible, and what followed surprised me. Her tone was hopeful when she spoke. "As in a very large dark haired biker looking guy?"

"Yeah, that's the one. I take it you know him."

She seemed embarrassed. "You could say that. He used to watch over me when I was a little girl." She suddenly sounded angry again. "I was so glad when Andrew was able to help him and his family."

Oh, damn! Alexander was the werebear that Andrew had freed twenty years ago when he changed the laws. No wonder he trusted them. "When are you getting out of there?"

She grumbled. "I'm hoping tomorrow." She whispered into the phone. "Do you think Andrew would let me come over and visit...maybe even spend a few days while I recover? Mom and Dad are in the middle of splitting up, so things are pretty ugly at home."

I nodded my head out of reflex. "I don't think that will be a problem. You can have my room and I'll take the couch if it comes to that."

She giggled. "So what's changed between Sunday night and today?"

Puzzled, I stopped pacing. "What?"

She cackled. "You weren't quite so anxious to get me into your bed the other night, but now it's all 'come sleep over for a few days.'"

My cheeks went flush, and I stammered, "That's not at all—"

She laughed even harder. "Oh, this is far too easy!" She paused as she composed herself. "Ask Andrew for me."

"I will."

"Good. If I don't hear anything I'll assume that it's okay and have Mom drop me off when I get out of here."

"Sounds good."

She whispered in the phone. "Thanks. I gotta go, someone's coming."

The line went dead and I pocketed the phone. I spent the next twenty minutes tidying the place up...just in case she showed up. After tucking the last of the dirty clothes into the basket and closing all the drawers, I headed for the living room. I was nervous and didn't know how to ask my uncle for permission to have a girl over, but it was for her own good. Her parents weren't in any condition to take care of her right now.

Andrew looked at me with curiosity on his face. "Something on your mind?"

Shuffling to one side, I felt my face get warm. "I just got off the phone with Heather. She asked if she could come by for a few days. It seems that Mrs. Broussard wasn't kidding about divorcing Robert." I felt my words get caught in my mouth as they rushed out. "She wanted to visit with Alexander as well. I told her it would be all right." I looked at my uncle, who was clearly enjoying my torment. "It's all right, isn't it?"

Andrew's smile quieted my fears and put me at ease instantly. "Absolutely. She can't very well make a full recovery with people trying to slit each other's throat at any given moment."

I felt myself relax. "That's what I said."

Andrew beamed. "I'll get one of the guest rooms available."

A part of me was disappointed that she wouldn't be staying in my room. "Need me to do anything before heading out?"

Andrew shook his head. "I think we got it covered." He pointed at the phone in my pocket. "Call us if you need anything."

"Sure thing."

Five minutes later I was pulling out of the gate as Alexander and two of his men waved me out. They were quick to lock up and vanish behind the thick gray cement walls. As for me, I had a few things I needed to run down. Pulling the card for Lieutenant Baptist out of my pocket, I dialed his number and got his voicemail. I asked if he could use department resources to track down the owner of the phone that was left at Walter's. It took another twenty minutes to reach the old DHL center in Elmwood.

I was hoping I could find some further information about Walter, and now I wanted to know more about Brad. Heather had never mentioned his full name during our conversations, but I was starting to get suspicious of the man. I wondered if I wanted him to be involved in this just to shove his face into a wall because of Heather or his hate of werewolves, or for any number of other reasons. Still, it would be a poor investigator who didn't follow up on a lead like this. How else would he have heard that Andrew was there?

Chapter 18

Friday June 5th

Leaning forward, I placed my head in my hands, forcing myself awake. It'd been a long day to say the least. Looking up at the clock, which read 12:15 a.m., I knew I was running on fumes. My hands were shaky and I was tired, and generally done for the day. Yet I could still feel a deep recess of untapped power.

Whatever I'd absorbed was now a part of me, and not something that could be taken away or used up, like the minor bits of magic used against me. The souls of the slain were now mine in a way that neither I nor the denarius could quite understand. Their power was a part of me, and would be at my disposal for the remainder of my life. In what capacity that would happen I was unsure.

Gabriel had taken his leave of me a few hours back to get some rest. I desperately wanted to find a comfy spot and do the same, but something about the office was nagging the crap out of me. Everything I'd found earlier was out in the open. Martha hadn't bothered to tuck anything away from possible prying eyes.

Not that I suspected she'd hide anything from her son on purpose, but it felt awfully convenient. I couldn't help but believe that I was missing some very important pieces of the puzzle. It would be prudent of her to keep a file on all the Archive's officials in her jurisdiction. I hadn't even found a file dedicated to Walter, a prime suspect. All the file cabinets seemed to be filled with pawns, but all the heavy hitters were missing.

Frustration was getting the better of me, and I got up and eased the door closed. I didn't want to wake Gabriel when the obscenities started to flow. I bowed my head and started grumbling every curse word that came to mind. Falling back into the plush office chair, I rolled it forward, placed my forehead on the edge of the desk, and stared at the tile floor.

The phone in my pocket rang, surprising me, and I nearly jumped out of the chair. Regaining some of my dignity, I sat up straight and answered the phone. "This is Gavin."

Andrew's voice was tired. "Just checking in. Everything all right?"

He sounded about as good as I felt. Leaning back in the chair, I tried to focus. "I'm fine. Get some rest…I'll see you sometime tomorrow."

Andrew sniffed and I heard him move, presumably to get up from his seat. "Stay safe and get some rest. I got a feeling you're going to need it."

Pitching forward again, I placed my elbow on the counter. "I got a feeling you're right."

Andrew let out a tired chuckle. "Good night."

"Night," I replied, and with that the line went dead.

Tucking the phone in my pocket, I rubbed my face, got back on my feet, and searched the office again. I knew that I had to be missing something. It took me a good twenty minutes to work my way around to the file cabinet next to the door.

I tugged on the top drawer, it was locked, but I felt the whole thing pivot. Allowing the cabinet to turn on the spot, it swiveled to the right and blocked the door as it snapped into position. There in the floor I found a heavy duty handle attached to a thick piece of steel. I grabbed the handle and pulled, allowing it to reveal itself slowly.

It was a fireproof—and by the looks of things, bombproof—file cabinet that appeared to be connected to some sort of counter weighted pulley system. Going to the others, I turned them to the side and found similar cabinets under them. The design was truly inspired; you had to lock yourself in the office, turn the first cabinet, and only then would it reveal its secrets.

It only stood to reason that if the key to opening the cabinets was the first cabinet, that was the place to start, and I was right. In the top drawer at the very front was Walter's file. Taking a couple of minutes to sift through the files and the next two drawers, I figured out the system. Active cases were in the top, while the older and unsolved ones were relegated to lower sections.

I grabbed the notebook she had tucked in front of Walter's file and sat back at the desk. She was very good at keeping notes. I suspected that I'd better start following her example, just not tonight. After I got through her notes and found some sort of understanding, then I'd start making my own. No need to jump ahead to conclusions only to have them proven wrong deeper into the notebook. Best to get all the facts first, then make a decision.

I was tempted to sift through the other cabinets, but I knew that I needed to take a small section and dig in. With that thought firmly in mind, I took Walter's file and spread it across the long desk before starting on Martha's notes. The first page out of the file was much like any police issue form, with a current photo clipped to the top right corner of the page.

After that the basics followed; his address, boring details such as race, eye color, etc., but what caught my attention was a list of business holdings and interests, which to my great surprise included a seat on the board of directors for Touro Hospital.

Martha had scrawled several notes that referenced the documents within the folder. The first and hardly surprising fact was that Walter was an only child from a broken home. From what I'd seen of the asshole he probably would've eaten his siblings, but that was hardly helpful. I continued to read that he'd been abandoned at the doorstep of a local orphanage that closed decades ago. She made several notes about him suffering from what she called a wasting disease, and his ability to manipulate the element of fire.

Martha described the wasting disease as the ability to absorb the essence of any living entity and pull that into himself, to be used to fuel other, darker magic. In her words he was a cancer upon the world that would need to be removed. Other notes showed Elizabeth Dodd intervening on Walter's behalf over the years, essentially blocking Martha's ability to incarcerate the man. An allowance that she had regretted recently and would not allow to happen again.

Turning the page, I found a marriage certificate clipped in place. Pulling it free, I gave it a thorough once over before deciding it was probably the original. I turned it around so I could read it properly. According to this, Walter had married a young woman named Mary Percy on May 21 of 1973. Flipping back, I reread the section that said he didn't have any living relatives before flipping the certificate over. Moving deeper into the notebook, I found a photo attached with a yellow Post-it note stuck over the face that read Mary.

I found it odd that she'd covered the face. Removing the yellow sticker, I suddenly understood. My stomach twisted; anger, resentment, and finally disgust won out. Still it took several more seconds for me to come to terms with the photo. Mary Percy was the spitting image of Martha, so much so they could've been identical twins.

That wasn't exactly true…even in the old black and white photo I could see the difference. It was the eyes…they were all wrong. Martha's eyes were full of life, intelligent, and genuinely happy. Mary's were dull, flat, and nearly lifeless. She had the eyes of someone who'd been broken in mind and body. I'd seen the same look on prisoners, drug addicts, and slaves.

Replacing the Post-it, I moved to the next page. The rest of the information I felt may have been speculative, but if not I had no idea how she'd come to the conclusions. According to Martha, Mary and Walter never lived with one another. There were extended visits, perhaps, but no actual cohabitation. During the investigation, Martha had found two birth records; one from July, 1974 for a Walter B. Percy, Jr., and one from December, 1985 for a J. Brody Percy. That, however, was where the paper trail ended. It was as if the kids had never existed in this world, other than on paper.

A sick feeling struck me, but I couldn't put my finger on exactly why. Maybe I was allowing my brain to race ahead, creating possible scenarios. It was clear he'd done something to Mary, but would a father really kill his infant children? Maybe that was when he got a taste for it. Maybe that was why he collected the stones. Maybe they were trophies, a keepsake that none but the Archive would realize was missing.

Huh...I'd never asked if it was guaranteed to birth a stone born from just one such parent. My grandfather had two with a human, and my father had me with a...I wasn't sure what my mother was. Perhaps a shaman? That would be something I needed to ask Andrew, along with several other questions given this new information.

Glancing over at the clock, I saw it was nearly 4:00 a.m. If I left now I might be in time for breakfast before catching a few hours' sleep. Putting everything inside the folder, I set about the office, putting it back the way I'd found it. With the last cabinet restored, I headed out the door and nearly ran into Gabriel.

He looked nearly as surprised to see me as I was to see him. "I didn't know you were still here."

Cocking my head at the exit, I said, "I was just heading back to Andrew's place. Need anything before I go?"

He simply waved. "Nah, I'm good."

Giving him two thumbs up, I grinned. "See you soon." Glancing back at the office, I let out a long breath. "I got a feeling there's a lot left for me to sift through." Holding up the file, I grimaced. "I'm hoping this will set me on the right track and I can put this thing to bed shortly."

Gabriel eyed the file with interest. "Good luck."

With that I was out the door and headed for home. Traffic was light this time of morning, and I pulled into the drive a half hour later. Alexander was, of course, there to greet me.

Alexander for his part looked well rested and happy to see me. "Long night?"

For the slightest of moments, I thought he took a long breath through his nose, but then again I was tired as fuck. I regarded him with a frank expression as I pondered the last twelve hours. "You could say that."

He thumbed back at the house. "I saw the lights come on a little while ago, so they're up."

"Good to know," I replied, heading for the back door. "Have a good morning."

"You too."

Not seeing anyone in the living room, I headed for the kitchen in the hopes of finding breakfast. I wasn't disappointed. Isidore was sitting at the table while Andrew stood watch over the stove. Both gave me a warm welcome and Isidore pushed out a chair with a foot.

Andrew called over his shoulder. "Hungry?"

"Absolutely!" I said as I sat at the table, sliding the file just to the left of me.

Isidore looked between me and the file and became curious. "Anything good in there?"

Remembering what I'd found my stomach turned, forcing me to fight back the sickness I felt. "I wouldn't say that."

Andrew dropped a heaping pile of eggs and sausages in front of Isidore, and a more manageable sized plate for me. He returned quickly enough with his own and took his seat. He gave me a quizzical look as he cut into his sausage. "I'm glad to see you made it back unharmed." His eyes flitted over to the file. "Find anything helpful?"

Chewing on a mouthful of food, I put a hand on the file and moved it closer to me in case either of them got too curious. "Before we get into what I found, I need to ask some questions."

Irritation crossed Andrew's face, clearly not used to being denied information he desired, the novelty having already worn off. "Shoot."

Seeing his expression, I thought I'd go for the easy questions first before lobbing a big pile of shit into the mix. "If one parent is a stone born and the other is human, what are the odds of that child being a stone born?" Taking another bite of food, I waited for him to answer.

He leaned back in his seat, thinking before he adopted a professorial tone. "While there is no such thing as a guarantee, the odds are fairly good that the resulting offspring will be stone born." He grimaced as an old pain gripped him. "It's not as if our kind is prolific in that aspect, but if we are able to create life and that life is brought to term, the likelihood is very strong, no matter the species, to result in a stone born. It has been known to happen that children are born human—which is exceptionally rare—or some other species, but again rare." His eyes trailed over to the file again. "Why do you ask?"

Needless to say I wasn't ready to share at this point, but a part of me felt compelled to give him something. It felt wrong keeping the information from him. But then again there was the whole creep factor of Walter marrying Martha's doppelganger....

Putting a hand on the file, I grumbled. "Combination of educational purposes and practical ones." It was then that I decided to fuck up everyone's day. Putting my fork on the plate, I turned to the file and pulled out Mary's photo, careful to leave the Post-it note in place. "Did you know that Walter was married?"

Isidore and Andrew both exchanged looks before shaking their heads no.

Andrew's face soured. "As far as I know he's never been married."

Laying the photo on the table, I scooted it towards my uncle. "Her name was Mary Percy and they were married in '73."

Andrew seemed angrier about the information than I believed the news warranted, but there was clearly some history there I wasn't aware of. He put a finger on the corner of the photo, pulled it closer, and removed the Post-it. A storm rolled across his features as fury welled up inside him.

His voice was full of anger and hate, staring at the photo. "The bastard just couldn't get past it." He slapped the yellow sticky over the face quickly, shoving it back in my direction. His disgust was all too apparent. "When she wouldn't have him for so many obvious reasons, he went out and found this poor thing." Still glaring at the yellow paper, he growled. "What does this have to do with your investigation?"

Shoving the photo into the folder, I let out a ragged breath. "I'm not sure, but it is more information than I had yesterday. To be honest, I was hoping that you knew something about it that would help narrow my search."

Andrew had clearly lost his appetite and pushed his plate away. "Is this why you asked about stone born children?"

It was more of an accusation than a question. "Only partially. I really did want to know how it worked. On the other hand, the reports show, at least on paper, that there were two children born to this union." Anger and hate danced across my uncle's face. "Martha wasn't able to track either of them down. There were birth certificates, but from what I can tell no actual child has ever been seen."

Andrew seemed pleased at the news. "It appears that no one's child is safe in his presence. Not even his own!" With that Andrew got to his feet and marched out of the kitchen without another word.

What the hell was that about? Turning to Isidore, I hoped he had the answer. "I've missed something fairly important; care to fill me in?"

Isidore's face sagged. "Martha was pregnant back in '68." He leaned back in his chair as he held out his hands in despair. "I don't know what happened exactly. No one does save for Andrew, Martha, and Walter. There was an argument or a fight that caused Martha to go into labor, but when they got to the hospital the baby was stillborn. Andrew hasn't spoken to Walter since, until the funeral. As you can imagine there is a lot of hate there."

It hit me like a ton of bricks. Walter was obsessed with Martha and had been for a long time. Not that it had stopped him from having her killed, but he was the kind of man who, if he couldn't have her, no one could. I had to wonder if the miscarriage was what broke Martha and Andrew up all those years ago. A lot of couples couldn't handle the death of a child. Who was to say they were any different? Then for Walter to have married her clone and had kids of his own was like a slap in the face to Andrew. All I'd succeeded in doing this morning was rubbing salt in a very old wound.

"I didn't know," I replied.

Isidore shrugged. "Not a lot of people do."

We finished our breakfast in silence and cleaned up the kitchen. I went to the living room in hopes of finding

Andrew, but he wasn't anywhere to be found. I was exhausted and needed a few hours' shut eye. Heading to my room, I locked the door and fell face first into the bed, falling right to sleep.

Chapter 19

It was 11:00 when I jerked awake, freeing myself from the hellish dream world I'd been living in for the last several hours. While the nightmares weren't new, they'd been given renewed life since my encounter with the stone. My mouth was dry, my head hurt, and my body ached. I hadn't realized that comfortable bedding could be used as a torture device. After years of sleeping on the floor, on the ground, or sitting up on cargo planes, this was beyond painful.

The first order of business was a shower to undo some of the knots. After that maybe I'd find someone in the kitchen with a hot lunch; okay, maybe I was hoping for a lukewarm lunch, but food was food.

Fifteen minutes later I was clean, dressed, and feeling somewhat better. Stepping into the hall I could hear voices, some of which were female, coming from the living room. Lunch would need to wait until I checked the guest list. The voices got clearer the further down the hall I went, and by the time I opened the door I knew I'd find Heather and her mother.

I saw Kimberly helping Heather into a chair in front of the desk. Andrew came out of the back and swept into his chair with a smile for both women. Two practical yet stylish suitcases and three smaller bags were on the floor.

Kimberly readily returned the smile before inclining her head in his direction. "Thank you for taking her in." She paused, biting her lip. "I'm sure it will only be a few days. I didn't feel comfortable leaving her alone at her place in case anything came up, and God forbid that I bring her to my place; it's a damn war zone."

Andrew nervously straightened up, the slightest touch of crimson in his cheeks. "What type of mentor would I be if I didn't help when I was able?" He made a show of waving away any further concern for the matter. "Consider yourselves welcome to stay for as long as needed. My home will always be open to those who are in need." Andrew's eyes fell on me as I stepped through the door, and he waved me over. "Glad you're awake." He pointed at Heather's bags. "Think you could lend a hand?"

Pushing back my shoulders, I nodded before turning to Heather. There was a tingle in my stomach when our eyes locked. Clearing my throat, I said, "No problem."

Kimberly cocked her head, her eyes appraising me once more. When I moved for the bags she cut in front of me. She moved quickly, gently lifting my right hand, moving it this way and that to inspect it thoroughly. Her eyes were wide and her mouth fell open before quickly closing again.

When she spoke, her voice was full of mirth and perhaps a little shock. "You're a *vigiles*?" Before I could answer, she held up my hand and turned to Andrew. "He's a *vigiles*?"

This time it was Andrew who turned several shades of crimson. "Yes."

Still holding my hand out, she asked. "When?"

Andrew turned a deeper shade of red. "Monday morning."

Never letting go of my hand, she threw her head back and let out a deep belly laugh that shook her whole body. "Oh my God!" She looked up at me, eyes glinting. "Not a werewolf after all." The smile left her lips and she took a quick step back. Her eyes searched my face once more before turning between Andrew and I. With that I knew she'd figured it out, even before she spoke her question.

"Gavin what, exactly?" Her tone was almost accusing.

A knowing grin crossed my lips and I couldn't help but snigger. It was clear to me, as it was to her, that the gig was up and she was onto my secret. "Randall, ma'am."

She cut her eyes back at Andrew and then looked up at me with the biggest smile on her face. "Very clever, young man! Very clever indeed." She turned her attention back to Andrew. "Robert is going to lose his shit when he brings his 'candidates' by on Friday, thinking they actually have a chance."

Andrew appeared not to be bothered at the comment. The crimson left his cheeks, quickly becoming serious. "In the words of my nephew, this isn't the first time, and considering the job it won't be the last."

Kimberly made a face that said she agreed. Grabbing her purse, she pulled out the phone I'd given Heather and handed it to me. "Thank you for letting Heather use it." Her joy faltered and frustration took its place. "I'm not sure what happened to hers."

It was clear that Heather hadn't shared her thoughts with her mother.

Kimberly spoke again. "I've ordered her a new phone, but it won't be here for a few days." She looked up at me with a softened expression that conveyed her thanks. "I figure you may need it more than she does."

Out of habit I'd stuck the phone in my pocket. "I've got another, and I was more than happy to let her use it." Looking over at Heather, I automatically pulled the phone out again, handing it to her. "You can keep it till your new phone arrives."

She blushed but didn't hesitate to take it from me and quickly tuck it under her thigh, being careful not to make prolonged eye contact. "Thanks."

The thought of Robert losing his shit when he learned I was the new *vigiles* didn't fill me with joy. I turned my attention to Kimberly. "Any chance I could talk you into not telling Robert about me?" I held out my hands in a halting motion. "I'm not asking you to lie, but if you could just omit this for now it would be very helpful in my investigation."

Kimberly considered my words. "I don't see that being a problem." Her expression serious, she glanced at Andrew and then me. "We aren't exactly speaking at the moment, at least not directly…the lawyers are sorting most of it out." She kept her eyes fixed on mine. "But you said this would help your investigation. Is Robert a suspect in something I'm unaware of?"

I flinched; that hadn't been the way I'd meant it to sound. "No, not at all. I just don't need the headache of him getting in the way." Remembering Brad's assumption that I was a werewolf, I growled. "It's obvious he likes to run his mouth, a lot. I don't need the people I'm investigating finding out there's a new *vigiles* until next week."

Kimberly quickly did the math. "So you've got a week to track down whatever is going on with the attack on Heather, and if I had to guess, Martha's death as well."

Andrew only raised his hands in mock defense. "I didn't say anything, but never let it be said that Ms. Broussard isn't one of the sharper tools in the shed."

Kimberly's eyes stayed focused on me. "Am I right?"

There wasn't any use in denying it. "Looks like the attack on Heather could be connected to Martha's death, and I really want to end this before ignorance is no longer my friend." It was then that I recalled a factoid from Walter's file. I was this far in…I figured I might as well jump. "I've got an odd question about Touro's board of directors."

Kimberly suddenly looked disinterested but waved for me to continue. "That's more of a Robert question, but I can try to answer."

Of course it was a Robert question. "Did you know that Walter Percy is on the board?"

Kimberly recoiled, anger and disgust painted itself across her face at the very idea. "That's fucking impossible!" She balled her hands into fists and I watched while she worked it out. "Goddamn it, if that's true, I can't begin to tell you how wrong that would be." With a shiver she got ahold of herself once more. "Any chance you got bad information?"

Good to see that Walter brought out the best in people. Shaking my head, I continued. "I don't think it's a mistake, but I'm trying to corroborate some facts I found in his file." Putting a hand on her shoulder, I tried to reassure her. "Thanks for the information."

She huffed. "Not sure how I helped, but you're welcome."

Turning, I noticed the bags were gone. All I could do was give Isidore a sheepish shrug to apologize for not helping. Turning my attention to Heather, I smiled. "Do you need help getting to your room?"

I wasn't sure what motivated Heather to keep so quiet, but it was clear she didn't wish to be involved in the conversation further. She nodded her head and tried to smile through the pain. Her effort wasn't as successful as she'd hoped and she grimaced, trying to push herself to her feet before collapsing back into the chair with her hand over her stomach. She didn't look at all pleased.

"I'm guessing I'll need a little more help than anticipated." As if to offer an explanation, she continued. "The meds are starting to wear off, and I want to be in bed before I take the next round of pills."

Without really thinking about it, I leaned over and scooped her out of the chair. To my surprise she was heavier than she looked. Not in a bad way, but in the sense that every inch of her was solid muscle. Taking her down the hall to the room across from my own, I found the door was open and I headed for the bed. Isidore had taken the liberty of turning down the blankets and stacking several pillows to allow her to sit up if she wanted. Laying her gently on the mattress, I couldn't help but feel slightly intoxicated by her form, even in this condition.

Standing upright, I offered her a big smile. "Anything else I can do for you?"

Heather looked down at her hands as she spoke in a low tone. "Think you could check in on me later?" Her gaze shifted from her hands, and she looked up at me with those sultry sea green eyes that gave me butterflies. "I know you've got things to do today, but I'd appreciate a visit from someone other than my mother."

I wagged my head in agreement. "Not a problem." Then a thought occurred to me that stopped me in my tracks, forcing me to shake my head. "If you're asleep I'm not going to wake you."

Heather huffed and folded her arms. "That's not really a visit then, is it?"

I felt a goofy expression overtake my features and I pointed at her stomach. "You need rest to heal up from being stabbed."

She rolled her eyes as she tucked the phone under her pillow. "Wake me if necessary."

Hanging my head in defeat, I let out a sigh. "Fine."

She gave me a look that said you-damn-well-better. "Good!" She looked at the door and shooed me out. "Go do some work."

With a bow, I rolled my hand in front of me. "Of course, My Lady."

Mock horror shone on her face, her eyes widened, and she fought off a case of the giggles. "Oh God! Don't do the Ren fair thing, ever!"

Swelling to my full height, I did my best to look offended, and failed. "Of course, My Lady."

Spinning on my heel, I closed the door behind me and heard the soft thud of a pillow hitting wood. Less than a minute later I was back in the living room, where I found Andrew, Kimberly, and Isidore at the desk talking in low tones. As soon as I arrived they suddenly stopped, which meant they were talking about me. Considering how I'd left the conversation earlier I couldn't blame them. Still, I felt my shoulders slump.

"Care to share?"

Andrew was the first to pipe in. "Why did you bring up Walter's connection to Touro?"

For a half second I thought about showing them the file, but that wouldn't help. "Honestly, I'm just reaching," I replied patiently. "At the moment I'm not sure it's important, but considering Timothy and Chan are dead and Martha's house is a charcoal briquette, I don't have the luxury of dismissing anything that might give me a lead on the man." I thumbed back at my room. "Speaking of which, I need to go over a few things before I head out. If you guys know anything about Walter and his whereabouts, this would be a great time to speak up."

Isidore, Kimberly, and Andrew all shook their head. Kimberly looked shaken. "I can check with the administration and see what they know. If it would help."

If she started asking questions and Walter found out it could spook the man, or worse, put her in danger. "No, not yet.

Let's see what I can dig up first, I wouldn't want you to catch any blowback from this."

She fell back in her chair, lost in thought. "Okay, but if you change your mind, just say the word."

"Sure thing."

Andrew's face hardened. "Anything I can do? And before you say no, remember I don't really give a shit about any type of 'blowback.' I want this settled!"

That made two of us. "The best thing you can do for me is stay put. Knowing you're safe will mean that I don't have to worry about trying to protect you."

Andrew sagged in his chair, clearly disappointed. "That's the dullest assignment you could possibly give me, not to mention no fun at all."

The comment made me more tired than I already was. "Yep, the joys of the dead coming back from beyond the grave to kill you...can't hardly stand it!" Shooting him a disgusted look, I admonished, "Do me the favor of staying safe so we can all get through this in one piece."

Andrew blenched. "I wasn't trying to make light of the situation. I'm sorry."

Casually flicking my wrist, I dismissed it. "Don't worry about it. I'm just tired. I really should get back to work."

I turned and headed back to my room. Once there I pulled the file off my desk and moved my Surface Pro into position. Reading the last of the notebook, I found an address for Mary Percy, but no number. Typing it into Google Maps, I found a street view of the place. It was an old run down farmhouse from what I could see. It wasn't as if they'd driven down the long drive to get a better view. Which meant that I'd have to go out there and see if Mary was still at the old address, because I was quickly running out of leads, leaving Walter in the wind.

Grabbing my phone, computer, and keys, I headed out the door. Sticking my head through Heather's door, I gave her a half smile. "Stopped in to say hi and bye."

Heather glowered at me while trying not to giggle. "So that's all I get is a quick hello?"

Opening the door, a little wider, I nodded. "Yeah, I've got to head to Destrehan to track down some information. I'll try to stop in later if it's not too late."

She pursed her lips and folded her arms in defiance. "We're back to that?"

With a quick wink and a nonchalant roll of my shoulders, I stepped back into the hallway. "What can I say? I did stop in and I did say hi. Now get some rest."

She cut her eyes at me with a big grin on her face, quickly giving me a very unlady like middle finger salute. "Smart ass. Go and do something productive."

Waving, I closed the door and nearly bumped into Kimberly, who smiled. "How's she doing?"

"Considering she was stabbed in the gut only a few days ago, she's doing fantastic."

Kimberly gave me a wink as she leaned in. "Shh. Don't tell anyone, but magic is a wonderful thing!"

That made me grin. I could only guess that Kimberly was doing something to speed up Heather's recovery process, but I didn't have time to find out what. "That's what I hear." Stepping around her, I waved. "I've got to head out…I'll catch up with you later."

She nodded. "Be safe."

"Thanks," I replied as I gave her a thumbs up.

Fighting the urge to pick up junk food on the way, I stopped in the kitchen to find Andrew at the stove. He looked back and nodded. "Burger?"

Food…real food at that! "Sounds good."

Andrew chuckled. "Heading out?"

"As soon as I finish my lunch I've got a few errands to run."

Andrew buttered the buns before placing them on the skillet, toasting them to perfection and then placing a healthy sized medium rare burger with provolone cheese atop the buns. All the condiments were sitting on the counter. "Help yourself."

I added a small bit of mayo, mustard, and ketchup before grabbing a thick slice of onion, a leaf of lettuce, and four pickles. Walking over to the table, I looked up at Andrew. "Mind if I go ahead?"

Andrew waved me onward. "Go ahead…I've still got to make a few more for Isidore and our guests."

Perking up before I took my first bite, I looked at Andrew. "Guests?"

Andrew bobbed. "Kimberly has asked to stay so she can tend to Heather."

That, of course, made perfect sense, and was something I should've thought of myself. I felt the blood run into my cheeks and the warmth emanate from my body. "Sorry about this. I should've given it some thought before agreeing on your behalf."

Andrew shook his head dismissively, placing two more burgers in the pan. "Hardly a bother. I'm glad to do it."

Taking my first bite, I felt my eyes roll back in my head a little as the sensation of the first real hamburger in nearly ten years rolled over me. God, this was good!

Andrew hooted, forcing me to open my eyes.

"What?" I asked.

Andrew shook his head. "It's really good, isn't it?"

I couldn't help but give him one of those fuck-yeah-are-you-stupid looks, before I said, "Yeah, it's good!"

Then I took another big bite, chewing slowly, savoring everything about it. The simplicity of the salt and pepper didn't overpower the fresh ground beef. "Isidore made this?"

Andrew nodded as he chuckled. "Ground it himself this morning."

God bless! I'd had hamburgers before, but nothing like this. "You'll have to tell him thank you for me."

Two more bites and it was gone. I wanted to stay and have a dozen more, but duty called. Picking up my plate, I washed it off in the sink and placed it in the dishwasher. "Thanks for lunch."

Andrew casually waved off the appreciation. "Anytime." He looked back as I turned to leave. "Where ya headed?"

"Destrehan; got a lead I need to track down."

"Call if you need anything," Andrew said as I headed through the door.

Two minutes later I was pulling out onto 4th Street, heading for the interstate.

Chapter 20

The scattered cotton ball clouds offered little relief from the glaring rays of the early afternoon sun in the bright blue sky. That being said, I was forced to flip the visor down. This was the first time I'd had the Tucker out on the interstate, and it drove like a dream. The steering was highly responsive and took the bumps in the road in stride, giving me the feeling of floating down I-310 at seventy miles per hour.

It struck me when I was about ten miles outside of Destrehan how very quiet it was inside the car. There wasn't any sort of road noise or sounds from the semi-truck that just passed me. Nothing really bled through, and it made me wonder if this was a design feature or another one of my uncle's enchantments.

Swinging off the interstate, I turned onto River Road, passing what looked to be some sort of massive apartment complex in the early stages of construction. Perhaps it was an office building, but whatever was going up had caused a good half mile of woodlands to be cut down and turned to a dirt pit. I was sure that the people who lived there didn't appreciate the fact that whatever was coming would surely lower the surrounding property values.

The library could be seen from the road, but my destination was just a little further down. I'd looked the place up after I saw it on Google Maps. It was an antebellum mansion of a pre-Civil War sugar baron. It had traded hands over the years until Mary Percy bought it back in the early '70s. The old photos taken back in the '40s showed the place in all its splendor…a massive white two story construction with eight large columns holding up the second story balcony and roof, sitting on about thirteen acres of land.

Pulling off River Road onto an old gravel drive, I dodged several potholes before finding a suitable parking space about a hundred yards in. The enormous oak trees dotting the yard were overgrown and unkempt, much like the yard. The rickety white picket fence had rotted out completely in several places, while the rest was a crumbling mess, including the rusted wrought iron gate that lay on the ground. Taking a long stride to try and avoid it, I had to duck to escape being throttled by a low hanging branch, and nearly tripped when my foot snagged itself on one of the iron bars.

Keeping my head down, I finally made it through the tree line. Standing upright, I took a good hard look at the rotting corpse of what used to be a home. The once impressive facade of the house was a putrefied ruin. The second story railing running between the first two columns hung precariously off the front by a single bolt…the next was missing entirely. Old plywood boards covered all the windows to keep vagrants, or more likely local kids, from breaking in. From the looks of several gaping holes on the first floor, the effort had failed miserably.

Making my way through the dusty, overgrown yard to the front door, I was sure that no one lived there, but one could never tell with these types of places. I might be lucky and Mary would be sitting there on the chaise with Walter, and I could wrap this whole thing up by dinner!

Yeah, that was never going to happen.

I was about thirty feet from the door when I heard gravel crunching behind me. With a longing look at the door, I considered ducking under the broken railing and giving it a good solid rap, but my gut told me that I needed to wait. Stepping back, I peered through the thicket and saw a white Dodge Charger, stenciled with St. Charles Sheriff's Office in blue and gold, pull in and park.

Well damn!

Keeping still, I watched a dark haired young man step out of the cruiser. The officer's movements were slow and methodical as he eyed the Tucker and put on his cap. Reaching through an open window on his cruiser, he pulled out a pad, noting my license plate. He casually tossed it into the car, then studied me through the foliage. Cocking his head to the side with a crooked grin, he waved for me to join him.

I made it back to the drive with only slightly more grace than before. Brushing off a few errant leaves, I had a moment to take in the deputy. He appeared to be older than I'd thought— maybe late twenties or early thirties—with dark brown hair and striking green eyes. It was all put together in such a way that if he'd been taller he could've been one of those male models. Unlike a lot of southern cops, he appeared to be fit under the dark blue, almost black uniform. His demeanor, clothes, and movements told me he took pride in his job and himself.

The big gold star on his chest read St. Charles Sheriff in deep black lettering, just underneath a matching nameplate reading J. Matherne. With a quick scan he assessed my threat level.

I was about a dozen feet away when he lifted a hand. His voice was calm, deep, and carried a thick bayou accent. "That's close enough." He cut his eyes at the run down plantation and then me. "You lost, or are you one of those movie scouts?" The latter thought brought a frown. "I can tell ya now that the owners have never agreed to let the place be used."

Shaking my head as I leaned against the Tucker, I smiled, trying to put the man at ease. "Neither. I was looking for someone who used to live here."

Officer Matherne made a funny face, apparently trying not to snicker. "Old Lady Percy?"

"Would that be Mary Percy?" I asked.

Officer Matherne shrugged and didn't look particularly interested in the conversation any longer. "Not sure what her full name was, but probably the same gal." This was obviously a well-known story in these parts and he was tired of repeating it. "Why would anybody be looking for her after all these years?"

Thankfully, I'd already prepared myself for such a conversation. One thing I'd learned over the years was to always have a plausible story ready in case you were stopped by the authorities. Today I was a blogger working on a story about the plantations of Louisiana.

Holding up my Surface Pro for the officer to see, I tried to look excited. "I just had a few questions about the old plantation for my blog."

That did the trick. His face went blank, then he sneered. The only thing worse than paparazzi were bloggers. Ten years ago I would've needed to set up an entire background with a real paper or a magazine, but these days all I had to do was say I blogged.

The contempt on his face told me all I needed to know. His interest in me had ended the moment I held up the computer. "Old Lady Percy won't be of much help." He lost himself to a memory. "According to the stories, she finally lost it about twenty years ago. The sheriff found her half naked, barefoot, and pretty beat up." He waved a dismissive hand. "From what I hear, it was clear to the folks around town back then that she wasn't able to take care of herself anymore." Genuine sadness crept into his face and settled in his tone. "The local church offered to come by and help her, but she refused them." An old pain crept through his eyes for the briefest of moments. "The story that's told says she kept repeating, 'He's taken the kids!'"

With an effort he shook free the memory. "Sad really. It's not like she ever had any kids of her own." He nodded at the house. "You'd be better off stopping at the library down the road for information about the plantation. As for Old Lady Percy, I heard they put her in one of those retirement homes somewhere in the city."

There went my chance of finding Walter on the chaise and being done by dinner. "I see." I really wanted to get in there but I doubted that was in the cards. "Any chance I could look around before I go?"

The look he gave me told me he'd rather shoot me than allow me access. "I'm afraid I'm going to have to insist that you don't." He pointed at a sign by the road. "It being private property and all. I wouldn't feel right about letting some stranger poke around."

Called it.

Pushing myself off the Tucker, I grunted my disappointment. "No problem; guess I'll be on my way."

Officer Matherne pivoted in place, eyeing the Tucker suspiciously. "That's a mighty fine piece of machinery."

Pride swelled in my chest and I patted the fender, giving the man a wink. "Isn't it?"

"Where can I find one?" he asked.

I snorted and tossed up my hands. "You got me; I haven't the foggiest. This one kind of fell in my lap last week."

He made a derisive huff and his eyes narrowed. "Blogging pays good these days, I take it."

Taking it for the accusation it was, I popped the door. "It pays all right." With a grin I held it open for the officer to get a good look. "I'd let you take it for a spin, but I need to get to the library before it closes."

He snorted at the offer. "I don't think my bosses would appreciate me joyriding on the city's dime." With a quick wave his smile faltered. "See ya soon."

Well that was creepy. Closing the door, I fired up the Tucker and pulled out on River Road. Having no choice in the matter, I headed for the library. With a little luck someone in there might know more about Old Lady Percy than Officer Matherne had.

The lady at the desk, while old enough to recall the incident concerning Mary, had no idea who currently owned the plantation or where they'd taken her after the "episode." I wasn't surprised to find Officer Matherne leaning against his car when I exited the library. He didn't say a word…only offered me a curt wave when I got into the Tucker and drove off.

Pulling onto I-310, I stepped on the gas and let the purr of the engine keep pace with my thoughts. The one thing I was quickly learning about the Deep South was how cliquish they were. Everyone they considered an outsider was stonewalled with great efficiency, or maybe I just didn't know the proper questions to ask. At the moment I was finding myself with more questions than answers.

By the time I turned onto St. Charles Avenue the sun was hanging low on the horizon. Pulling up in the drive, Alexander and two of his men were there to greet me. Well, it was more like a quick visual inspection. After it became common knowledge about Chan being a shapeshifter, Alexander had stepped up his security. I found it curious that they made a point to sniff me upon my return. I wasn't sure if it were a wereperson thing or not.

Getting out of the car, I quickly called out. "Alexander."

The big man turned with an inquisitive expression. "Yes?"

It felt like a stupid question, but I had to know. "Please don't be offended, but is it some sort of custom for werepeople to smell others in some sort of greeting or something?"

Alexander's face tensed. He lowered his voice, glancing from side to side as he stalked over. "Is that some sort of dog joke? Are you suggesting that we go around sniffing each other's asses?"

My heart skipped a beat. Fuck, I'd just insulted the man. "No...that's not what I meant. I—"

His big form quivered and his face turned pink before laughter spilled out his mouth. "Oh God, this never gets old!" It took several seconds but he calmed himself. "It's because of the shifters. They give off a strong floral scent before, during, and a half hour after a change." He fought off another fit of giggles before continuing. "They can't mask it." He pointed at my right hand. "I've never heard of one being able to duplicate the *vigiles* scarring either, but that's within the realm of possibility."

That explained why I'd smelled jasmine the night of the attack. "Good to know...thanks."

He clapped me on the shoulder before turning to leave. "If you need anything you've got my number."

I patted my pocket. "I do."

It was already after 5:00 p.m. and I'd need to hurry if I was going to catch dinner. Walking through the living room, down the hall, and into the kitchen, I found Kimberly, Andrew, and Isidore sitting at the table. Andrew glanced up and thumbed over his shoulder. "There's a plate and some roast on the counter."

Thank the gods. Giving them a thumbs up, I grabbed a plate. "Thanks."

After a quick dinner I made my way to my room, depositing the computer and papers I'd copied from the library before making my way over to see Heather.

We talked about my visit to Destrehan and she giggled. Her tone was haughty when she spoke. "You have to wonder if Brad and your new police buddy are related."

I sniggered. "Because they're both assholes?"

She guffawed, grabbed her gut, and winced. "Don't make me laugh!" She calmed herself and shook her head. "Because they're both Matherne's." Closing her eyes, she shifted a couple of pillows in an effort to get comfortable. "Of course, in this part of the country you can't throw a rock without hitting a Matherne or a Boudreaux, or even a Broussard for that matter!"

"I suppose."

Heather pushed herself up with a grunt. "Of course, Brad is from Destrehan, so the odds are pretty good they're related somehow. Probably distant cousins." She pursed her lips in thought. "Ya know, I've never really heard him speak about his family other than his father." She glowered at the memory. "That boy has some serious daddy issues. Probably why he's so attached to mine."

Not wanting to open that can of worms, I steered her back on topic. "Maybe next time I drive out that way I'll call him for tips on where to eat."

She smacked me playfully on the leg. "Don't be an ass." She started to titter and her chest heaved. "God, I'd love to see his face though." She gave me a hopeful glance. "If you ever do call him, make sure to push his buttons by using his full name."

"Which is?" I asked.

Her face soured. "Walter Bradley Matherne."

The name hit me hard in the gut and I froze. "Seriously? When's his birthday?"

She shot me an odd look. "Why? Planning on getting him something?"

Shooting her a dirty look, I shook my head. "Doubtful."

She let out a long breath. "July 31."

This wasn't possible. Seriously? One thing sure, but there were just too many coincidences for it not to be true. "I've got to go."

I got to my feet to leave when Heather waved a hand and the door swung closed. "Wait a second. You start asking questions about Brad and you've suddenly got to go? What's going on?"

I'm a terrible liar but I did my best to feign ignorance. "Nothing…." That's when it dawned on me what had just happened. Eyeing her, I didn't find the ring she normally wore, or any ring, necklace, or anything that could be used as a focusing item. "Where's your ring?"

She turned a sickly shade of alabaster, panic set in, and she moved her hand under the blankets. "I don't see what that has to do with my question."

Sitting on the edge of the bed, I stared at her curiously. "Let's start with the ring and then we can revisit your question."

She scowled, reluctantly pulling her hands out. "If I had to guess it's with my phone."

It took a second but then I understood. She believed her father had it along with all her other personal effects from that night. I didn't have a clue what use Robert would have with any of it, but that wasn't my concern at the moment. "If he has it then how are you able to use your abilities? I was under the impression you needed to be in possession of such items for them to work."

Her unease continued to grow, and she had the distinct look of a kid who'd been caught with her hand in the cookie jar. "Maybe because I don't need one."

From everything I'd read all witches needed a focusing object. Leaning back, I folded my arms and waited. "Go on."

Heather's form deflated and she closed her eyes in defeat. "Damn it!" She glared at the pill bottles on the nightstand for their betrayal. "I can't believe I slipped up so badly." With a heavy breath her eyes pleaded with me. "No chance you'd be willing to forget about it?"

Okay, now I felt like an asshole, but I needed to know what was going on. "I'd like to, but all things considered, I can't."

Reluctantly she nodded. "You're not the only one with secrets." Her weariness was apparent. "This can't leave this room. Swear to me."

I shook my head. "Let's hear it first. I'm not willing to put myself or my uncle at risk over a promise I may not be able to keep."

Heather sagged but understood. "My mother's father was a sorcerer." It was easy to see how nervous she was. "With my mom and dad both being witches, the odds were I'd be a witch as well."

Then it dawned on me. "You inherited your grandfather's gift of sorcery."

Relief and sorrow shone in her face. "Yeah."

Wow, okay; good for her. "Why lie about it?"

Her eyes bulged and the panic returned. "Well for starters, witches hate sorcerers." Seeing that I was slow on the uptake, she continued. "You've met my father; that man is a racist through and through. If he ever discovered I was a sorcerer, he'd kill me. I'm not talking about the yelling and screaming thing…I mean he'd literally kill me."

Now that's father of the year award material right there. "I'm sorry."

Her shoulders slumped forward and she did her best to become as small as possible. "It's become second nature to hide my talents." Her eyes pleaded with me again. "Promise you won't tell anyone."

She had nothing to worry about from me. I'd always felt bad about my situation growing up, but I'd never hid who I was. This was so much worse. The strain it must've put her under all these years. "You have my word."

Relief swept over her. "Thank you." She gave me a sheepish look and asked, "Think you can trust me with your secret now? What has you so hot and bothered about Brad?"

That was a cheap shot and one I probably deserved. "Sure." Glancing back at the door to make sure we were still alone, I sat up straight. "Martha had a file on Walter Percy in her office."

Her face scrunched itself up at the mention of his name. "What's that bastard got to do with it?"

It was good to see the man had fans. "I'm not sure that he does, but in the file was a marriage certificate and a couple of birth records...one of which was named Walter B. Percy, born on July 31, 1974."

She sniggered. "That's what has you all worked up? That's a huge jump."

The theory already had more holes than swiss cheese, and here she was poking a few more. Trying to sound more confident than I felt, I mounted a defense. "You have to admit that it's suspicious that Brad's name matches so closely. What are the odds of two boys being born in such a small town with the same first and middle names on the same day?"

That put her on the ropes but certainly not out. "I'll give you that...it's unlikely, but it's not out of the question."

I might as well stamp my feet and hold my breath at this point because she was right. It wasn't impossible. "But what if I'm right? I know it sounds desperate, but it's all I got."

There was pity in her eyes when she spoke. "You find more and I'll believe it; but if that's all you got, you're pretty screwed."

At least she wasn't sugarcoating it. "You're right, I'm screwed, but let's see where this goes before we totally discount the idea."

She pursed her lips and snarked, "You know that's not really a lead, it's more of a hunch. One that I'm guessing is wrong."

Chuckling, I nodded. "Could be, but I'm still going to check it out."

She threw up her hands in defeat. "I suppose it couldn't hurt."

Getting to my feet, I looked at the door and then her. "I should get going."

Her easy smile was back. "Good luck." With a flick of her wrist the door opened. "Stop by later if you want."

Seeing her happy again did quite a lot to improve my mood. "I'll see what I can do."

I was out of her room and into my own a few seconds later. Grabbing my computer, I started typing. If Brad Matherne and Walter B. Percy were two different people, it should be easy enough to figure out.

Chapter 21

Saturday June 6th

By the time the sun peeked over the horizon it was obvious that I'd overestimated my ability as a digital sleuth. All my attempts at tracking down Brad's past or even his present were proving to be fruitless. From what I could tell he didn't have a use for the Internet, meaning no social media, no credit cards, bank accounts, or even the slightest hint of a digital footprint. Of course, I could be looking in all the wrong places.

Truth of the matter was I didn't have the same credentials I'd possessed a month ago. A mere thirty days ago I could've made a call and had his entire life story by the end of business. Now I was relegated to doing Internet searches and paying for third party services to get the slightest bit of information, of which there was none. This was certainly not my finest moment, to be sure.

My phone rang just after 9:00 a.m., and to my great surprise it was someone who may be able to help…Lieutenant Baptist.

Sitting up straighter at my desk, I answered, "Good morning," trying to keep the exasperation out of my voice.

Baptist's thick accent carried over to his rich laugh. "You sound terrible. Long night?"

Deception wasn't ever one of the strongest abilities in my arsenal. Probably why I'd never moved out of my position in twenty-eight years. "You could say that." I paused. "To what do I owe the pleasure of your call?"

There was a sharp intake of breath and the rustle of papers in the background. "I tracked those numbers you gave me."

Some detective I was turning out to be; I'd totally forgotten about them. The value of Martha's meticulous note taking habits was becoming painfully apparent. "Let me guess…nothing?"

"Da," he said in a bored tone. "They appear to be burners purchased out of state." He paused and I heard more papers being moved. "You have one of them…correct?"

With a flick of a finger I knocked the burner into a nearby pile of books. It turned out to be another dead end. I could use it for a paperweight for all the good it was doing me. "Yeah."

He grunted his satisfaction. "Good. One of the techs gave me Andrew's address for the first number."

"And the other?" I asked, already guessing the answer.

He gave a contemptuous grumble. "Nothing. Dead as a doornail."

Snatching the phone off the table, I tossed it in the garbage. "Great!" Where I failed, perhaps the UCD would succeed. "I need you to look into a couple of names for me as soon as possible."

Baptist sniggered. "You're not wasting anytime in tapping the UCD's resources before officially taking the job."

He was right, but at the moment I didn't have a lot of options. "Yeah, sorry about that."

He calmed himself and I heard the sharp click of a pen being readied. "No worries. Who are you looking for today?"

Picking up Walter's file, I flipped through the notebook, stopping at the marriage certificate. "The first name on the list is Mary Percy, former resident of Destrehan. Not sure where she is now…perhaps a retirement home, but I can't be sure. I don't have a birthday, but I've got an old address."

There was a flurry of scratches before he spoke again. "Address?"

It took another ten minutes to go through what I needed on Mary, Brad, and Brody Percy. I knew it sounded crazy, but if I could connect any of the Matherne's to the Percy's I might have a chance. Of course Baptist wasn't happy, and he filled me in on Walter's vast political connections. While the UCD wasn't a fan, that didn't mean that the mayor's office agreed, and due to his involvement, it would slow the process down.

Ending the call, I stood, stretched, and headed for the door. I couldn't stop fidgeting; the frustration of not knowing what to do next wore on my nerves. I'd spent the last three decades being the solution to the problem, not ferreting it out. My handlers had done almost all the legwork prior to my involvement. Sure there were times I had to change things on the fly, but I always had a solid target and the resources of an entire government at my disposal.

I found Heather, Andrew, and Kimberly sitting around the table in the living room. I wasn't really in the mood to socialize, but they'd already seen me. Fuck! The last thing I wanted to do was get stuck in a conversation with anyone, even them. Too late now. Fighting off the wave of antisocial behavior, I waved and faked the semblance of a pleasant mood.

Pushing the thoughts of Brad, Walter, and the others to one side, I lumbered towards the table, trying to sound casual. "Good morning, folks."

Andrew seemed surprised at my presence. "When I didn't see you at breakfast I thought you'd already left for the day."

The mention of food made my stomach growl. "Sorry about that, I must've lost track of the time."

Heather's gaze locked onto me. "How's the hunt?"

She was obviously more than a little curious about Brad and so was I, but for very different reasons. I couldn't hide my frustration. "Terrible." Turning to Andrew, I shrugged. "The lack of any official resources is drastically hindering my progress."

Understanding flooded Andrew's face. "I'm sorry about that, but there isn't a lot I can do till Friday rolls around. If we did anything now it would only alert the others about your post."

Kimberly's displeasure was clear when she turned to Andrew. "That's true, but keeping it a secret until then is going to go over like a lead balloon." Her eyes were full of pity when they turned to me. "Nothing against you, but...."

I gave her an indifferent roll of my shoulders. "Don't worry about it. What's done is done, and remember, we have a tactical advantage at the moment. We can worry about the political fallout later."

Kimberly didn't appear convinced and turned back to Andrew. "The fact he's your nephew will only make things worse." She stopped, delight creeping onto her lips when she turned to me. "Is it true that Ms. Dodd refused to register you?"

The way she asked the question made me uneasy. Shuffling to the side, I felt my chest tighten. "She may have asked me to leave her office a bit hastily."

Andrew didn't appear bothered. "Ms. Dodd will be fine. Nothing to worry with."

Kimberly's eyes widened in disbelief. "Of course, because Elizabeth is known for her humility and taking responsibility for any shortcomings." Her disappointment mounted. "Andrew, you know she's going to take every opportunity to make him pay for her oversight."

That unsettled him and he considered her words. "Perhaps, but it can't be undone now." His face hardened and his voice turned to ice. "We couldn't allow Robert's candidates to take over as *vigiles*." He'd said Robert's name like he'd just tasted shit. "It would be a huge setback for everyone."

Kimberly fell back, acquiescing the point. "That's also true." Her weary gaze shifted to me. "But he's the one that has to live with the consequences."

Andrew couldn't argue the point. "I suppose it's a good thing Elizabeth has plenty of time to get past it."

Nodding at my uncle, I stepped closer. "Andrew's right, she'll just have to get over it. It's not like I can quit." I felt my resolve harden. "Considering she isn't my boss, interference in my affairs could be considered a crime." Seeing I had their attention, I continued. "Simply put, if she gets too far out of hand, I'll break it for her."

Kimberly teetered between astonishment and hilarity. She adopted a patronizing tone. "Perhaps you don't understand your position."

Before she took the conversation too far down that road, I cut in. "Perhaps it's you who doesn't understand the role of the *vigiles*." With the aid of the denarius, I set to work correcting her misunderstanding. "Prefects rule the triumvirate and the day to day actions of their territories, but their authority isn't greater than that of the local *vigiles*. It can't be…otherwise I'd be nothing more than a hired thug to be used at the prefect's whim."

The three of them looked at me in shock. The denarius was incensed by the outright lack of respect afforded my position, and we both swore to rectify it in the coming months. What I'd left unsaid would've caused chaos, but if Ms. Dodd didn't come to terms with the situation quickly, I'd be forced to strip her of the ability to interfere.

Kimberly found her voice, shaky as it might be. "You'd be the first *vigiles* that I've ever heard of to exercise those rights."

That revelation sent the denarius over the edge. It was fuming that the position had been allowed to fall into such a pathetic state. I didn't know why, but my anger flowed right alongside the coin's. "I haven't the faintest idea how things got this bad, but I can assure you that it'll change."

The embarrassment on Andrew's face was evident. "Perhaps we've all fallen into a convenient status quo…." He trailed off, ashamed. "If this is how you want to proceed, you'll have my support."

The denarius, satisfied with Andrew's answer, checked his name off a list of potential obstacles. Not that I had any idea of what I'd do about it even if he was opposed to the idea.

Heather didn't look well when she got my attention. "I could use a little help getting back to my room."

The political debate over, I gave her a smile. "Of course."

In one fluid motion I leaned over and scooped her up. Heather cocked an eyebrow at her mother. "What?"

Kimberly fought back a grin. "Oh, nothing dear. You just look so sweet in his arms."

Heather's face turned beat red, and tucking her head into my shoulder she mumbled, "Mother!"

Kimberly made a show of eyeing me up and down. "Careful with my little girl."

Blushing, I stepped around the table and padded off to Heather's room. "Yes ma'am."

Kimberly chuckled. "No need to be shy. It's not every day I let a strong handsome man carry my daughter off to bed."

Heather's nails dug into my back and she pulled her head out of my chest. "For God's sake, please shut up."

Trying to make our exit an expedient one, I picked up the pace.

Kimberly's voice carried after us, full of mirth. "What? If you're not interested, just remember I'll be single soon."

That put a hiccup in my step but I pressed on, keeping my eyes focused on the wall in front of me.

Heather's head collapsed into my chest again. Her voice full of horror, she said. "Oh God, kill me now."

Andrew and Kimberly's laughter followed us down the hall. Once we were safely in her room I nudged the door shut with a foot. Placing her gently on the bed, I pulled the blankets over her legs.

Heather was still crimson and terror filled her eyes. "I'm so sorry about my mother. She's...she's all sorts of embarrassing. Please don't judge me by her actions."

My cheeks still felt hot and the tightness in my throat wouldn't go away. "I wouldn't worry yourself about it. Other than the horrible embarrassment at my expense, it was kind of cute."

Heather averted her eyes, suddenly finding the spot on the floor next to my feet very interesting. "She may have gotten the idea that I thought you were attractive."

The tightness cut off my ability to take a breath for a split second. "You think so?"

She chewed her bottom lip, keeping her eyes on the floorboards. "Yeah; you're kinda cute in that weird, tall-dark-and-handsome way."

Sweat beaded on my forehead and I suddenly felt like a teenager. "Thank you, and if it makes you feel any better, I think you're gorgeous in that way-out-of-my-league kind of way."

Tearing her eyes off the floor, she tossed a pillow at me, turning so red I thought she might pass out. "You should probably go work, and we'll sort this out-of-your-league thing out later."

Thankful for the excuse, I gave her the thumbs up.

That's right, I'm super smooth. What the fuck kind of move was that? God, I'm such a dork.

"Absolutely...I mean, yes, I've got work." Stumbling backwards towards the door, I stammered. "See you later."

She didn't make the situation any less awkward when she returned my thumbs up with her own. "Bye," she said playfully.

To make things that much worse, I actually backed into the door and fumbled with the knob a few times before finally getting it open. Yep, smooth! Thankfully, in the safety of my own room I closed the door and leaned against it in desperation. That could've gone way better.

There was a chime and I opened my eyes to see the Surface Pro light up and the mail icon hovering on the screensaver. Grateful for the distraction, I snatched it up and saw the email was from Lieutenant Baptist. Damn, that was fast.

Gavin,

I made a cursory check on the four names you gave me, and three out of the four are a bit strange. The fourth one for James Matherne, who doesn't appear to have a middle name at all, checks out. He was adopted at age ten by the Matherne family living in Destrehan. He went through school without issue and joined the St. Charles Sheriff's Office right after high school. From what I've been told he's on vacation somewhere in Ireland for the next few weeks. I'll make a courtesy call when he returns.

As for Mary Percy, I'm still doing some research on her. Same for Walter B. Percy Jr. It's like they came out of nowhere and vanished nearly as quickly. I'll keep digging in the meantime.

As for Walter Bradley Matherne, his past is a bit of a mystery at the moment. No driving record, taxes, or any of the regular paper trails you'd expect to see.

I did find a warehouse out on the riverfront that appears to belong to him. It's located at 198 Mississippi River Trail, Jefferson, LA 70121.

Let me know if anything pops up for you when you go for a visit. I'll be in touch when I have more information.

Lt. William Baptist UCD

Considering I had to make a trip out, breakfast would have to be on the go. I'd picked up a backpack at Office Depot last night so I wouldn't have to lug everything by hand. Stuffing the Surface Pro into the front pouch, I grabbed the files, my notes, and shoved them down into the bag hastily.

Grabbing the gladius and the wakizashi, I looked around the room to make sure I had everything before heading out. Passing through the living room, I waved, chomping on a piece of dry toast on the way downstairs.

Chapter 22

The trip to the riverfront was blissfully uneventful…after that, however, I may've gotten myself lost. Okay, so I was lost, but not really…Google gave me poor directions. The problem was that the warehouse sat on the other side of the levee, making it impossible to see from the road. Perhaps it was pilot error, but there weren't any witnesses so nothing to worry about.

Considering how easily Brad spooked, I thought it best to park across the street at the self-storage center. After stowing my gear, I had to play a life size version of Frogger when I crossed the heavily traveled River Road. These drivers weren't playing…they flew by doing considerably more than the posted thirty-five miles per hour, and not one of them gave a fuck about pedestrians. After a few near misses I was across without any bodily injury; mentally, however, may have been a different story.

The paved drive and official looking gate gave the place a local government kind of feel. If I had to guess it was once a pumping station that had been phased out. I wouldn't have thought Brad clever enough to buy such a place. I'd seen the U.S. Government use the same strategy overseas. They would buy a place that was either official or made to look that way to keep the locals away. No one wanted to deal with government employees if they didn't have to. It gave an area or building extra security that it wouldn't otherwise have.

Moving up one of the paved branches of the Y shaped drive, I crested the levee to find two separate complexes. The nearest one, which was maybe forty yards away, consisted of a single story dilapidated red brick building and three large storage silos. The silo nearest me at this end of the lot was a dull gray thing that stood twice as tall as the building itself. The two older silos sat at the opposite end of the broken brick building, matching its height.

Standing at the top of the levee I took in my surroundings. Off to the left, leading up from River Road and rising out of the ground, cresting at the top of the levee, were four massive pipes running to a modern red brick structure another thirty yards in that looked to be completely intact. That was probably where I'd find Brad, but first things first…the smaller structure needed to be cleared before moving forward. I swung the backpack off my shoulder, pulled the gladius out, and fastened it to my belt. I'd tucked the computer, along with the other files, in the trunk of the Tucker before crossing the street.

The entrance was a pair of old white rotting wooden doors with a large pane of filthy glass about head high. Light poured in from the shattered and broken metal roof above, revealing its dark interior in shafts of brilliant white. Stepping up, I gave the first door a solid tug, and as expected it didn't budge. The next door, however, was unlocked and swung open, with a great deal of effort on my part, about a foot and a half before getting lodged against the pavement. That clearly wasn't going to shut again. Just what I needed, proof that I'd been there.

While it was clear from the state of the interior no one had traipsed in or out of this place in years, I would be remiss if I didn't verify its threat level. Again, not that I thought there was a problem, but years of training took over as I cleared the building. It took less than a minute of poking around inside to see the most danger the place proposed was me impaling myself on a rusty nail or being cut by some random piece of debris that littered the floor.

Stepping out, I shoved on the door to no avail. It was stuck there, and there was nothing I could do about it. With a hapless shrug, I focused on the building further up on my left. Where the first had been a shack in need of demolishment, the second warehouse was sturdy, secure, and slightly imposing. The deep red brick two-story building looked almost new, and its metal roof gleamed in the afternoon sun. I could see an overly large roll up garage door of flat gray metal prominently positioned in the middle of the building, facing a tiny yet empty parking lot.

A smaller gray metal door that looked more at home on a firehouse or school emergency exit stood next to it. Matching gray steel slats shuttered the front windows. It had a bland utility feel to go along with the entirely uninviting vibe it gave off in waves. What in the fuck would interest Brad about the place, other than the seclusion and the ability to hide evidence in the Mississippi River, a mere twenty yards away? Then again, I could be reaching for yet one more reason not to like the guy.

After giving the building a good once over, I ruled out gaining access through the long, narrow, horizontal windows since they were on the second floor, and sealed with gray metal shutters that matched the doors in front. There was always the novel approach of the front door. Stealthy it may not be, but it was the only way in or out of the fucking place. Stepping forward, I grasped the handle and pushed down on the thumb mechanism, and to my great surprise it pulled open. That was easy…but nothing good ever came from easy.

I flinched when the overhead florescent lights sprung to life. The harsh white light highlighted the room in glaring detail. I was shocked to see an immaculate two story open loft. About midway down on the right was a brushed silver metal spiral staircase leading to the floor above. The polished cement floor ran the length of what I would consider a cozy home. The furniture was comfortable yet modern, and I couldn't help but think back to Isidore, who would think he'd died and gone to heaven. To my right sat a vintage late '60s model GTO, fully tricked out. The deep purple paint glinted in the overhead lighting, with that fresh from the factory look.

The hairs on the back of my neck stood up as I felt energy coursing through the air. The denarius recognized the power and whispered *werebeast!* Everything went still and I felt more than heard someone coming up fast behind me. Shifting my weight, I spun, stepping to the side, barely able to keep my footing. I wrapped my hand around the hilt of the sword.

A massive gray and silver werepanther wrapped itself around my midsection, pinning my arm in place. He hefted me easily into the air, spun, tucked his shoulder in, and ran us into the solid metal door, using me like an airbag. I heard the sickening crack of at least one of my ribs snapping from the impact. Before the stars and darkness could leave my eyes, I suddenly felt weightless as he flung me through the air a good ten feet, then the worst part of any free flight came into play…the landing. I stuck it, with a solid eight point two, landing on my face and cracking a tooth, smearing blood only to slide to a halt a few feet further in.

The secret to winning most fights was simple. It wasn't about how good you were or how strong you might be; it was about how much punishment you could take and still get back up. Of course, while skill and power could win out, the ability to get up and fight after being crushed and tossed across the room was enough to scare the shit out of most people.

However you wanted to look at it, be it a good thing or a bad, I'd had a lot of experience with pain. This sucked, and before it was over it was going to suck even more, but as long as I drew breath and could move there was a chance.

The big man stalked forward slowly, more out of overconfidence than concern. When he was close enough I spun, taking his legs out from under him, and he hit the floor hard. Getting to my feet, I pulled the gladius free of its sheath. That's when I finally got a good look at the thing. It was biped, with two arms that ended in great gray claws. Its face was a horrible mashed up thing, something between a man and a great panther.

Its big yellow eyes flicked closed and he gingerly rose up, clearly not used to being on the receiving end of…well, anything. Hunching over, he growled and shot forward, raking his claws across my chest, ripping long deep gashes. But he wasn't the only one who'd drawn blood. He hissed and spat, howling in pain as he tried to hold his gut closed. The gladius had found its mark and the panther's blood ran freely to the floor.

Anger clouded his judgement and he charged again. I went low, diving to the side, swinging the sword with a powerful backhand, slicing through the calf muscle and sending him to his knees. Spinning to my feet, I lunged, driving the gladius through the back of the creature's skull, down through his neck, and out his chest. Yanking it free, I drew back and sliced through the neck, cleaving his head from his shoulders. There was a wet thud when it hit the floor.

The body changed from the great werepanther to an older looking gentleman. Of course, I was a firm believer we all looked much older than we were when we had surgery, unconscious, or in this case, were dead. This man was no different. Looking around for something to clean up the mess, I quickly realized that there was little hope of covering it up. That was the thing about concrete; no matter how much you polished its surface, dump a corpse worth of blood on it and you were sure to get a stain.

Putting aside any thought of hiding the mess, I took stock of my personal situation. Things weren't looking good...I had at least one broken rib, deep gashes ran the breadth of my chest, and I was going to bleed to death from it or one of the internal wounds. There wasn't a chance in hell that I'd be able to fight off another surprise attacker, and with that in mind I stanched what bleeding I could and proceeded to clear the building.

With every step pain shot through me; each breath was labored, ragged, and wet. If I got help soon I'd probably live. Pain I could handle...a random attack, even from someone like Brad, and I was a goner.

Keeping the gladius out, I willed the discomfort to one side before slowly making my way through the loft. The second floor was interesting to say the least. At the far end I found a state of the art security system. Thankfully the cameras were on a closed circuit, which meant I only needed to remove the hard drive from the computer to ensure my anonymity.

The real question was, who in the fuck did I report this to? The denarius responded that I answered to no higher authority before remaining silent. It sounded strained, as if it were in pain. Its response wasn't exactly helpful. Should I call Andrew, or did I call the UCD?

Honestly, calling the UCD wasn't really an option, so I pulled out my phone and dialed Andrew's number. It rang twice before he answered. He was laughing as he put the phone to his ear. "Were your ears burning?"

What? I didn't really want to know nor did I care. "Forgive me, but this isn't a social call." Yeah, that came out like I was an asshole, but I was bleeding out, so he'd have to get over it.

Andrew's voice turned somber and there was an urgency in his voice. "What's wrong? Are you all right?"

Trying to stifle moans of pain, I slowly made my way into the nearest chair. "Where to start? There's a dead guy on the floor, I'm pretty beat up, and I didn't know who else to call."

It took a couple of minutes to get it all out between the blood loss and the difficulty breathing, but he got the idea pretty quickly. He barely paused after I'd finished before he spoke in a rush. "You still have Alexander's number on you?"

"Yeah," I replied.

"Call him now and tell him to come by and clean up the mess," Andrew ordered. "After that I want you back here…I'm pretty sure Kimberly can help."

Made sense. Of course, I wanted to tell him to call Alexander, and then I realized Andrew didn't know the address. "I'll be in touch."

A quick phone call and thirty minutes later Alexander showed up. I'd moved the chair closer to the front door to wait. He looked at me and then down at the corpse, and his astonishment and awe were easy to see.

"You did this?" he asked.

His tone was odd and I couldn't tell if he was angry or impressed. I was hoping for the latter because I was in no condition for round two. With great trepidation I got to my feet. "Yeah, but I swear it was in was self-defense."

Alexander's mouth fell open, then a low, soft, rueful chuckle escaped his lips. "Goddamn!" His gaze searched for understanding. "Do you have any idea who this is?"

With a quick glance, I shook my head. "He's just another dead guy."

Alexander huffed, shaking his head in disbelief. His eyes were full of an unwarranted awe that I couldn't readily explain. "Damn! Did I ever misjudge you."

Shaking my head, I said, "It was complete self-defense…I've got the hard drive from the cameras to prove it."

Alexander laughed, and held his hands out. "No, no. Not what I meant."

"What did you mean?"

Alexander leaned over and poked the dead man's cheek, presumably to make sure it was real. "This was Marcus Gray, one of the oldest, if not the oldest, werepanther in the world." He stood and slowly wiped the digit against his pants. "He had to be closing in on three hundred years old." Squinting, he pointed at my chest. "That's all he did?"

That was absolutely hysterical, considering all he did was practically rip me in two. "I have a couple of broken ribs to go with this beautiful reminder." Eyeing the corpse, I shrugged. "Probably beats being dead though."

Alexander snorted his disbelief. "Ya think?" He shot Marcus the finger before kicking the lifeless body hard enough to scoot it a half dozen feet. "Fucker was a world class douche, with a long list of grave markers to his credit."

"Oh," was all I could manage.

Alexander pulled his cell out of his pocket and gave the all clear signal. Then he looked at me. "Are you finished here?"

Considering I was about to pass out, I nodded. "Yeah."

Alexander stepped forward and snatched my bag off the floor. "This is yours, right?"

The ability to speak was quickly leaving me and I nodded.

Alexander swung a big meaty arm under my shoulders, holding me upright. "Good. Andrew's in a bit of a rush to get you home." He hefted me up when I started to sag. "I'll drive if that's not a problem." He moved us around and took in the place. "Your uncle is going to be shocked about Marcus."

Maybe it was the blood loss, but part of me felt a little bad for the man. "I'm starting to feel a little bad about killing the guy."

Alexander's tone was harsh when he said, "Don't. He was a complete bastard who enjoyed being a slave to what he called his 'betters.'"

"And who did he serve?"

Alexander grimaced. "Walter Percy."

And we have a winner! "Well, that means I'm on the right track." Looking around the loft, I growled. "Is there any chance that you guys can hold this place till I can get back and make sure I didn't miss anything?"

Alexander cackled. "Oh, we can do that. I've been looking for a place for the rest of my clan to hold up until things calm down."

Giving the man a curt nod, I nearly jumped out of my skin when I heard the door pull open. Reaching for the gladius, I felt power ripple off Alexander as he prepared to turn. We both relaxed when we recognized the man coming in as one of the guards from Alexander's crew. Five minutes later I was in the passenger seat and headed home. Hopefully, Andrew had something that could fix me up quickly so I could get back on the road again.

Chapter 23

We were about ten minutes into the drive when we hit a vicious bump in the road and I felt a rib puncture my lung and another edge up against my heart. I screamed and time stopped...not the you're-about-to-die-and-your-life flashes-before-your-eyes kind of stopped. I mean it stopped. I couldn't move and I heard a whisper behind me.

The creature spoke in a cold, haunted flat whisper. "The little spirit inside you thinks you're going to die."

It paused, and I felt something slip through the flesh of my back and boney fingers protruded from my chest. "It's correct." It hesitated, flexed its fingers, then pulled back, rearranging the broken ribs. "That is something I cannot allow!"

Then time resumed its natural course. I howled in agony when the power of the denarius sprung to life and brilliant blue flames erupted from the gashes on my chest, cauterizing them instantly.

Alexander nearly wrecked the car when my shirt caught fire. He might have done less harm to me if he had. Instead he waved a big meaty hand in my direction, beating the flames into submission and me along with them.

Fifteen minutes later we arrived at the old house. One would think that with the rib out of my lung and off my heart things would be better. They'd be wrong. My ribs were still broken, two at least, and while I wasn't losing blood any longer, I hadn't exactly replaced it either. Then there was my burned chest and my smoldering shirt. Add that to the fact I had to climb the stairs to the second floor, and it made for a very long painful trip.

Every breath sent waves of pain through me and every step jarred my body, but this wasn't my first rodeo. I grunted and shuddered with each and every step. Alexander patiently walked behind me to make sure I didn't roll down the staircase.

When I pushed the door open Kimberly stopped mid-step. I saw a moment of shock on her face, quickly replaced by a blank, all business expression. The woman must have been a trauma nurse at one time and her training kicked in. She waved me into the nearest chair, taking stock of the visible damage. When I didn't immediately respond to the nonverbal order, her expression hardened and she pointed at the chair once more.

Kimberly's voice carried an edge I'd never heard before. "You need to sit and let me look at you."

Andrew swung around to stand over me, taking in the damage. "What the hell happened to you?"

Thankfully, Alexander grabbed Andrew's elbow to pull him out of the way and answered the question. He pulled his mobile out and clicked through a few photos before holding it out to Andrew. "Gavin and Marcus Gray went ten rounds, and Marcus lost."

Andrew's shock was complete, his eyes wide, ignoring the phone and focusing on Alexander. He pointed at me and fury filled his voice. "He did this? Where did that son of a bitch slither off to?"

Alexander wisely kept his mouth shut, tapping the top of the phone and forcing Andrew's eyes onto the screen. Andrew recoiled at the sight of the severed head.

Alexander hooted, mirth in his tone. "I'm happy to say Marcus didn't make it."

Andrew took the phone and stared at it a long time before turning his attention to me. "You did this?"

Kimberly, meanwhile, was poking and prodding at my chest. Swinging around, she pushed Andrew out of the way with a grumble, disgust written across her delicate features. "Get the fuck out of my way! You can gossip later, but right now I've got a patient to attend to." She gave Alexander and Andrew a pointed glare. "Unless either of you want to be second and third in line, find somewhere else to be!"

Even the slightest pressure caused my chest to vigorously object, so I kept mostly quiet minus a couple of grunts as she continued her examination. "Think you could ease up a little? I just got a rib out of a lung…I don't need another."

She acquiesced to my request, then she grabbed a pair of surgical scissors out of her bag and cut away my shirt. She winced at the burned mess on my chest. "What the hell did you do?" She wheeled on Alexander. "Did you take a goddamn blow torch to him?"

With a weak wave, I pointed at the mark on the back of my right hand. "This isn't Alexander's work. It was the denarius."

He paled and looked down at us. "I don't know what happened, but it scared the shit out of me. One second he was sitting there bleeding, the next he was on fire and the car filled with the scent of burning flesh." Alexander's pallor worsened and I thought he might puke. "I've never seen anything like it."

Andrew stepped closer, handing the phone to Alexander. This new information had garnered his full attention. He got close enough to get a good look at the blistered and melted skin, but stopped far enough away to not impede Kimberly's work. "Fascinating," he mumbled. "The denarius did all that?"

I didn't understand why he was suddenly so interested. I rolled my shoulders noncommittally. That was a mistake…pain coursed through my body in long nauseating waves. Trying to keep the contents of my stomach off the floor, I tensed and held my breath until it passed. "Thankfully. I may've bled out if it hadn't."

For a split second I considered telling them about the boney hand that fixed my ribs, and the denarius panicked. *No, that wasn't my doing.*

Then who? I wondered.

I don't know, but that information is not for them.

The denarius was certain on that fact, and who was I to question it further?

Andrew was curious when he turned to Alexander. "How serious were the wounds?"

Alexander didn't look well, and his voice was low when he spoke. "I'm not sure how Gavin was conscious when I arrived. I've seen men die from far less."

During the conversation, Alexander and Andrew had drifted too close for Kimberly's liking and she growled. "If you don't step back I'm going to cut the both of you!"

She pulled an ancient brown vial and a couple of cotton balls from the open bag on the table. Removing the stopper, the room filled with a foul stench as she poured a thick, green ichor onto my chest. Replacing the stopper, she used the cotton balls to smear the near vomit inducing fluid over the charred wound.

The green ooze suddenly started to crackle and bubble. Kimberly fell back in surprise, and my chest felt like it was on fire for the second time in less than an hour. Sickly gray and black smoke rose into the air and the last of the ichor boiled away, leaving my chest covered in a thin layer of ash.

Everyone stood there, dumbfounded. It took nearly a minute before Andrew turned and disappeared, returning quickly with wet washcloths and a towel. Kimberly held out a hesitant hand to take the washcloth before regaining her composure. Once she was fully in control of her body she started wiping the cool cloth against the wound.

The sensation of the cold cloth against the hot skin felt good, and then I realized I wasn't in pain. Testing a theory, I took a deep breath…nothing. With each stroke, Kimberly revealed the bright pink of new skin. Sure it was in the form of four really nasty jagged scars, but I was healed.

"That's fucking awesome!" I said, mouth agape.

I'd expected to find satisfaction on Kimberly's face, but instead she looked confused and perhaps a little frightened. She peered up at me, her voice barely above a whisper. "How do you feel?"

Taking the towel from Andrew, I wiped the rest of the ash away and tentatively leaned forward. My ribs still ached, but it was nothing a hot shower wouldn't cure. The room was quiet and I craned my neck around to see their stunned faces. "What? I'm fine. Hell, I'm better than fine. I feel great."

Kimberly tucked the vial away and scrambled to her feet. "You shouldn't. The salve was meant to speed up the healing process only slightly, fight off infections, and ease the pain." She gestured at me and her face scrunched up in disbelief. "Nothing like that was supposed to happen."

"Oh," was all I could manage. Getting my head on straight, I looked at Alexander. "Think you could give us a minute?"

Alexander was only too happy to comply. Personally, I thought he'd seen enough weirdness and only needed an excuse to leave.

Kimberly kept her distance but I could see curiosity getting the better of her. "That's just so odd."

I got to my feet and looked at them. "I'm sure everyone has questions, me included, but if there are no objections I'd like a shower."

Not hearing any, I went to clean up. Twenty minutes later I was clean, and to my surprise my ribs were no longer an issue. I still hurt, but it was more of a forgettable dull ache. Grabbing a clean set of clothes, I made sure everything was a George original. If I'd been wearing one of his shirts this morning, I wouldn't have had my chest torn open.

Stopping in the kitchen, I found Isidore and Alexander standing over the counter, whispering. They nearly jumped out of their skins when I popped in. Isidore looked at me, shaking his head. "Do you ever make noise?"

Grunting out a, "Meh." I craned my neck trying to see what was on the counter. "Occupational hazard."

Isidore stepped aside to reveal the heaping plate of burgers and grumbled. "Normally I'd tell people to mind themselves so as not to get hurt, but I think I'll keep my mouth shut."

Alexander chuckled. "Wisest thing you've said in years."

I suppressed my amusement and tried to do a little damage control along the way. "Ever think I might've gotten lucky?"

Isidore snorted. "Please! I've seen Marcus. Nobody's that lucky!"

I could see by the looks on their faces there wasn't a chance in hell of convincing them otherwise. My stomach growled and I pointed at the burgers. "Any chance I could get one of those?"

Isidore thumbed at the table. "Take a seat and I'll make you one."

That was an offer I couldn't pass up. "Thanks."

Isidore set about making the burger with all the trimmings, allowing me to eat in relative silence as he and Alexander discussed house security. Finishing up, I headed into the living room to find Kimberly and Andrew having a heated discussion at the desk.

Kimberly waved a triumphant hand in my direction. "Do you believe me now?"

Andrew's eyes fixated on me. "I'm not convinced."

Kimberly's mouth fell open in disbelief. "Seriously?"

It couldn't have been more plain to see that I was the subject of conversation and they were having a serious disagreement on theories. I'd never liked being the center of attention, and I liked it less when people talked behind my back. Strolling over, I gingerly sat in the chair next to Kimberly. "Anyone care to fill me in?"

Irritation covered Kimberly's face, and glaring at Andrew she waved for him to interject. "Yes, Andrew, please tell Gavin what we've been talking about."

He looked more than a little put out at the suggestion. "I'd like to know how you're feeling first, if that's all right?"

Gesturing at my chest, I scowled. "I'm a little sore in places, but otherwise fine."

Andrew contemplated my words for longer than it took me to speak them. Turning to Kimberly, he shook his head. "If your theory was correct he'd be completely healed by now." He paused, gaining strength for what must be his defense. "Think about it...the entire grounds are covered in enchantments, which I might add haven't lost an ounce of their potency since he arrived."

Kimberly didn't appear to be convinced, but his words had clearly shaken her confidence. Turning to face me, she pushed herself up in the chair. "But you are feeling significantly better since I applied the ointment?"

"If you mean have I improved since then, the answer is no." I felt a need to clarify the situation. "All my relief came from the ointment itself. Sure, the hot shower took away the aches, but then again that happens for everyone."

She deflated at the words. "I see."

Even with the defeated look on her face I felt like they were pushing me into a corner. "I have no idea what you guys are talking about. Maybe if one of you came out and said what was on your mind I could help."

Kimberly dug up the courage to speak first. "With everything I've seen recently, and after a long discussion with your uncle, I was starting to think that you were a siphon."

The denarius woke up at the words, and it urged caution.

"What's a siphon?" I asked.

Andrew glowered at Kimberly. "They're a myth and nothing to concern yourself about." His gaze never left Kimberly when he spoke. "There's never been recorded proof of their existence."

That was a fucking dodge and not helpful. "That didn't answer my question."

Andrew tore his gaze from Kimberly. "A siphon absorbs power from the world around them. They can use any sort of magical energy to heal themselves, and they drain the life from those around them at an astonishing rate." He turned to Kimberly. "That is if you believe the legends."

Draining the life out of everyone around me and transforming magic into healing properties. I could definitely check one of those things off the list. But my gut told me that I wasn't a siphon. I may have some of their traits, but it was obvious even to me that she was wrong. "Granted I may heal quickly when exposed to certain types of magic, but I think we can all agree that I'm not sucking the life out of you. Think about it…if that were the case Heather wouldn't be getting better."

Kimberly blinked at the words, slowly nodding her head. "That's true, but you have to admit," she waved a hand at my chest, "whatever that was is weird."

What could I say? Hell yes, it was weird, and I didn't have an explanation for it. "You'll get no argument from me." Tapping my temple, I continued. "Even the denarius knows that I'm not a siphon. But it isn't sure what I am other than a stone born."

Kimberly was alert and she looked between Andrew and myself. "You can speak with it?"

"Of course." For the life of me I couldn't figure out what I'd said that rated the shock they wore.

Andrew looked confused. "I knew it was a warehouse of knowledge much like my own coin, but I've never heard of anyone being able to communicate with it."

I had the sudden feeling that I'd just told the room I had an imaginary friend. "Maybe the others haven't ever actually voiced it. I mean it sounds a little peculiar…."

Kimberly's face was hard yet somehow more welcoming. She gestured at my right arm. "Andrew tells me that isn't the only unusual thing about your bond with the coin."

The Aquila…one more item in a long list of eccentricities. Pulling up the sleeve high enough for her to see it, I said, "I suppose it isn't."

Kimberly got to her feet and for the first time since my chest was covered in ash she got close enough to touch me, running a finger around the scar tissue. "Could it be?"

Andrew was on his feet and next to her nearly instantly. "Like I said earlier, I really don't think so."

The way she ran her finger around the symbol was almost reverent in nature. "Well, I do."

Her words hit Andrew hard enough to make his body slump. "It couldn't be."

With a jerk of my sleeve I covered the mark. This whole talking about me like I wasn't in the room really pissed me off. "I hate coming in late on a conversation because I miss all the important shit, like the context in which any of your words make sense."

Andrew looked worried, but kept his eyes fixated on the sleeve of my shirt. "I'll look into it." In an afterthought he brought his gaze up to mine. "She believes that you wear Caesar's seal." He looked at her pointedly. "If that were the case, Lazarus would've been here by now."

Kimberly collapsed into her chair with a sigh. "Who says he isn't on the way?"

Andrew's annoyance was getting the better of him, and he raised his voice. "Let's start with the fact that Europe hasn't lost their shit. Seriously, if he so much as moved a toe outside the Vatican, people would be shouting about it. Secondly, there hasn't been a *vigiles* strong enough to take over for Naevius since his death at the Battle of Hastings, and you somehow think that my nephew is going to walk in and suddenly pick up the mantel?"

Kimberly was ready for the argument and pointed at me again. "He wears the Aquila, and I've never heard of another vigiles having such a mark. You really need to accept the fact that Gavin isn't normal by any stretch of the imagination."

While this was fascinating, I had things to do and sitting here wasn't getting it done. I got to my feet and let out a long breath. "Thank you for the compliment, but none of that is really important right now. Let Andrew dig into the mark if you want, but right now I've got to go."

Quickly saying my goodbyes, I hastened off to my room in an effort to get my head around the possibilities. If Lazarus did show up it would only complicate things, and I didn't need that right now. I found it curious that the denarius was choosing now to be silent on the matter. Great, even my imaginary friend wasn't talking to me. I needed to go to Elmwood and check on Gabriel, and maybe if I were lucky, I'd find something helpful on Walter in the process.

Chapter 24

Cooler temperatures were ushered in by the setting of the sun. It was dark by the time I reached Elmwood. The denarius did it's best to alleviate my concerns about siphons. While they were dangerous to all life, they were especially so to those who wielded magic. There was no recorded occurrence of such a creature, but the tale had been passed down in legend from one generation to the next. From what I could gather it was the magical world's version of a Krampus, something told to children to ensure they behaved.

According to the myth, their power was such they'd drained the very life from the land they lived on, creating the great deserts of the world. They were destroyers of entire civilizations, and their bones continued to take life even after their death. I, on the other hand, was limited to absorbing magic and perhaps the souls of the dead.

It occurred to me to ask the denarius about the peculiarity of our ability to communicate with one another. At first it was quiet, but after a few seconds it spoke.

I've been silent for more than a thousand years.

Since Naevius? I asked.

I felt the denarius bristle at the name. *Naevius was the last to hear me speak, but I stopped talking with him hundreds of years before his death. He was an unworthy choice, one that I vowed never to make again.*

That made me pause. This being, person, creature, had waited for more than a thousand years to choose someone worthy. *Why me?*

The denarius laughed joyfully as it flitted around my mind. *You are more powerful than you know. A part of your soul is ancient, and the blood that runs through your veins is of the gods above!*

That made me chuckle at the absurdity of the comment. *Whatever you say.* I paused. *What do I call you?*

I felt it puff out in pride. *I am the denarius, for now at least.* It paused as if it were trying to recall something. *That's all I remember of who I am for now, but once I'm fully awake and we tap into the others, my memory will be restored.*

The others? I asked.

Yes, the other denarius. We are all separate, but we are all one, the denarius said quietly. *It's as if I'm cut off from parts of myself, but that's changing now. Thanks to you.*

Something inside me told me the conversation was at an end. Just as well, because I was pulling into the parking spot outside the old DHL center, better known as the House of the Dead to Gabriel.

My questions about Lazarus were met with silence…the denarius refused to deny or confirm our connection. The one thing I felt from the coin was the fact that it wished to wrap this situation with Walter up as quickly as possible. In that we were in total agreement; the other things could wait until such time we had a moment to take a breath.

Even with the distraction of the denarius, I had a feeling of being followed. Traffic had been virtually nonexistent, and I doubted it was possible that I'd been physically tailed. Of course, with magic in the mix that may not have been necessary.

The business park was dead to the world at this time of day; even so, I gave the area a hard look before making my way to the door. Pausing, I looked around to ensure I was alone before I punched in the code, then waited for the click of the magnetic lock to disengage before stepping inside. Gabriel stepped through the double glass doors leading to the back, eating a sandwich with one hand while holding a Glock in the other.

Sucking something out of a tooth, he holstered the Glock. "Evening."

With a wave of my bag, I asked, "How are things?"

He held the door open as I passed. "Everything's fine here. You, on the other hand, look like you've had a rough day."

That was a nice way of saying I looked like roadkill. "Yeah, it's been a rough one." Glancing over my shoulder, I took one more look at the doors.

Gabriel followed my gaze. "What?"

Frustrated, I shuddered. "I'm not sure. I had the sense someone was tailing me, but I never caught sight of them."

Gabriel had an uneasy look on his face. "Let me grab some gear and I'll make a pass of the grounds."

Unable to fight off the sensation, I gave him the thumbs up. "Sure, I'll be in the office."

Gabriel turned on the spot and headed to the armory, sandwich in hand.

Setting the backpack on the desk, I shut the door and tugged on the first cabinet. It had no more than swung to the side when all hell broke loose. The lights went out and the place went dark. Pulling the cabinet into place, I stepped back to grab the wakizashi out of the pack. Emergency lights flickered into dim existence while gunshots rang through the facility. I didn't need all my years of experience in gunfights to tell that there was only one shooter, most likely Gabriel.

I quickly made my way through the poorly lit halls, clearing rooms as I went. Rounding the corner, I found the source of the commotion. Two dozen specters were closing in on a glowing Gabriel. The man was surrounded by a brilliant white light that kept them at bay. Every time they pressed forward, his aura shrank by several inches. It would only be a matter of seconds before they were on him.

Remembering my previous encounter with the specters, I recalled with clarity how their claws punctured thousands of tiny holes throughout my body. No matter how strong Gabriel may be, I was sure he wouldn't survive the encounter.

Picking up speed, I felt the pull of the beast deep inside me. Raising the wakizashi, I brought it down in a vicious angular slice, cleaving two of them in half. The remaining embers of the destroyed souls was all the beast needed to become manifest. I roared as the flowing robe swept over me, absorbing the last of their power. A wave of pain hit me hard and I felt my right hand transform itself into an onyx glove as the left elongated into a blue flaming gauntlet.

Sweeping the blade wide I caught two more. I spun and caught another in the face with the silver blade. There I could see my reflection in the glass door. The shadows wrapped themselves around me in a way that made me look like the mythical Grim Reaper. The robes appeared to be alive, swirling around me of their own accord. I thought I could see the souls of the damned bound to me in this tattered form. The hood was a ghastly thing that kept my face hidden in a pool of darkness. The only things visible under it were the glowing orange-red orbs where my eyes should've been.

With a shiver I turned back to the battle, but not before the first of the specters drove their hands deep into my back. Tearing myself free, I spun and cleaved the offender in two and pulled its power into my own.

Slamming my left hand into the specter speeding towards me, I stood there and watched it burn. Tendrils spread out from the billowing reaper's cloak and tore apart the last of the specters in seconds, devouring even more power. I felt my aura expand and it flared when it touched the gleaming white light of Gabriel. The resulting discharge sent him hard into the wall, knocking him unconscious. At least it erased the look of fear and horror in his eyes. I had a feeling that he wasn't taking this whole Grim thing very well.

With the specters gone the beast inside receded, leaving me to clean up the mess. Gabriel had punctuated their arrival with gunfire, and I'd ended their visit with a clash between light and darkness. Kneeling, I got my arms under the big guy, and to my amazement lifted him easily. I made for the armory and the large conference table, where I deposited him. Grabbing a Coke out of the nearby fridge, I popped the top with a crack and a hiss to wait for his return to the land of the living.

My wait wasn't a long one, maybe fifteen minutes...time I spent checking the facility to insure we hadn't missed any of our guests. The last five minutes were the longest by far, waiting for the man to stir. And stir he did! His eyes popped open and he frantically looked around the room as he did a crab crawl backwards, falling off the table, punctuated by screams of terror.

After nearly a minute of him cowering in the corner, he straightened up and got to his feet, nervously looking around for unseen enemies. His voice was hoarse and it cracked with each syllable. "We were attacked!" Gabriel looked at me with fear in his eyes. "How did you survive the reaper? It tore the souls apart, and I thought I was next...." He paused, searching for words. "A fucking reaper! Why am I still alive? They aren't even supposed to exist!" He paused and looked at me again. "How are you even here?"

A reaper? What the fuck! I could feel the denarius become alert before vanishing from my senses. Great time for it to suddenly want a vacation.

Taking a drink of the dark bubbly overly sweet liquid, I shook my head. "If they aren't supposed to exist, how do you know it was a reaper?"

Gabriel staggered. "Part of my heritage.... The angel side of my parentage has an innate ability to recognize such a creature. That's all it screamed in my head when I saw it, and then I was down. I was sure it was going to kill me." He looked at me curiously again. "You haven't told me how you survived the creature."

Grabbing a clean glass off the counter, I moved over to the refrigerator and opened the freezer. I pulled out a chilled bottle of vodka I'd seen earlier and poured him a very healthy glass and handed it to him. "You should have a couple of drinks and sit for this."

Gabriel hesitantly took the glass and fell into his chair. "Why?"

If the denarius wasn't going to help, then I'd need to get the information the old fashioned way and ask someone who knew more about the subject than I did. "Tell me about the reapers."

Gabriel took a large gulp before grabbing the bottle and topping himself off. "Reapers are myth...well, I thought they were mythical, but now I'm not so sure."

Trying to keep the impatience out of my voice, I urged him to continue. "That doesn't really tell me about them."

Gabriel took another hit and then let out a long breath. "I don't know much." He must've seen the irritation on my face, so he continued. "They are brutal, terrible creatures that show up every so often throughout history when the dead walk the earth. They serve as some sort of barrier between the living and the dead."

I leaned forward, suddenly more interested. "Could they show up because of a single powerful necromancer?"

Gabriel shook his head. "I don't know, but that doesn't feel right. It would take an army of necromancers raising the dead to bring forth a reaper."

I tried to remain calm but I felt panic in the recesses of my mind. An army? That wasn't good. "Gabriel, I need you to remain very calm. Think you can handle that?"

Gabriel didn't look so good and he pounded back a bit more vodka. "Probably, but I'm not promising anything if The Reaper shows up."

That kind of sucked considering what I was about to say. "I'm not sure how you saw the fight, but if you think about it carefully, you'll notice that 'The Reaper' kept the specters from killing you. You might even say he saved your life."

Gabriel scoffed at me and slammed down the last of the vodka. He paused before pouring himself another drink, his face turning sour. "You weren't there…it was only me and The Reaper. Even if you had been there, what makes you think it was there to save me?"

Keeping calm, I waved a hand for him to continue. "Think it through a bit further. You didn't see me but you saw The Reaper, and yet I saw the fight."

Gabriel upended the bottle and swallowed several times. Bringing it down, he looked me in the eyes. "That was you, wasn't it?"

"It was," I said calmly.

He took another drink from the bottle and then poured some into the glass. "No, that's not possible. I've shook your hand, for God's sake. I would've known. Hell, I'm still breathing. No. It's not possible. You're lying."

Huh? The man clearly didn't want to believe me. "What reason do I have to lie? And how would you know from shaking my hand?"

His speech was slurred and the laugh was dark. "Angels and nephilim are life, but reapers are our exact opposite. They bring death. We cannot touch without hurting one another by our nature."

"Perhaps the information you have is wrong, because I assure you that was me. Think about it, Gabriel. Think back to the fight, The Reaper. I was using the wakizashi," I said as I patted the sword.

He looked at the sword, then me, and then the sword. "Holy shit!" He jumped to his feet. "You're a goddamn reaper."

I shook my head. "I'm a stone born. It seems that I have the abilities of the creatures you call a reaper, but I'm nothing to fear. If I were the creature you described, why would I bring you here and wait for you to wake up, only to try and kill you?"

Gabriel thought about it for a long while, keeping his grip on the pistol. Finally, after nearly a minute, he took his hand off the grip and collapsed into his chair. "You may be a stone born, but I promise you that you're a reaper as well. The fear of you is instinctual but one I can get past. As you pointed out, you did save my life. That's twice now, and for that I owe you my loyalty and my respect."

This could've gone very differently, but it hadn't and now I had more information than I'd previously possessed, and Gabriel was still willing to serve as centurion. I would count that in the win column.

Keeping my voice low, I dared a grin. "Think we could keep all this between us?"

He pounded back another gulp of vodka before fixing me with a straight face. "Well, with all the friends I have hanging around I'm not sure how that's going to be possible."

Sarcasm, fantastic.

"Thing is, if we are going down the path I think we are, your secret will be out sooner rather than later," he said.

If we were going down that path, there would be an army of necromancers blocking the way, and I didn't care if they knew who I was or not. I'd only met one of their ilk and I already didn't like them.

With a tired shake of my head, I shrugged. "Maybe, but right now I've got other problems."

Gabriel gave me a look that told me he understood, yet wished to reassure me. "I'll keep your secret and my promise to serve as Caesar's centurion."

I was not sure why but the words gave me comfort. "Thanks." Looking over at the clock, I turned back to Gabriel. "Will you be all right?"

He gave me a drunk sneer and a wave of his hand. "I'll be fine. We nephilim heal quickly, even from learning that our new friend is a reaper."

Friend? I couldn't recall the last time I'd had a friend. It wasn't like anyone from the reservation qualified. The most I could hope for there was silent animosity. This was a first for me and it felt good. "I don't think I've ever had a friend before...I like it."

Gabriel snorted into his drink. "That would make two of us." He held his glass up. "To new friends." He nudged the bottle and sucked on his lip. "Next time you come back, think you could bring a bottle?"

I sniggered. "Of course!" With a big thumbs up, I headed for the door. "I've got some reading to do in the office before I head back."

His eyes were glassy and he looked exhausted. "The fight earlier and maybe the booze after have taken its toll on me." Getting to his feet, he made to follow me out. "I'm going to crash for the night."

With a small nod I headed back to the office. By the time I finished putting everything away it was nearly eight Sunday morning. I was sure that Andrew would have questions. It was then that I realized that living with my uncle wouldn't work for the long haul. After this was over I'd need to find something of my own so I could come and go as I saw fit without having to answer to anyone.

Piling into the Tucker I drove home. Needless to say I was exhausted, grumpy, and generally giving zero fucks about anyone. I desperately needed a hot shower, a decent meal, and a good solid eight hours of sleep. I guessed two out of three wasn't bad, but the sleep would need to come sooner rather than later.

To my surprise Alexander wasn't at the gate when I arrived. Instead, two of his clan pulled the gates open, and quickly closed them behind me. A bright red BMW was parked in front of the garage, which meant we had guests. I pulled in and parked, doing my best not to block anyone in before heading upstairs.

About halfway up I heard the unmistakable voice of Elizabeth Dodd yelling her displeasure at what I could only guess was my uncle. Pushing the door open, I had the unfortunate view of Ms. Dodd's backside as she ranted at my uncle, who sat at his desk. Alexander and Isidore stood flanking him, ensuring the vampire didn't have a chance to harm him.

She turned on me the instant the door opened. Recognition flickered in her eyes and she pointed an accusing chubby finger in my direction. "About time your filthy human errand boy showed up!" She stopped her rant, sniffed, and her fangs snapped into view. "Nephilim!"

Quicker than I'd thought her capable she crossed the room. Instinct kicked in and I slammed a hand hard into her throat and lifted. Her feet dangled off the floor and I shoved my right hand into view. "Hold your tongue before I rip it out!"

Shock registered on her face. She struggled but couldn't free herself, and panicked.

With a sharp slap to her forehead, I raised my hand for her to see once more. "Stop struggling and look at my hand," I ordered. She stopped and her eyes focused on the Pax Romana seal, and her whole body went slack. "I'm going to let you down now and you're going to behave. Am I clear?"

When I released her she landed on the floor with incredible grace for such an ugly little woman. She straightened her suit jacket and sneered up at me. "I don't know what's going on, but if you're truly the newest vigiles you had better learn your place."

The denarius flared at the insult. Great, now the little fucker was talking to me.

Glaring at the little vampire, I stepped forward, readying myself for battle. "You need to take a deep breath and relax, because if you keep pressing your luck with me, I'm going to burn you to the ground right where you stand. The previous vigiles may not have exercised their full authority for one reason or another. I, on the other hand, will."

She snarled in frustration, whirling on Andrew. "I suppose you're to blame for this!"

Andrew shook his head. "You know as well as I do that the denarius chooses its host. I had nothing to do with it!"

She stomped her foot into the hardwood floor, spinning to face me. "You've been causing me no end of problems, *vigiles*," she spat.

Giving her one of those, "Oh, do tell" looks I shook my head. "Please, go on."

She growled. "It appears that you've slain a full member of the Archive. Care to explain yourself?"

Glaring down at her, I glowered. "It's a *vigiles* matter, but I'm going to give you a bit of advice, Ms. Dodd."

Arrogance poured out of her as she snorted. "Are you now?"

Faster than the vampire could move I snatched her off the floor again and raised her to eye level. "I am, and you'd damn well better listen." My voice was hard and came out in a snarl. "You've allowed a necromancer to flourish in your territory, not to mention a city that you call home." She ceased struggling and her eyes went wide as fear took hold. Any prefect allowing a necromancer to live in their territory was subject to summary execution if they had even the slightest of hints of their presence. "I'm going to work on the assumption that you didn't know. Pray that I don't find out otherwise."

I sat the pudgy woman back on her feet and released her.

Her voice quavered when she spoke. "I didn't know…who is it?"

Shaking my head, I said, "I'm not willing to discuss it with you at this point. I don't know you well enough to trust you with such information. That means if the necromancer in question is suddenly warned, you knew them." I let my aura flare out and I saw the others shiver in response. "If that happens you won't live to see a new day." She turned an astonishing shade of white and trembled. "Furthermore, everyone who knows I'm the new *vigiles* is sequestered to this house, save for you. You have two options…either keep my secret, or I'll have to ask Andrew to prepare a room for you." I paused for a second, glaring down, and made it clear that I wanted nothing more than her dead. "I suppose there is a third option."

She visibly gulped at that before her face hardened. "I think I can keep a secret."

Allowing my body to relax, I stepped back. "Good to hear."

The arrogance returned to her voice. "I live to serve."

Staring a hole through the woman, I nodded. "See that you do. For the record, you should be aware that I've killed three Archive members, only one of which was under your jurisdiction."

She blinked at the information and turned to Andrew for confirmation. "Is this true?"

Andrew slowly nodded. "All in the course of his duties."

She swallowed hard and turned to face me with defiance written across her smug little face. "Anything else I should know?" Venom dropped from every word.

This was a game I would tire of quickly. "Stop thinking that I'm some insubordinate underling. Go polish up on the law and understand that if you do anything to interfere with my investigation I'll deal with you accordingly."

She paused, reaching out with her senses. "What are you?"

"I'm the *vigiles*, and that's all you need to know."

She straightened her suit jacket as she turned back to Andrew. "I'm sorry to have disturbed you with what is obviously an in house issue. I would ask that the governor not take it personally since I've got a new *vigiles*." She turned back to me. "May I at least get your name?"

Smirking, I said, "Gavin Randall."

Her mouth fell open before closing. She turned and glared at Andrew. "Any relation?"

Clearing my throat, I forced her attention back to me. "I'm his nephew. Will that be a problem?"

She shook her head. "Not at all." She took a deep breath and stepped around me. "I'll be going now if there is nothing else."

Stepping aside, I kept my eyes on her. "There isn't. I'll see you Friday for the ceremony."

She glared up at me, hate shining in her eyes. "It appears so."

She passed through the door, and with what I was guessing took a great amount of effort, refused to slam it. I gave her a good minute before turning around to face Andrew and the others, who were doing their best not to laugh.

"What?" I asked.

Alexander strode past me and clapped my shoulder hard enough to send me forward several steps. "Damn good show! I'll see that she leaves without destroying anything."

Andrew waved me over to the desk just as Kimberly made her way into the living room. She looked around to make sure we were alone before wrapping her arms around my neck and hugging me tight. "Thank you so much!"

Giving her an odd look, I turned to my uncle. "What's going on?"

Andrew chuckled. "Ms. Dodd was here to force Kimberly and Heather out of our home, saying that I was interfering in a family/ triumvirate dispute." He threw his hands up. "A request that I would've been unable to refuse had you not intervened."

Raising a surprised eyebrow at her, I shrugged. "Not sure what I did, but I'm glad to have done it."

Kimberly giggled. "I don't think I've ever seen that woman at a loss for words before."

Andrew shook his head. "Neither have I."

Isidore stood frozen behind Andrew. He sniffed the air loud enough for us all to hear. "In her frustration she forgot about the nephilim."

With that everyone turned to me expectantly. Holding up my hands to calm everyone, I said, "No need to worry about the nephilim; he works for me in much the same way Isidore works for Amelia."

Andrew placed his elbows on the desk. "You've been here less than two weeks and you've already met and employed a nephilim?"

Avoiding the question with a noncommittal shrug, I said, "It was a very odd day."

Andrew nodded. "Care to share?"

Shaking my head. "Not particularly, no."

Andrew chuckled. "I could order you to tell me."

I countered, "Actually, you couldn't. Amelia could order me to tell her, and if she felt like it was important could share it with you, but I'm betting good money she'd keep her mouth shut."

Andrew raised an eyebrow and hooted. "Fair enough. I'm sure it'll all come out in the wash."

"I'm sure given enough time that you're right."

With that Andrew filled me in on what brought Ms. Dodd to our doorstep besides the Broussard's and Marcus Gray being killed. She was upset that a filthy human was somehow involved with what she considered a messy situation. Ms. Dodd had implied that Andrew had overstepped his authority in the matter by involving a human, i.e. me. This was further confirmation that I'd need to move out and find a place of my own sooner than later. I couldn't have people running to my uncle's place every time they got their panties in a wad.

Chapter 25

Sunday June 7th

The encounter with Ms. Dodd and the ensuing conversations left me spent. The fact I smelled of nephilim concerned me, but probably not as much as it should've. Extricating myself from my uncle and the others, I slogged off to my room for a nice long hot shower and a few minutes of peace, followed by a good night's sleep.

The one thing I hadn't expected was the level of violence contact with a nephilim brought out in others. Ms. Dodd had been absolutely murderous merely at the scent. No wonder Martha had kept Gabriel hidden and away from the Archive. I doubted seriously he would've survived if his presence had been common knowledge. I'd have to bring Gabriel into the open soon to ensure the others knew he was under my protection.

His heritage would need to remain a secret from everyone, save for myself and Gabriel, until such time as we could ease the news to all of those involved. If Andrew were to find out at the wrong time it could be disastrous. His father may be an unknown factor, but Martha being his mother would most likely upset Andrew no matter when he learned the information.

Turning the knob in the shower and allowing almost nothing but hot water to spray over me felt remarkable. It wasn't nearly long enough, but then again my knees kept buckling under my weight as I nodded off several times. I took the hint, toweled off, and pulled on a pair of jeans before falling face first into the soft, cushy mattress, letting sleep take me almost instantly. Truth be told, I didn't recall hitting the mattress. The dream, or perhaps it was a vision, was upon me in seconds.

What I saw before me was not the world I knew. It was younger and far more primal than anything in recorded history.

Gods and devils walked the earth, warring with one another on a scale I couldn't comprehend.

The god Ankou rose up out of the darkness to create the armies of the undead, ripping souls from beyond the veil to serve him here and now. Ankou, in that moment, created the blackest of arts that we call necromancy. His hate and anger at the light drove him to break the laws of creation itself.

Lugus, god of light, saw this abomination, and in his arrogance created life where none should ever exist and brought forth warriors of pure life against the soldiers of death. The battle was terrible to behold. Shadow and light weaved in and out of encounter after encounter, neither side gaining an upper hand.

Both gods stooped lower and lower, creating even more abominations and in turn tearing the very fabric of the world apart. The other powers of the land created pockets of reality as they tried to flee the terrible war. In time the world seethed and tore at itself, as it couldn't withstand much more of this conflict of life and death.

As the earth itself cried out in terror and pain, it created a being of such power that nothing could withstand it. Thus The Reaper was born. The Reaper stood in the midst of a great battlefield, with Lugus on one side and Ankou on the other.

The Reaper looked out towards Ankou high up on the ridge above. The Reaper's voice shook the earth as he spoke. "This will end now. Withdraw your forces and leave this world, or I'll be forced to involve myself in such matters."

Ankou laughed, as he did not understand the situation. "Why would you fight for Lugus? Tell me your name so that I may make it legendary with your death for such arrogance."

The Reaper sighed as he looked back to Lugus. "I make you the same offer. Withdraw and leave this world." He paused as he glanced at each god in turn. "Or I'll be forced to remove you both."

Ankou and Lugus were so enraged they ordered their forces against the solitary figure. The Reaper held out his hands at either side and ripped the souls out of both armies as he swelled to his full height.

In his rage, The Reaper bound archangels and arch demons to the land as protectors to ensure the balance. His power tore at both gods, stripping them of all their authority and sealing them behind the veil, never to enter this world again.

The Reaper turned its face to me and I screamed.

Sweat poured off me and I shook, replaying the dream over and over again in my head. A soft knock at the door roused me from my vision. Looking over at the clock, I saw that it was 1:15 p.m.

"Come," I said.

Heather pushed the door open and gingerly hobbled into the room before closing it behind her again. "You all right?"

Pulling myself upright, I stood and padded over to the dresser, pulled out one of my old T-shirts, and quickly pulled it over me before flopping back onto the bed. "Fine. Why do you ask?"

She blushed, chewing on her lip. "Modesty?" She giggled and then her face turned serious. "I thought I heard you scream." She waved a hand at the nearest chair. "Mind if I sit?"

Getting myself together, I sat up straight on the edge of the bed. "Bad dreams. Nothing to worry about." Trying to ease her concerns, I painted an easy smile on my face and gestured for her to sit. "Help yourself."

Heather carefully lowered herself into the chair with only a slight grimace. "Thanks." She made herself comfortable…which was a relative subject after being stabbed in the gut. "I hear you ran into Marcus Gray."

Falling back in bed, I said, "We had a lengthy conversation in which he tried to kill me. As for the modesty thing, I guess I'm not used to attractive women showing up in my room when I'm half asleep."

Heather's embarrassment grew, and her tone was apologetic. "Sorry, I didn't mean to wake you."

Popping my head off the mattress, I shook my head. "You didn't." I shivered when the dream rushed into my mind. "Honestly, I wouldn't have minded if you'd woken me up a few minutes earlier." I could see she wanted to talk about something other than my nightmares. "What's up?"

She bit her lip again. "I heard about Marcus, and then there was the shit with Ms. Dodd, not to mention the fact a nephilim is somehow involved." She looked at me in a strangely hopeful yet fearful manner. "Is it true? About the nephilim, I mean."

Sitting up again, I stretched. "If by true you mean that I have a nephilim in my employ, then yes, it's true."

At the confirmation her eyes went wide and her mouth dropped in the cutest little "oh." She gathered herself and curiosity laced her voice. "Wow!" she said quietly, then her voice raised an octave. "I've never seen an actual nephilim. Are the stories true? Are they massive? Powerful? What's he—or is it she— like?" Her fast paced questioning stopped as her face turned sour. "I've heard they are dangerous. Are you sure it's safe?"

Myths, legends, and complete ignorance of someone led to base human reactions of fear and anger. Sitting up straight, a bitter cackle escaped me. "The same could be said about sorcerers, werebeasts, witches, and other members of the Archive. They could all be considered dangerous to the normals of the world."

Her mouth fell open, realizing how she'd sounded. She shrugged helplessly as she let out a long breath. "I don't think I've ever thought about it in that light before." She shook her head. "I never meant it like that…I was curious, then I spouted the shit I've been told all my life before ever meeting them." She looked hurt and disappointed in herself. "I'm sorry."

I did my best to look reassuring. "Don't worry about it. You wouldn't be the first person to fall victim to such a thought process." Thinking back to my own childhood, I couldn't hide the pain on my face. "People don't realize how much it hurts to be discriminated against for things that aren't your fault. Things that you personally were never responsible for."

That hadn't helped and she looked more hurt than before. "I'm really sorry. I never meant it that way. I swear."

Squeezing my eyes closed, I shook my head, trying to clear it so I wouldn't be such an asshole. "I'm sorry if that came out wrong."

Heather's smile was bittersweet. "No, it came out right. The truth is rarely kind, and even rarer still gentle."

I frowned at the words. "You're right."

Shifting in her seat, she changed the subject quickly. "Where did you find Marcus and why did he attack you?"

The memory of Marcus sobered me, snapping the cobwebs out of my head instantly. There was the truth and then there was what she wanted to hear. I'd already promised her I wouldn't lie, so I went with honesty. "Have you ever been to Brad's place?"

At the mention of Brad's home, she looked completely repulsed. "That creepy place on the river?" She looked sick for a moment before shaking her head. "He's invited me, of course, but the place gave me the willies. Why do you ask?" Then it dawned on her. "Marcus was there?"

Trying my best not to come off like a jerk, chanting I told you so, I forced an even tone. "Yeah."

Heather's face clouded with confusion. "Why would Marcus be there? Do you think he was looking for Brad?"

Swinging my feet off the bed, I let them down to touch the cool hardwood. Taking a deep breath, I let the coolness of the floorboards seep in and I hung my head before raising it again to meet her eyes. "I'm not sure, but it looked like he lived there."

She was fighting hard not to see the obvious and I couldn't understand why. She looked like she was going to lose her lunch when she spoke. "That's not possible. Everyone knows Marcus works for Walter. Why would you think he lived there?" She suddenly looked scared and considerably younger. "Are you sure?"

That was quickly becoming my number one most annoying question. Why did everyone doubt my word? Still, I needed to put my anger in check to see why she was fighting so hard against the idea of Brad being involved. "I'm pretty sure."

Heather's composure cracked at the words and tears threatened to fall. "God, I really want you to be wrong."

"Why does it matter so much?" I asked.

Her head fell forward and her shoulders slumped. "Because if he's with Walter, where does that leave my dad?" She sniffed, fighting back the tears. "I know he's a world class asshole, but he's still my father. And I just have a hard time believing that even with all his faults he'd be the kind of man that would have any dealings with Walter Percy!" She sagged, the possibility of such a thing rolling over her. "At this point I could still forgive him, but if he were somehow working with Walter I'm not sure I could ever look at him again."

The heart of the matter was, if he was involved what would I do? He would have to be brought to justice, especially after what I'd said to Ms. Dodd. She would insist on it. "One thing at a time. Let's find out if there is even a connection. After that we can see where it takes us."

Heather's face hardened. "If he's tied up with a necromancer there aren't a lot of options." She straightened herself, getting to her feet. "If that's the case, make it quick. Don't drag it out. Just end it."

That was a tall order and an even more difficult request, but one I'd honor. "I can do that."

She leaned over and wrapped her arms around me in a weak hug. "Thank you."

With that she was out of my room, across the hall, and closing the door before I could get my thoughts together. Just as well...what the fuck was I going to say? "Thanks for giving me permission to kill your old man"? Or "Gee, thanks for letting me do my job"? Yeah, my options just got worse from there.

Closing the door, I sat on the bed and placed my head in my hands, trying to work up the nerve to get back on my feet and do what needed to be done. My phone chimed, letting me know I had a new email. When I pushed the icon, the mail from Lieutenant Baptist popped into view.

Gavin,

I wanted to give you a heads up. While information on Walter Bradley Matherne is scarce to say the least, I had a little more luck with Mary Percy. I won't bore you with the details, such as me having to trek down the to the records office to find the actual marriage certificate, which forced me to drive to Baton Rouge for a birth certificate.

Turns out Mary Percy's full name is Gretchen Mary Matherne Percy. With a name like Gretchen I might want to lose it as well, but I digress. Mary Matherne changed her name when she got married to Walter.

Turns out that one Mary Matherne was admitted to a secure nursing home in 1995, where she died in 2005 due to the flood waters of Katrina. With the lack of information on Walter Bradley Matherne, I backed into a few files under Walter Bradley Percy.

The news isn't great. He was given up for adoption shortly after birth but was never taken in. He spent a great deal of his childhood and teenage years in the foster system. That is until he turned fourteen, when he was hospitalized at Touro. Once there it turns out that he was treated for his injuries and brought on as a volunteer by Robert Broussard.

The next four years are sketchy, but it appears that Robert and the boy stayed close. His name is buried deep in the purchase of that place by the river that I sent you to. BTW, how did that turn out?

For now, I have to run…still tracking down information that might be useful. Be in touch soon.

Lt. William Baptist UCD

Looking up at the door, I sighed. That effectively ended the question of Brad being Walter's son. What it didn't answer was if there was still a connection between Walter, Brad, and Robert. That in and of itself was the only good news I could see. It meant that I didn't have to take Robert's head and put it on a pike for everyone to see, yet. My gut was telling me that the man was dirty, and the evidence was piling up that he was more involved in this than anyone guessed. Well, maybe

Heather had guessed, and that was why she was so adamant about Brad.

Finally getting to my feet, I grabbed my boots and other items to finish getting dressed. There was a lot to do, the first of which was to discover how Ms. Dodd had gotten the news about Marcus Gray. I was fairly certain that no one at the house was feeding her the information. My best guess was the CCTV station wasn't as closed off as I'd suspected.

Of course, having a massive wound in my chest and a couple of broken ribs to boot may have had something to do with that. If it was connected to the Internet, Walter probably had a live show of the whole event. Thank God I didn't go all shadow form on the bastard. That was one secret I'd like to keep to myself for now.

Heading into the kitchen, I found a covered plate of food with a note from Kimberly in a beautiful flowing green script.

Gavin,

Made my famous beef stroganoff in honor of you helping Heather and I this morning. We are eternally grateful for what you did.

P.S. I can't guarantee there is anything left for you. Isidore and Alexander look very hungry.

Pulling the cover off I was pleased to find a generous helping of the dish in question. I guessed Isidore and Alexander had seen fit to save me a healthy portion. Eating what I could, I put the rest in a plastic container before placing it in the fridge. I strode into the living room that was blissfully empty; after my conversation with Heather, I wasn't exactly in the talkative mood. Something about a person having to come to terms with someone else killing their father kind of killed the whole conversational vibe.

Five minutes later I was pulling out onto 4th Street heading for Elmwood. I still had the files I'd pulled from the office earlier. I hadn't read them, mind you, but I had them. I wanted out of the house as quickly as possible. I needed to breathe without having someone standing over me. After decades of virtual solitary confinement, the pressure of having such a large number of people around me at all times was draining.

The one on one interactions I had with Gabriel were taxing enough, but the parade of individuals through Andrew's house was going to kill me or simply drive me insane. An odd thing occurred to me. My commute to Elmwood was something I looked forward to, since it was the only time I was ever truly alone.

I needed to check on Gabriel; after that I'd sift through the files before stopping at Brad's to see what else I could find. Something needed to turn loose, and I could only handle one thing at a time, meaning that my main goal hadn't changed...I needed to find Walter. After that I'd sort through the aftermath. I couldn't risk him disappearing on me, and if I started taking out his kid, and possibly Robert in the process, he might run before I got my hands around his neck.

That was something that couldn't be allowed to happen. Walter needed to believe that I was as clueless as ever. One of the most valuable lessons I'd learned while I was away was a simple one: Let everyone think you're stupid, even if you're the smartest person in the room. That meant that I never lost my accent. American's with accents were thought of as stupid. It was amazing what people would say in front of you when they believed you were too dense to understand them.

Chapter 26

Monday June 8th

The sun was hanging low in the afternoon sky as I sat in the car, adoring the last few seconds of being completely alone. If this was how the outside world was, I wasn't sure how people coped with the constant input of information overload. Mentally I was tired from meeting new people, constantly having to evaluate their every action to ensure they were not a threat. I was quickly realizing that living alone would mean more than not having to answer to someone, but would also be a chance to recharge without constantly being barraged with people.

Adding to my stress was the fact I hadn't been able to shake the dream from earlier. Even the denarius was at a loss to explain what we'd been shown. It was so real, but as the denarius told me there wasn't any possible way for me to know what was true and what wasn't. The denarius was an ancient creature, yet it had no memory of such a battle. It was partially convinced that this was my subconscious' attempt at making sense of all the events since my arrival in this new and foreign world. I was inclined to agree.

Pulling the keys out of the ignition, I stepped out of the car and headed into the old DHL building. I was maybe three steps inside when Gabriel rounded the corner with his gun drawn. Once he saw it was me he holstered the weapon quickly.

"Good evening. Are you always going to greet me with a gun or has this got anything to do with last night's visitors?" I asked.

Gabriel grunted. "You'll have to forgive me, that's the first time I've been attacked in my home."

He fell in step with me as we headed for the armory. Looking up at the big man, I patted him on the shoulder. "Hopefully it won't happen again anytime soon." Thinking back to my encounter with Ms. Dodd, I sighed. "They know about you."

He stopped at the door and turned to look at me with the slightest hint of fear in his eyes. "Who knows about what?"

Waving for him to let us in, I continued. "Ms. Dodd, Andrew, and several others know that I've employed a nephilim and that you are under my protection."

Gabriel didn't stow his weapon as he had previously, but rather kept it holstered and took a seat. "Do you think they'll be all right with that?"

Thinking back to Ms. Dodd being suspended in the air, I chuckled. "I don't think I left them much of a choice." Shaking off the memory, I found my seat as I leveled my gaze at him. "They won't touch you…that's one thing I'm sure about. It might help me deflect some things if I knew more about you other than Martha was your mother."

His frown grew and shook his head. "More specifically, you'd like to know who my father is."

Giving him a "Well yeah" look, I nodded. "It would be a lot easier to tell them about your father than your mother."

He made an "Oh, well" gesture when he flopped into his chair. "I won't argue the point. Thing is, I don't know. Mom wasn't exactly forthcoming on the subject."

Well fuck! That shot all sorts of holes into my first plan to deflect a steaming pile of shit off our doorstep. "That sort of fucks things up for us." Keeping my eyes locked on his, I shook my head. "Andrew won't be happy—or hell, maybe he will—that Martha had a child with someone else."

He looked confused. "Why wouldn't he be happy?"

"They were married; you knew that right?" I paused long enough for him to nod his affirmation. "Martha lost their child due to some sort of accident. From what I understand their marriage fell apart after that."

His mouth fell open as realization settled over him. "I see how this could be a bad thing, and for once it would have nothing to do with me being a nephilim."

Touching a finger to my nose, I nodded. "Exactly."

"Anything else?" he asked.

Shaking my head, I said, "Not right now, but there's going to come a time when you leave this place, and when that time comes—"

"You want me to keep Martha out of it." He finished for me.

I shrugged helplessly. "At least for now. I'd really appreciate the time to break it to the old man when someone isn't trying to kill him." Flopping back into my chair, I let out a breath. "It won't make it any easier, but he might react to the news better. There is so much of this world I haven't gotten a handle on yet, and pissing off my uncle wouldn't help matters."

He snickered, smacking a meaty hand against the table. "Not to mention he might kill us both out of shock."

There was that. Sitting there, I took in Gabriel and realized how most people felt around me. He was huge. How many times had I nonchalantly smacked a table, making it shudder, or clapped them on the back, only to knock the wind out of them? Gabriel was several inches taller than me, with a good hundred pounds of muscle to boot. Not to say that I was a slouch. I was in great shape and stood six feet six inches tall, but damn! This guy took the cake.

Thumbing back at the office, I said, "Now that I'm sure you're okay, I'm going to see what I can dig up in the office."

He gave me a big thumbs up. "You going to be here for dinner?"

Stopping, I turned around and looked at him curiously. "No idea."

Gabriel nodded. "I'll order an extra pizza just in case."

Pizza sounded good to me, but I had work to do so I left Gabriel alone to do whatever it was he did. It occurred to me that one day soon I'd have to figure out what that was. From what I could tell his life was as sheltered as the one I'd left not long ago. These thoughts rattled through my mind as I sat at the desk and started sifting through the files I'd pulled last night, and I found my mind drifting.

Then something in the paperwork caught my eye. Martha had scribbled an address in the margin of one of the pages: 723 Congress Street, New Orleans. Punching the address into my phone, I zoomed in to see it was in a section of the city called the Bywater. From the looks of things this wasn't the best of neighborhoods, and the address in question appeared to be a boarded up heap of shit.

I grabbed my gear, which at this point included both swords shoved into a backpack, along with a few other essentials. Time to go see what was so important about this run down piece of shit across town.

Stopping at the armory, I stuck my head in. "Looks like I won't be here for dinner after all."

Gabriel gave me a wave. "Good hunting." He paused, looking a little anxious, almost as if he'd heard my thoughts earlier. "Would you like me to tag along? I don't exactly get out a lot."

Shaking my head, I replied, "Tell ya what; after I wrap things up on Friday afternoon, we'll go grab a drink and have a good meal somewhere in the city." Thinking back to my earlier encounter with Ms. Dodd and even Heather, I frowned. "Today, however, I believe having you out and about might cause more trouble than I'm able to handle at the moment."

Gabriel's smile was a knowing one and he took the rejection in stride. "I understand." His voice perked up as he spoke the last bit. "I'll hold you to the whole drink and dinner after Friday, though."

Giving him a wink, I grinned. "Wouldn't have it any other way."

I felt bad for leaving the kid, but if everyone responded to nephilim the way Ms. Dodd or even Isidore had, I'd spend more time explaining his presence than getting anything accomplished. With that thought depressingly fixated in my mind I headed out. Frankly, I could use the backup, but that couldn't happen until after Friday.

Traffic wasn't terrible, and dusk was rapidly approaching by the time I pulled up outside the matt gray shotgun double thirty minutes later. Shotgun houses were narrow houses only one room wide, with rooms arranged one behind the other. They were very popular in the south, taking hold after the Civil War. Northerners might be familiar with something similar called railroad apartments. Either way, they were normally in the poorer sections of town, and this wasn't the exception to the rule.

The windows were boarded up with rotting plywood, but the transom over the 723 entrance appeared to have a curtain. The 721 entrance had a padlocked metal security gate, with foil in the transom. The decaying wooden door had the doorknob cut out but was closed. Turning my attention back to 723, I saw that the green solid wood door still looked functional. A part of me was horrified that people would still live in this sort of squalor here in the States. I'd, of course, seen much worse when I was overseas, but those were Third World countries, or literally in the middle of a war zone.

The air was still, thick, and hot. The stench of death hung all about the house as if it were seeping out of every broken and battered board lining the loathsome home. As I stepped closer a chill ran up my spine and the little hairs on my arms and neck stood on end. Pulling the gladius from the bag, I slung the backpack over my shoulder, pounded on the door, and waited like an idiot for something to happen. Nothing did. The hilt of the gladius became uncomfortably cold when I turned the knob, and with a push I let it swing open on its own.

The place was a mess and smelled of feces, death, and vomit. Stepping inside, slowly allowing my eyes to adjust to the gloom, the uneasy feeling about the place ramped itself up into something otherworldly. Pressing my back against the wall, I remained cautious, clearing the first room before proceeding through the narrow hall that contained an entrance to the tiny bath that took only seconds to clear.

Taking a tentative step into the kitchen, a shiver ran up my spine and the denarius screamed out the wrongness it felt in such a confined space. The filth was one thing, but there was something hidden. Instinct forced my eyes up, where something shimmered into view and dove at me, claws outstretched. Diving to the side, I slashed out with the dark blade of the gladius. There was a hiss like steam and I felt the blade bite into flesh, followed by an unearthly howl of a deranged beast.

Scrambling to my feet, I turned and got my first good look at the thing. It was a filthy, twisted version of a woman, with long razor sharp talons on both her boney fingers and elongated feet, sharp pointed teeth, feathers for hair, and a hard horned colored beaklike mouth. One of her golden eyes was missing, and there was a long jagged scar across her throat. The denarius whispered in my mind that I was seeing what was left of a harpy.

Her movements were slow; I'd managed to slice through several muscles on her right thigh. Thick black blood ran freely down her leg as she stood defiantly between me and the final room. She swiped out with her overly long arms, her claws narrowly missing me. Moving forward, I planted a boot in her chest, deflecting another blow with the gladius, nearly slicing one of her hands off in the process.

Stepping back, I held my right hand out. "I don't want to kill you, but if you continue I'll have no choice."

Her one good eye looked at me as if she understood my words. She fixated on the blade, gave me a toothy smile, and charged. Lifting the gladius, I caught her full in the throat, the force of her weight pushing the point through her neck and out the other side. For the briefest of moments, I swore I thought I saw a smile before death took her.

I gave the blade a hard jerk to one side, freeing the blade from the harpy's neck, nearly decapitating it in the process as I let its lifeless corpse hit the floor with a splat and a thud. I checked the room for anything else and found nothing. Approaching the final room, I found it padlocked shut. My patience for this shit was at an end, and I backed up and planted a foot against the door, sending it splintering open.

I found the source of the smell. A small man lay slumped over a desk, and it was clear that he'd been dead several days now. Moving the bloated body aside, I nearly gagged on the stench. He was leaking onto the papers on the desk, but it didn't take a genius to figure out they were blueprints. To what I didn't know. I snapped several photos before dialing Alexander's number, which was quickly becoming a habit.

Alexander answered on the first ring. "Good evening, Gavin. How may I help you tonight?"

"Evening," I replied. "I'm in need of your services again."

I could hear him stepping outside before answering. His voice was low, nearly whispered into the phone. "What's going on?"

It took several minutes to fill Alexander in on where I was and what was going on. He seemed surprised. He flat out didn't believe that I'd encountered a harpy within the city limits, since they weren't known for being city folk or even indoor folk. Personally, I was starting to think that she was just as much of a prisoner as the man had been. Alexander agreed to bring a few guys out to secure the scene and clean up the bodies. One day soon I was going to have to find out what he did with them. That, of course, could wait until this situation was tied up. So much of my life now hinged on tying up this case and the ceremony on Friday.

Sifting through the wreckage of the room, I found several drawings of the dagger that the shapeshifter had used at the wedding. I would lay good money that the dead man was the missing enchanter, Aaron Lopez. I took the diagrams of the dagger and folded them up, stashing them into my bag.

Digging through the papers that weren't stuck together with human fluids, I didn't find any other weapon designs, which meant that he'd only made the one. Good to know. Then again, he may have only designed one type of weapon and they mass-produced the thing. That would be bad. Either way, daggers were about as easy to hide as the gladius and the wakizashi.

A half hour later Alexander showed up with half a dozen clan members. He stepped inside and I guided him through to the kitchen. He stopped in his tracks, stunned to see exactly what I'd described to him lying dead on the kitchen floor.

He shook his head in disbelief. "Goddamn, boy! You've had a real interesting first few weeks on the job. First Marcus, and now a fucking harpy! Jesus Christ, you like your prey on the lethal side."

What was I supposed to say to that? All I could do was muster a weak smile and nod. "I guess this last week or so has been eventful. As for the prey, I don't go looking for fights."

Alexander couldn't take his eyes off the fallen creature. "Maybe not, but you sure as hell finish them."

Waving him back to the last room I showed him what I'd found. "I'm betting this is the missing enchanter Martha was looking for." Pulling out the blueprints, I let Alexander get a good look at them. "I'm not sure what these belong to."

He followed my finger to get a good look at the papers. He studied them for several minutes before looking up at me. "Appears to be an old set of prints of Charity Hospital."

The name didn't sound familiar, but then again I was new to the city. "Never heard of the place."

His smile was bitter when he caught my eye. "Not surprising since it closed after Katrina ten years ago."

"There ya go." I shook my head in frustration. "Fat lot of good that'll do anyone."

Alexander nodded. "Want me to send someone to check the place out?"

"I'd rather you didn't. If anyone's there I want first crack at them."

Alexander looked back at the kitchen. "You've got a knack for making a hell of an impression."

I gave him a thumbs up, headed for the door, and stopped suddenly. "What do you do with the bodies?"

Alexander grinned. "How about we chalk that up to one of those mysteries in life?"

It was clear he wasn't inclined to tell me, and I couldn't risk him not handling the situation. "For now that'll be fine."

"You going back to Andrew's?" Alexander asked.

"Probably."

"Good. I'll catch up with you there when I'm done here," Alexander said.

Getting into the car, I turned the key and drove to Andrew's. I got about halfway there when I saw a local bar and pulled into a parking space out front. I walked in, ordered a double, and downed it before making my immediate exit and heading home.

Chapter 27

Tuesday June 9th

Rousing myself from bed, I glanced at the clock: 4:30 a.m. I'd spent the majority of last night going over blueprints for Charity Hospital. Much to my displeasure, it was a massive complex. The surrounding area wasn't much better, as it was a maze of buildings and an active medical facility, Tulane Hospital.

The one good thing about the evening was the fact I'd turned in at a decent hour, rested well, and didn't have any freaky dreams. Maybe the denarius was right and it was just my subconscious clearing away the old nightmares with the newest boogeyman.

Picking up the Surface Pro, I clicked through the Wikipedia page for Charity Hospital. The place had gotten its start in 1736, making it the second oldest in the nation. It had gone through several incarnations, the sixth and final being in 1939, with 2,680 beds making it the second largest at the time. From the sounds of things, they were all about being second to everyone else.

Like a great deal of the New Orleans area, Katrina inflicted heavy damage on the hospital in 2005, and it had never reopened. The presence of Tulane Hospital, which was practically across the street, would make it tough for anyone to just walk in and take over a section of the abandoned monument without discovery. Then again, stranger things had happened.

Unfortunately for me, I didn't have access to real time satellite feeds or even basic intelligence on the place. What I did have was a bunch of notes, some blueprints, and a shit ton of ground to cover. Basically blind as a bat who'd lost its voice.

After a quick shower, I got dressed and headed for the kitchen, and found it to be overly crowded. Heather, Kimberly, and Andrew were sitting at the table, while Isidore prepared sausage, eggs, and toast for breakfast.

Isidore glanced over his shoulder and thumbed at the table. "Find a place to sit and I'll bring you something shortly." He flashed me an evil grin and looked back at the pan. "Hope you like scrambled eggs."

Someone was full of themselves this morning…the joke was on him though. While it was true I preferred fried eggs, I'd spent years eating scrambled in the mess hall where ever I was stationed. It would take far more than scrambled eggs to put a speed bump in the road I was traveling. Let's face it, going to find an evil bastard who could summon spirits from beyond the veil was shitty. Scrambled eggs, not so much.

While I wasn't sure who, someone had stocked the kitchen with several metal folding chairs, which made for a tight fit. Andrew scooted to one side, allowing me to move my seat between him and Heather. I caught the sly smirk on his face as he and Kimberly exchanged knowing glances. Fucking great, now they were playing matchmaker. That' was the last thing on my mind at the moment.

Isidore broke the scowl I shot Andrew when he leaned over to serve me a plate with two fried eggs, three sausages, and a couple of strips of bacon for good measure. When I glanced up at him, he waved with a flourish at the plate. I mumbled my thanks and he turned to finish breakfast.

Thankfully, the others were busy talking amongst themselves, leaving me to eat my feast in peace. Well most of them anyway…Heather was noticeably quiet. Every now and then she'd catch my eye before glancing between Andrew and her mother. Kimberly and Andrew couldn't have been more obvious about their intentions without taking a full page ad out in the paper announcing our engagement.

When I finished, Andrew put aside his attempts at matchmaking and steered the conversation into a fishing expedition. "So, what's on the agenda for the day?" He paused, grabbing his half-empty plate in a ruse to join me. "Anything I can help with?"

I felt bad for the guy; he wasn't used to being in the dark about anything. People were always so willing to tell him their secrets. With me being immune to his talents, he had found it a blessing at first, but now the burning desire to know that which he was denied appeared to be putting a strain on his normally pleasant demeanor.

Trying to sound disinterested, I said, "I've got a couple of boring errands to run. If you really want to help you could check the local DMV and see what I need to do to get a driver's license." He looked crestfallen at the request. Taking a deep breath, I softened my tone. "I know this is hard for you, but you running around out there only gives Walter a target. Besides, leg work rarely produces anything interesting."

Andrew's expression turned into a scowl. His voice loaded with sarcasm, he said, "If that's what you call your visit to the Bywater or even the river, then yes, by all means, don't bore me."

Like I said, this was hard on the guy, and I probably deserved worse than a good tongue lashing. Rallying my defenses, I did my best to play it off. "That's unfair." It really wasn't. "That's like watching a football team's highlight reel." Crossing my arms, I did my best to appear convincing, if not a little offended. "Those incidents are the exceptions to the rule. Most of my time is spent pouring over paperwork, stopping at libraries, and generally spinning my wheels. If anything important turns up, I'll tell you."

Andrew cocked his head to the side. "What about Charity?"

Goddamn Alexander!

I huffed and grabbed a piece of bacon. "What about it?"

Andrew wasn't deterred. He was desperate to find a way to help even if it meant putting himself in harm's way. "Charity is a massive place. It would be difficult for anyone to search the place thoroughly alone." He gave me one of those casual shrugs, like he was doing me a favor with his next words. "If you wanted an extra set of hands, I've got plenty of time."

He had to go and fight with logic, what an ass. "While I appreciate the offer, I couldn't possibly let you go anywhere near that place. On the off chance Walter is there, it would be the equivalent of walking you straight into the hangman's noose."

Isidore cut in, anger rippling through his words. "You aren't going. Give it up already."

Andrew shoved his dish in the sink hard enough to break it. Glaring at me, he said, "I'm not a helpless old man. I can handle myself."

This whole dealing with family thing was far more difficult than I remembered. Having to fight him every step of the way made me uncomfortable. I hated telling him no, but it had to be done. I had a job to do whether he liked it or not. Holding my hands up in surrender, I sighed. "I never meant to imply that you were, but if you're out there it would make what I have to do that much harder."

The fight left him and his body sagged. "All right, but if you need me promise you'll call."

Putting a steady hand on his shoulder, I said, "I will."

Andrew reached over and patted my hand. "I suppose that's the best I can hope for."

I felt like a heel, but there wasn't anything to be done about it. "For now I suppose it is."

With that I was out the door and back into the blissfully quiet hallway. I had no immediate plans to visit the abandoned hospital. If necromancers were strongest at night, then the sun being at its pinnacle should negate some of their power. And then again, it may not do shit, but it would provide me with enough natural light to search the place without too much trouble.

Stopping, I turned around and stuck my head through the kitchen door. "Andrew, there is one other thing you could do for me today."

His eyes lit up and he stood a little straighter. "And what's that?"

Damn, he was getting his hopes up. "I'm going to need George's services for a special project."

Andrew's face fell, his expectations dashed. "That shouldn't be a problem. Any specifics I can give him?"

My cheeks flushed and I found myself unconsciously tugging at my shirt. I couldn't believe how awkward I felt. "It would appear that I'm hard on clothes." Sweat beaded on my forehead. "I was thinking he could design a uniform and perhaps some work specific gear."

Kimberly gawked at me. "A uniform? Why?"

I felt perspiration on the back of my head and the burning on my cheeks intensify. "If I had one I could destroy those instead of my street clothes." My throat was dry. "If they were perhaps more rugged they'd last longer than a week."

There was that, and then there was the real reason. I may not have served any specific branch of the military but I'd definitely had a uniform, even if it was a dark suit and tie. The concept of any uniform was to convey acceptance by a larger force, a support system. That message would tell others that I was not alone and there would be others should anything happen to me. It was empowering. But saying that out loud would just sound stupid.

Andrew chuckled. "I'll make the call." He paused, thinking about my words, and frowned. "I'll need to order some Kevlar and other armored material to protect you from more mundane weapons."

"Thanks."

The thought of rifles, knives, and pistols being mundane were amusing considering how I'd spent the last several years. Stepping back, I let the door swing shut behind me. A couple seconds later, I heard the door swing open. Turning, I saw it was Heather, who'd followed me out. "Good morning."

She beamed, caught up quickly, and kissed me on the cheek. The touch of her lips against my skin sent a rush of blood throughout my body.

Heather's eyes fixed on mine. Pulling back, she sucked in her bottom lip in a way to let me know she'd enjoyed herself. She glanced over her shoulder before locking her arm around mine as we made our way down the hall. "Those two old betties need to mind their business." Her voice dropped to a whisper. "I know you don't have any intention of calling anyone for help, and I think that's a mistake."

Tugging her closer, I tsked. "What makes you think I won't call?"

She clucked, turning her fierce gaze on me. "Don't lie to me or to yourself."

I was both happy and a little irritated that she knew me so well already. Not wanting to ruin the moment, I kept my voice low so only she could hear. "I'm not lying." I paused, enjoying her warmth against me. "Even if things got bad, who would I call? It's not like I'm going to invite Andrew to his own execution."

"We aren't helpless, you know!" she growled.

Her words took the wind out of me. "I never thought you were, but you're injured."

She took a long breath and leaned her head against my shoulder. "That's true, I'm on the disabled list currently, but there's always Alexander."

That was true, and after the ceremony I'd be able to call on Gabriel. Squeezing her arm, I opened the door to her room. "I'll call him if the need arises. I'm not above asking for help."

With a squeeze in return, she slipped past me and sat on the edge of the bed. "You never said anything about my mother and Andrew playing matchmaker."

"Not much to say about it. I'm with you, though; they should mind their business." Daring to push my luck. "I'm sort of hoping their involvement isn't necessary."

She bit her lip, blushing hard. "It isn't…."

Well, there you go. I'm a grown man who just asked a girl if she likes him. "Good to know. Maybe once this is over we can go out on a proper date. You know, one where you don't end up getting stabbed."

Her mouth fell open in shock and then she started to giggle. "Ass!" Still beat red, she nodded. "I'd like that."

This felt odd. I'd spent most of my life without friends or girlfriends, and here I was in the course of a couple of weeks picking up both. The years I'd spent doing the hard things people didn't want to talk about seemed suddenly far away. Life was changing, and all I could do was hope I could keep up.

Her amusement faded and she frowned. "What's on your mind?"

It was alarming how observant she was. "I was just thinking how different the world is here on the outside."

She didn't press, simply stood and gently kissed me on the lips before wrapping her arms around me in a powerful hug. "I hope you find the change a pleasurable one."

I'm not sure my heart skipped a beat, but it certainly sped up, and I fought the urge to let things go any further...she was injured, for Christ's sake. Stepping back, I placed my hands on her shoulders. "That was never in question." Cocking an eyebrow at her, I grinned. "Get better fast, and maybe no drinks at our dinner."

She smirked. "I can do that."

"I should go," I stammered.

With that I turned and headed for my room, then grabbing my gear I made my way out to the car. Five minutes later I was out on 4th Street heading for Elmwood. I kept going through my mind, deciding what to take to with me. It wasn't as if I even knew what I was running into. That's when I decided to turn the car around to head for Charity Hospital. How could I make a plan if I had no frame of reference for what I was getting myself into?

Andrew was right earlier; I'd need help securing the place, so I pulled out my phone and dialed Alexander's number. I needed to find a way to turn the odds in my favor, and he could help with that. The call itself took less than five minutes. He and his men would secure the perimeter, ensuring no one escaped while I cleared the building. He assured me he would have a crew there in twenty and set up in thirty. The man was efficient, I had to give him that. At this rate I needed to find a way to put him and his people on the payroll.

The ride back through the city took nearly half an hour, but I found my way to the front of the hollowed out hulk that had once been a place of healing. It took another twenty minutes to find a decent parking spot. I may have cheated on that, considering I paid to park in Tulane's garage across the street.

I didn't see any obvious signs that Alexander and his people had arrived, but taking it on faith I made a quick perimeter check of Charity Hospital. The place was fucking massive. The gray cement walls jutted some twenty plus stories out of the broken and overgrown medical campus like a crumbling monolith. Everything about it gave off waves of pain and death. Even if Walter wasn't here, there was enough misery in this place to fuel the nightmares of anyone near a state of sanity.

Thunder rolled through the sky above as a storm moved in. Just what I needed...rain and a cloudy day to boot. Whatever added benefit high noon was supposed to offer me was probably off the table now. On the other hand, the pouring rain and added darkness made it easier for me to cross onto the property, hopefully unseen.

Simply walking up to the Ambulance Only ramp, I found a metal door slightly ajar. Pulling the door just enough for me to duck inside, I was cast into utter darkness. The dark hall was hot and humid, and the air was stale. Sweat instantly made its way to the surface of my skin, coating me in a slick sheen of perspiration.

Swinging my pack around, I secured the swords before pulling out an LED flashlight. It took me a good forty-five minutes to sweep the vacant first floor. I heard a knocking sound that I first thought was some random piece of metal on the side of the building being caught in the wind. It didn't take long for me to catch the rhythm of it.

Following the sound up and up, I cleared floor after floor in quick succession. The one thing I couldn't shake about the place was the feeling of being inside a corpse. The building was dead and had been that way for many years. I wondered if it had a similar feeling prior to Katrina or if this was a recent addition.

On the twelfth floor I found a functioning server room with Internet access, along with a security station. Multiple cameras were trained all over the building, including a camera that would have caught my entrance. I didn't need to rewind the tape to know that someone had seen me coming from a mile away. Fuck! Not only did this mean that I'd been seen, but someone was most likely waiting on me.

The note attached to the farthest monitor only confirmed my assumption. There on a bright yellow Post-it note was scrawled a message.

Please make your way to the 13th floor so we can be properly introduced.
W. P.

Well, that was just fucked up! He literally left me an invitation into his inner sanctum. All I could hope for was that Alexander and his men were in place by this point. I took the liberty of taking the servers offline and cutting the Wi-Fi and Internet access points, essentially blinding anyone watching elsewhere. Then I made my way up to the thirteenth floor of the middle tower. My mouth fell open as I took in the sight before me...row after row of stones much like the setup Andrew had at his house, but on a far grander scale. It looked as if someone had removed several walls in every direction to make this one giant room dedicated to trophies of the dead.

Walter sat at the end of the rows waiting for me to step out of the shadows. Getting to his feet, he smiled and waved me forward. "Glad you could make it."

Chapter 28

Just fucking great! It was obvious he knew I was there, and staying in the shadows sweating my ass off wasn't going to help. Even so I kept stock, still looking around for any danger other than the obvious. Again, I took in the vast number of stones laid out in nice neat rows. Martha obviously hadn't even scratched the surface of this madman's antics.

Speaking of which, I watched as Walter pulled his cane out and slowly made his way to his feet. He took a couple of steps away from his makeshift throne before waving at me and shooting me the biggest shit eating grin I'd ever seen.

His laugh was dark, ragged, and much more chilling than a man of his stature should be able to command. "Come out of the darkness, boy. You look ridiculous standing there with your mouth hanging open."

Closing my mouth, I stood upright and stepped into the lit room. With an exasperated look I cocked my head to the side. "Neat trick." Thumbing back from the way I'd come, I said, "I'm guessing the camera's downstairs gave me away."

Walter's cane tapped the floor and he gave me a knowing wink. "When it became obvious you were a professional I guessed you couldn't miss them. With that being said, you did disconnect them and disable the Internet access?"

The fact that he wanted me to disable the cameras and cut off the Internet was disturbing in and of itself. The fact he was nearly insistent about it sent a chill up my spine. Still, I painted on the most confident expression I could muster and waved with a flourish. "But of course!"

Walter's smile was dark and his thoughts seemed to turn introspective. His eyes focused on me again and his voice went flat. "Good. I didn't really want to share this moment with the others."

"Others?" I asked.

Walter waved a gnarled hand dismissively, turning his attention to the cases around the room. "Nothing to worry yourself with, boy." When he turned his dark brown eyes towards me, they looked almost black in the lighting. "You've been a very costly misjudgment."

Sarcasm at the ready, I said, "I aim to please."

Walter made a side step with a loud click of his cane against the floor. His frustration level seemed to be growing. "When we first met I assumed you were human, but your resourcefulness tells me otherwise." His expression turned almost pleasant. "I'm unsure what Andrew is paying you, but I'm sure I can more than match it. My budget has suddenly become flush with the loss of Chan, Timothy, and Marcus. Name your price and we can move forward as partners." He shrugged off their loss easily. "What do you say?"

Trying to keep the astonishment out of my voice, I asked, "You're offering me a job? I thought you'd be a bit more upset."

Walter's cackle was cut short and it turned into a ragged wheeze. "Kings don't get upset about pawns."

He obviously wasn't lacking in the confidence department. Still it unnerved me. "King of what exactly?"

He puffed out his chest and gestured at the room. "Behold, my loyal subjects." With a clack he moved closer to his chair. "Can you see them?" His voice dropped and he stared at me. "It's Gavin, isn't it?"

It appeared that Walter was well informed. Keeping my features serene, I stepped closer. "It is."

In the most serious of tones, he asked. "Well, Gavin, are you interested in the job?"

Jesus Christ, this guy was out of his fucking mind! "I'm not sure I like the benefits package." I shook my head. "I've got to know. When did you realize I was here?"

Walter huffed. "We can negotiate the perks, if that's what interest's you. As for when, you're driving my old friend's car around the neighborhood. Once you parked across the street it was only a matter of time before you wound up here." He seemed lost to memories for a moment before speaking again. "I remember riding around town in the old girl." His smile faded as he shook himself free of the memory. "That was a long time ago, with a man very different from the one that owns it now." He looked at me curiously. "Why would you drive such an antique around town?"

Keeping a healthy distance, I shrugged. "It's what I've got at the moment."

I couldn't help myself, my eyes fell on several of the cases between he and I. There were just so fucking many. Jesus Christ, how long had he been at this, and just how many people had he killed?

Walter followed my gaze and waved a gnarled hand out at the thousands of display cases. "Aren't they beautiful?"

Following his hand, I finally took in the scope of the place. It was mind boggling and sickening. The number of people that had died for this man to have such a trophy room was staggering. The only thing I was sure of was the number of souls we'd removed from the earth would've made a healthy sized city.

I wasn't able to keep the bile and anger out of my voice when I spoke. "Very impressive."

He hobbled back to his seat, making himself comfortable with hardly a care in the world as to me being there. "It's my turn for you to satisfy my curiosity. How did you find me?"

There wasn't a point in lying to the man. It wasn't as if it were going to make a difference in the long run. A chuckle escaped my lips as I realized the absurdity of the clue that led me here. "Believe it or not, it was a random note on the corner of a piece of paper that led me to the place on Congress."

Walter made a derisive snort, his mood becoming foul. "Obviously my shit for a son didn't clean up the house like he was supposed to."

"Family. Whatcha gonna do?" I cut in.

Walter's face twisted itself into a combination of disapproval and agreement. He growled. "I suppose you dispatched the creature guarding Aaron?" He snickered. "Or what was left of him anyway."

Jesus, the guy really liked killing people. I maneuvered through the cases to the expansive middle aisle. My voice was flat and I gripped the wakizashi. "I'm afraid so."

Walter clucked and shifted in his chair. I heard the puff of an oxygen machine as he leaned over and took a deep breath. "You haven't said much about my offer," he growled. "You've killed several of my employees, and one way or another you're going to make that right."

I had to give him credit for being a persistent, crazy bastard. Keeping my hand on the sword, I frowned. "I've already got a job."

Walter snorted. "As one of Andrew's sniveling servants?" He slammed his cane into the floor with a loud clack. "I offer you a chance to lead, boy! I offer you a place in what's coming! You have no idea what's about to happen. You better believe you want to pick the right side of the line to stand on."

Holding up my right hand, I shook my head. "The job I was referring to was the one you relieved Martha of."

Walter glared at me at the mention of Martha's name. "You aren't worthy to speak her name! Andrew wasn't worthy of her! How dare you?!"

Deep down inside I was probably a bad person, because I felt an unyielding desire to poke the wound, just because I could. Raising my voice, I said, "And you were? Is that why you settled for the imitation version? Just what did you do to Mary all those years ago to make her lose her mind?"

Walter's expression turned hard and he wheezed, anger filling him. "You are very well informed." He shook his head. "She was a means to an end and gave me what I needed."

"Kids?" I growled. "Kids you gave up? Well, at least the one." I paused, glaring at the old man. "I've met Brad, and believe me I understand why you didn't want him." Waving a hand out at the stones, I let my anger flow through my voice. "Which stone belongs to your other son? The one you killed."

He put his anger in check, and snarled. "What's your last name? I need to know where to send the flowers."

And that was confidence for you. Misguided as it may be, he was convinced that I was going to die there.

Allowing the Grim to take over my senses, I felt a calm come over me. "Randall."

Walter's eyes went wide and he nearly choked on his own tongue. "I should've known that Andrew had fucked around on Martha! The worthless bastard." He glared at me. "Who's your mother, boy? I want to know who to kill next."

Anger threatened to overtake the calm at the thought of this man threatening my parents. Forcing it aside, I said, "You're about thirty years late for that party."

Walter's features went blank at the news, then shock, followed by understanding, washed across him. "He's your uncle. Wow, I have to admit I didn't see that coming." He paused, lost to a memory. "Zach and Jennifer's kid. I hadn't realized they even had a child." He leaned his head from side to side, trying to size me up once more. "It's obvious you're not one of the filthy werebeasts, or even worse, a human. Care to clarify your species for me?"

Clucking my tongue, I shook my head. "I told you before that information is going to cost you."

Walter sneered. "You're always good for a laugh. It's a shame that you're about to die." A wicked smile crossed his lips and he shook an accusing finger at me. "You are a very interesting man. I've consulted those beyond the veil, and I have it on very strong authority that you've been very busy." He nearly crumbled to the floor when pain wracked his body. "Gods have mercy!" He gasped. "You dare judge me after the death you've brought to this world?" He cried out and fell out of his chair onto his knees, panting. "You arrogant, hypocritical bastard!"

I'd been constantly moving, making my way closer and closer to Walter. Now that I was midway, a familiar sensation flooded me as a cold power swept over me. The denarius growled out a warning that something was terribly wrong. Thing is, I was past caring.

My voice was hard as I felt the beast inside me begging to be set free. When I spoke next the words came out hard, flat, and in a voice not entirely my own. "I'm aware of my past sins, if that's what you are referring to."

Walter tapped the cane on the floor and the shadows all around us took shape. "All these years I thought I was a master of death, but compared to the lives you've taken, I'm a rank amateur." He chuckled. "Of course, the ones I've slain can't harm me." Arrogance painted itself across his features and he waved a lazy hand in my direction. "A benefit of being one of the chosen, a necromancer."

The way he said necromancer made my skin crawl. The fact that some asshole could call up the spirits of the dead to make them do his bidding was disgusting. It may have been more impressive if I hadn't already seen this trick twice before.

Shaking my head slowly at the old man, I sighed. "Walter, I'm going to offer you a one-time opportunity to surrender. If you do so I'll make sure your death is quick and painless."

Walter's snarl was apparent when he got to his feet. "And if I don't?"

Pulling the wakizashi out, I stood there facing the man. "If you don't, what happens next is entirely on you. What I will do to you in this place will become legendary, on earth and beyond the veil. In the end you'll beg me for death."

Walter's anger faded, replaced by his own self-importance. He returned to his makeshift throne and shook his head. "You're as arrogant as your uncle." He waved a hand and I felt the power move through the room. "When I'm done here I'll ship back pieces of you for the next hundred years, just to torment the bastard."

Walter waved his hand again and the specters poured out of the darkness. As if God himself was conducting a symphony, thunder struck and the building rattled. The storm outside raged in rhythm with the swirling mass of souls before me. They closed in on all sides by the hundreds, and they all came seeking their pound of flesh and vengeance upon the man that had taken their lives…me.

I didn't need to count them to know how many there were, at least in round numbers. If Walter had summoned them all there would be close to 6,600 of them, all wanting nothing more than to finish what I'd started nearly thirty years ago. Stepping into them, I brought the wakizashi down in an angular slash, destroying three of the broken souls.

Their power turned into tendrils of smoke, wrapping themselves around me in the death shroud of the Grim. I felt the power course through me as the tattered robes shot out in every direction, tearing the enslaved souls apart. My view of Walter was obscured by the mass of specters swirling between us.

Sweat stung me as hundreds of claws ripped through my back and chest, but the wounds closed almost as fast as they were opened. The power of so many specters pouring into me was intoxicating.

I wanted to lose myself to the Grim, but I knew instinctually that I couldn't let that happen. I couldn't lose control, but it became more and more difficult as they were torn asunder and absorbed. I knew that if I lost myself to the Grim, I'd become far worse than Walter.

With every soul I destroyed rumbles of thunder crashed against the building in rapid succession, creating a crescendo. The violent music flowed through the city, rocking its very foundation. I felt the souls of the living thrumming in the background as their pain echoed the battle all around me.

Slowly but steadily I worked my way through the horde of ever thinning specters, until I broke through the line separating me and Walter. By the look on Walter's face he hadn't seen my transformation, and now that he got a good look, he turned an impressive shade of white. Walter gathered himself up to his feet, hefted his cane like a baseball bat, and swung it at my head. He was surprisingly fast, and I barely ducked out of the way.

Walter shoved a hand into his jacket pocket and dove at me, forcing something smooth and hard into my left hand and clamping his around mine in a vice. Instinctually I knew it was Walter's stone and if what Andrew told me was true I wouldn't be long for this world. My head exploded in pain. Screams echoed through the room, and it took several minutes to realize they weren't my own. Not that I wasn't screaming, but I wasn't the only one.

The few remaining souls in the room howled, all the individual cases calling out in pain. My hand was locked around a smooth hot stone that funneled power from the specters, the stones, and Walter directly into me. Writhing on the ground, I couldn't actually see what was going on, but from my vantage point I could tell that none of them were moving to attack me. One by one they faded from sight as they simply ceased to be.

I felt Walter's life ebbing away when I heard the others, the stone born, stepping from their display cabinets and moving toward Walter. The specters were gone now. Still unable to move, I lay on the ground helplessly as I watched the stone born advance on the dying Walter. One by one they ripped a part of their souls from him then returned to their cabinets, until there was only one left.

I felt the pressure around me ease as Walter whimpered one last time before going limp. The last of the stone born stood there and gave me a slight bow. "We belong to you now."

Then he vanished back to his display case. Power flooded through me as I got to my feet, towering over the broken form of Walter Percy. My left hand shot out and the blue flames wrapped themselves around his neck as I jerked him off the floor. He howled, windows shattered, and I felt the warm moist air flood the floor all around us. Thunder struck and shook the building as a blinding white light crashed through the room.

Squeezing tighter, I knew that his body had given up on life several minutes ago, but his soul was still trapped inside. I tore it free and felt the building shake again, the psychic trauma bleeding out into the open. I heard people screaming in the street below, crying for mercy. They wanted it to stop. Then I remembered Alexander and his people were down there. The helpless sick and dying in the nearby hospital writhed in the background. They could feel this…they felt the anger and pain. Finally, I tore Walter's soul free before devouring it, allowing the Grim's eyes to turn scarlet. Then it was over.

Chapter 29

Friday June 12th

What took place immediately afterward was hard to explain. The Reaper, for lack of a better term, faded back in on itself and I went to check on those below. Alexander and two dozen of his clan were still wobbly but getting back to their feet. They never spoke of what they saw and never asked what happened.

A part of me knew they'd felt and experienced Walter's last moments before his soul had been torn asunder. How much of what they knew was a mystery, and one they didn't seem keen on sharing with me. They were afraid, yet brave enough to do what needed to be done. And what needed to happen was a cleanup of the entire facility.

It took the better part of two days, with men and women working in shifts for nearly forty-six hours, to move all the stones and the rest of Walter's things out of Charity Hospital to the Elmwood facility. They would stay there for safekeeping until I could find a more suitable place. Gabriel wasn't exactly pleased to have Alexander and his brood traipsing in and out of his domain. Alexander had to keep a close eye on things since his people weren't real keen on working with a nephilim.

The one overriding factor for Alex and his people was the fact none of them wanted to cross me. That was both a blessing and a curse. It was clear that any chance at a friendship with the man was gone for the moment. Whatever had transpired down there was enough for him to want to keep things on a purely professional level. His normally jovial attitude had been replaced by caution and trepidation.

I'd visited the DHL complex since everything had gotten settled in at the far end of the warehouse. Everything was incredibly quiet as none of the stones had spoken to me since my encounter with Walter. Something told me that once we were all settled that would change. I wasn't sure that was a good thing. Only time would tell.

Today was a big day however. The meeting was scheduled for 10:00 a.m., and I was told that the ceremony would be held after. Andrew assured me that it would all be wrapped up by early evening at the latest. And yes, that statement was ambiguous as hell and I told him so. Andrew had asked about Alexander's change in attitude several times. I wasn't in a position to speak for the man, so I always directed his questions back to Alexander.

During the move from Charity Hospital to Elmwood I'd had time to review the security footage from Walter's lair. He'd been kind enough to keep a log of what he called "the highlights." One of those highlights was Robert Broussard plotting his daughter's death, along with that of his wife. Robert had hired Chan to remove his daughter and wife at the wedding in hopes of gaining access to the wards around Andrew's property via some sort of key.

Because of this news I'd barely left my room in days, avoiding Heather and Kimberly. I wasn't sure how I'd be able to face them after I was forced to pass judgement on the slimy bastard. I'd intentionally waited for today to reveal the information to make a statement to the others. I wanted this to be a public execution. I needed them to see that crossing this line would mean their death. Most importantly though, I needed to cement myself as the *vigiles* without question. My authority after this would be absolute.

It would be a hard thing but it was necessary. Being the new kid, I had to find the biggest, baddest asshole in the group and give them a bloody nose. After that things would get considerably easier. And because of this decision, things could get very strained between me and the two remaining Broussard's.

For now, however, I had less than an hour to prepare for the meeting. I was hoping that Robert and Bradley would get nervous and skip it entirely. If they went on the run, I could track them down and deal with them quietly. That wasn't going to happen though. I knew that. I'd planned for it.

Staying in my room till just after 10:00, I slowly made my way through the house and to the large meeting room. Alexander and Isidore were dressed in dark blue suits on either side of the door as silent sentinels.

Isidore reached for the knob and I shook my head. "Did Robert show up?"

Alexander growled as he gave me a curt nod. "Him and his little man servant Brad."

"You two should be aware I'm not going in there just to be recognized as the *vigiles*. I'm going in there as the *vigiles* to pass sentence on those involved with Walter." Letting that sink in for half a second, I nodded again. "Call whoever you need to ensure that no one leaves here until I'm done. Am I clear?"

Alexander stood up straight. "I'll see to it."

Isidore put a hand out. "It's my duty to protect Andrew."

"You're welcome to come in with me. I got a feeling things will go south very quickly. So quickly, in fact, no one will have much time to complain about a werewolf in their midst."

When I pushed the door open, the conversation in the room stopped as they all turned to look at me, with Isidore trailing behind. "Sorry I'm late." Keeping a steady pace, I headed straight for Robert and Bradley. "For those of you who don't know me, I'm Gavin Randall, your newest *vigiles*."

Robert got to his feet and slammed his fist into the table. "Werebeasts can't be *vigiles*! It's against the LAW!"

Holding up my right hand for all to see, I kept marching towards Robert. "Good thing I'm not a werewolf." He became flustered and stammered to say something. "You assumed I was a werewolf. I never actually said that was the case."

Robert strode around the table, his face turning from red to purple as anger welled up inside him. "How dare you?! You're nothing! How did you fake the mark?" Robert pulled in power as he readied himself to attack. "I'll destroy you!"

I felt power wrap itself around me. Since my encounter with Walter and the horde of specters, I had been able to transform myself into the shadowy grim at will. Robert threw power at me and his face froze in horror at what he saw. I felt the impact rolling over me like a gentle breeze, only to be added to my already bolstering form.

A glint of sunlight reflected off the long silver blade Bradley pulled out of his bag. Long strands of shadows stretched over the distance between us, slicing off the offending hand and dragging him closer. I slammed my flaming left hand against his throat and he howled in pain. His body began to burn and power poured from him into me as I absorbed all that he was, leaving only the charred skeletal remains of a man.

Robert dropped to his knees, pleading for forgiveness. "You don't understand. Walter forced me into it." He pointed at the still upright smoking form of Bradley. "That was his son...he was sent to keep tabs on me!"

My voice boomed through the room. "Lies." I pulled the Samsung tablet from my pocket and placed it on the table. My onyx index finger tapped the screen and it started to play. "Was it his idea to send Chan after your daughter and your wife?"

Robert's form shook as he looked back at his wife and daughter. "Yes!"

Again my voice echoed through the room. "Lies!"

Robert's voice broke through the speakers of the tablet and the scene played out. Robert had practically begged Walter to kill Heather and Kimberly. Walter actually refused the man's request several times before Robert convinced him of its benefit, a key into Andrew's home.

Robert's face turned into a sneer, and he glared from me to his family and back to me. "What of it?" He glowered as he looked at the shocked faces in the room. "I'm a member of the triumvirate, and there isn't anything you can do about that."

I flashed across the room, slamming my right hand into him and pulling him off the floor. A second later there was a clink and tinkle of a coin hitting the floor as the ancient piece of metal rejected its host. "What I did to Walter will be merciful compared to what I do to you!"

Robert struggled free of my grasp, scrambled back, grabbed the silver dagger I'd freed Bradly of, and shoved it through the side of his neck, sending a spray of arterial blood throughout the room. I reached out, plucked his soul from his body, and tore it into hundreds of pieces while the others were forced to watch the spectacle.

That's when I heard the door open behind me and I turned, ready for any sort of surprise that may come. At least that's what I thought at the time. What I saw was Gabriel striding just a few steps behind another man who was tiny by comparison.

The man was unnaturally pale, so it was hard to determine his actual heritage. The sides of his head were nearly shaved with the dark brown hair at the top swept back, giving him a very early 1920's kind of vibe. He wore a long brown robe that trailed on the floor behind him. He was so thin as to appear frail, but the light gray eyes told me he was a vampire.

He held up a hand and everyone in the room took a knee almost instantly. Looking around I could see everyone was frightened. Taking a step forward, I allowed the shadowy grim to fade from sight.

"And just who in the fuck are you?" I demanded.

His face twitched as it clearly wasn't accustomed to smiling, and then he opened his mouth and a big deep belly laugh erupted from his lips. He got control of himself quickly as he straightened his robe, still trying not to smile.

He pointed a bony finger at Robert's prone form and shining silver manacles appeared on his wrists and feet. Looking back at Gabriel, he nodded. "Take him away. I would like some time to speak to the dead man." He paused as he looked at the body again and then back at me. "It appears that won't be possible." Another flick of his wrist and the manacles were gone. "Remove it and have it burned." Then he turned his attention back to me. "As to who the fuck I am...you may call me Lazarus. The others know me better as Caesar."

You ever have that moment when you know you fucked up in a big sort of way? Yeah, that's how I was feeling just about now. Looking around, I didn't know what to do. I started to take a knee and he sped forward and caught me. The guy was surprisingly strong.

He shook his head. "You don't kneel." He looked at the others. "You may rise and bear witness." He looked up into my eyes. "You are my vigiles *urbani*, and as such you do not kneel to me."

I looked at him, completely dumbfounded. "What?"

Lazarus looked around the room until his eyes fell on Andrew. "Step forward." Andrew did as he was told. Lazarus gestured towards me. "I understand that he was to be one of your *vigiles*."

Andrew nodded. "He was to take over the position from Martha O'Neil, who passed away recently."

Lazarus nodded. "I also understand that Gavin is new to the Archive."

Andrew looked over at me and nodded. "A recent recruit due to circumstances beyond my control."

Lazarus smiled. "You'll need to find a suitable replacement for Martha, but in the meantime Gavin can do the job while you train him in our ways." Lazarus waved Ms. Dodd over as he shook his head. "Ms. Dodd, as you can see by Gavin's actions today you can be removed from your position, and if you continue to harass me with petty disputes, that's exactly what will happen. Am I clear?"

Ms. Dodd swallowed hard and nodded. "I understand."

Lazarus swept the room once more with his gaze before waving a languid hand at them. "The rest of you may go about your business. I need to speak with Gavin alone."

Other than Isidore and Andrew, people couldn't exit the room fast enough, but even they left without a word. Caesar had spoken and they could do little else but comply.

Lazarus gestured for me to take a seat, and he did the same. He made himself comfortable and smiled in my direction. "Did you know it's been 949 years since I've had a *vigiles*?"

Giving him a slight shrug, I kind of did the half nod, half shake thing that made no sense whatsoever. "I'd heard it was something like that."

Lazarus leaned back in his chair, looking around the room. "It's been longer since I've left Rome." He was curious as he eyed everything. "Do you have any idea why that is?"

This time there was absolutely no hesitation. "No, I don't."

He turned his full attention to me. "Because I created the coins, but they were meant to work in tandem with a *vigiles*. Naevius went rogue on me centuries prior to his death, crippling the Archive's power. Until the coin found a new host we were only limping along on what was left of my life-force."

"I don't understand," I told him.

He fell into a long explanation, which I still didn't really comprehend. The gist of the situation was this; Caesar needed to be paired with an equally powerful *vigiles*. They would in turn power the other coins to better govern and run the Archive. The mental connection that had once been common between the governors and prefects had long since dissipated as the Archive's power dwindled.

The coins were all living beings, with their own unique personalities and knowledge to be passed on to the hosts. Now that I was there to counterbalance Caesar, things would start to fall into place. How long that would take he didn't know. It had taken centuries for it to get to this point; common sense told us that it could take nearly as long, if not longer, to repair the damage.

An hour later I guided Lazarus into the living area to find Andrew, Isidore, Heather, Kimberly, and Alexander waiting for me. They all took a knee at the sight of Lazarus, who quickly told them to get to their feet.

He looked around the room. "Any chance you've got something to drink?"

Andrew looked a little pale. "Like what?"

Lazarus licked his lips and beamed. "A good red wine…no, how about something else…something harder." He clapped me on the back with surprising strength. "I've got cause to celebrate."

Looking from Heather to Kimberly, I picked up on their concern as Kimberly put a voice to it. "What about us?"

Lazarus made an unpleasant face. "I've instructed the nephilim—Gabriel, I believe is his name—to handle Robert's remains. As for you, I have no quarrel with either of you. It's clear that Robert acted of his own accord against the Archive."

Kimberly nodded. "We are free to go?"

Lazarus smiled, sat, and waved for Kimberly to do the same. "I may be the caesar, my dear, but even I'm not so cruel as to punish a woman and her daughter for being unfortunate enough to be related to a traitor." His voice was kind and soft as he spoke. "You have my full support in all matters." Lazarus gestured for Heather to step forward, and he held out the old Roman coin that I'd dislodged from her father earlier. "Sorceress, I'd invite you into the circle if you are willing."

Heather paused before stepping forward. "You believe I'm worthy?"

Lazarus laughed and shook his head. "I see power in you the likes of which your father never possessed. I also see a heart that has been wounded." He placed the coin in her hand and clamped it shut. "You and your mother are far better people than the man you knew as your father." Lazarus smiled once more and turned to Andrew as he patted his stomach. "I'm starved; any chance of dinner?"

Andrew grinned and nodded. "About that…I'll have to order in for all of us."

Lazarus smiled. "Sounds good. In the meantime, drinks?"

Andrew ducked out of the room only to reappear moments later with several bottles of Dalmore in hand. Isidore was close behind with a tray of sparkling crystal glass tumblers. A drink was poured for everyone, and for the first time in fifteen hundred years Lazarus relaxed and let his hair down, so to speak. It would have been great to see if he didn't scare the shit out of everyone.

The evening grew late and Kimberly and Heather were the first to leave, returning to their home to deal with their loss. Lazarus didn't so much leave as much as he vanished a few hours later, with a promise to be in touch soon. Alexander and

Isidore smartly left Andrew and I to sort through our issues alone.

Over the next month things returned to normal. Well, as normal as they could be now that Lazarus was out walking the earth again. Alexander and his clan were now officially on the payroll as centurions in much the same way Gabriel was. Several of them were using Brad's place on the river as a makeshift headquarters to be close to the Elmwood facility without having to live with Gabriel.

I was in the process of purchasing a condo in the CBD when I got the call from Heather. "Hello," I said into the phone.

Heather smiled. I didn't need to see her face to know that was what she was doing. "Sorry I haven't been in touch lately. It's just been a little strange since that day."

That day being the day I'd ripped her father's soul apart. That was the day I'd turned into a reaper. That day was the day she'd become a member of the triumvirate. That day was a LOT of things.

"I understand," I said hopefully.

"You still owe me a dinner," she said quietly.

"I do."

She snickered. "There's a great little place I know in Gentilly. Do you like sushi?"

"I love sushi."

Her voice was full of mirth as she spoke. "Meet me at Good Time Sushi at seven tonight." She paused. "That is, if you're free."

That made me laugh. "I'm finishing up some paperwork now, and of course I'm free. I'll see you at seven."

With that I hung up the phone, signed for my new home, and gave the realtor a big fat check. Being the caesar's *vigiles* came with 949 years of back pay. Who knew?

Proof

Made in the USA
Charleston, SC
05 April 2016